"Green nails all four voices of her alternating narrators: women knocked down by disappointment who find hope and unlikely camaraderie through the pages of a book. This is an uplifting read for dark times, featuring strong and unique characters uniting toward a common goal. It also has crossover appeal for fans of historical fiction from Jennifer Ryan and Kate Quinn."

—*Library Journal* starred review of *The Blackout Book Club*

"The characters' trajectories from strangers to close friends will warm readers' hearts. Bookworms will take to this."

—*Publishers Weekly* on *The Blackout Book Club*

"Green proves to be a first-rate author in her remarkable first novel about humanity and patriotism. . . . Green brilliantly creates a limitless and captivating reading experience with the nuance and wisdom of a seasoned writer. The timeless dichotomy of forgiveness and justice rings with contemporary relevance, and Johanna will be a well-loved heroine for her gumption, humility, and wit."

—*Booklist* starred review of *Things We Didn't Say*

"*The Blackout Book Club* is a fabulous novel that will warm the hearts of readers everywhere. Amy Lynn Green gives us a poignant look at life on the home front during WWII and how comfort and camaraderie can be found in the shared love of books. This will be a wonderful book club read!"

—Madeline Martin, *New York Times* bestselling author of *The Last Bookshop in London*

"*The Blackout Book Club* is an ode to books and libraries, but it's also an ode to human connection. Amy Lynn Green's entire cast of characters comes vividly to life, each woman with a distinct voice that makes the reader feel as much like her friend as her fellow book club members are. I couldn't put this book down!"

—Addison Armstrong, author of *The Light of Luna Park* and *The War Librarian*

"*The Blackout Book Club* is an engaging story that illustrates the power of books to unite and encourage us in trying times. The wonderfully diverse cast of quirky characters brings to life the shared worries and hopes of people on the WWII home front. A wonderful read."

—Lynn Austin, author of *Long Way Home*

"A salute to the power of books and of friendship! Not only does the writing sparkle with Green's trademark wit, but the characters become your dear friends, slowly exposing the hurts and secrets that have shaped them. Come to *The Blackout Book Club* for the fun—stay for the depth."

—Sarah Sundin, bestselling and award-winning author of *Until Leaves Fall in Paris*

The
CODEBREAKER'S
DAUGHTER

Books by Amy Lynn Green

The
CODEBREAKER'S
DAUGHTER

AMY LYNN GREEN

BETHANYHOUSE
a division of Baker Publishing Group
Minneapolis, Minnesota

© 2025 by Amy Lynn Green

Published by Bethany House Publishers
Minneapolis, Minnesota
BethanyHouse.com

Bethany House Publishers is a division of
Baker Publishing Group, Grand Rapids, Michigan

Printed in the United States of America

ISBN 9780764242991 (paper)
ISBN 9780764245022 (casebound)
ISBN 9781493450794 (ebook)

Library of Congress Cataloging-in-Publication Control Number: 2024041938

This is a work of historical reconstruction; the appearances of certain historical figures are therefore inevitable. All other characters, however, are products of the author's imagination, and any resemblance to actual persons, living or dead, is coincidental.

Cover image by Marie Carr / Arcangel; cover design by Mumtaz Mustafa

Baker Publishing Group publications use paper produced from sustainable forestry practices and postconsumer waste whenever possible.

25 26 27 28 29 30 31   7 6 5 4 3 2 1

To Lucy and Emma,
with all my love.

Dinah

As the bell above the drugstore door gave its apologetic half jingle, Dinah Kendall turned casually on her stool to see who else had ventured out on such a blustery winter afternoon. She smiled at the trio in drab olive wool coats. Yes. These had to be her assigned marks, though they'd arrived later than scheduled.

The first man was older, tall and thin enough to place at least third in a Lincoln look-alike contest if he'd only grow a beard. He surveyed the drugstore with a frown, as if disappointed by how utterly twentieth century their surroundings were. A younger fellow stumbled after him, the tortoiseshell glasses on his round face obscured by the sudden fog of warmth. The third man, a college linebacker sort with perfectly coiffed blond hair, let the door fall shut behind them.

While they bantered and stamped slush from their boots, Dinah noted her first impressions—in her memory, of course. It would look suspicious to take out her notebook. All she knew for sure was that they were agents of the Office of Strategic Services. The first two might be diplomatic spies or radio technicians, but probably not commandos parachuting into danger to support resistance groups. The third one with the blond hair and loud laugh . . . well, he had the build of a field agent, at least.

Time to insert herself into the conversation. Dinah smiled warmly as the three army men approached the counter. "You're brave fellows coming out in this weather."

"We were hopin' for a battlefield tour, but the park's closed for snow," Glasses said. His Southern accent made her wonder which side of the war his great-grandfathers had fought on. "Our bus driver recommended this place instead."

The blond linebacker glanced around doubtfully. This close, Dinah could catch a whiff of his spicy cologne, something most rural boys wouldn't be caught dead wearing. "He said it used to be a hotel, and Lincoln stayed here."

"He did," she assured him, knowing that the maze of boxes and bottles flanked by an ordinary diner counter would be a disappointment. "In fact, President Lincoln wrote the Gettysburg Address in a bedroom upstairs."

The older man's eyebrows shot up. "No kidding?"

She nodded. "Some nincompoop stripped the building of its brick and made it into a soda fountain. It's really too bad." The storefront ought to at least have a historical plaque, rather than windows plastered with advertisements for magazines and mouthwash.

Gettysburg was the only place in America in 1944 where if someone talked about "the war," you had to ask which one. If you closed your eyes to block out the cars and electric lights and newspaper headlines, it was easy to hear echoes of the Civil War all around town.

Come on, Dinah, you're not a tour guide. She'd given up on that dream. "Anyway, the Wills House can't be beat for a cheap meal."

They seemed to have a hearty appetite, placing hefty orders with the soda jerk and ribbing one another about how much they could consume in one go.

Dinah had to fight the feeling that, under ordinary circumstances, she'd enjoy a chat with these three without ulterior motives. Thoughts like that might make her go easy on them.

"Miss?" The freckle-faced jerk proffered a glass of root beer brimming with foam, and Dinah whisked it away.

In a confidential tone, she leaned toward the soldiers. "I came in to pick up a prescription for my mother, so I thought I'd drown my sorrows while I'm at it. I'm a student at Gettysburg College, and my last exam went rather poorly."

That was a lie, but at twenty, Dinah was the right age to be enrolled in college, and she couldn't have them think she was a flirty bobby-soxer still in high school or they wouldn't give her the time of day. And she needed some explanation for her presence in the empty drugstore on such a gloomy winter afternoon.

"Get them talking as soon as possible," the colonel had instructed her when he'd explained her unique volunteer assignment two months ago. *"Any fellow who can't hold his tongue and keep up his cover on our soil is likely to put his team in jeopardy once he's overseas. We need you to be thorough, Miss Kendall. Lives are at stake."*

"That's tough." Dinah blinked back to her current reality, where the older OSS recruit was nodding sympathetically. "I always thought things got easier toward the middle of term."

So he was college educated—and an optimist. "That's very kind of you to say, Mr. . . . ."

"Stanley Hewitt."

"And I'm Milton . . . Milton Hardy," his bespeckled Southern friend was quick to add. She noted the slight pause before his surname.

When she glanced at the blond linebacker, he gave a movie-star smile marred only by one crooked front tooth. "Ralph Baker."

A strong start. Those were names on the list she'd been given—not their real names, only the aliases these men used during training.

The men took stools next to her, so far the only other customers, and the soda jerk hunched over the grill on the far wall to fill the extensive order. Dinah had found that, lacking alcohol to loosen tongues, a sense of privacy was the next best thing.

"My name is Dinah Kendall. And *do* call me Dinah." She beamed at them. "Thank you so much for your service. It's been wonderful having men in uniform around town."

The men straightened, looking flattered, which was exactly her plan. Some of her targets made it clear they wouldn't mind a little flirtation to get things started. Others were guarded, so getting them to talk usually meant an introduction on some practical pretext, like needing a nickel for a pay phone. Today, Dinah had gone with the part of the friendly girl next door.

They spoke of the ordinary things: where they were from, whether they had ancestors who fought in the Civil War— Stanley's great-grandfather was a Union cavalry officer—and the snowy weather.

"I'm from Texas, y'see," Milton continued, as if his accent hadn't made that obvious, "where it's only cold inside a Frigidaire, the way God intended."

"Here, it never thaws until at least April," Dinah admitted. "But our spring is lovely."

Ralph snorted. "We'll have to take your word on that, I'm afraid."

She didn't allow herself to react to that. Ralph had as much as admitted they'd be going overseas soon. "We'll be sorry to see you all go. There's something so patriotic about having handsome men in uniform striding through town. Surely it's not so bad back at your base."

"Oh, I'll miss a few things," Ralph said. He held up his thumb, counting off the list on his fingers. "First, the chow isn't half bad. Second, some of our training is exciting. And third"—he paused to aim a wink at Dinah—"we get to drive across the state line for some quality time with beautiful girls."

The blush that Dinah felt creeping over her face wasn't feigned, although she was more embarrassed for poor Ralph than herself. If he thought about what was he was saying, he'd realize he'd given away the approximate location of his training camp—south of Gettysburg in the mountains of northern Maryland.

Stanley's eyes flashed with alarm, and he leaned toward Ralph, whispering something—in French? "Aw, can it, will you?" Ralph muttered in response. "She's just a local girl."

If only he knew. Dinah pretended to be occupied gathering napkins from the nearby basket, addressing Milton this time. "You've got to be awfully tired of conditions out in Camp Sharpe by now." Better to pretend she hadn't noticed the "state line" comment. "I'm sure the CCC didn't make those buildings for winter use. What's it like?"

By now, the soda jerk had shoved burgers before them, and Milton dug in with enough vigor to land a mustard stain on his collar.

"Just what you'd expect," Milton said, shrugging, after he'd swallowed. Had he taken a bite to give himself more time to answer? A good tactic. "Sparse and drafty."

No one corrected her false assumption. Dinah knew that they were not from Camp Sharpe, located a few miles outside of Gettysburg. Stanley, Ralph, and Milton had been bussed in from the Catoctin Mountain OSS training camp in Maryland. No one was even supposed to know they were there.

No one, that is, except for army officials, OSS brass . . . and the daughter of the camp's lockpicking and safecracking instructor.

As Dinah thought through her next question, Milton pushed his basket of fries her way to offer her one, which she accepted.

Was that . . . a hint of guilt mingled with the salt?

All for the cause. Besides, you might get to make a good report for at least two of them.

"I really am grateful for your sacrifice," she said, with a bit too much of a flutter in her voice, but Milton and Ralph seemed to be eating it up. "We all are."

"We do what we can," Ralph said, wiping greasy fingers on his napkin. "For our country . . . and for you ladies back at home, of course."

How far could she push them? Ralph had already shown he didn't think much of his secrecy oaths. Time to press for some real information now. "You army boys are all the same," she teased. "Why, I just met a group of your kind last month at a New Year's dance. They worked as radio broadcasters, but that's all they'd tell me. I imagine you're doing similar work?"

This time, the pause was longer. Stanley was the first to speak. "I don't think we should say much about that."

She tilted her head so her light brown hair fell over her shoulder and smiled. "Oh, don't mind me. I just can't help being curious."

Time to direct the conversation to their training exercises— something that might make them reveal what sort of mission they were preparing for. "You know, I spend most of my days volunteering with the Red Cross, knitting and such, so I hear all about what they put you boys through in boot camp."

"When you're not in classes, you mean," Stanley interjected.

Dinah blinked. "Excuse me?"

"I'm sure most weekdays you're at the college, busy with your studies." An innocent-enough comment . . . except that Stanley was staring her down like she was on the other side of one of the interrogations the OSS recruits practiced on their instructors.

Smile, act natural. She could recover from a minor slip like that. "Oh, sure. But we've got loads of free time for volunteering, especially over the holiday break."

"Sure." Stanley swiveled his stool slightly to face her more directly. "Say, I find it a little odd that the door over there had a notice posted that the pharmacist was out today, yet you said you picked up a prescription for your mother."

Drat. Why did Colonel Forth have to send the smart ones her way? If the soda jerk had been standing farther away, she might have tried to claim he had filled it for her, but he was washing a stack of dishes within easy earshot.

Milton and Ralph were both frowning at their friend, clearly not following the point of these statements, but Dinah gave Stanley an assessing glance. Yes, he'd figured her out, and he wasn't backing down. Good thing she wasn't a real spy, she had to admit, because she'd just blown her cover, tangled up in the half-lie part of her half-truths.

"But mostly, what I want to know is," Stanley continued, "why are you asking all these questions?"

There was nothing for it now. Dinah made a note to be more careful in the future, but for now, she might as well make her point perfectly clear. "Did you gentlemen know that before the war, not far from here, there was a summer camp run by the German-American Bund? It trained boys and girls in the principles of Hitler Youth, children who would now be about my age."

Milton scrunched his nose beneath his glasses, clearly missing the implication, but Ralph's eyes had gone wide with alarm. Clearly at least he recognized the name of the homegrown Nazi organization that Roosevelt had banned after Pearl Harbor. "You don't mean . . . that is, you weren't one of them?"

"No. But for all you knew, I might have been." She'd known a few local boys, in fact, from German families, who had attended, coming back spewing propaganda and bitterness. "During wartime, there are no guarantees that the enemy isn't listening. No place is safe, and especially no person . . . no matter how much she might seem like a sweet, innocent local girl."

Ralph shut his gaping mouth long enough to look chagrined at that.

She lowered her voice. "You know Colonel Godfrey Forth? War hero with the build of a grizzly bear and the voice of rooster?"

Milton choked out a laugh at this description of the camp commander and his braying tones, but Stanley only nodded at her to continue. "He mentioned in his orientation speech that you would be closely monitored during your training, and that you were to keep to your cover stories at all times."

The fact that she could quote this speech seemed to confuse Milton further. "But . . . how does . . . ?"

"You're working for Forth," Stanley guessed. "You were trying to get us to reveal secret information while on leave." He made connections quickly, a useful asset in someone who worked in espionage. There was leadership potential in him. She'd put that in her report.

Dinah shrugged. "Better me than a friendly Axis gal . . . or a home-front fifth column spy."

"Then it looks like you're the one who blew your cover," Ralph teased, but there was a hint of nervousness in his cocky demeanor. As well there should be. He was the one of the trio who hadn't passed the test. Would it be enough to dismiss him from the OSS?

Dinah smiled wryly. "Let my mistakes be a lesson to you." Underhanded as it might seem, she felt no shame about her role. Like the colonel had pointed out, these men were only months away from carrying confidential information in and out of enemy territory. It was vital to know they could maintain secrecy.

"Do not speak to your fellow soldiers about this." After a half dozen tests, these three were the only ones to have found her out. "There are a few of us placed about town for this assignment, and we haven't gotten to all of your cohort yet."

"I should have known you'd be beautiful *and* clever." Ralph leaned closer to aim another wink her way, hitting her with the full force of his cologne. "But we did all right, didn't we?"

"I thoroughly enjoyed our conversation," Dinah said, dodging the question. "And I mean that, all pretense aside."

Ralph's tense shoulders relaxed, as if he thought a bit of flattery had struck his mistakes from the record.

Not a chance. Whatever Colonel Forth did with her report, she had to write it honestly, including his slipups. *Sorry, Ralph. But careless talk costs lives.*

Milton swallowed hard, eyebrows still shot up his forehead. "Golly. You mean, this whole time . . . you're really . . . ?"

"That's right. I spy on the spies." Dinah couldn't resist a smug smile as she stood. "Enjoy your leave, gentlemen. And I do hope you have time for a proper tour of Gettysburg. There's always another secret to uncover."

2

Lillian

SATURDAY, FEBRUARY 26, 1944

Lillian Kendall shivered as she pried the frozen mailbox open, once again forced to take on Dinah's usual tasks, since she still hadn't returned home.

Colonel Forth had assured them that her daughter's "missions" would not be dangerous, but they were also supposed to be brief. Dinah had been gone for almost two hours now.

As she trudged back, she sorted the envelopes with mittened hands, smiling when she saw a heavy ivory envelope. It was always a good day when the mail contained something for her, not just her gregarious husband or mother-in-law.

Once inside, Lillian set aside the puzzle she'd been creating for *The New York Times*—only a few stubborn three- and four-letter clues to fill in before she'd mail it to the editor—and settled into her favorite chair by the fire.

Elizebeth Friedman's spidery cursive greeted her with characteristic warmth from the first line. Lillian could almost hear her friend's voice narrating the chatty letter.

Her smile faded a few paragraphs in. *We are extremely understaffed at work. I know you told me you were not interested in a job, but so much has changed since Pearl Harbor. Have you ever considered reentering the game?*

This again. Lillian skimmed the rest before returning the letter to the envelope. No matter how Elizebeth pleaded, she was *not* willing. Those days were long behind her.

And yet . . . wouldn't it be nice to do something that mattered?

Absurd. Any position would certainly require her to move to Washington, DC, for the duration of the war. Roger couldn't leave his locksmith shop, and she couldn't leave him, not for that long. What Elizebeth was asking of her was simply impossible.

Lillian sighed, knowing she'd delay writing her response for weeks, dreading the chore of turning her friend down tactfully. That was work better suited to someone like Dinah, who could deliver refusals with grace.

Just then, the stiff-jointed front door creaked open and banged shut, a harbinger of Dinah's arrival. Relief mingled with annoyance as Lillian heard a clatter of heeled boots. "Dinah, please. Your grandmother is taking a nap upstairs." Though her husband's mother had lived with them for four years now and "rested her eyes" each afternoon, Dinah never could seem to remember. "You're later than I expected."

There was a pause before Dinah appeared, brown hair in a disordered frizz about her head. "Just a few . . . complications today. I had to make more notes than usual too. There's no point in waiting around for me, tapping your foot."

Complications. As if that wasn't supposed to make her worry even more. Even when Lillian gave her a pointed look,

Dinah didn't add anything further, tugging off her boots while dripping slush onto the carpet.

"I supported you accepting as a favor to your father's old military friends, as long as you're not put in a compromising situation."

That code phrase meant Dinah wouldn't be asked to hang about in one of the Gettysburg bars. Perhaps it was a lingering effect of coming of age during Prohibition, but Lillian was wary of the potent cocktail created by youth and alcohol.

"But you have to remember," she continued, even as she noted Dinah's eye roll, "this isn't actual espionage. These tests are a game for the recruits, a training exercise. If you need to leave early or call home on occasion, well, the colonel must understand you have a real life as well. We do worry about you, you know."

"Yes, Mother," Dinah said, her voice as flat as if she'd ironed it—which, a glance at her daughter's ensemble indicated her tone would be the only thing she'd ironed lately. She crossed her arms, belying any respect the polite agreement might have communicated.

Bely.

That was a good crossword choice, short and filled with common letters that could be used in intersections. The clue might be *contradict* or *cancel out*. Trying not to seem obvious, Lillian jotted it down in her open notebook.

Dinah glanced at the empty chair near the fireplace before draping her mittens near the hearth. "Where's Dad?"

"An emergency over at Reaser Furniture."

Dinah sighed as if this was a personal inconvenience to her, though by now she ought to know her father could be called away at inconvenient hours when keys were lost or locks broken into. As she headed to the hallway, probably to get lost in a novel up in her room, she pointed to the blanket over Lillian's lap. "Who's the letter from?"

"Never mind." Lillian snatched the envelope and tucked it into her notebook. "Now, don't forget to clear a path to the porch before dinner."

For a moment, before she turned away, Lillian saw a spark in her daughter's eyes as they lingered on the hidden envelope. Curiosity . . . or suspicion?

Land sakes. It was a mistake letting Dinah playact as a spy. It had made her see mysteries behind every innocent request for privacy.

All the same, Lillian locked the letter in her jewelry box before starting dinner preparations. There was nothing sinister about Elizebeth's request, but it was a reminder of a chapter of her life that was behind her now.

It would be better for everyone if it remained closed for good.

As Lillian entered Colonel Forth's office, an explosion shook the building. She flinched. Did they need to flee for cover? She could feel the buzz of panic begin to build, pricking at her like pins into a cushion.

Breathe deeply. Think logically. Observe. These were the tools she'd developed over the years to slow the anxiety that sometimes threatened to overwhelm her. And in this case, neither her husband, Roger, nor the grizzled officer opposite them shouted an alarm, even when a second explosion caused a few pens to tumble off the colonel's desk in a drum roll of thuds.

"My apologies for the noise," the colonel said in his usual strident voice, indicating two seats in front of his imposing desk. "It's demolition day."

"I see," Lillian said, as if this explained everything. She crossed her ankles neatly, glad she'd worn her best tweed dress and Sunday pearls. It gave her comfort to be well-dressed, especially not knowing why they'd been called to a private meeting with the OSS commander "as soon as convenient."

"What's this about, Forth?" Roger asked in the straightforward way people in town seemed to appreciate. "Have the boys been complaining my class is too tough?"

Colonel Forth chuckled. "Not a bit. They love it, the rascals."

As well they might. Roger instructed each graduating class that passed through Catoctin Mountain in the basics of lockpicking and safecracking. *"Like an accountant running a course on tax evasion,"* he'd joked. Lillian had only to glance to her right to see the agents' final exam: breaking into Colonel Forth's office, then springing the combination lock on his steel wall safe.

"There's something I'd like you to see." The colonel pushed two papers their way, one typewritten on bland memorandum stationery, the other inked on lined paper torn from a notebook. "Both are descriptions of Albert Ramsey, an OSS trainee. Tell me what you notice."

Lillian took the typewritten page first. It appeared to be an official evaluation, detailing Albert's best qualities, potential weaknesses, reception by his peers, and work he would be best suited for.

When she'd finished and traded with Roger, she blinked in surprise. "This is Dinah's handwriting."

Colonel Forth inclined his head.

So this meeting *was* about their daughter. Lillian had suspected as much. Otherwise, Roger would have been called to the meeting alone. Other than the time two weeks before, when Dinah had come home late and in a bad temper, the OSS missions seemed to have gone smoothly. Was something wrong?

With the drapes drawn, the light in the office proceeded murkily from a lone desk lamp. Lillian held the note close. As usual, Dinah's hurried strokes and creative spelling made a cipher of sorts. *Al has a forgettable face and manner, plain as vanilla ice cream. But he's careful, almost fastidious, and never turns his back to the door. Slower reaction times, especially to questions, but smart enough. Instead of lying, he shut down my questions with "That is not information I'm allowed to share." Maybe not squad leader potential, but he'll follow any order you give him.*

It went on for a few lines, but Lillian had already realized what the colonel wanted her to see. "They're similar descriptions."

Colonel Forth gave a sharp nod. "Correct. Your daughter described a man she'd spent a half hour in conversation with. The other was his assessment by a team of psychologists after three days of intensive interviews, tests, and exercises."

"Ha!" Roger burst out, practically beaming. "Dinah's always had a good sense for people. Goes to show that you don't need all that Freudian nonsense."

Lillian took a breath to change the subject before Roger started on a rant about modern psychology, but Forth beat her to it. "Your daughter has a remarkable gift. Not only has she lured eight of our candidates to reveal sensitive information, but over the past three months, she's also given us accurate and perceptive profiles of dozens of recruits."

Lillian exchanged a glance with her husband. "I assume there's more to this meeting than simple praise."

"Quite right." Colonel Forth leaned forward. "Last week, I made a recommendation to the OSS's headquarters in Washington to find a fit for your daughter."

"Well now," Roger said, leaning back in the chair, his voice trailing off as he processed this news. "A job with the Office of Strategic Services. My, my."

"Are you sure she's qualified?" Lillian had seen Dinah's grades in her commercial department class. "She's never taken a civil services test, and I doubt she's prepared to."

"Paperwork and gatekeeping," the colonel grumbled, as

if the entire bureaucracy could be circumvented with a well-placed telephone call. "Dinah has the raw talent we're trained to look for in agents."

Another demolitions test shattered the quiet. Gracious, how could anyone *think* in this racket?

"There's one thing I'm confused about," Lillian said, only belatedly realizing she'd cut off the colonel during another monologue.

Ever the gentleman, he paused regardless. "Yes?"

"Why are you discussing this with us? Surely Dinah ought to be in this meeting."

Under her scrutiny, the colonel seemed unable to find a comfortable position in his well-worn chair. "Well, I . . . I suppose I thought, since the girl—er, young woman lives at home . . . and as Roger is a friend of Lieutenant Colonel Henson, I ought to speak to the two of you first."

"That was real thoughtful of you, Forth," Roger said, smoothing the jagged conversational edges she'd left behind, as always. The colonel relaxed, and Lillian gave her husband a significant look. "But Lily's right. It's up to Dinah to decide. Just . . ." Roger paused, chewing on his lip before pressing on. "You don't mean . . . she'd be sent overseas?"

Lillian found herself interested in the colonel's answer. She hadn't lingered on lurid accounts of seductress spies like Mata Hari in the last war, but the femme fatale image was difficult to shake . . . and though Dinah was warm and amiable, it was one she did not fit.

The colonel waved cigar-stub fingers in dismissal. "Goodness, no. We have very few openings for female international operatives. Besides, a role like that requires mastery of at least one European language. I believe Dinah speaks only English?"

"That's correct." Lillian had tried in vain to educate her in both French and German from an early age, the first of many failures in sharing any of her own interests with her daughter.

Forth continued, "This is an office position—research, creation of materials pertaining to our international interests, that sort of thing."

It was a vague description, but that was no surprise. Lillian remembered what it was like to have information handed out in dribs and drabs on a need-to-know basis.

"When would she start?" Roger asked.

"Early April. The OSS can't keep desks open for long. There's usually an exam to take, an oath of security to sign, and a few days of psychological evaluation for new recruits, as I mentioned before."

Lillian stiffened. *Psychological evaluations?* She found herself strangling the chair's wooden arms with a grip that wouldn't have been out of place in the recruits' hand-to-hand combat classes.

Roger was still nodding placidly, not looking her way, and for a moment she resented the fact that he wasn't alarmed.

"I don't think that will be necessary," she interrupted, the words tripping off her tongue in a frustratingly disordered way. "The evaluation, I mean."

Calm down. This can be explained rationally. Lillian forced a smile. "Based on what you've said, Colonel, I doubt Dinah would be under the strain your operational groups and intelligence agents are."

To her relief, Colonel Forth nodded. "True. Besides, in the case of a personal recommendation, I daresay we could skirt around that step."

Lillian relaxed, suddenly unsure what to do with her hands, and settled on folding them in her lap.

"Though I have to say," the colonel continued, "the boys find the tests rather fun. Mostly team exercises and obstacle courses, though I'm told the women only create their own filing cabinet organizational systems and answer interview questions."

Heavens. It was a good thing she'd spoken up. Dinah's idea of an organizational system was sticking reminders to her mirror with chewing gum.

"All those details can wait," the colonel said, standing. He likely had a full agenda: lessons to plan, reports to dictate, hand grenades to restock. "It sounds like my next course of action will be talking to the young lady herself."

Lillian restrained herself—barely—from saying it ought to have been his first.

Once inside Roger's beloved Buick touring sedan and past the checkpoint at the park's entrance, her husband let out a low whistle. "Well, well. Our daughter is going to be a spy."

"She's going to be administrative support for spies," Lillian corrected, her mind full of lists of things that must be done in a few short weeks. Because Dinah would accept, eager for adventure as anyone her age.

Gradually, she became aware that Roger was speaking in that soothing, low voice of his, pitched so that the noise of her own thoughts sometimes overwhelmed it. ". . . and besides, she's so young, Lily."

Having not heard his other objections, she could only respond to this last one. "So was I, when I first left home."

He, graciously, didn't point out that had been a very different situation. "Dinah didn't even want to go to college, just started clerking for the locksmith shop. To be so far away for the rest of the war . . . She's never traveled alone either. It's an awfully big city to navigate."

Part of Lillian wanted to scoff, attributing Roger's worry to his hesitance to be separated from his only child. A bus schedule was as easy to read as a recipe card.

And yet . . .

This was the same Dinah who had crashed the car into their mailbox during her first driving lesson. And who had been lost for six hours on their vacation to Virginia Beach because she had wandered off to reenact the battle between the *Monitor* and the *Merrimack*. And who barely achieved Cs in her high school classes because she regularly forgot about her assignments.

Perhaps Roger had a point.

"I wonder if Margot has an opening in her boardinghouse," Lillian mused. Her old friend had converted a stodgy brownstone into a lodging house to accommodate the influx of single women into the capital for war work.

"That's right," Roger said, brightening. "I'd sure feel better if Dinah was staying there."

Another idea began to form, and Lillian stared at the bleak landscape of early spring before speaking. "It's possible I could go with her. I'm sure I could stay with Elizebeth for a week, possibly two. Just to see Dinah settled in safely."

"The Friedmans, of course! It's been ages since you've visited."

Both Friedmans were quite busy, but surely they'd be willing to host her for a short time. That way, after helping Dinah move in, Lillian could retreat a safe distance away. Close enough to reassure Roger, far enough away to let Dinah feel independent.

"I'll telephone Margot and Elizebeth tonight to ask."

Lillian's mind, already hurrying ahead with plans, paused over one last question. She and Roger might agree it would be wise for Lillian to accompany Dinah to Washington, DC, a seemingly practical and simple solution.

But what would Dinah think?

Dinah

Dinah folded her new brown crepe suit, picturing herself striding confidently into a Washington, DC, office wearing her tallest pumps. After all, the Office of Strategic Services wanted *her*, and not just in a "Your Country Needs You" poster sort of way.

It felt like one of the daydreams she'd indulged in at the locksmith shop during slow times. She could still picture the suppressed smile on Colonel Forth's face when he'd said, "There's an opening in our Morale Operations division."

"Morale Operations? You mean . . . creating posters and slogans?" *Don't look disappointed*. That sort of work was important, if dull.

"Goodness, no." The colonel gave an exaggerated shudder. "That's the Office of War Information's territory. Our MO division is concerned with the morale of the *Axis* forces—specifically, damaging it."

28

That sounded a great deal more fun. "How?"

He had shrugged. "I'm only aware of one specific example—branches tend to keep to themselves—but generally, they prepare what's known in the business as black or gray propaganda. Black being information that purports to come from an Axis nation, such as rumors or leaflets, when we are actually the originators. Gray being information from an unspecified source, like a radio broadcast."

"Fascinating," she said, though she wanted to ask a dozen questions all at once. "What's the specific example you know of, if you don't mind?"

This time, Colonel Forth smiled in earnest. "An old friend of mine sent me a mockup of a design used earlier this year. Nothing secret about it now." He opened a drawer and drew out what looked like a disposable napkin. When he held it across the desk to her, Dinah could see German words printed on it, along with a swastika. "Custom toilet paper, distributed secretly to German officers. The text points out that Hitler's ideas are . . . well . . ." He coughed, whisking the paper away, his neck coloring with sudden red. "I suppose this isn't a topic for mixed company, eh?"

Dinah didn't bother to conceal her laughter. "Never mind that, Colonel. That story raises *my* morale, at least."

A twinkle crept into his blue eyes. "You'll do just fine with MO, Miss Kendall. They'll be glad to have you."

Even now, as Dinah chose an outfit for the train ride to the capital, she repeated that reassurance to keep from becoming overwhelmed. *"They'll be glad to have you."*

There was a job out there that was a perfect fit for her . . . and it would require her to sign an oath of secrecy. How perfectly delicious.

It wasn't her first choice of careers, but stern Dr. Tomlinson had made it clear that becoming a battlefield guide for Gettysburg National Military Park would be out of reach—at least for her. The idea of her getting a college degree, much less a master's degree in history . . . well, it just wasn't possible.

"How's this for a job well done?"

She glanced up to where Dad proudly displayed her sock drawer, which had gone from looking like a squirrel's nest of assorted junk to something that might pass a barracks cleaning inspection. "Wonderful."

"I found about three packets of hairpins too." As he nudged her open suitcase aside to make room on her bed for the drawer, he paused, gawking.

Dinah turned to see what had caught his eye. Nestled on top of the blouses and skirts that Mother had deemed "professional" was the photograph she kept on her vanity: Dad standing next to a skinny, freckled version of herself at the Shiloh National Cemetery.

"Ah," he said, deep smile lines raised to life all over his face. "You're bringing it."

"I have to bring some memento from the Union summer, don't I?" A graveyard might be an odd choice for a sentimental snapshot, but Dinah couldn't bear the thought of leaving it behind.

For nearly two months after her twelfth birthday, her father had left the locksmith shop to Grandpop's care to go tromping around "points of interest" in Gettysburg and beyond, just the two of them. They had explored monuments, listened to guides recount thrilling battles, and held makeshift picnics where, decades ago, men had given "the last full measure of devotion." All without Mother around to complain of blisters or ask if they'd remembered to bring an umbrella.

"Those were good days," Dad said fondly. The iron frame of her twin bed groaned under his weight as he sat down. "Though I tested the limits of meals made from canned beans."

Dinah laughed. "Mother would have been appalled if she'd seen how we ate on that trip."

"Hopefully you'll fare better in DC."

"Apparently Auntie Margot has a decent cook," Dinah said, tucking a sewing housewife into her suitcase. "I got the whole spiel from Mother last night, along with a map of the government worker bus schedule, our train tickets, and a paper with my brassiere size written on it, in case I'd forgotten."

Dad glanced up, but she wouldn't meet his eyes. "Some people say 'I love you' with hugs and kisses, others with train timetables and shopping lists and reminders to bring an extra pair of gloves."

"I know." Dinah hefted a teetering stack of records onto the window seat to make room to open Grammy's old steamer trunk. That didn't mean she had to like it. "Anyway, thanks for the help." She caught him up in a hug, savoring the smell of his Aqua Velva aftershave, mingled with metal from key engravings at the locksmith.

"Anytime, little Yankee." For once, she didn't protest the nickname, watching him leave with a smile.

Too bad Dad isn't the one escorting me to Washington. But a business as booming as their little locksmith shop didn't run itself, and he still had his training at the OSS base.

Oh well, it couldn't be helped. Dinah stretched her back, surveying her bookshelf. It probably wouldn't be worth lugging many books to Washington, since the Library of Congress was only a streetcar ride away. Still, Dinah pulled out the first few volumes of THE BLUE AND THE GRAY series, smiling at the familiar engravings before returning them to their place.

And stopped.

Was that . . . ?

She stooped over and reached until her fingers brushed a slim clothbound volume that had fallen behind her copy of *Brother Against Brother*.

No, she corrected herself, once she held the familiar burgundy

binding, memories flooding back. This book hadn't fallen behind. It had been hidden.

More to the point, she had hidden it, years ago.

For a moment, Dinah paused, like she was about to open
a treasure chest or a crypt, even though she knew what was
inside.

Sure enough, when she brushed off the dust and eased open
the cover, there it was: line after line of text in her mother's
beautiful, neat handwriting.

All of it unintelligible.

The same disappointment she'd felt years ago when she'd
opened her twelfth birthday gift from Mother pricked at her.
Maybe she'd hoped that growing older would mean that she'd
be able to decipher the codes her mother had written so long
ago as a test for her daughter.

But as she stared at the lines, none of them rearranged themselves into something useful. Only a few dates, from July 1917
to the early '20s, appeared to be written in the ordinary way.

"It was a stupid idea, anyway," she grumbled. All she'd
wanted for her birthday that year was a pet rabbit. And what
had Mother given her? A book of gibberish wrapped up in
golden paper with a red bow.

A week later, she and Dad had left on their trip, and Dinah
had brought the journal with her, full of dreams of Civil War
spies like Elizabeth Van Lew transmitting critical information
across enemy lines. During that whole two months, Dinah
couldn't solve a single one of the puzzles. Pages of her guesses
that were jammed inside the back cover, covered in pencil
scrawls, eraser smears, and even a few tears of frustration,
testified to that.

Dinah shut the book, ready to return it to its hiding place
for another decade. Maybe by then she'd live up to Mother's
expectations.

Except . . . wouldn't the OSS break codes? Dinah tossed the book onto her suitcase beside the Union summer photograph before she could change her mind. What could it hurt to bring it along?

Maybe now that she was going off on her own, she'd unlock the secrets of her mother's journal once and for all.

Lily

"It is easy to say, in hindsight, that I felt a sense of foreboding from the first headlines about the Zimmerman telegram. But the day of the rally at Riverbank felt weighty in a way I'd never experienced before."

— Excerpt from Lillian Kendall's journal

SUNDAY, JULY 8, 1917

Lily Nilsson placed her steps carefully, her boots squelching with each step, to keep the hem of her skirt out of the mud. That, at least, was one way in which this rally resembled conditions for the doughboys over in France.

Riverbank was dressed for war, the hastily erected platform dominating the lawn decked in patriotic bunting that sagged after an untimely morning drizzle, typical of rural Illinois. Not even George Fabyan's millions could bully the weather into cooperation. The brassy notes of the national anthem carried to her on the sharp-edged breeze, and Lily chafed her hands against her arms to stay warm, searching the crowd to see if she recognized any of the young fellows from the nearby town streaming toward the enlistment tent.

There. She spotted the hawkish profile of Bert, the estate's iceman, apparently game to trade his saw and cart for a rifle and a gas mask.

Not long ago, everyone was using words like *neutrality* and thanking God for President Wilson's assurance that America wouldn't interfere in another continent's troubles. That was before the broken cipher of the Zimmermann telegram had revealed the Germans' treachery, using Mexico to threaten America's borders. Now, even all of Mr. Fabyan's wealthy, famous friends were doing their bit. Charlie Chaplin sold war bonds, Lillian Gish starred in silent propaganda films, and rumor had it that Teddy Roosevelt had tried to persuade Wilson to let him follow his old Rough Riders to charge into glory. All of them had been spotted at Riverbank for social calls on lazy Sundays, but no longer. There was a war on, and everyone felt the need to be involved.

"Hello there!" The cheerful call repeated twice before Lily glanced to find its source, never dreaming it was aimed at her. Maud Smythe, dressed in a pretty sailor dress instead of her usual maid's uniform, stood outside of the rally's main tent, waving her over.

Their eyes had met, and Lily knew it would be rude to turn away. She might as well stand with Maud as anywhere else.

Maud clutched Lily's arm as soon as she was within reach, smiling rapturously. "Have you ever seen such a crowd? They say three thousand people turned out."

"Oh?" Lily managed, trying to seem appropriately impressed. Everywhere she looked, friends waved and shouted to one another, mothers corralled rowdy children, and gangs of teenage boys gaped at the machine gun set up on the hill.

35

So much noise. Lily wished she'd used the day off to take a nap in her quarters.

As Maud tugged her past the stage, Lily could hear the auctioneer-like voice of the recruiter, an army captain dressed in olive drab. "Better to go and die than not go at all! Who will step up for our country's hour of greatest need?" Behind him, the rally tent ballooned to the stormy sky like the circus had come to town.

Maud's voice rose to be heard above the speech's swell, squeezing her arm in a way that made Lily flinch. "Isn't it exciting, Lily?"

"I'd say it's rather ominous."

At this, Maud's pert nose wrinkled. "What's that supposed to mean?"

Lily could have said it was the answer to the clue "dire" in last week's *New York World* crossword puzzle, but that likely wouldn't clear things up. And expressing her worries for the young men who bragged about guns and glory would make her seem unpatriotic. "Just that it looks like rain."

"No need to be all fancy about it." Maud shook her head, though her teasing smile seemed slightly off, like a pitcher of curdled cream. "Honestly, Lily, sometimes talking to you is like talking to an encyclopedia set."

It was an insult, Lily knew. And yet . . . encyclopedias were beautiful. Her employer, the eccentric millionaire George Fabyan, had full shelves of them, including all twenty-nine volumes of the *Encyclopædia Britannica* Eleventh Edition, the spines smooth and unbroken. Lily had slipped into the den at the Villa once to touch them.

Someday, she'd have a set just like that. Never mind that on her current salary, she'd have to save for years.

". . . there's no sense putting on airs," Maud was saying, and Lily realized she hadn't been listening, too caught up in her own thoughts. "We all know where you . . ." Her cheeks pinked, and she cleared her throat. "Anyhow, you're no better than the rest of us."

Lily had encountered far worse in her early days at River-bank, from muttered gossip to rude names spoken to her face. Even now, after a year working in the kitchens, with her once-bobbed hair nearly grown to her shoulders, many of her fellow servants remembered where she'd been before Riverbank. "I didn't mean to imply otherwise."

But Maud was grabbing Lily's arm again, pulling her on-ward. "Come on, let's go see the trenches."

Lily hadn't been up to this side of the estate for weeks to see how the trenches had expanded, dug by Mr. Fabyan's gardeners. Once just a few piles of dirt on the lawn, now they cut across the property like a jagged scar, a series of passages tall enough to shelter a full-grown man. Several dozen people had climbed down into them, and more waited with tickets in hand.

Lily squinted to see more of the view, then frowned. "Does no one realize it's only a very long hole?"

"Lily!" Maud exclaimed, clearly scandalized. "They're rais-ing money for the Red Cross."

"That's something, I suppose." Still, why pay for a tour when the army officer narrating it spoke loudly enough to be heard on the other side of the three-hundred-acre estate?

"As you may know," he bellowed, "our artillery does not need to be re-aimed after each shot. Due to the hydraulic recoil, our soldiers can bombard the enemy's fortifications with a howitzer over and over again."

He did not, Lily noted, mention that the Germans could do the same thing to them.

Maud's eyes widened. "My stars! Can you picture all those brave boys, fighting down there for days at a time? What must it be like?"

Lily took in the effect the weather was having on the model

trenches despite the boards that reinforced them, keeping them from caving in. "Muddy, I expect."

This prompted another despairing look from Maud. "You have no romantic imagination."

"War isn't romantic."

This simple declaration of fact seemed to tear into Maud's cheery mood like one of the mortar shells the officer described.

"Well, I'd better be off," Maud said, turning on her kid boots. "Enjoy the rest of the rally." With that, she jaunted away, not attempting an excuse.

To find more pleasant company, Lily supposed. She couldn't really blame her.

Well, now Lily had seen the rally, or at least as much of George Fabyan's patriotic tableau as she cared to. Perhaps there was still time for that nap.

The muddy slog back to the cottage was rough going, but at least no one responded to her call of "Anyone about?" when she entered. Peace and quiet were difficult to come by when one had to share a small second-story room with two other unmarried women.

Once she'd scraped her boots and set her uniform skirt out to dry, Lily perched on the edge of her narrow bed, reaching under her pillow to take out the Fun page of the *New York World*, still folded in quarters after she'd salvaged it from the Lodge's fireplace this morning.

Mr. Fabyan was proud of the newspapers he had mailed to him from his textile company's offices in New York, Boston, and St. Louis, and the residents of the Lodge enjoyed debating the headlines before discarding them next to the coal scuttle. Even though she knew they'd be used to line the cages of Nelle Fabyan's exotic pets, Lily always returned this section after borrowing it. She knew employers took theft among those in service seriously, and unlike other unmarried girls working here, she had no family to fall back on if Mr. Fabyan turned her out.

With a rustle of newsprint, she unfolded the diamond-shaped grid of the weekend crossword puzzle, full of neat, blank potential, her eyes scanning the clues . . . until she noticed a small square of white paper pasted just beneath the puzzle. When she read it, her breath caught.

Miss Nilsson, Will you kindly consider meeting me by the reflection pool in the Japanese garden at noon on Wednesday, July 11? I should like to ask you a few questions. Sincerely, E. Friedman.

Though the wording of the note was polite, Lily couldn't help feeling a spike of anxiety. Someone knew she took and completed these puzzles. Was she in trouble? Surely not. After all, there was no harm in what she was doing.

Lily studied the signature again. *E. Freidman.* She couldn't match it to a face. Surely it couldn't be one of Mr. Fabyan's famous guests? No, not if they'd found out her name. It must be a resident here at the Lodge.

As Lily folded the note to tuck into her pocket, a nudge of memory solved the mystery. *Of course.* The note must be from Elizebeth Smith, the young scholar who worked with the imposing Mrs. Gallup. She'd changed her surname only a few months ago when she married a Jewish scientist breeding fruit flies at Riverbank.

Lily tried to picture Elizebeth in more detail and failed. Gallup's Gals were interchangeable, an entourage of white shirtwaists and upswept hair peering at old manuscripts through magnifying glasses. From the snatches of conversation she'd overheard when Mr. Fabyan paraded guests around the grounds, it seemed they were searching for secret ciphers in the plays' manuscripts to prove Shakespeare wasn't the real author.

Now that she knew the note writer was a woman . . . meeting with her was something to consider, at least. What could

Elizebeth possibly want? Perhaps an academic like Elizebeth simply found this new type of word puzzle fascinating.

Curiosity warred against Lily's love of routine and control. She folded the newspaper page and tucked it under her arm.

Would she take the risk?

5

Lillian

Lillian stood, brushing the dirt from her hands. *There.* She'd removed all the matted leaves from the walkway garden. Roger certainly wouldn't remember to do so while she was gone, but he commented every year on how much he loved the early bloom of the yellow tulips she'd planted shortly after they married.

With her bags packed, Lillian's only task before Dinah's last dinner at home was to make her famous Dutch apple pie. Lillian had memorized the recipe long ago, one of the few good things Mama had passed on to her, and she ran through the steps in her head as she opened the front door.

And stopped short. Because a few quick whiffs brought her the unmistakable cinnamon-sweet smell of something baking.

Sure enough, when she hurried to the kitchen, there was Martha, bundled into a flour-dusted apron, humming to herself as she placed a perfect lattice pie on the counter.

Her mother-in-law must have heard her enter, because she

turned, beaming. "Ah! Well, this was meant to be a surprise, but I suppose a pie's hard to hide."

Lillian tried to work up a convincing smile. "That was . . . thoughtful of you." Though now she had nothing to do with her afternoon, and her spices would be left helter-skelter instead of properly in alphabetical order.

As Lillian scrubbed the remnants of dirt from her hands in the kitchen sink, Martha looked up wistfully. "Ah, me. The house will be so quiet without Dinah about, won't it?"

"I suppose it will." There had been so much to do in the past few weeks that Lillian hadn't stopped to think about what would happen after she came home from Washington, DC, without her daughter. Certainly, since high school, Dinah had often been out with friends or one of her clubs, but without her teasing at the dinner table, her sporadic declarations of Civil War minutiae, and even her shoes scattered in odd places . . . well, things would be different, that was certain. How had her daughter grown up so quickly?

". . . insisted that we keep her room just the same, for visits," Martha was saying. "Although I suppose she won't mind if I tidy the place up a bit."

"I'm sure she'd be grateful. Are you sure you'll be able to manage while I'm gone?"

"Puh!" Martha clattered her pie into the pie safe with enough force that Lillian worried for the crust's structural integrity. "It won't be a problem, dear. Roger and I will get on just fine. I cleaned a house and fed that very man for twenty-four years before you came around, and I can do it again."

Lillian turned away to keep Martha from seeing her bristle at the blatant reminder that she was replaceable.

Stop being sensitive. Martha meant well. She always did.

Clearly not perceiving the direction of her daughter-in-law's thoughts, Martha waggled a mock-stern finger in her direction. "Don't spend a scrap of worry on us, Lillian. You focus on getting Dinah settled and having a good time with your friends."

"Thank you, Martha." That, at least, was something to lift her mood. Elizebeth had sounded excited to see her again, though she had warned that *"William and I work beastly hours these days."* Lillian had assured her that she still had the *Times* crossword deadlines and was fully capable of keeping herself busy. "It will be good to do something useful for a change."

"For a change?" Martha tsked, rattling a pot onto the stove. "Lillian, dear, what do you think raising a child and keeping a household together counts for? Nothing?"

Lillian sighed. She had not budgeted time for a lecture this afternoon. "I didn't mean it that way."

"It's all those important friends of yours," Martha grumbled, beginning to peel a mound of potatoes, her slapdash approach missing large sections of skin. "Those women working in the government, getting written up in newspaper articles and traveling all about. That's all well and good, of course, but it's enough to make anyone feel a bit envious."

"I'm not jealous of anyone, and certainly not my oldest friends." That would be childish. It was true that Elizebeth Friedman and Margot Schnieder had exciting careers, but she'd chosen a different path.

"Good, because you've got no cause to be. The good Lord knows we can't all change the world, and we're not meant to." Martha shook her paring knife at Lillian for emphasis. "Never forget, there is great honor in being an ordinary woman."

"That's an admirable thought." Whether there was any kind of honor in Lillian's rather dull life or not, she'd chosen it willingly.

After being shooed away from the roast, Lillian wandered into the front room, starting a grocery list for the next week's meals, noting where ration coupons would need to be turned in. Halfway through the produce, she was surprised by a hearty "And here I was hoping to catch you with your feet up for once."

Roger stood in the doorway, taking off his suit coat with a fond smile in her direction.

"Never. Especially now, with so much to do." Lillian glanced at the mantel clock before rising on her toes to accept his peck on the cheek. Only a quarter past three. "Home early, I see."

He winked. "Well, my two best gals are heading out tomorrow. I thought I'd steal all the time with them I could."

Despite herself, Lillian couldn't help smiling. Roger really was still a boy sometimes. She wished that she could have his carefree air. It felt sometimes as if she'd been born forty-four.

"You'll only get time with me, I'm afraid. Dinah is out paying farewell calls to the Quincy sisters and the O'Rileys and who knows who else."

"Ah, sure. Our social gal." The cheerful smile on Roger's face faded as he pressed his lips together, the same worried look he'd worn in the early days of the Depression when it had been hard to make ends meet. "Say, Lily, I've been meaning to ask. Is everything all right with the Friedmans?"

Lillian blinked at the sudden change of subject. "As far as I know. Why?"

Her husband fiddled with his suspenders, harrumphing deep in his throat before continuing. "It's just . . . their Christmas letter was awful sparse. They usually do something fancy, like that cipher wheel or the Hittite hieroglyphics."

"Mayan pictographs," she corrected absently, taking the booklet of ration coupons out of the credenza. He had a point there. This year's holiday letter had been disappointingly quotidian. "They're quite busy with work, which, you understand, they can't say much about." That silence even extended to each other, since Elizabeth worked for the navy, and William for the army, and secrets couldn't be shared between the two branches.

Roger settled into his usual chair, tugging the footstool closer. "And what about that bit where Elizabeth said William was removed from active duty military status for health reasons?"

She hadn't remembered that detail. "Well, he's not as young as he used to be. He had some kind of illness a few years ago, related to his heart, but I'm sure it's nothing to worry about. In any case, Elizebeth would have told me if my coming were inconvenient."

"Maybe."

Lillian set down the list and put her hands on her hips, turning toward him. His expression was as bland as the tentative response he'd just delivered. "All right, Roger. What is this *really* about?"

"It's only . . ." Roger's voice dropped lower. "I heard something from Bob Weeks, you remember him? I wasn't sure if I should mention it, since normally, I don't pass along gossip—"

"Oh no?" Roger wasn't mean-spirited, but he was as much a small-town boy as any other Gettysburg native, far too interested in the personal lives of others.

He ignored her barb and plowed on. "Weeks told me that William cracked some important cipher . . . and then he cracked himself. Went doolally, as our Tommy friends would say. Spent the first several months of 1941 in Walter Reed's mental ward. That's why the army made him a civilian—they're not sure when it's going to strike again."

Lillian didn't respond, her mind spinning like the wheels of a mechanical cipher machine, trying to determine what she was feeling. Surprise, possibly, but also . . .

Anger. Yes, that was it. Anger that, after so much time, so little had changed. That William's years of faithful service had been set aside because of a crisis. That even Roger spoke of someone's suffering as if it were no more than sensational scandal.

And perhaps, anger that Elizebeth, her oldest and dearest friend, had been through something so terrible and never told her.

"Even if that's true, the mind is complex," she said, keeping her tone guarded, "and I'm sure the stress of William's position is beyond what most of us will ever experience."

Roger had turned to glance out the window, or surely he would have noticed her sudden stiffness. "Maybe, but if he can't handle it, he ought to leave it to the young fellows."

"Roger, perhaps you've forgotten that William Friedman is a friend of mine." Lillian clasped her hand in a fist to keep it from trembling.

Now Roger turned back to her, and this time when he spoke, his tone was gentler. "I'm sorry, Lily. I didn't mean anything by it. I know with your mother . . ."

"This has nothing to do with Mama." Though Lillian had to wonder, would she be so sensitive about the gossip without her own personal history?

After watching Lillian for a long moment, Roger shook his head. "No, I guess it doesn't. Anyway, I'm sure William's doing the best he can, and Elizabeth too. Maybe he's healed up just fine."

Calm down. It's just his way. Early in their marriage, Roger had read a volume of Wilfred Owen's poetry aloud to her, full of grisly, hopeless, trench-scribbled verse. When he'd gotten to "Mental Cases," with its description of "men whose minds the Dead have ravished," Lillian had begged him to stop.

Military men, she'd learned, felt pity for any they considered mentally unstable . . . but they often didn't understand them, could find no place for them. It was no wonder Roger couldn't muster the same sympathy she felt for William—if what he'd heard was true.

"I just worried that your being there might put a strain on them, especially William," her husband went on. "That's all."

"I think you're letting an exaggerated tale turn your head."

The more she thought about it, the more Lillian decided Roger and his friend must be mistaken. There was no need to jump to conclusions based on rumors from someone who might simply be jealous of William's success.

"I'm sure you're right, as always." Roger tugged her down toward him and pressed a kiss to her forehead, then her cheek. "Now, just promise that you'll miss me at least a little."

She shook her head at his antics. "I'll only be gone for two weeks. I am confident you'll survive."

"Only if you call me so I can hear your voice," he said seriously.

"Perhaps I'll write you a letter, for old time's sake."

The reference to their courtship made Roger smile. She'd seen his collection of the letters she'd sent him while he was stationed in France, tied up with a ribbon.

"At least this time there won't be an ocean between us," he said, pulling her close.

Lillian allowed herself to be kissed, enjoying the familiar smell and feel of the man she loved. Yes, she would miss her husband, though she wouldn't tell him so after he'd fished around for a compliment. It wouldn't do to feed his ego.

Once Roger released her and began to search for his slippers, Lillian slipped away to her room, opening the nightstand drawer where she kept letters from her friends. It didn't take long for her to find what she was looking for.

Interesting. Elizebeth hadn't written to her at all during January of 1941, or for two months after. From Margot, such a delay wouldn't be unusual. She'd often traveled about the country for her work as Congresswoman Rogers's staff assistant, but Elizebeth was usually punctual with her monthly letter.

Elizebeth's next letter, dated April 3, 1941, was shorter than usual and contained an introductory apology for being slow to write, blaming it on "a taxing time at work, coinciding with sickness in the house. William's heart continues to trouble him." The rest of the letter was a glowing report of her daughter Barbara's academic achievements.

Lillian hastily folded the letter and tucked it into the box.

Yes, William had been sick, but there was no evidence that Roger's spurious explanation, rather than Elizebeth's own, was the correct one. Her husband was making her doubt one of her best friends, causing her to see trouble where there was none. Surely there was nothing to worry about.

Dinah

Dinah wiped condensation from the cab's rain-spattered window, trying to get a glimpse of the Washington Monument, or any other landmark. No luck. Washington, DC, was somber and pitch dark, like a nation in mourning—or in hiding. "I heard they had to turn off all the spotlights on the buildings. Afraid of Germans bombing the White House."

Mother hid a yawn behind the back of her hand, unimpressed by this bit of trivia. "I should think so."

It was far later than they'd planned to arrive. Their train had pulled in on time at ten o'clock, but in the jostling to recover their luggage, the fight through Union Station crowds, and difficulties finding an available taxi, it was now nearer to midnight.

"I wish I could have sent word to Margot not to wait up," Mother fretted, leaning against the seat so the streetlights flashed a pattern across her weary face.

"It'll be fine, Mother." Dinah had uttered that same phrase at least ten times on the trip already.

Soon enough, they arrived at a nondescript brownstone in the Dupont Circle neighborhood, three stories tall and boasting a prime position on the corner of the street.

Dinah wrangled their luggage up a few steps to the porch—her steamer trunk and suitcase, and Mother's carpetbag, a relic from the turn of the century—while Mother paid their driver. Holding the brim of her soggy hat so it would repel at least a little water, Dinah used her other hand to give a firm rap on the door.

A few moments later, Margot Schnieder threw the door wide open. "Darlings!" she cried at a volume that Dinah worried might wake the neighbors. She seemed perfectly comfortable revealing her coral kimono to anyone passing by, draped around the tall, willowy silhouette popular in the '20s. Her blond hair, without a streak of gray, brushed against Dinah like cornsilk as she was forcibly wrapped in a hug.

"We are so sorry to be late," Mother said. "The inconvenience . . ."

Auntie Margot waved her off. "Oh, pish. I'm more night owl than early bird anyway, you know that. Come in, come in!" She helped heft Dinah's trunk into the foyer, letting it drip on the parquet flooring. "It's so good to see you both again."

"Thanks," Dinah said, as always finding it difficult to get a word in edgewise with the effusive Auntie Margot, as she insisted Dinah call her. The thawing warmth of the house wrapped around her, and Dinah sighed, tension easing from her shoulders. . . .

Until she turned to see a simian face leering at her from the wall.

Only a stuffed monkey, she realized, mounted between the light sconces in the entryway.

Mother gawked openly at the unusual décor choice. "What is *that* monstrosity?"

Auntie Margot only chuckled. "Oh, that? I call him George. I found him in a curio shop, and he reminded me of those awful monkeys at Riverbank. You remember, don't you?"

"Unfortunately, yes," Mother said dryly, turning her back on the thing. Dinah did the same. There was something downright creepy about the taxidermy head's marble eyes.

What was Riverbank? Had Mother ever mentioned it before? Dinah tried to think back to the stories she'd demanded as a child from Auntie Margot when she and Mrs. Friedman had come to visit. No mention of a place called Riverbank came to mind, just the stories of Auntie Margot's travel and adventure as a translator and attaché to Edith Nourse Rogers, one of the first female members of Congress.

Now, for some reason, Auntie Margot had decided it was time to leave her job in politics and settle down, a lucky break for Dinah. The housing shortage in DC and other "war towns" had made the news for years now.

As Auntie Margot led them deeper into the entryway, Dinah gathered her first impressions of her new home. At first glance, it mimicked any Victorian-style row house, with a staircase rising to the second floor and flocked velvet wallpaper framing the archway into a parlor furnished in polished cherrywood. Yet, here and there, she could see touches of Auntie Margot's flamboyant personality: a cabinet of multicolored glassware, walls painted mint green, and a lampshade embellished with thick gold tassels.

Inside, Auntie Margot's voice had lowered at least a few decibels. "I only keep one spare room for guests, and it's as small as a closet, but it'll do until . . . when are you going to the Friedmans', Lily?"

"Sunday morning. That's the only day they get off."

That earned a tsk from Auntie Margot. "My word. It shouldn't be legal, the way the military works even their civilians to the ground. But that's wartime for you." Now Auntie Margot turned to address Dinah. "Myrtlewood Hall is the proud home of six government girls—seven with you."

"Myrtlewood Hall?" Lillian said dryly. "Are we in a Daphne du Maurier novel?"

"Oh, stop, Lily. It's a fine name. You're just allergic to whimsy." With that, Auntie Margot offered to help Dinah haul her trunk up to the second floor, where she was given the key to her room. Not much to look at—just a narrow bed, desk, vanity, and closet—but not unwelcoming. And best of all, it was entirely hers.

After hanging up her coat and shaking the rainwater from her hair, Dinah realized she hadn't said good night to Mother and Auntie Margot. The floor felt cold even through her socks, and Dinah paused on the landing. Auntie Margot probably thought she was using a low tone, but it had the effect of a stage whisper, carrying clearly. "Say, Lil. Are you in town for . . . anything related to your first career?"

"No," Mother said firmly. "Roger wanted someone to accompany Dinah, and I felt it would be a good time to visit you and Elizabeth. Then I'll be away."

First career? Dinah frowned. Other than the crossword puzzles she turned in monthly to *The New York Times*, Mother hadn't ever worked outside the home.

No, wait. She vaguely remembered Dad saying Mother had worked in a rich man's kitchen before they met. *"That's why she can bake worth millions,"* he'd joked. Still, that didn't fit with Auntie Margot's air of secrecy.

With effort not to let the boards beneath her creak, Dinah trudged back up the steps, covering a long yawn. *In the morning. I'll ask Mother about it in the morning.*

───────

At breakfast, Dinah sat with the other young women before a tower of waffles perfectly centered on the serving dish, along with plump, spicy sausages and quarters of pink grapefruit pooling in juice.

After Auntie Margot pronounced grace, Dinah tucked into her first bite of waffle—crisp, then chewy where the drizzled honey had seeped in. *I'm going to have to watch my waistline, or my new clothes won't fit.*

Mother sat beside Auntie Margot, conversing with her in low tones, leaving Dinah to introduce herself to the others. Once that was done, Betty, a freckle-faced girl to her left, jabbered about her work at the Records Office without once asking Dinah a question in return.

"It sounds like important work," Dinah said politely, pouring a glass of milk. "I'd love to hear more about it sometime."

Betty beamed. "Glad to have ya, new girl. You'll fit right in."

She would have thanked her, but a sound at the doorway interrupted her. A young woman wearing clunky laced brogues tromped into the dining room like she owned the place. She wore a neat blouse and checked skirt, but her thick, black hair looked as if it hadn't seen a comb in days, maybe weeks. Or maybe it had simply gotten lost deep within the tangle.

Auntie Margot glanced up at the noise but didn't comment on the boarder's tardiness, only inclined her head slightly in greeting. Everyone else seemed to stiffen, like a gunslinger had just walked into the saloon in a Western film.

The newcomer sauntered more than walked to the only empty seat—right beside Dinah.

"Good morning," Dinah said, smiling.

The other boarder slouched forward in her chair and . . . grunted?

Maybe she wasn't a morning person. Dinah decided to pass her the coffee without further comment.

After the brief disturbance, the other boarders continued to chatter eagerly to one another, though no one seemed interested in including the newcomer in the conversation.

She, in turn, sucked in massive gulps of coffee and large bites of her sausage, treating her utensils like pitchforks, as if this were a race.

Say something to break the ice. Dinah cleared her throat to get the woman's attention, indicating the spread before her. "Is breakfast always this elaborate?"

The grunt she received seemed to be one of affirmation. "Miss Schnieder thinks anyone who skimps on breakfast is trying to look like 'some emaciated flapper.' Better eat up."

Except when she was imitating their landlady, a broad Boston accent tinged her vowels, some of her *R*'s dropping off entirely.

"Well, I can certainly do that." Dinah gave her fellow boarder her most winning smile. "I'm Dinah Kendall, by the way."

The other young woman jutted her chin in Dinah's direction, apparently a substitute for a return smile or handshake. "Winora McMahen."

Dinah blinked in surprise. "That's an unusual name."

Winora let out a weary huff. "My ma wanted to name me after her mother, Winifred. Pops felt the same about his mother, Elenora. There was an ear-splitting row till my older brother piped up and said, why not smash them together?" She ended her story with a challenging tilt of her head, as if daring Dinah to comment further.

"Well, I think it's lovely," Dinah ventured. Anyway, it had prompted three full sentences of dialogue, which felt like a success.

"Better than Elefred, I guess." Winora speared a sausage link. "So, whaddya doing in DC?"

"I . . . I have a government job."

"No kidding. So do all of us." Winora waved a fork vaguely at the five other women, all dressed in cardigans, their hair rolled, suddenly looking indistinguishable. "What sort of work?"

"Oh, clerical." Dinah took a gulp of milk to give her time

to change the subject. "I'm not starting until Monday, though. Auntie Margot thought it would be good for me to have the weekend to get settled."

Winora cocked her head. "Funny that you call her that. Auntie, I mean."

"She and my mother are friends."

Winora grunted again, giving her a look that said something like, *Great, a teacher's pet.* She pulled out her chair with a scrape, tossing her napkin on her empty, sticky plate. "Well, see ya around."

It wasn't the best start, Dinah supposed. But there was still time. Perhaps Winora was simply having a bad day or had stayed up late the night before.

In any case, she wouldn't let it bother her. She'd finally arrived in Washington, DC. It was time to make her mark.

7

Lily

Eeeee! Ooooeeeeeee!

Lily shuddered as she hurried down the path, averting her gaze from the monkey's bright eyes and bared teeth gleaming at her from behind the bars of its cage. Whether Nelle Fabyan's pets were smiling or sneering at passersby was a matter of debate.

At least the path to the gardens didn't pass the bear cage. Whenever Lily had reason to visit the northern edge of the grounds, she gave their barred pavilion a wide berth.

As she hurried by, the stench of the miniature zoo faded, overpowered by the sweet perfume of the rose arbor, its archway beckoning her toward the peaceful Japanese garden beyond. Lily hesitated, as if being near the flowers would help overpower the smell of sweat and soap flakes that clung to her after scouring breakfast dishes. From her vantage point, she could see over the fence into the garden.

Just as she'd thought. Elizebeth Friedman, looking composed and cool in a white dress with graceful lace sleeves, stood by the shrine on the edge of the pool. Waiting for her.

Lily kept quiet as she approached, watching Elizebeth mount the footbridge and peer at the water's lily pad–dotted surface. She seemed to be in her twenties, only a few years older than Lily. Curly brown hair framed a pretty profile, though she had none of the flashy elegance of the New York heiresses and Hollywood starlets who roared up to Riverbank in their automobiles.

Coming closer, Lily cleared her throat, hovering at the edge of the bridge like one of the butterflies attracted to the feathery pink wildflowers. "Mrs. Friedman?" When the other woman looked up, Lily held out the completed crossword puzzle. "I'm Lily Nilsson. You asked to see me?"

Her heels rapped against the bridge as she walked toward Lily, arm extended. "Delighted to meet you. And please, call me Elizebeth. I haven't gotten used to people addressing me by my married name."

Any worry that she was due for a reprimand faded under the young woman's warm manner. "Then you must call me Lily."

"Very good, Lily. I'm sure you're wondering what all this is about."

Lily nodded. If she hadn't been so curious, she might not have shown up at all. As it was, she'd almost backed out on the way, making the excuse that it might not be worth wasting the short lunch break allotted to her. But she knew if she didn't find out what the mysterious note writer wanted, she would always regret it.

"Weeks ago, I first noticed someone had returned an old copy of the *World* with its crossword puzzle completed—flawlessly." Elizebeth smiled wryly. "I discovered it quite by accident, as I'd gone back to a discarded newspaper to settle a debate with my husband. After that, I made a habit of rummaging through the papers to see if the solver would strike again. Each week, the puzzle was completed perfectly, and even once corrected a typographic error. None of my fellow breakfasters would confess to the deed—and they're not the sort to feign modesty."

That seemed true enough. The Riverbank crew was an elite lot of biologists, psychologists, professors, and academics of an indeterminate nature, all of them working on projects commissioned by Mr. Fabyan.

Lily had fallen into step with Elizebeth, away from the bridge and beneath the cluster of conifers, their dappled shade a welcome respite from the heat.

"So I watched long enough to find out who it was. You were the one who completed all of them, correct?" Elizebeth prompted. "The handwriting seemed consistent."

Lily nodded, searching for something appropriate to say. "I-I enjoy a challenge."

"That's what we were hoping." Before Lily had time to wonder who *we* might be, Elizebeth continued, "Several of us have been assigned a . . . research role that requires attention to detail and a familiarity with words, both of which you clearly possess. Mr. Fabyan is desperate to procure additional minds to work on our team so he can deliver what he's promised."

This was not at all what Lily had expected. "Are you . . . offering me a job?"

"If you'll have it."

"On the basis of a few months of completed puzzles?"

"Not only that," Elizebeth admitted. "When I spoke to Mr. Fabyan about you, he looked up your employment file."

Only the continued peaceful smile on Elizebeth's face checked Lily's desire to flee. "What—what did he say?" she managed.

"That you'd scored quite highly on something he called a Binet-Simon Scale, as reported by your school. 'Exceptionally bright,' he said they'd called you. He became very animated about it."

"I'm sure," Lily managed, through a mouth that suddenly felt drier than the dust on the path. What seemed, on the surface, to be a compliment, might be her undoing.

"He ended up flying out of his office, eager to speak to some doctor in Chicago about the psychological tests administered to army officer recruits before I could finish asking him about hiring you to our unit." Elizabeth shook her head at their employer's eccentricities, and Lily felt her tense muscles begin to ease. "Regardless, I took that as enthusiastic support of our decision to hire you."

So Mr. Fabyan hadn't mentioned the reason the girls at Lily's school had been subjected to testing—to detect telltale signs of "feeblemindedness." If he had, Lily was sure, Elizebeth would not be so eager to associate with her now.

"What sort of job?" Lily asked, still cautious.

There was a glimmer of the theatrical in Elizebeth's eyes. She knew what she was about, letting Lily ask questions as suspense built. "One quite different from what you're used to. Our employer is somewhat demanding."

"You mean Mr. Fabyan?" She already knew that; the millionaire was known for his outbursts of rage over anything or anyone that didn't meet expectations.

"Not exactly. When America entered the war, Mr. Fabyan let President Wilson and anyone else know the services of anyone at Riverbank were at their disposal. Which means that now we answer to the United States military."

Lily swallowed hard. It felt like she'd unwittingly tumbled into a strange, new world, where anything at all could happen next, like Alice into Wonderland. "Which branch?"

"All of them," Elizebeth said, her voice and demeanor the very picture of calm. "We're all they have in terms of codebreakers at the moment, the dozen or so of us over in the laboratory."

Codebreaking? For the United States military? Lily wasn't

even sure what that meant. "There must be some mistake. I-I work in the kitchen."

"And I'm a farmer's daughter," Elizebeth said, shrugging. "There's no class hierarchy in this new code bureau. There can't be. There are perhaps only three or four other people in the entire country who can do what we're being asked to accomplish."

If that was supposed to make her feel less overwhelmed, it missed the mark. "Which is what, exactly?"

"Take the encrypted messages our radio technicians have intercepted—from foreign armies, diplomats, and spies—and translate them into plaintext."

That sounded to Lily like something out of an ancient myth, medieval alchemists turning lead to gold.

"For now," Elizebeth went on, with a matter-of-fact air that didn't belong to that genre, "the only qualifications for our codebreakers are cleverness, patience, and determination."

The question hung in the air between them: Did Lily have those qualities?

She wasn't sure herself, so instead she asked, "Why doesn't the government or the military already have an office for code-breaking?"

Elizebeth gave a wry smile. "A question I asked myself." She gestured for Lily to join her on a stone bench overlooking the garden, its feet carved to look like dragon's claws. "Some government officials felt that 'reading others' mail' during peace-time was ungentlemanly. As well, technology has changed. A Civil War spy might have tucked a message into a hollowed-out egg, or within the lining of his saddlebag, or in the case of a woman, under the boning of her corset. The messages were rarely intercepted, and so the ciphers encrypting them were rarely complex."

Lily nodded, following this logic, though she knew little of espionage's history.

"Now, we have radio. All one needs is an antenna to intercept an enemy communique. But understanding what it says has become much harder. We Americans, protected so long from the squabbles in Europe, haven't bothered to keep up with the times of more advanced encryptions."

"But *you* know how to decrypt these messages?" What sort of institution trained someone—especially a woman—for that field of work?

"I learned when Mr. Fabyan hired me to search Shakespeare for hidden ciphers."

So that was the connection, the far-fetched Francis Bacon scheme led by Mrs. Gallup. "Are you saying that a handful of English coeds are being entrusted with the country's intercepted war transmissions?"

It had come out more rudely than Lily had intended, but Elizebeth only smiled good-naturedly. "Essentially, yes. My husband William and I are in charge of our operation." She went on to explain the pay, the hours, and the room and board provisions.

"But what is it *like*?" Lily finally asked.

That caused Elizebeth to pause, tilting her head like she was listening to the quiet ripple of water around them. "All I can say is . . . codebreaking is method and madness, both at once."

Lily shivered, banishing the images that rose up whenever madness was mentioned, but Elizebeth must have mistaken her response. "Exciting, isn't it? Although, to be frank, most days are full of dreary trial and error between breakthroughs. Nothing happens, followed by everything happening."

Which, Lily was sure, made it far more taxing than her days rolling out pastry in the kitchen, but perhaps also more meaningful.

"So, how about it?" Elizebeth asked, her bright eyes full of hope. "Will you join us, Lily?"

8

Lillian

No one answered Lillian's first knock on the Friedmans' front door, but that was no surprise. After all, she was nearly an hour earlier than she'd told Elizebeth to expect her. Being perpetually early was one of Lillian's incurable personality traits, though usually moderated by Roger's difficulty getting out the door.

As Lillian waited for a response, she smoothed the skirt of the Swiss dot dress she'd modified to fit this decade's fashion. Not that she had to impress Elizebeth, but there was something about her friend that made her want to look her best. Elizebeth had managed to raise two brilliant children while keeping up her career. During the '20s, while hunting down rumrunners with the Coast Guard, she'd been the subject of interviews in national publications about "the woman expert on puzzles." And somehow, she still found time to take graduate classes in archeology, practice piano, vacation in Mexico, and collect rare books for her personal library.

Meanwhile, Lillian had spent her years since Riverbank creating crossword puzzles, gardening, and sewing endless party dresses for her fashion-obsessed daughter. It was difficult, at times, not to feel inferior.

Lillian knocked again. In the pause, she took in the rich scent of the Talisman rosebush by the door, William Friedman's pride and joy. Unlike her last several visits over the years, it was a bit droopy, an indication that its fastidious owner had not been out with a watering can lately.

A fluttering at the curtains indicated subtle reconnaissance, and a few moments later, the front door creaked open. "Lily!" Elizebeth said. "What a surprise."

"I'm sorry for being so early. It's hard for me to judge how long taxi rides will take." The words came automatically, as something to fill space, because Lillian knew it was bad form to tell a woman she looked "worn-out." Yet she could hardly pretend that her friend was her usual polished self. Tendrils of curly brown hair poked out in all directions, and the sagging darkness beneath her eyes testified to nights with little sleep.

"Come in," Elizebeth said, an odd note of hesitation in her voice, glancing over her shoulder before opening the door wider. "The guest room isn't ready yet, I'm afraid."

"Don't worry about that. I can make it up myself if need be. I don't want to trouble you."

"Oh, it's no trouble, really." Elizebeth led her into the parlor and perched on the edge of the sofa. "It's so good to see you again."

"Likewise," Lillian assured her, sitting beside her. As she did, she frowned, unable to keep from giving her surroundings a quick, assessing glance.

A thin layer of dust coated the furniture, and a stack of newspapers had piled up on the credenza. The ashtray in the corner was nearly overflowing, and the windows that let in the golden afternoon light were streaked and smudged.

Something was wrong here. She'd known from past letters that Elizebeth's housekeeper had taken a welding job shortly after the start of the war, and that cleaning help was impossible to find in Washington these days, but still. The state of the place, given Elizebeth's fastidious reputation, was shocking.

"I thought perhaps we might go out for dinner tonight, just us girls," Elizebeth went on, her voice bright as the chrome that Roger so carefully polished on his sedan. "Like old times. Perhaps we could invite Margot."

"That sounds lovely. She sends her greetings, as does Dinah." Lillian tore her attention away from the smudged windows and studied Elizebeth carefully. "And where's William on this fine spring day? I brought a box of cigars for him—a gift from Roger."

This time, Lillian was certain she wasn't imagining the hesitant pause. "He's . . . not well today, I'm afraid."

It was enough of an eerie echo to make Roger seem a prophet. *"I just worried that your being there might be a strain on them, especially William."*

"Goodness, Elizebeth, why didn't you tell me? Is it something serious?"

"Nothing contagious. You know . . ." She let out a sigh. "His heart has always been weak. And he's just so very tired."

Her shoulders slumped, and Lillian shifted closer on the sofa. "It seems he's not the only one."

"I'm managing. But the work never seems to end, and . . ." Her friend's voice trailed off when she noticed Lillian's own sober expression. "It's all right, Elizebeth," Lillian said softly. "I'm here now. You can tell me anything."

The polite veneer that had suspended Elizebeth in hostess form seemed to disappear, like a coat slumped off its hanger, and she crumpled into the embrace Lillian offered.

Now what? Lillian patted her friend's shoulder awkwardly. A moment later, though, Elizebeth moved aside, sniffling slightly. "Goodness. I didn't mean to . . . it's simply been a difficult week."

"Is this about the stress placed on William?" Lillian tried, hoping her words were tactful enough. "I'm sure it's quite taxing for his health. Physically and . . . mentally, I mean."

The widening of Elizabeth's eyes showed she knew what her friend was getting at. "How did you know?"

Unwilling to fully betray her husband, Lillian replied with, "Remember, I was involved in codebreaking for a time too, though with much lower stakes than William is facing now. It seems only natural that these grueling years in his position during wartime would take a toll. And he's always been a touch melancholic."

"Yes, of course you'd understand." Thankfully, Elizabeth seemed relieved to unburden herself on someone. "No, William isn't well. He hasn't been for some time. I wanted to tell you, but William . . . he doesn't like people to know when these episodes fall on him. This is the first he's had in some time. We thought maybe . . ." She gave a shake of her head and an anxious glance toward the stairwell.

"How long do they usually last?"

"Sometimes only a few days. But he was admitted to Walter Reed General Hospital for over two months during his worst period, so it's impossible to know."

In the pause, Lillian wondered, *What would Roger say at a time like this?* Very little. That was his gift, what endeared him to so many people in trouble: Roger was an excellent listener. "That must have been very difficult."

"Yes," Elizabeth said, straightening with the "soldiering on" bearing that Lillian recognized when Roger didn't care to open up about what he'd seen in the Great War. "I'm so sorry. I ought to offer you lunch." She glanced over at the clock on the mantel. "That is, tea. I'm sure I could find something . . ."

"I'm not at all hungry," Lillian said, motioning for her friend to stay seated. "How are you holding up?" Was that the proper way to phrase it? Goodness, Lillian was failing rather badly, tiptoeing around like Elizebeth was a bereaved widow.

"All right, as far as things go, though . . . life piles up." She gestured to the clutter around them, finally acknowledging the state of the place. "I considered calling one of the children home to help, but it's John's senior year at boarding school, and Barbara is in Panama with her new job at the Office of Censorship."

"Young people shouldn't have to shoulder such concerns." Then she added quickly, "Not that William is a burden. I didn't mean—"

But Elizebeth only massaged her temples, giving her a weary smile. "No, no. You're right. Both of us have tried to keep the severity of William's condition from the children. He calls it 'the heebie-jeebies' when he writes to them about it at all, as if it's a monster under the bed. It feels that way, sometimes. A shadowy beast keeping one up late at night, whether from its actual presence or the fear of its return."

She explained more, confirming the general outline of the rumors Roger had heard. After a particularly stressful project, about which he could say nothing, William had a nervous breakdown. With the army's knowledge, he checked himself in to Walter Reed for experimental treatment, which only seemed to make his melancholia worse. After his recovery, he was dismissed from active military status, and though he continued to serve in his role as a civilian, the threat of compete dismissal always loomed over him. This resulted in his desire to battle his occasional "fits" of depression alone.

"So, then, have you told the army that William is missing work due to travel?" Lillian asked.

For a moment, Elizebeth only looked at her blankly, then shook her head. "Oh, no. William's still going to work. He's only taken one day of vacation in years, for our twenty-fifth anniversary."

"You can't be serious." Hadn't Elizebeth just said that William had difficulty getting out of bed, trembled with nervous energy, and hardly slept at night? It simply wasn't sustainable.

"It would only reinforce their idea that he's unfit for his work, and the country needs him now more than ever."

"But . . . surely someone must notice?"

"In the army's codebreaking unit?" Elizebeth's chuckle was brittle. "Everyone is exhausted, run-down, and either riddled with ulcers or addicted to cigarettes. William hides his fits as best he can. Besides, he still has pills to take from his last attack. Amytal, the kind they use for soldiers with battle fatigue. They help, somewhat. At least he gets a few hours of sleep." She spoke the words with practiced confidence, but Lillian noticed that the breath she took in quavered slightly.

"We'll pray he gets better soon," Lillian said, trying to sound confident. She knew Elizebeth believed more in a general creator than one who intervened in their world. But sometimes, life was so very far out of one's control, and there was no one to appeal to but God.

To her surprise, Elizebeth stood and clasped Lillian's hand, tears in her eyes. "Thank you, Lily."

"For what?" As far as Lillian could see, she'd come in uninvited and forced Elizebeth to speak of things she'd hoped to keep concealed, all without offering a single practical solution.

"For not being horrified, or even shocked."

Lillian frowned. "Why should I be? William is responding in a logical way to the strain he's been put under. It's a testament to his strength of mind that he's endured so long, certainly not a weakness."

"I can't tell you how good it is to hear you say so. I have felt the same, myself, but sometimes I wonder . . ." Elizebeth stepped to the side, glancing back toward the stairs again. "Regardless, I nearly telephoned Margot to tell you not to come, but I had a desperate hope that William would be stronger by today."

"If it's a bad time for me to be here . . ."

Elizebeth cut her off with a firm shake of her head. "Certainly not. Where would you go? The hotels around town have been converted into apartments, and there's scarcely a room free unless you're a major general." She gave Lillian a cautious look. "Besides, I thought perhaps . . . you would understand better than most."

Lillian's breath caught. Both Friedmans knew as much as Roger about her past with a mentally ill mother, confided in them during her years at Riverbank, though they hadn't spoken about it in years, as if by silent pact. Their unconditional acceptance and friendship had once both surprised and encouraged her. Now it was her turn to be of use to them.

And, for the first time, Lillian had a reason to be grateful for the childhood she'd endured, born to a mother only half present in reality, who stumbled through work and disappeared into darkness for days, even weeks, at a time. Mama had been troubled in a different way than William but had faced a similar lack of solutions.

Lillian often found it difficult to read others' emotions, but this time, Elizebeth was right: She could identify with the fear the Friedmans felt. She *understood*.

This time, Elizebeth reached across the space between them, squeezing her hand. "Please, Lily. I want you to stay. It would be . . . a comfort to me."

Lillian met her gaze. She seemed sincere, all social niceties aside. "All right. But I give you fair warning: As long as I'm here, I intend to be of some use."

For the first time since opening the front door, Elizebeth seemed genuinely at a loss for words. "Oh, but I couldn't . . . You are a guest here, Lily."

"A guest whose only skills are cooking and housecleaning.

Don't take offense, Elizabeth, but you look like you haven't eaten a decent meal in a month."

"Only a week." The feeble protest felt like a confirmation.

"In addition, I could handle your bills and checkbook. Respond to business correspondence saying that William is ill and will reply when possible. Stand in ration lines on your behalf when the good cuts of meat come in. Anything at all."

Lillian hadn't given this much thought, and yet the more tasks she listed, the more sensible it sounded. She stood, mentally making a list of all that could be done.

Elizebeth chewed on her lower lip, then looked up. "That sounds . . . wonderful, actually."

Lillian felt a burst of triumph. Useful. She could be useful, in some little way, to the friend who had opened a whole world to her. "Then consider it done. I can stay for a month, at least." That was longer than planned, but surely it wouldn't be difficult to make arrangements. Roger would be delighted that she'd be able to check in on Dinah a while longer.

Her friend seemed to weigh this, shifting on slippered feet. "I suppose you think I ought to insist that William leave his job for his health. But I can't do that. He's doing good work, Lillian. And so am I."

Good work. What manner of secrets lay behind those simple words, Lillian might never know.

"Besides, on a more mercenary level, we have mortgage payments. John's private school is quite expensive, and with the tuition we paid for Barbara's degree at Radcliffe . . . Losing an income now, either William's or mine, might mean losing our home, the life we've built here."

"As I said, I understand, Elizabeth. And I'm here to help, for as long as you need me. It's what friends do."

"All right," she finally said. "If you're certain."

Lillian felt a warmth inside of her as she climbed the stairs with carpetbag in tow, a sense of purpose she hadn't felt in years, ever since Roger began working longer hours and Dinah went out with friends most evenings.

Roger always spoke of the hand of Providence placing people where he designed. *"Like we're pawns on a chessboard?"* Lillian had joked, though the idea was faintly distasteful.

"No," he'd said, taking her seriously. *"More like characters in one of those Shakespeare plays you're always reading. Timing the entrances and exits for the perfect story."*

It was a nice sentiment, but this was the first time Lillian had really felt as if some higher power had placed her in the wings, right where she needed to be. Maybe this was the reason she'd come to Washington, DC.

Dinah

By her third stack of documents, Dinah had gone squinty and cross-eyed. She blinked a few times, trying to get some moisture back, and forged on.

In addition to the marking requirements prescribed in sub-section 4-103, the warning notices prescribed in this section shall be displayed prominently on classified documents. . . .

"Don't tell me you're actually reading that drivel." Her guide, who had introduced himself as Barry Longstreet, smirked at her, leaning against the generic beige wall. "Let me help you out: *Confidential* means don't talk about it, *Secret* means *really* don't talk about it, and *Top Secret* means don't talk about it even to God."

"I have a feeling God already knows." Dinah had spent enough Sundays in her little Gettysburg church to understand that much. According to Dad, God was somehow big enough to know everything and small enough to care about everyone. Her

71

father was convinced the hand of the Almighty had brought Dinah to Washington, for instance. *"You'll see,"* he'd said when they hugged good-bye. *"You're in the OSS for a reason."*

Mr. Longstreet laughed longer than the little quip deserved. "Go on, then. Give us your autograph."

Not wanting to look like an egghead, Dinah skipped the last several pages and added her signature with a flourish.

"And there you have it, Miss Kendall." Mr. Longstreet swept up the paperwork like it was nothing more than junk mail. "You're one of us now." He shook her hand, and, rather than letting go, smoothly transferred the gesture into taking her arm to direct her out of the conference room.

"Delighted," she said, trying to sound as professional as her new brown suit and pumps made her look. "Are you responsible for training me?"

"Unfortunately for both of us, no. That would be one of our chiefs, Mr. Frasier Agnew." Mr. Longstreet made a face like he'd gulped orange juice directly after brushing his teeth. "He'll go over the department basics before turning you over to Olivia Masterson in Rumors."

Dinah tried to ignore a flutter of misgiving from the sour way Mr. Longstreet had pronounced both names and focus on the fact that she worked in an office that had a division called "Rumors."

"Agnew's last hire eloped with a streetcar driver," Mr. Longstreet went on, guiding her around a corner with a light touch to her waist . . . a bit too low for Dinah's comfort. "He's sensitive about it. You can't help being gorgeous, but don't talk about seeing a beau." An insinuating wink indicated that Mr. Longstreet would be more than happy to fill that role.

As they walked down a long, office-lined corridor, Mr. Longstreet lowered his voice. "Agnew was a top news correspondent in Berlin before he had to be hustled out in the late thirties.

Frederick Oechsner—that's MO's director—put him in charge of propaganda. It pays to stay on his good side."

He stopped talking altogether when they got within earshot of a woman who was presumably Mr. Agnew's secretary, a stern-looking matron who appeared vaguely irritated that they had interrupted her machine-gun pace at the typewriter. She stood to show them inside the office at the end of the hallway.

Mr. Longstreet gestured for Dinah to precede him, giving her a good first look at Frasier Agnew, standing beside his desk. He was only an inch or so taller than Dinah, and quite pale. His mild brown eyes were magnified by spectacles, and he looked to be in his fifties or early sixties. There was nothing physically intimidating about him, and yet . . . Dinah felt smaller in his presence, somehow.

Maybe it was the way he paced the room like it was a cell rather than an office, or the precise trim of his receding hair, or the fact that his desk was organized with everything at right angles, neat enough to seem disused. A hint of smoke lingered, and the curtains over the lone window were partially drawn, giving the air of a noir detective's lair.

"Miss Kendall, here for her first day, sir," Mr. Longstreet said in a voice several notches too loud.

Dinah blinked, suddenly aware that Mr. Agnew was taking a direct path toward her with the determination of Sherman marching to the sea. Not knowing what else to do, she stuck out a hand.

He took it, and she matched the firm pressure as best as she could.

Then he returned to his desk, settling heavily in his chair. A map of the world dominated the wall behind him, making him look, absurdly, like he was trying to place himself at its center. "You wear far too much lipstick, Miss Kendall. I hope you won't spend all your time stepping out with young men."

Mr. Longstreet gave a strangled cough that might have been a laugh.

"No," Dinah said, keeping her voice even, "I imagine I'll spend a good portion of it here."

When his stare refused to produce the blush he was apparently looking for, he grunted. "Well, you have my sympathy."

"I'm sorry?" she blurted, wondering if she'd mistaken his meaning.

"Surely you've heard at least *some* tittle-tattle about our department. We do, after all, employ people for their ability to create convincing rumors."

She didn't respond. Silence felt better than stammering another question.

"No? Then allow me to welcome you to the dregs of the OSS." Mr. Agnew let out an audible sigh like he was auditioning for a role in a Shakespearean tragedy. "Where we linger so far at the bottom that we taste more like oaken cask than fine vintage."

"Don't sugarcoat it or anything," Mr. Longstreet said sardonically. If Mr. Agnew realized he was being mocked, he gave no sign of being offended. In fact, the one glance he aimed at Mr. Longstreet was as curt as a spoken dismissal.

"Good luck, doll," Mr. Longstreet muttered. "See you around."

As he slammed the door behind him, Dinah hesitated. There must be a reason Mr. Agnew categorized Morale Operations so negatively, but asking why felt a bit too forward for a first day. Instead, she set her handbag down, then edged toward her new boss.

"Please listen carefully, as I don't like to repeat myself." He drew out a plain black notebook and handed it to her. "Since you don't seem to have brought anything to take notes."

She nodded her thanks and perched in the wooden swivel chair in front of his desk, crossing her legs at the ankles the way Mother had taught her.

"As I'm sure you know, I administer the Publication and Campaigns Division of Morale Operations. Allow me to lay out a few expectations." Despite its slightly nasal quality, there was something mesmerizing in Mr. Agnew's voice, booming out to mere mortals like Oz the Great and Terrible. "First, on days when you're not being paraded about by every Tom, Dick, and Harry with childhood aspirations of being a spy, I expect you in your assigned desk at eight a.m. Not merely in the building. In the Rumors office."

He gave a pointed look at Dinah's notebook, breaking the spell, and she ducked her head down and jotted, *Don't be late*, even as Mr. Agnew went on, "Do you smoke?"

She frowned. "No."

"A pity. You won't mind if I do." Dinah glanced up to be sure she'd heard correctly, and that the words were not phrased in the form of a question. Given that he was reaching for a lighter and that the discreet ashtray just to the right of the leather desk pad was full, she suspected she had.

Mr. Agnew went on to specify the lunch hour, forbid the chewing of gum, and give her a list of OSS, Army, and British Intelligence acronyms to memorize.

She'd just begun to scan the alphabet soup of entries when Mr. Agnew tossed a slender booklet on her desk with the carelessness of a boy delivering a newspaper, labeled *Morale Operations Field Manual*. "You'll spend the rest of the morning reading this. There's no sense in disturbing other people's productive work to hear names that you'll forget instantly before you've learned the basics."

"Understood," Dinah answered, taking advantage of the pause, "but would you mind giving me more details about my daily tasks?"

Mr. Agnew stared at her for a moment, as if to determine whether she was joking. "I suppose it was too generous to assume someone would have informed you already." His weary head shake indicated just what he thought of OSS hiring practices. "You have been assigned to the Rumor Department, headed by the estimable Mrs. Olivia Masterson. Her team's particular line of professional devilry is wading through information from overseas news sources and our own Research and Analysis Department to produce nuggets of false news to confuse and dishearten our enemies."

This, at least, vaguely resembled the work Colonel Forth had described, though he'd made it sound like a much greater adventure. "As such, you'll read and prepare reports, study Axis radio broadcasts, and type up endless drafts of rumors, programs, and whisper campaign ideas, many of which will never be used."

Dinah dutifully jotted these tasks down in her notebook, despite her sinking sense of doom. It sounded just like school, only with higher stakes.

Still, this was vital work, and they'd chosen *her* for it. *I'll just have to learn.* Maybe they wouldn't realize how little experience she had.

The morning passed quickly in a barrage of new information from the manual and a more detailed twelve-page memorandum detailing the Rumor Department's mission. During lunch, Dinah stayed in the office and tried to sort out the Morale Operations organizational charts while choking down a soggy egg salad sandwich.

The moment Mr. Agnew returned to the office, slamming the door behind him, he burst out with, "Tell me, Miss Kendall, what are the six principles for creating rumors, as found in the *Morale Operations Field Manual*?"

Dinah straightened her spine, feeling like she was back in Camp Fire Girls, reciting the Gettysburg Address for her Citizenship honor bead. "A good rumor must be simple, plausible, vivid . . ." She tried to remember the exact wording found in the handbook. It had been interesting reading, but she hadn't expected to be tested. "Effective, memorable, and dramatic?"

"The last three are suitable to the task, suggestive, and concrete."

Well, her answers hadn't been *so* far off. "I'll read the manual again tonight," she promised. So much for a relaxing evening after her first day.

"I wouldn't bother."

Her eyes flashed upward, but her employer was flipping through a multipage memorandum, seemingly content with his brief exhortation. "Sir?"

"Most of its content is to differentiate our territory from that of the Office of War Information. The section on rumors might be the only bit of practical training for you in the whole thing." Mr. Agnew sat heavily in his chair. "Apparently, most people need careful instruction to cast 'a net of deep deceit, a gilded hook that holds a poisoned bait.'"

Dinah tilted her head slightly, not recognizing the reference. "No belief in 'the truth will set you free' around here, I take it?" The Bible, at least, was one book she knew well enough to quote. Maybe that would make her sound at least somewhat intelligent.

"On the contrary. I'm a journalist first, Miss Kendall." He seemed genuinely offended, ready to whip out his press pass at any moment as proof. "As such, I believe truth is the most powerful force on this earth. Still, the lies we manufacture in Morale Operations might give us the edge we need. Because sometimes, the truth is that our enemies are winning the battle. If we let them know it, they might win the war. And we can't have that, now can we?"

"No, sir," Dinah said, though she'd never really thought about it before.

"I want to be clear, particularly since you'll be working in Rumors." Mr. Agnew signed a document in front of him, then set his fountain pen down with a flourish, his attention focused on her like the sights of a rifle. "We are not ladies and gentlemen here in MO. We use nearly the same techniques that outraged Americans when the Nazis employed them to conquer nations."

"Surely not," Dinah blurted, before she could stop herself.

"Oh, yes." He ticked off examples on his fingers, his tone as even as if he were reciting the daily special from a dinner menu. "We are liars and scoundrels. We spread panic among civilians. We blackmail and bribe and loot identity papers from corpses. We insinuate German wives are unfaithful and forge poison-pen letters and stoke prejudices. In short, we stoop to anything that will cause our enemies to lose the will to fight." He paused, watching her for a reaction. "There is also an absurd amount of paperwork." This last addition earned a brief shudder.

Dinah couldn't quite determine whether he was joking. The expression on his face was as blank as a new sheet of typing paper, making him harder to read than any of the OSS recruits she'd spied on in Gettysburg. "I . . . I think I understand."

"Please sit up, Miss Kendall. Slumping is a habit difficult to unlearn."

Dinah jerked to attention like a green boot camp private who'd fallen asleep during roll call. Mother would have been horrified.

"Now then. There were a few details missing from your file that I would like to add." Mr. Agnew held up his pen, perfectly poised, like a dagger. "I understand you were hired primarily because of your performance in an assessment task at the Catoctin Mountain Training Area."

"That's correct."

"I'd like to hear more about your formal training. Typing speed?"

She hadn't been prepared for this. "Average." *I hope.*

"How many words per minute, Miss Kendall?" he clarified flatly.

"Oh. I . . ." Dinah had attempted a commercial typing course during her junior year of high school but had barely emerged with a C. Her work at the locksmith shop had mostly involved scheduling repair appointments and greeting customers.

Better to be honest than make up a number that might not be within a plausible range. "I haven't timed myself. Sir."

He made a note of this, though what it was, she couldn't see. "Then what was your score on the civil service exam?"

"I-I was told I didn't need to take an exam." Had Colonel Forth exaggerated the number of strings he could pull? "I wasn't aware this was a secretarial position."

"It isn't, per se, but Rumor workers do all of their own typing, and they haven't time to waste on silly errors." *The sort you're likely to make,* he seemed to imply. "I suppose it's too much to hope that you have at least a year of experience in journalism, or at junior college in a commercial department?"

Each question made Dinah want to sink lower in her chair. "No. I . . . took a few courses in high school . . ."

Mr. Agnew's sigh was so gusty it could have triggered monitoring by the Weather Bureau. "Then you won't have used a duplicating machine before, or had any of your writing published, or made use of information from scholarly research?"

Each phrase felt like an attack. *Not good enough.*

"I know some shorthand," she said, in frail defense. "And I have nearly two years of experience as a clerk at my family's locksmith shop."

"I see." His reply was unimpressed, which felt appropriate, as Dinah had never felt so unimpressive in all her life. "Miss Kendall, the OSS, like many organizations, is steeped in the ancient Washington custom of nepotism. This means I am quite used to dealing with employees hired for personal connections rather than qualifications—your earlier acquaintance Mr. Barry Longstreet being a prime example. But I assure you that while

I can accept a certain amount of on-the-job training, I expect to find competence and initiative."

This comparison to entitled politicians' sons, more than anything else, brought a hot reply to Dinah's lips. "Wait just a moment, sir. I may not have the experience you're looking for, and you may not approve of my lipstick or posture or anything else about me, but make no mistake: I *am* a hard worker." She formed a thin line with her lips, holding her head high. "I suggest you let me prove myself before passing judgment."

"Hmm. Duly noted, I suppose." He looked at her over the rims of his glasses, his slim silhouette framed by light from the window. "I can only repeat the eternal demand made upon us all, Miss Kendall." He pounded a fist on his desk, rattling the ashtray. "*Improve.* Soon, please. And for goodness' sake, find a more professional color of nail polish. None at all would be preferable."

"Are you sure you don't want to fire me now? I'd rather know before I settle my arrangements here."

She realized that, for the first time, Mr. Agnew was *smiling.* Just barely, but there was an upward tilt to his thin mouth that couldn't be denied. "It is to your benefit," he intoned, "that I hold to the antiquated principle that pluck shows promise." He stood and handed her a hefty folder from his desk. "Tomorrow, I will introduce you to Mrs. Masterson and the rest of her team. It would serve you well to be prepared. You must be bold *and* useful."

"I'll do my best." What more was there to promise?

What am I going to do now?

Certainly not tell Mother. Dinah was sure she had never been overwhelmed about anything as ordinary as a difficult first day of work.

No, she'd find some way to press on and make good. Until then, no one needed to know.

10

Lily

"I'd never felt quite a part of Riverbank, but once I joined Elizebeth and William's crew, for the first time, I had a purpose."

—Excerpt from Lillian Kendall's journal

Monday, July 16, 1917

Lily stared up at the Engineering Building, a tiered cake made of bland beige blocks, each floor smaller than the last. She deliberately averted her eyes from the laboratory in the east corner.

So this is it. Could she walk up these stairs without fleeing to the safety of her new quarters? She took one last deep breath and marched forward.

"Oh, we don't work in there, Lily." Elizebeth steered her away with a smile. "That's for Mr. Fabyan's military researchers and anatomists and the like."

"Oh," Lily said, the only word she could manage through her relief.

"You should be grateful." Elizabeth shuddered. "They say there's a laboratory that displays actual human skeletons with spinal deformities and distortions."

"I had heard." Lily wasn't about to tell Elizebeth that she had been given a personal tour of the Chamber of Horrors, shuddering at the grotesque forms hung there and trying not to listen to the narration delivered by one of the posture scientists.

"They say the rich fellow who lives here hires graverobbers to snatch the bodies for him," one of the other girls had whispered in her ear, a gleam of malice in her eyes. *"Buries the corpses in unmarked graves around the estate and hangs the bones here. Maybe he'll do the same to us when he's done with us, eh?"*

Whatever the truth was about the Chamber of Horrors, it was certainly best not to speak of it. Elizebeth treated her like an equal. Lily could only assume that meant she didn't know about the experiments that had originally brought Lily to Riverbank, a secret Lily meant to keep hidden.

Elizebeth led her past the Engineering Building and the Acoustics Laboratory, currently under construction, to a two-story building she referred to as Engledew Cottage, though calling the sprawling outbuilding a "cottage" felt like an insult to the fairy tales that Lily had treasured as a child.

"It's not much," Elizebeth said, climbing up to the porch. "Drafty in the winter and stuffy in the summer. The first floor is our code room, the second is divided into living spaces. William and I have a suite there."

She probably felt these accommodations were austere, but when Lily had moved her few belongings into the Lodge from the tiny room she had shared with other unmarried maids, it had seemed like a palace. Every night, a glass of ice water and a plate of fruit was laid out for each resident on their nightstands.

At Elizebeth's prompting, Mr. Fabyan himself, large and imposing in a white suit coat and striped trousers, had explained to his disgruntled cook why a member of his serving staff was being requisitioned for war work. *"Now then, Miss Nilsson,"* he'd barked, the first and only time he'd addressed her directly, *"go out and be* spectacular.*"*

Now here she was, ready to become a codebreaker.

Elizebeth opened the cottage's front door, and Lily hovered in the doorway, her eyes flitting over the scene inside the code room.

Desks and several long tables turned the hardwood floor into a maze, with all other furniture pushed toward the wall. Men and women hunched over papers, paced by the windows, or pecked furiously at typewriters. Every now and then, a burst of nonsense would usher forth from a group crowded around a workstation. "Yoke, easy, jig, cast!" was met with a rapid-fire reply of "Fox, vice, cast, pup, oboe."

It was difficult not to stare, but Lily schooled her expression and attempted to look, if not confident, then at least competent.

She listened more carefully, noting the repeated words. *It's an alphabet. They're spelling something.* She'd heard of military men using such a system to make sure messages were transmitted accurately.

A quick count revealed there were no more than fourteen workers in the code room, including a few who seemed to be clerks or stenographers. Elizebeth had not been exaggerating their need for more help.

"Good morning, Margot," Elizebeth said over the noise to a young woman stationed by a desk near the door, her hair a shade of blond so pale it was nearly white.

"I'll call it good when this heat wave breaks," Margot grumbled. She flicked her eyes up to greet them, and Lily had time to wonder if she'd gotten the job based on her looks alone. She had a confident glamor that wouldn't be out of place at the soirees Mr. Fabyan threw, full of famous songstresses and starlets.

"This is Miss Lily Nilsson," Elizebeth volunteered as Margot went back to work, slicing through envelopes pulled from a large canvas sack as if fileting fish.

"How do you do," Lily offered.

Another quick, assessing glance from the secretary's kohl-lined eyes. "You've dug up a new one?"

"Thankfully, yes." Elizebeth turned to Lily, who must have been staring at the piles of paper. "The ciphers come by post or telegram from Washington, and Miss Schnieder sorts ones whose origins indicate they will be in German, her native language. A couple of the other clerks are competent in Spanish, the other main language of the transmissions we're sent."

"As you can see, we're falling behind," Margot pointed out, not a trace of a German accent in her voice. "Or, rather, you lot are. I only translate real words, not this code jumble."

The situation wouldn't be helped by Elizebeth taking the time to train her. Yet again, Lily felt panic push on her sternum like a weight. Maybe she shouldn't have agreed to this.

"Then we'd best get started." Elizebeth nodded at Margot, then ushered Lily deeper into the long, open room, past a blackboard filled with scribbled letters, sharp and white against the ashy remains of work completed—or failed—and erased. "I'm afraid your education will be brief. Codebreaking can only really be learned by doing. In its simplest form, it's a process of asking two questions over and over again."

That, at least, suggested a method, something more concrete than the near-magic Elizebeth had described before. "And those are?"

"What do you know? And what does it mean?" She gestured to a rare chair, and Lily took it, staring at the paper Elizebeth had placed before her, full of letter clusters, as if someone had tested a typewriter by pressing keys at random.

Elizebeth stood at her side, her voice becoming professorial as she indicated the paper. "There are two main types of ciphers: transpositions and substitutions. Transpositions rearrange the letters of a word. Substitutions replace one letter with another. The first step in solving a cipher is determining which sort is used."

"How do we do that?"

"By writing out each occurrence of a letter in a worksheet column." Elizabeth pointed to the jumble before her. "We call this a frequency analysis. If the most common letters appear most often—vowels, for instance—then a transposition is most likely."

In the corner of the paper was a notation in fountain pen, *Berlin, April 20, 1917—Practice Cipher*. Lily felt a welcome rush of relief at the lowered stakes. They had already solved this one. "What are the most common letters in German?"

Elizabeth nodded in approval, and Lily felt a burst of pride that she'd asked an intelligent question. "*E, N, I, R, T,* and *S,* in that order."

After Lily dutifully jotted down each letter of the message in the proper column, Elizabeth went on to explain how to use letter and word frequency to gain a starting point, the signs of a more complex polyalphabetic cipher, and the difference between a code—ordinary words substituted for compromising ones with the meanings agreed on in advance—and a cipher. Through it all, she patiently answered questions Lily feared sounded foolish.

Even an hour into the lecture, Elizebeth's eyes were bright with excitement, and Lily couldn't help feeling some of her own. Here was a woman who not only loved breaking ciphers, but who also loved teaching.

"William and I read a recent study published by a Harvard professor about the ten most common English words to occur in conversation—"

"Did I hear my name?"

The sudden intrusion of a male voice startled Lily into re-membering that there was a world beyond Elizebeth's instruction and the papers before her. She looked up to see a young man in a suit with a crisply starched collar and smart bow tie approach to stand beside Elizebeth.

Lily had seen William Friedman around the Lodge breakfast table, though he wasn't one of the flashy, outspoken types. Of average height, with mild, round features, and precisely parted hair, he was more likely to fade into the background.

Elizebeth shifted to make room for him. "Indeed, you did. Though unless you're bearing a German-English dictionary, I'll thank you not to interrupt our lesson." Her words held a teasing lilt, despite William's dramatic clutch at his heart.

"You wound me, my love." They exchanged a glance filled with such affection that Lily looked away. "This is our crossword recruit, I take it?"

"The very same," Elizebeth confirmed. "Lily, my husband, William."

"Good to meet you," Lily said shyly. William offered his hand to shake, and her grip wasn't as firm as it ought to be. "Only . . . I thought you were one of the scientists, Mr. Friedman, not on Mrs. Gallup's crew."

"I was," William said, smiling at his wife again. "Lured away from my fruit fly genetic experiments by this beauty and her puzzles."

Elizebeth laughed. "Don't listen to him. Mr. Fabyan assigned him to this project himself." She pressed the flat of her hand to her husband's chest, playfully pushing him away. "Back to work now, Billy Boy. We've got to get Miss Nilsson ready to join us in earnest."

"Yes, Mrs. Friedman." He pressed a kiss to his wife's forehead before slipping away, and Lily blushed at the public show of affection.

How lucky for Elizebeth to have found a man who so clearly adored her. Lily felt a twinge of jealousy in spite of herself. Her mother had tried to instill a suspicion of men into her, a result of too many failed relationships of her own, but Lily had seen enough healthy marriages to realize a happy ending was indeed possible.

Not for her, though. The dream of a husband and children had been destroyed for her years ago. But for someone.

Step by step, Elizebeth walked her through the example, pausing to let Lily work out conclusions alone and showing her examples of ciphers further along in the decryption process.

Finally, Lily glanced at her pages of notes. After assigning the most frequent letters and word pairs to their likely plain-text equivalents, with Margot looking over her shoulder and a dictionary at her side, words began to emerge. Each new likely assumption led to a dozen others, written lightly in pencil first, then traced over when she was sure they fit. With Elizebeth's guidance and hints, she soon had one whole sentence, then two.

. . . *so schnell wie möglich*, which meant, according to Margot, *as soon as possible* . . . As her pencil flew over the paper, Lily felt a smile tug at her lips. This feeling . . . it reminded her of the day she'd found a doll buried in the mud near one of their many temporary homes. The riverbank was downstream from a dump, and Mama sent her there sometimes after a hard rain to look for metal, glass bottles, or crockery that they could sell to the junkman.

That day, Lily had seen a few china fingers sticking out from the soil like the shoots of a pale wild onion. She'd clawed the whole thing out, a mass of mud, waste, and rotted vegetables with only the vague form of a doll beneath it. Back at their tenement, she'd scrubbed the filthy thing, and when wide blue glass eyes had looked at her, she'd felt the same thrill—of discovery, of clearing away the dirt to reveal a hidden treasure.

This treasure, however, wouldn't be tucked into dresses made of rags. Lily's decoded messages could spare a convoy ship, predict a battle, or save a battalion.

She wrote the last of the missing letters, passing it to Elizebeth without a word. She was rewarded with a warm "Well done" from her teacher.

I can actually learn this.

After a not-so-leisurely luncheon, Margot sidled over with tips on how to crack a cipher in German without knowing the language—a condensed list of common words and letter pairings would help until it became rote—and then Lily was invited to watch several codebreakers she had yet to meet tackle a complex cipher together. This resulted in the alphabetic shouting she'd heard earlier and the use of a blackboard alongside worksheets of grid paper.

This had quite a different feel from simply being matched against a test puzzle. Louder. Less organized. More stressful. Even hearing the chaos and watching the focused, yet frenetic, actions of the other codebreakers made Lily breathe faster. The humid, almost airless room seemed to close in around her, and her heart tripped to the beat of the first buzz of panic.

Not here. Not now. Please.

Mama's terrors were back again, surfacing, as they often did, in moments of stress or exposure to the unknown.

"We ought to put the girl in an institution," the doctor had argued, not knowing she was listening, *"at least until she's twenty. Diseases of the nerves often manifest quite early, particularly the cycle of mania and melancholia exhibited by her mother."*

But unlike Mama, Lily could fight these moments of panic without allowing them to turn into days or weeks of uncontrolled emotion. She had before, and she *would* now.

She tried taking deep breaths, focusing on one thing—the box of large white gum erasers on the table—and repeatedly denied the instinct to flee. Still, even as her heart rate slowed, she had to wonder: Had taking this job been a terrible mistake?

"This idea of codebreaking as a solitary job is patent nonsense," Elizebeth said during a brief lull. By then, Lily had taken a seat beneath one of the cottage's open windows and felt somewhat better. "Several people often work out a cipher to its conclusion. We find the answers together, or not at all."

"What if we fail?" Lily asked, her voice quiet and tense.

"We will not," Elizebeth said simply, setting a new cipher before her. "More accurately, we cannot. Too much depends on us."

It seemed too simple, except that Lily could see it was working. Armed with only a few books on codebreaking and time staring at typefaces in Shakespeare folios, Elizebeth and William were becoming the nation's expert codebreakers. And she was joining them.

Lily picked up the paper with its garble of letters, licked her dry lips, and began.

11

Dinah

There. It's over.

Dinah felt a sense of relief as she sat on her bed and slid off her pumps. Climbing down the steps of the OSS headquarters in three-inch heels had been murder, though it was better than the shoddy leather "bootees" issued to Union soldiers. They were often poorly sized, so to get them to fit, soldiers would soak them in water and walk in them to reshape them as they dried. Dinah didn't suppose that technique worked with pumps.

At least Mother wasn't here to say, "I told you to buy the flats instead," with her eyebrows if not in words. Dinah had half expected to be accosted by Mother in the parlor on arriving back at Myrtlewood, but all she'd gotten was a phone call from the Friedmans' home. Dinah had been able to answer a barrage of her mother's mundane questions easily enough —"Did you meet your supervisor? Are there other women working in your department? Do you have an adequate understanding of the position?" Dinah hoped Mother would attribute any vagueness to the secret nature of OSS work and not her desire to get off the line and escape to her room.

"I hope to stop by sometime this week," Mother had said before ringing off, "although I'll have . . . tasks to see to here, so I won't be available as often as I thought."

"That's all right, Mother. I'll be just fine," Dinah had said quickly—too quickly, maybe, because Mother's good-bye after that had sounded a bit wounded. But really, whatever was keeping Mother away would give her some space to be independent. It was for the best, for both of them.

After changing into her favorite pair of slippers, Dinah stifled a yawn—how could she be so tired after a day behind a desk?—and headed downstairs, hoping to find some of the other boarders in the common spaces. Unlike her mother, who, once she had made friends with Elizebeth and Margot in her twenties, didn't seem to need any others, Dinah didn't intend to isolate herself from Myrtlewood's social life.

But when Dinah hurried downstairs, the only other occupant of the parlor was Winora McMahen, seated with a large sketchbook clutched in her arms. She glanced up when Dinah entered and turned pointedly away.

Well. So much for that.

Dinah glanced around for some excuse to be present in the room. Not the piano, its keys yellowed like unwashed teeth—her lessons at age eight hadn't advanced much beyond a mangled "Frerè Jacques." She could call Dad and Grammy on the phone in the hallway, but then Winora might listen in. Finally, Dinah settled on perusing the books crammed into a built-in case on the south wall.

She took down a tome with a charming motif emblazoned on the spine in gold. *An Introduction to American Civilization.* "Has Auntie Margot actually read any of these?" she muttered.

"They came with the house."

Dinah spun around, but Winora hadn't looked up, her pencil moving across the paper with deliberate strokes. "She'll probably renovate them eventually like she does everything else. Better watch out . . . if you hang around here with nothing to do, she'll put you to work stripping wallpaper or something."

That sounded just like Auntie Margot. "I take it you've lived here a while, then?"

Winora shrugged. "Almost a year."

It wasn't much of an answer, but it was something. Maybe this was the other girl's way of making an effort. "What do you think of the place?"

"It's fine, I guess. The rent is cheap. Curfew's too early, though." She shrugged. "And Schnieder leaves me well enough alone." Winora eyed Dinah meaningfully. The implication was clear. *You'd better do the same.*

Well, that was a dead end. Still, Dinah wasn't accustomed to being ignored. She'd been on her high school's yearbook staff, taught Sunday school to children at church, and served as secretary of her senior class. She never failed to win others over—eventually.

Everyone liked talking about themselves, didn't they? So long as the questions weren't about anything too personal or controversial: family, politics, religion, the war . . .

Goodness. What does that leave?

"So . . . have you been around to see the sights?" she ventured.

"Some." Winora hunched over, shading a small area with her pencil in a particularly forceful motion.

Keep trying. She can't maintain one-word answers forever. If Winora truly wanted solitude, she could have done her sketching in her room. "I was hoping to visit the Constitution at the Library of Congress this weekend. Have you been?"

Winora's bushy hair trembled as she shook her head. "No go. They snuck out all of the important documents—Bill of

Rights, Gettysburg Address, even some old Bible—just after Pearl Harbor. Put 'em on a train in the dark of night to hide somewhere in case the Jerries bomb us."

"Wow." Dinah tried to think of how to continue the conversation, but all that came to mind was the latest Western film she and her friends had gone to together. "Imagine if you'd been a train robber just trying for an honest day's theft and ended up with the Constitution."

This time, at least, Winora actually looked up at her. Granted, it was with an expression of incredulity, but still. "That's not how robberies work."

"It would make a great comedy is all I'm saying. Sort of a reverse heist." She could just see it: Gary Cooper cast in the lead role, realizing his mistake, trying to return the documents without getting caught, falling in love with a beautiful train attendant . . .

Winora squinted at her. "Where did you say you worked, again?"

Dinah perked up. An actual question, the sort conversations were made of. And yet . . . how was she supposed to answer? "I didn't, actually."

"That's all right. I already know."

The smug look on the other woman's face made Dinah blanch, certain she was somehow telling the truth. Had she followed Dinah to the OSS headquarters? Why? What would Mr. Agnew say if he found out?

"I don't understand," she tried, though it sounded unconvincing even to her ears.

Winora made a low, gravelly sound that Dinah finally identified as a laugh. "No need to fake it. We're both OSS. Even in the same department. I walked past you this morning, getting the rundown from Longstreet."

If Winora had told her she was a member of Roosevelt's cabinet, Dinah couldn't have been more surprised. "*You* work in Morale Operations?"

She shut her sketchbook, tucking her pencil in her hair, where it all but disappeared in the dark tangles. "Yep. I'm a few halls down, in Forgery. Better keep your jokes about stealing the Constitution to yourself. From what I hear, Agnew wouldn't like it."

"What fun!" Dinah clasped her hands together, suddenly brimming with things they could talk about, as long as the others weren't around. "I'm so glad you told me. Are you a secretary?"

"Me?" A scornful look puckered Winora's lips. "Not a chance. I'm an artist."

"Oh." That would explain the sketchbook, but what use would the OSS have for an artist? Perhaps she illustrated the pamphlets they dropped over enemy lines. Dinah suppressed the urge to ask her if she'd sketched Hitler's face for the toilet paper. "Have you been drawing for a while?"

"Almost eight years in the family business," Winora said, a flicker of pride giving character to her monotone Boston accent. "Although technically, it's more engraving."

"Is that . . . sculpting with metal?" Dinah now wished she'd taken art electives at school, though she would probably have been hopeless at those too.

"Something like that." Her tone made it clear Dinah was wildly off, but that she didn't want to take the time to explain to a complete ignoramus.

"How long have you ___?" Dinah began.

From deeper in the house, a bell rang out a call to the dining room, reminding Dinah more of the sprawling farmsteads outlying Gettysburg than a city apartment building. Upstairs, feet pounded in the hallway and doors slammed as the other boarders hurried down to dinner. Winora stood with her sketchbook clutched protectively against her chest.

Dinah caught her free arm before she could reach the door, smiling warmly. "I'd love to talk more tomorrow. Could I join you for lunch?"

For a moment, Dinah thought Winora was going to turn her down flat, but then she shrugged. "I guess."

"Wonderful! Stop by Rumors at noon tomorrow, then?"

Winora didn't look thrilled, but Dinah knew she'd win her over in time. If she was going to be with the OSS for the long haul, she'd need to get to know a few coworkers, perhaps even make some real friends.

Things were already looking up.

12

Lillian

Lillian drew the drapes forcefully enough to unleash a whirl-wind of dust, triggering a fit of sneezing. The lemony light of late morning revealed the state of the Friedmans' study. The unwashed dishes, overflowing ashtray, and daunting stack of unopened mail bore testimony to the months the Friedmans had neglected this corner of their home.

And yet, for all its lack of priority for cleaning, Lillian knew Elizebeth had let her into the inner sanctum. For years, this was where her friend had completed her cryptography work when her children were young and she worked from home. This was the location of their collection of rare books on cryptography, some dating to before the Civil War. And, based on the full waste bins and cups ringed with long-dried coffee or chamomile, this was where one or both of the Friedmans spent much of their leisure time.

All good reasons to make sure it was put to order. As Lillian's pumps sank into the study's thick carpet, she could spot scattered hints of what Elizebeth and William had been up to lately:

a family photograph with Barbara smiling brightly in graduation robes; a wooden plank carved with Mayan pictographs;
and, perhaps most telling, several Spanish textbooks, including a
well-worn Spanish dictionary marked with stumps of torn paper.

Next to it on the desk, a book of poetry lay with pages
splayed open: Siegfried Sassoon, another one of the macabre
Great War poets Lillian had tried to appreciate for Roger's sake.
She was about to return it to its place on the shelf when she
noticed the last stanza on the open page was scored with dark
underlines. *Do they matter?—those dreams from the pit? / You
can drink and forget and be glad, / And people won't say that
you're mad; / For they'll know you've fought for your country
/ And no one will worry a bit.*

"Poor William," she whispered, closing the book. What he
and Elizebeth must have gone through these past few years.

"Now, where to begin?" Lillian asked the empty room. Her
tasks the day before—cleaning the kitchen, planning meals,
and restocking the pantry—had been straightforward. Now
she took silent inventory of the room before nodding. The desk
clutter would be the first to go; then everything else would seem
more manageable.

The day before, Lillian had assured Elizebeth she could
handle filing bills, addressing envelopes, and replying to mail.
Elizebeth had given her a crib sheet to guide her in this last task.
Most would receive a generic message that the Friedmans had
received their letter but due to illness would be delayed in responding. The note to personal friends was somewhat warmer
but also less truthful, implying general busyness was to blame
for a lack of response. *"We don't want to bother anyone,"*
Elizebeth had insisted.

"That's the trouble with people these days," Roger had said
when she'd called him to tell him of her change in plans. *"No
one wants to be a bother. Don't they realize asking for help is
a way of giving someone else a chance to care for them?"*

Enough thinking. Time to begin. Lillian sat in the worn leather chair behind the desk, and, after some rummaging, located a letter opener. Underneath it was a folder overflowing with clipped newspaper articles poking out temptingly.

I did tell Elizebeth I'd straighten things up, Lillian reasoned, giving in to the curiosity to open the file. As she arranged the clippings in a tidy stack, a cursory glance revealed they were all about the arrest of Velvalee Dickinson, known as "The Doll Woman."

Lillian remembered the sensation from a few months ago. Mrs. Dickinson was an innocuous-looking middle-aged doll seller, accused of using coded messages about doll shipments to convey information about naval production and coastal defenses to the Japanese.

Lillian's eyes darted over the articles, looking for mention of one of the Friedmans, but found nothing but J. Edgar Hoover declaring he and his G-men had kept America safe from the danger on their own shores.

A likely story.

If Elizebeth was saving these clippings, that meant she or William had been involved, and they'd been written out of the record once more. Whether credited or not, Elizebeth may very well have found evidence that would convict a spy ring and protect thousands of American lives.

And what had Lillian done over the past few years?

It's not to be dwelt on. We all have our parts to play.

By afternoon, the study was already vastly improved. Lillian straightened a stack of envelopes, taking a moment to enjoy the smells of furniture polish and the meatloaf baking in the oven. An odd mixture, to be sure, but one that testified to a good day's effort.

"Already finding much to keep you busy, I see."

The voice from the doorway was so thin and pale that for a fleeting moment of fancy, Lillian expected the chained ghost of Jacob Marley to confront her about her past.

Instead, she glanced over to see William Friedman . . . though not William as she remembered him from the last dinner party she and Roger had attended, when he'd worn a dapper suit with a striped bow tie and given a toast "to the best, which is yet to come."

From the haggard lines of his face, heavy with stubble, to the bowed shoulders in civilian duds rather than his old army uniform, it seemed that the best might never come again.

She banished the thought and mustered up a polite smile. "Good evening, William. I didn't realize how late it was."

"Elizebeth told me you'd come."

How his voice creaked, like an old piece of furniture. And he seemed to lean against the wall for support, though his clutched briefcase indicated he'd just returned from the office. She hadn't heard him slip out in the morning.

"There's no need to play the host," she said. "I'll bring you up a tray for dinner if you'd rather eat in your room."

"Please don't go to any trouble."

"It's no trouble," she assured him. "I'm here to help. Please, William. Rest."

He seemed almost to protest, as his wife had, but instead his gaze dropped downward. "Thank you. It—it has been a hard year. A hard several years."

"It can't go on forever, this war." Lillian had repeated this phrase to many a worried mother and young wife, waiting for word of their soldier. It was as close to optimism as she could bring herself without feeling trite. "It will end."

William had already begun to shuffle away, but he paused before adding, finally, "The last one did, didn't it?"

"Yes." At great cost, but they wouldn't speak of that now. It was an awful burden, being witness to two world wars, with their modern weaponry and unspeakable death tolls. "We can only hope the end comes soon."

13

Lily

"All summer, there was no message our team could not solve, though working hours were long until the first breakthrough. The military hailed us as a success. Still, part of me longed to be individually useful."

—Excerpt from Lillian Kendall's journal

WEDNESDAY, AUGUST 29, 1917

Margot leaned across her desk, her slender arms visible through sleeves of diaphanous blue silk, as Lily hurried into Engledew to escape the rain. "Did you hear the news? William and Elizebeth cracked the Tommies' machine yesterday."

"Did they?" Lily had looked at it only briefly before being called away to another project. It had the distinction of two separate sliding disks, a double layer of protection. The British had sent it to their American compatriots before using it for war communications with instructions "to ensure that it truly is unbreakable." That is to say, they hoped the Riverbank team would fail.

Even Lily had expected that, at best, it would linger on the blackboards for days, with letter patterns tried one after another by brute force until one finally worked. "What were the two code words they used to encrypt the wheels?"

The glimmer in Margot's eyes told her this was going to be good. "You'll never believe it. *Cipher* and *machine*."

Lily groaned. "Really?"

She nodded gleefully. "The person who chose them for this test was a government bloke, not involved in espionage, but still. You'd think he'd have some common sense."

As Elizebeth always said, the human element of encryption always proved to be the weakest link. No matter how many layers of complexity a machine had, a person was choosing what words to input to begin the scrambling.

And every now and then, even the cleverest people made mistakes.

"It took a while, but William guessed one word, then Elizebeth guessed the other based on that," Margot went on.

That was no surprise. All of the codebreakers collaborated on ciphers, but there was something about the synergy of the husband-wife team that was near miraculous.

Margot evened out a stack of papers with a triumphant tap. "It's a finger in the eye of those stuck-up Room 40 blokes who think their codebreakers are better than ours."

Lily couldn't deny that was the impression she'd gotten too, though it likely had more to do with the British having a few years' head start in codebreaking. When pioneering a field, years, even months, of experience made a substantial difference. Lily ought to know. She still felt hopelessly behind the others at Riverbank, often watching and joining in only when the first bit of work on a cipher had already been done, rather than making a substantial original contribution.

"Come now, Margot," Lily tried to temper her friend's smugness. "Wouldn't it have been better if it had been unbreakable? The British are our allies. Now they'll have to spend months starting over."

"Better us than the Boche," Margot said, the military slang sounding harsher knowing she applied it to her own former countrymen. "Say, you want to go swimming tomorrow?"

The non sequitur—a clue in last week's crossword that had nearly stumped her—flustered Lily for a moment. "I . . . I don't own a bathing suit." Outside of the included room and board, her salary was slim, and she'd already bought one new skirt and two shirtwaists from Marshall Field's in Chicago, as Mr. Fabyan had insisted, claiming his employees must wear "only the best." A skimpy bathing costume, where her shins and shoulders would be completely exposed, would be an unthinkable waste of money.

"Fine, shopping first, then swimming." Clearly noticing Lily was a hard sell, Margot added, "You haven't been out to the island, have you?" Lily shook her head. "Well, the colonel's pool is modeled after a Roman bath, with columns and everything. It'd be practically like going to a museum."

"That can't be," Lily interjected, recalling the book on Roman history she'd skimmed when a crossword clue had referenced the Peloponnesian War. "Men and women didn't bathe at the same time in the Empire, except, of course, prostitutes."

Had she really just said that out loud? Lily glanced around, making sure no one else had noticed, but the rest of the staff seemed to be busily about their work.

"Is that so? Boy, you sure do know a lot, Lil."

There she went again, spouting off more than others cared to know. Lily winced and was about to make a hurried disclaimer . . . until she took in Margot's expression and realized she'd said it with appreciation. "So, how about it?"

Lily ought to say yes, probably. How many times would

Margot reach out in friendship if she kept refusing? "I-I'm not sure. Maybe . . ."

She was rescued by a call of "Miss Nilsson!"

It was Mr. Ford, one of the other full-time staff members, also recruited from Fabyan's roster of scientists. He was an excitable middle-aged fellow with a background in analyzing acoustics, the complex patterns of which had trained him to be sensitive to detail.

She gave Margot a little wave and left her to her filing, watching as Mr. Ford held something behind his back with the air of a ringmaster like P. T. Barnum. "Ready for the latest curiosity?"

She nodded, and he set a telegram before her, a series of numbers and dashes, quite short compared to some of the multiple-page ciphers they were asked to solve, and not a letter in sight.

"What is its provenance?" It was Lillian's favorite question to ask, one that, if answered properly, could include all the context needed for understanding where to start with a message.

"It was intercepted from a group of activists in New York suspected of working with Indian separatists to cause unrest in the British colonies, possibly with German assistance. The language is likely English." Mr. Ford leaned back in a chair, loosening his tie, his neck already glistening with sweat. "This is the first message from this sender we've encountered, although we have an inkling of what kind it may be."

Before she could figure it out for herself, Mr. Ford pointed to the rows of numbers. "These patterns, numbers in three groups, almost always indicate a book known to both sender and receiver, with the first number being the page. That makes it far more random than any transposition or substitution cipher, yet simpler for the recipient to translate without error."

"Clever." Now Lily could understand what he meant. The first number in each sequence varied widely. "And yet the second number in each group is always a one or a two. A book printed in two columns?"

His ruddy cheeks stretched into a smile. "Exactly what we suspected. Though that narrows it somewhat, it might be an encyclopedia, a dictionary, a Bible, or a book of Hindu prayers. We've contacted the local authorities asking if a search of the activist's library might produce a well-used volume fitting that description and are awaiting their reply. They may not have enough evidence to issue a search warrant. Until then, it makes a nice curiosity, but I don't imagine we'll get anywhere with it."

Perhaps a messenger boy would arrive at any moment with the answer they needed, direct from New York via telegram wires. Still, Lily couldn't keep herself from scanning the text.

"What do you know? And what does it mean?"

Those two questions, Lily had found, helped settle her nerves and keep the terrors away . . . most days. It was only when the noise and temperature of the room rose, corresponding with the pressure to crack a particular cipher, that she found herself spiraling into a panic. Twice in the past month, she'd had to make a visit to the privy as an excuse to break away and get her emotions under control. Lily did her best work in the morning, when her mind was fresh and the heat in the room hadn't begun to rise.

Wait. What about . . . ? The longer she stared at the short message, the more sure she felt. "It's a dictionary."

Mr. Ford, who had already begun to walk away, blinked rapidly, as if communicating in Morse code. "Pardon?"

She held up the paper and tried again. "I think—that is, the patterns indicate . . . and if it is, we can make progress without having the book. Can't we?"

"I'm not sure what you mean, Miss Nilsson." She couldn't blame him for his skepticism. Though the men of the code room generally treated the women as equals, Lily was still new and the most softspoken in the building.

Lily indicated two instances of 1-1-1. "What could this be but the word *A*? Common enough to be used twice even in a short message."

If he had begun a frequency analysis as was standard procedure with substitution ciphers, Mr. Ford would have seen it himself. Despite the unusual source, the correspondent had composed a message like any other, which meant repeated words.

Mr. Ford accepted her conclusion with a nod. "Let's say it is. Go on."

She pointed to a pattern that occurred three times in the message, one with the highest first number of any of the trios. *354-2-78.* "Might this not be *you* or *your*, a word at the end of the dictionary that often reoccurs?"

Mr. Ford, who had been mopping his brow with his handkerchief, now wrung it anxiously, staring at the letters with bulging eyes. "Yes, yes, I see."

Lily began jotting down these notations on a worksheet. "The more we speculate, the more we can test the words by context."

"It might just work." His grin was broad and unaffected, and Lily felt a new burst of energy. She might really be on to something. He called over the dark-haired Alberti sisters, and Lily, flushed at the attention, explained her theory to them. Together, they began charting the most likely options for each trio, testing combinations on separate sheets of graph paper.

Bit by bit, phrases emerged, then lines as options were ruled out or judged more likely. Lily flitted from person to person, combining and testing suggestions against each other, crossreferencing the dictionary, and adding to the master document, scrawled on one of the chalkboards.

Hours later, they had their message, or as close as they could come to it. There were still a few words that could not be reliably decrypted—references to a specific place, or more likely, an agent's code name—but they'd left only three gaps in an otherwise straightforward and damning bit of evidence.

"I can't believe it," Lily whispered, staring at the document in her hand, recopied from the many smudged drafts. She collapsed onto a bench, suddenly realizing she was famished. Was it lunchtime? Or had that long since passed?

"Good work, Lily," Elizabeth said, squeezing her arm, her voice warm with pride, and Lily blushed. Her mentor had been busy elsewhere during most of the process, and Lily wondered if that had been intentional, to let her protégé take the lead.

"We did it together." It was true, and yet Lily allowed herself to bask in the triumph, at least for a moment.

Lily glanced out the window, where life at Riverbank in the height of summer went on as usual: gardeners trimming the greenery; children of the staff frolicking around the estate; Nelle's ridiculous monkeys wandering free, diapers tied around their waists. "They'll never know what we're doing, will they?"

Elizabeth followed her gaze. "Who?"

Lily felt foolish all at once, but surely, Elizabeth would understand. "Anyone, outside of the people in this little room."

"Maybe not," Elizabeth looked around at their motley crew with a fond smile. "History has a way of forgetting all but the emperors and generals . . . and the occasional brilliant playwright. Women in particular often change the world quietly, without recognition." She took Lily's hand and squeezed it. "But we're doing what needs to be done and doing it well. That's all that matters."

Dinah

Dinah took the steps to Morale Operations' intimidating pillared structure two at a time. *I will not be late.*

The OSS headquarters was made up of a U-shaped complex of brick buildings, each three stories with windows blinking out on a central courtyard. Who knew what the other divisions were up to behind those panes? Research and Analysis alone, she'd been told, had a staff of nine hundred professors, economists, and diplomats doing things like piecing together submitted vacation photos to create a map of Japan's shorelines, combing German newspapers for unrecorded obituaries of Wehrmacht officers, and assessing foreign intelligence.

But out of all those people, the one who happened to be blocking the hallway to Mr. Agnew's office was Barry Longstreet, arguing loudly with another man about whether the army or navy football team was likely to win out this year. As she approached, he stopped mid-rant about the number of All-Americans at West Point, catching her eye and turning abruptly from his buddy to saunter toward her.

Dinah tried to keep moving at a businesslike pace to show she didn't have time for a long conversation. "Good morning, Mr. Longstreet."

"Sure is. And you're looking mighty fine today, Dinah." She didn't particularly like the way he eyed her up and down, like he could see right through her cable-knit cardigan. "How'd you get stashed away in a dull little office like this? You should be headed to Hollywood."

Since Mr. Longstreet didn't seem genuinely interested in the events that had led her here, Dinah only laughed wryly. "Not a chance. You clearly haven't heard me sing or seen me dance."

"Why don't we fix that, eh?" He took another step closer to her. "Come out with me tonight to the Mayflower. They've got a swing quartet playing."

Had he just asked her on a date? Participating in an activity she'd just said she didn't enjoy? "Thank you for the offer, but I feel it's better to keep my work and personal life separate." That was true, and an answer that might not hurt Mr. Longstreet's ego.

His photo-ready smile eased into a pout, and she had the sudden thought that the clean-shaven look currently in vogue didn't do his baby face any favors. "Aw, come on, Dinah. Think about it, won't you?"

She shook her head. "I'm afraid my mind's made up."

His jaw twitched slightly. "Someone else already asked you, didn't they?" When she didn't immediately deny it, his expression turned dark, and he swore under his breath. "I knew it."

"No," Dinah protested. "I don't know who you'd be talking about." Her whirlwind of a first day hadn't left her with time for socializing.

He laughed bitterly. "C'mon, you have to have noticed you're one of the best-looking gals around the building. I heard there's a fellow down in Radio who's been asking around about you, and did you see those R&A eggheads stare when you climbed up the steps this morning?"

Dinah had not, but the fact that Mr. Longstreet had been watching from a window as she entered the building gave her the creeps.

"As I already said," she repeated, giving her words more force this time despite the color that rose to her cheeks, "I have no interest in dating coworkers."

"I'm not some wet-behind-the-ears upstart." Mr. Longstreet took a step closer, backing her toward a row of filing cabinets and cutting off an easy means of escape. "My father is a partner at his own law firm. Everyone says he's got a shot at becoming attorney general."

"I can't see how that's relevant," she interrupted, sidestepping him. The door to Mr. Agnew's office was open. If she could only reach it . . .

As if following her glance, Mr. Longstreet sneered. "It's Agnew, isn't it? He's trying to keep you to himself."

"Excuse me?" she sputtered. He couldn't mean that the way it sounded.

Mr. Longstreet leaned casually against the cabinets, giving his eyebrows an insinuating slant. "Guess his invalid wife isn't enough for him these days. I didn't take you for the type to try to climb the ladder by carrying on with the boss."

There was a calculated look in Mr. Longstreet's eyes that told Dinah he didn't really believe the nonsense he was spouting. He only wanted to get a reaction out of her.

But a man who had to goad a woman into saying yes to a date didn't deserve one.

Though her cheeks burned with embarrassment, Dinah forced herself to deliver a cutting glance his way. "I'm aware our department specializes in creating vicious rumors, Mr. Longstreet, but allow me to suggest you save your lies for the Nazis."

Leaving him standing agape, knowing his shock wouldn't last long, she rushed down the hall.

Despite the fact that the clock's hand crept toward the hour, Mr. Agnew's secretary wasn't yet stationed in watch, so Dinah knocked on his door herself, entering without waiting for an invitation, the better to shield herself from Mr. Longstreet's view. Behind his desk, Mr. Agnew was already scribbling on a document placed in front of him, eyebrows furrowed in concentration.

"Good morning, Mr. Agnew." She took a deep breath, trying to regain her composure.

He looked up from his work and stared at her a moment, as if unable to place who she was and what she was doing here.

"You said you'd see me to the Rumor Department and make introductions today?" she continued.

"Ah. Yes. I suppose I must." He stood, capping his pen and leaving it at a perfect right angle. "I'm off to a committee meeting anyway, to deal with allegations from the Office of War Information that we're infringing on their territory." He gave a scowl of Shakespearean proportions. "If I could string them all up with the red tape they foist on us, I'd do it."

"A committee meeting sounds like a dreadful way to spend a morning."

"Yes, well, 'Theirs not to make reply / Theirs not to reason why / Theirs but to do and die.'"

"Into the valley of Death rode the six hundred," Dinah burst out. She'd learned that poem in school—part of it, anyway—because it reminded her of Pickett's Charge. The surprise in Mr. Agnew's eyes before he harrumphed and turned away might go down as her most impressive work for the OSS.

Now to do the same to Mrs. Masterson. Clutching her handbag like a shield, Dinah marched down the stairs to the next level, where Morale Operations' rumor team held court next to the Radio Department.

Based on the dubious source of *His Girl Friday*, the open office space looked to Dinah like a small newsroom, with workers typing away at rolltop desks arranged in two lines, with an aisle leading to a massive oak slab where Olivia Masterson presided.

There was no mistaking her. Rather than sporting the dull-hued wools and cottons of the others in the room, Mrs. Masterson was dressed in a teal taffeta dress that rustled as she moved, gold earrings dangling halfway to her shoulders. She looked every inch a socialite queen who had been drafted into office work, which, according to Mr. Agnew, was exactly what had happened.

A poster behind her desk read, in bold type, *When you strike at the morale of a people or an army, you strike at the deciding factor.—William J. Donovan*

Dinah could do that. She knew she could . . . if only she had a chance to prove herself.

Mrs. Masterson looked up as she approached, lifting an eyebrow thin as a piece of spaghetti. "Miss Kendall, I presume," she pronounced, her voice a throaty alto. "Frasier told me you would be coming."

"Yes, he . . ." Dinah glanced over her shoulder. Mr. Agnew had disappeared, either too busy to make introductions or disinclined to socialize with the intimidating Mrs. Masterson, Dinah couldn't guess which. "That is, I'm excited to get to work."

"Let's hope that mood lasts at least a few days. With the schedule they've foisted on us—it's absolutely mad—we need all the fresh blood we can get." Mrs. Masterton picked up a thick file folder, then gave Dinah an assessing glance. "Although I think you'll find that there's a great deal of difference between what we do here and batting your eyelashes at greenhorn recruits to get them to spill classified information."

So Mrs. Masterson had read her file as well. "I wouldn't have assumed otherwise. I'm here to learn."

"And you will. By doing." Mrs. Masterson swept across the room without checking to see whether Dinah was following, then gestured with a clatter of bangles to an empty desk tucked into the corner of the room. "We're of the sink-or-swim persuasion around here."

She set the file folder down on Dinah's desk with a solid thud. "These are the competition—transcripts of recent Axis radio broadcasts doing to us what we're trying to do to them. Tokyo Rose, Axis Sally, Lord Haw-Haw, and the like. Even a few translations from propaganda stations over in France. Read them, take notes, and type up a report by the end of the week."

"What sort of notes?"

She waved the question away like it was a mere detail. "Standard analysis. The amount of negative or positively nuanced language, number of jokes thrown in to keep soldiers listening, anything that stands out. The brass thinks we need to up our game now that the British gave us the job of scripting the most listened-to Allied propaganda station, which means learning from the enemy. Waste of time, if you ask me, but I promised I'd put someone on it. And since you're our newest recruit . . ."

So she was being assigned to a trivial task, ticking a box to make Mrs. Masterson look good to her superiors. Not exactly what she had hoped for.

And yet . . . this was her chance to learn something about rumor creation and scriptwriting, and from experts, even if they were hostile experts. When Dinah was asked to create her own content for the Allied programs, she was determined to be ready.

"I'll do my best," Dinah said, infusing her voice with more confidence than she felt.

Mrs. Masterson gestured at the room with her perfectly manicured nails. "You'll have to do better than that, sweetheart. Look around. We've got the top academic expert on propaganda and its effects, a congressman's campaign manager, two former dip-

112

lomats, and fluent speakers of every combatant country, besides our writers in the field."

For the first time, Dinah glanced about at her new coworkers, all hunched dutifully over their work. They did seem to be a varied lot; five men and two women, all of whom seemed to be at least two decades older than her. She felt like a coed among professors, unprepared for her first day of classes.

Read and take notes. That's all I have to do for now. Suddenly, her irritation with the mundane task felt more like a relief.

"Oh, and welcome to the team, dear." Mrs. Masterson's smile as she flounced away reminded Dinah of the taxidermized crocodile she'd seen at the Natural History Museum. "We're delighted to have you."

By the time lunch came around, Dinah was more than ready to escape the Rumor Mill, as her colleagues referred to their office. The monotony of the radio commentary she read through was beginning to get into her head, a litany of bad news for American troops. The Axis broadcasters were accomplishing the goal of lowering her morale, at least.

During the course of the morning, several coworkers had taken the time to greet her and ask a few polite questions, but they'd all left for lunch together without issuing her an invitation to join them. Apparently, her answers had given them the impression that she was a nobody—which, in fairness, wasn't inaccurate, given the credentials of the rest of the OSS staff.

Of course, she didn't unload any of that on Winora when she went to find her fellow boarder for lunch, just asked her cheerful questions that garnered a smattering of brief answers.

The courtyard Winora led her to wasn't far from the grand Federal Reserve Building—"Being close to all that money helps my digestion," she claimed—but despite its central location, it seemed deserted. This was, Dinah decided after a glance around, because there was no formal seating, only decorative bushes and a bevy of geese peering sinisterly at them as they entered.

"But where do we sit?" Dinah asked, confused.

"Over there," Winora said, jutting her chin in the direction of a concrete flower planter, filled with a line of straggly pansies.

This place was nearly as uninviting as Winora herself. *Maybe she took me here hoping I won't want to come back.*

Maybe I shouldn't. After all, there had to be more pleasant people about OSS to lunch with.

Dinah scolded herself for thinking that way. Winora might be prickly, but she clearly needed a friend, and sometimes the people most difficult to get to know proved to be the most fascinating. Besides, she'd never met an artist before.

That, at least, gave her a starting point. "Tell me more about your art. Are you self-taught, or did you attend art school?"

"Art school's not cheap." With a crinkle of brown paper, she opened one of the sacks Auntie Margot provided for boarders to use. "Maybe someday. That's why I'm nickel-and-diming my way along here. Soon as the war's over, I'm off to California."

"Sounds exciting," Dinah said, sitting next to her and unwrapping her sandwich from a square of wax paper. "And warm." The concrete planter was just wide enough to provide a comfortable seat, relatively speaking, though she could feel the cold through her skirt. The lone entrance made the courtyard into a wind tunnel, chilly on the overcast day.

"You bet," Winora said, taking a bite out of something glistening and brown.

Dinah frowned. "Is that a . . . MoonPie?"

"Moon *sandwich*," Winora corrected with dignity, despite spewing crumbs on the ground. "Not as good as a bakery whoopie pie, but you take what you can get, y'know?"

Dinah checked the wrapper, abandoned next to the now-empty lunch sack. It was a plain old MoonPie—layers of marshmallow and graham cracker dipped in chocolate. "And that's all you eat for lunch?"

"Listen, it's cheap, it's delicious, it's none of your business." Winora shrugged. "Sometimes I wash it down with a cola."

Dinah was sure her disgust showed on her face. "That can't be good for you."

"Worse than your bologna? You got any idea what goes into that stuff?"

"No," Dinah said primly, taking a bite, "and I'll thank you for *not* telling me."

Winora laughed, startling a nearby goose. At least she had a sense of humor buried under that tough façade.

"So, how did the OSS recruit you, Winora?"

From the way she stiffened, it seemed even this basic question wasn't welcome. A quarter of the MoonPie disappeared before she shrugged. "I've got some relevant experience. The OSS found me while I was spending the year living northwest of Baltimore."

"Really? I'm from Gettysburg. We might have been only fifty miles apart." Dinah was about to ask whether Winora had ever visited nearby Antietam when she paused. A shadow jutted across the entrance to the courtyard, long and broad-shouldered, crowned with a brimmed hat.

She watched it closely for a few moments, but instead of signaling a newcomer's approach, the shadow didn't move for several seconds . . . until it suddenly disappeared back into the alley with a distant rush of footsteps—or, at least, that's what she thought she heard. It was difficult to tell over the sound of the courtyard geese beating to the sky like gangsters after the cops had been called, squawking noisily.

"Did you see that?" Dinah asked.

Winora was staring at the feathers and droppings the geese

left behind. "Sure. They're everywhere. You've just gotta yell a little to get them to scatter. And never feed them."

Dinah frowned. "For a moment, I thought . . . well, that someone was watching us. A man, I think."

Winora grunted, picking up and crumpling her MoonPie wrapper. "Rookie syndrome."

"What?"

The other woman waved her hand dismissively. "It's all that secrecy talk they spoon-feed us early on, the papers you sign. Makes you think you're someone important. Listen, Dinah, if there are any spies worth their salt around DC, there are a thousand better places for them to be than watching two broads like us eat lunch."

That was logical, and yet . . . Dinah crossed her arms, staring toward the alleyway. "I was sure I saw a person start to approach, then stop and hurry away."

"Probably only Barry Longstreet waiting to ask you on a date once you were away from me."

Dinah pulled a face. "He already tried. I said no."

"Good for you." Winora stood, making it clear that lunchtime was over. "Seriously, don't let it get to ya. Come on. It looks like rain. I'll give you a look around MO, show you the interesting stuff."

"That sounds lovely," Dinah said, and meant it.

Still, as she walked back to headquarters with Winora, Dinah couldn't help giving a glance over her shoulder. No figure lurked in the shadows.

Winora was right. Surely, if anywhere in the city was safe, it would be the headquarters of the OSS.

15

Lillian

SUNDAY, APRIL 23, 1944

"Greer Garson," Margot said, propping her feet up on the coffee table. She was still wearing her trim, stylish Sunday dress, which made the picture all the more absurd. "Make sure you spell it right."

As if Lillian needed a reminder to be thorough. She dutifully jotted the contribution down in her notebook, glancing to see where it might fit. She was dreadfully behind on her latest crossword assignment because of her work at the Friedmans, so she'd come to Myrtlewood for help.

"Now I need a movie title with at least two *E*'s with one other letter between them."

"Oooh, a tricky one." Margot twiddled her finger in the air, spelling out invisible words, her lips pursed in thought. "I know! *The Maltese Falcon.* You could make the clue 'Spade digs up a statue.'"

"Perfect, puzzlers adore puns."

"Is this why you really came over for Sunday lunch?" Margot affected an exaggerated pout, straightening an avalanche of magazines with movie stars beaming on the covers—hers or the boarders, Lillian couldn't say. "To milk me for crossword clues?"

"Of course not." Lillian tucked her notebook into her pocket. It had also been a good chance to talk to Dinah, give the Friedmans an afternoon of privacy, and enjoy some delicious deviled eggs. "But there's no sense in wasting a chance to consult with my very best source of Hollywood clues."

"I am a sucker for flattery," Margot admitted. "But honestly, Lil, it's a Sunday. Can't you leave off work and rest a bit?"

"We went to your church already this morning. I'm sure God is quite satisfied." Dinah had been delighted to attend New York Avenue Presbyterian Church once she found out Abraham Lincoln had a family pew there during his presidency. She'd crept up to it, almost reverently, after the sermon to stroke the wood. "Besides, I feel like the apostle Paul would appreciate a good crossword puzzle."

"You are impossible." Margot gestured around the room. "Now, you haven't told me yet what you think of what I've done with this place."

Lillian took a moment to regard the room. There were traces of its old self in the hardwood floors and wallpaper, but given the garish floral throw pillows scattered about and ceramic deer stationed on the radio cabinet, she wondered how long they'd last. "They're not choices I might have made, but the décor suits you, Margot."

Margot tossed her blond hair with a laugh. "I can always count on you for honesty, Lil. And thanks. It's a change, working on renovating this old place instead of traveling and translating and running myself ragged on Capitol Hill. For one thing, it's easier to see the difference you're making."

Something about her friend's light tone seemed forced, and

she was staring wistfully out the window. "Do you ever miss your work in Congress?"

"Every day." Margot again adjusted the stack of magazines on the side table. "I'm hoping to go back to it, you know, after all this dies down."

Based on Margot's letters, Lillian could guess what "all this" meant. On paper, Margot had left her position as an aide to Representative Edith Nourse Rogers voluntarily. In reality, she'd quit to protect the congresswoman's reputation when some political rivals had started spreading rumors that Margot, born in Germany, might harbor secret fifth column sympathies. Absurd as the idea was, Margot hadn't wanted to threaten Representative Rogers's chances for reelection.

"That's all I ever wanted to do, you know. Important work, something that would create real change." She raised a hand to sweep away a few strands of flyaway hair, and it lingered there, pressed to her temple. For a moment, the tired gesture made Margot look her age, though her makeup and jewelry remained immaculate.

"And you have," Lillian assured her. But she also remembered how upset Margot had been in the late thirties when the Wagner-Rogers bill had been voted down. Roused by reports of the expulsion of Jews from Germany, Representative Rogers had advocated strongly for a bill to allow twenty thousand refugee children into the United States, and Margot had spent weeks preparing research and translating German documents for the committees to look over. Still, too many voices clamored "America first!" and the bill had failed. "Though I'm sorry it didn't turn out like you'd planned."

"Me too. Now, don't frown at me like that, Lil," Margot said lightly, straightening up. "Like I said, the change isn't entirely bad. The girls here keep me feeling young. It's been especially fun to see Dinah all grown up too. She's a great gal. You should be proud."

"I don't see how I've had much to do with it. She's always taken after her father."

"Oh, she has some of Roger's traits, but I see her mother in her too." She stood, drawing the curtains against the afternoon sun, before adding, "Do the two of you . . . talk much?"

What sort of a question was that? "Enough. As you mentioned, she's at an age where she would prefer I keep my distance."

"Oh, I'm sure." Margot tilted her head back at her. "But you've always been . . . distant. Not so much to your closest friends. But even we are sometimes left to guess what you're thinking."

Lillian narrowed her eyes at her friend. "Margot, are you meddling?"

Margot splayed a hand dramatically beneath her throat. "Me? Not a bit. It's just that sometimes, Lily, my dear, you tell others you care about them in cipher when they need it in plaintext." Her lips quirked up at the reference to their old work. "In any case, one can never be too effusive."

"A motto that comes from too long working in politics." Lillian said it lightly, but she couldn't stop a flash of annoyance. What right did Margot have, as someone who had never raised a child, to comment on her parenting?

Margot tittered out a laugh. "Darling, *I* never ran for office. I'd have far too many gray hairs if I had."

"Come on, now, we both know you dye it," Lillian teased.

"Of course not!" Margot huffed. "I *pay* someone to dye it. Haven't you heard of a salon in that two-horse hamlet of yours?"

"I haven't been inside a real salon since the incident with the eyebrows," Lillian said, knowing this reference would guarantee a change of subject.

Sure enough, Margot burst out with a merry laugh. "I had almost forgotten about that. Life seemed so simple in those early days at Riverbank, living in luxury with all of you genius codebreakers." Margot sighed wistfully, like she was lounging in the shade of the marble pillars that surrounded the Fabyans' swimming pool once more.

"Maybe it was simple for you." Even then, Lillian had questioned whether she was making the right choice. It was different for Margot, she supposed, getting her first taste of freedom away from her large German immigrant family, tasked with clerical work and simple translations from her native tongue. "Riverbank did have a dark side."

"I know," Margot said, pulling a face. "No need to be a wet blanket about it."

But Lillian knew it was dangerous to romanticize the past. Far too easy to remember only the triumphs and forget the troubles—even the dangers—they'd been through together. She, at least, chose to remember.

16

Lily

"As months flew by, my skill with codebreaking grew. Those days of feverish work seem almost a dream now. But William Friedman always hoped to do more."

— Excerpt from Lillian Kendall's journal

SUNDAY, OCTOBER 21, 1917

Lily let the smell of warm cocoa swirl inside her until she could almost taste the rich chocolate on her tongue.

"Keep stirring," Elizabeth exhorted Margot, who clattered a wooden spoon around the interior of a tin pot balanced precariously over a miniature alcohol burner. "The heat has to be distributed evenly."

None of their other surroundings belonged in a confectionery. As a married couple, William and Elizebeth had one of the larger accommodations on the second floor of Engledew Cottage, with its own sitting room adjoining their bedroom. This provided privacy for their weekly Sunday afternoon gatherings, to avoid being interrupted by cigar smoke or discussions of sound waves in the Lodge's parlor. A snug chaise lounge and armchair tucked near the fireplace provided the ideal setting for conversations and cards.

"Are you sure this is going to work?" Lily asked dubiously. Despite the heavenly smell, the mixture in the small pot looked more like sludge from the trenches on the front.

"We did it all the time at college," Elizebeth assured her. "The upperclassmen would host elaborate midnight spreads of treats we'd cook in secret in our rooms. Once, I speared oysters with hatpins and roasted them on the gas jets of my lamp."

Margot let loose a boisterous laugh. "Does William know you were such an anarchist in the wild days of higher education?"

Elizebeth gave a secretive smile. "There's a reason we waited until William was going into town."

"You just don't want to share the fudge," Lily teased. "So much for romance."

"Speaking of which," Margot said, her voice heavy with mischief, "any young gentleman in your life, Lily?"

Irritatingly, Lily could feel a blush start to rise in her face at yet another round of Margot's nosy nonsense. "No," she said shortly. One of the young scientists had offered to take her for a ride in his auto, but she'd turned him down. The idea of driving at speeds like that terrified her—or maybe it was the thought of having to make conversation with someone with a PhD. "And I don't think there will be."

At Elizebeth's direction, Margot added a trickle from a milk bottle that Lily resolved not to ask her where she'd gotten it from. As former kitchen staff, she couldn't endorse pinching anything from the Lodge's stores.

Never one to be deterred, Margot returned to her previous line of questioning. "That's just fine. I say, don't let anyone sweep you off your feet too quickly. A girl with a brain like yours shouldn't waste it scrubbing floors and minding children."

Lily remained silent. She hadn't thought much about her plans after the war. Elizabeth, at least, would expect her to pursue a career in codebreaking. And she *would* enjoy that . . . wouldn't she? At any rate, she was good at it. That was better than anything she could have hoped for when she was sent to the reformatory school.

Still, the doctor's warning echoed back from a few years ago. *"Those prone to neurotic attacks ought to avoid significant stress. Your mother's fate doesn't have to be your own."*

No matter how often she'd tried to find information in books or through questions at the reformatory, Lily had realized medical professionals didn't yet know what caused her mother's illness or know how to cure it. At least, there was no clear consensus. If Lily continued in the high-stakes world of codebreaking and began to manifest those familiar symptoms, there might be no way to stop them, and that was the fate she dreaded most of all.

"William assures me there will be no shortage of opportunities in our field after the war," Elizabeth put in. "Joseph Mauborgne—the army officer who approved Riverbank for cryptography—all but promised us jobs in Washington. And there's always the private sector, developing commercial ciphers for business secrets."

"Yes," Lily said vaguely. "I'm sure."

She hadn't told Elizabeth, but lately, if she had to walk away from a cipher at the end of the day without a breakthrough, Lily could barely sleep at night, the letters and patterns running through her mind in a loop. That, she was sure, was why she'd had more nervous attacks during the day.

For now, she considered her work a sacrifice for her country. But after the war? She wasn't sure she wanted to continue with ciphers. And yet, what would Margot and Elizabeth think if she said so? Particularly when the alternative—Margot's scorned idea of settling down and starting a family—wasn't an option for her.

"Sounds dull as paste to me, but you two will be smashing at it," Margot said cheerfully, showing Elizebeth the fudge for approval, the mixture now creamy and smooth.

"And I suppose you'll live the bohemian life you've always dreamed of, Margot?" Lily said, eager for a change of subject.

"Naturally." Margot batted her eyelashes like a damsel in a silent film. "I want to travel. Across the country, maybe across the world. Can you imagine the thrill of dashing over the ocean in a biplane?"

Lily didn't attempt to conceal her shudder. That sounded even worse than rattling around in an automobile. "I'd rather not."

Margot shook the spoon in remonstration, dropping a speck of simmering fudge on the carpet. "Now, see here, Lil. Sometime or other, you'll need to take a risk instead of always playing it safe. And the way I see it, all of us ought to start making plans. Our work is going down to a trickle."

That much was true. Fewer and fewer ciphers were coming into Engledew Cottage as the various branches of the army assembled their own experts. They'd actually had time for real lunch breaks recently, and even ended work early last Friday to take a boat out on the river, perhaps for the last time this year before the autumn turned bitter.

"That may change soon," Elizebeth said, a smile tugging at her lips.

Margot managed to hold out all of three seconds before demanding, "All right, Liz, spill. We know you and William have Fabyan's ear. What's new?"

She shrugged. "They're announcing it next week, so I don't see any harm in telling you. The army is coming to us."

The army? "What do you mean?"

"They're sending at least four dozen Signal Corps officers, maybe more in the future. We'll train them to decrypt messages in the field, saving critical time wasted in transporting messages to us." Elizebeth's gaze became distant, as if she were picturing herself with chalk in hand, using her teaching degree once more. "We'll start with a simple, bilateral cipher, then go on from there."

"Do we have room?" Lily felt foolish immediately after blurting out the question, but Engledew Cottage already felt crowded when one wanted a moment alone, and she couldn't imagine a few dozen men tramping into their makeshift headquarters.

Elizebeth shook her head. "Mr. Fabyan plans to both house them and hold classes at a hotel in town."

Margot stuck her lips out in a fake pout. "Too bad. We could use more single men around here."

"I wouldn't have thought the strict, formal military officer would be your type," Lily teased.

Her friend waved that objection away. "Oh, I'm sure they can't all be that way. After all, as William always says, 'You don't have to be crazy to be a codebreaker . . . but it helps.'"

The words stabbed at Lily like a needle into a pincushion. "Don't say that," she blurted, adding when both women's attention turned to her, "please."

"It was only a joke," Margot huffed, and even Elizebeth's brow furrowed at Lily's outburst.

Yes, but a joke that made light of something very serious, something that dragged up dark memories, wasn't funny. Not to her.

"Margot, would mind going to the Lodge to fetch a pat of butter from the icebox?" Elizebeth interjected, saving her from coming up with a coherent response. "As soon as the fudge cools, we'll need to mix it in."

This time, Lily didn't protest the clandestine raid, grateful for the change of subject, but the moment Margot shut the suite's door, Elizabeth turned back to Lily. "I know talk like that must be difficult, with your mother's . . . health struggles."

Lily sucked in a breath, waiting for the first signs of panic—the racing heartbeat, the desire to flee—but was surprised that she felt none. "How long have you known?"

"Mr. Fabyan told William weeks ago about the history detailed in your employment file, and he told me," she admitted. "I hadn't felt the need to say anything before, but I thought perhaps now might be the right time." She turned to take the fudge off the burner, as if to avoid Lily's gaze, though her voice remained calm. "You see . . . mental neurosis runs in William's family as well. Two of his brothers have sought treatment for debilitating melancholic moods, with varying success. It's a rather difficult subject, isn't it?"

"Yes," Lily managed to say, overcome by an odd sense of relief. Why?

Maybe because someone she respected knew about Mama . . . and it hadn't ruined her life. Or because there was someone close to her who understood what it was like to fear the unavoidable consequences of heredity, to hide from shame and stigma.

Old habits prompted Lily to blurt out, "I've seen no signs of her frailty in myself, however. That is, it hasn't affected my ability to work."

Granted, it had only a few months before, but now, with their decreased workload, surely it was true enough not to count as a falsehood.

"I wasn't worried." Elizebeth laid a hand on her arm. "We don't think any differently of you, Lily. Just as I know you won't think any differently of William."

"Of course." Lily blinked back a sudden wetness in her eyes. Elizebeth's simple declaration went against years of warnings from Mama about what would happen if she ever spoke the word *madness* aloud, or even confided in another on personal matters.

The difference, Lily realized, with the same bittersweet regret that often accompanied memories of her mother, was that she had found something Mama never had.

Someone she could trust.

———

An hour later, Elizebeth cut the cooled fudge into squares. Lily had only just taken her piece when the door to the sitting room swung open and William stormed inside, his hair whipped into a frenzy by the fierce Illinois wind.

"He's done it again. The scoundrel. The absolute . . ." William, ever the gentleman, broke off where Lily had braced herself for a string of cursing.

Elizebeth was on her feet in a moment, reaching for her husband, who accepted her hand on his arm, still tense with anger. "Whatever is the matter?"

It was as if the other two women weren't even there. Margot leaned forward, eager to hear the latest, but Lily felt she could die of embarrassment. If she stayed absolutely still, she might disappear into the wallpaper.

"A heart condition, they said." He scoffed. "I thought it was only a mistake. But I never expected him to go so far."

This, at least, Lily understood. William had recently returned dejected from his army physical. The doctor had diagnosed him with a slight heart murmur, enough to declare him unfit for military service. He'd been useless in the code room for days, clearly brooding.

"William. Calm down," Elizebeth soothed. For the first time, she cast a quick glance at her friends but went on without asking them to leave. "What can you possibly mean?"

"Do you know who the commander at Camp Grant is?"

Elizebeth shook her head. Even Margot, who usually knew all there was to know about people in Riverbank and the surrounding area, only shrugged when Lily glanced her way.

William clenched his hat in his hands. "He's George Fabyan's brother-in-law."

Quiet fell as the revelation settled in. Elizabeth shook her head. "William, you don't think . . . ?"

"Oh, but I do." He laughed bitterly. "Now we know why Fabyan suddenly acceded to my request to join the army after three straight months of denials. Because he found a way to prevent me from going."

How awful that must be. Even Elizabeth had lamented the way this diagnosis made William fall into a slump of moodiness. *"It makes him feel like less of a man,"* she'd confided to Lily, worry creasing her brow.

"He's trying to trap us here," William said, his voice climbing in pitch. "We'll never leave, Elizabeth."

She stood and moved to his side, placing a hand on his arm. "That's not possible, love. I'm sure when the war's over . . ."

"It will be too late. I'm needed *now*." He paced the room in a half dozen measured steps. "Only last week, I was harassed by a vigilante from the American Protective League when I went into town. All the other men my age have enlisted, and I have a skill that's desperately needed at the front. But I can't go because a stubborn old millionaire is moving us about like pawns on a chessboard."

He trailed off, staring at their pan of fudge without seeming to realize it was there. "After we train the army fellows, there won't be much left for us to do. Then he'll shuttle us back to that Shakespeare-Bacon conspiracy theory."

Elizabeth made a face like she'd eaten something pickled. She had told Lily in confidence that she and her husband were convinced Mr. Fabyan's pet theory was nonsense. "We simply won't work for Mrs. Gallup."

"Oh? Where will we work, then? Fabyan has the whole military attached to his suspenders, maybe most of Washington.

And who do you think gives jobs to codebreakers?" He shook his head in disgust, stomping back toward the door.

"William. Don't leave like this."

He thrust his arms through his coat, shaking off Elizebeth's pleading. "Don't worry, I won't charge into the Villa and accost Fabyan with his own samurai sword. I simply need to go for a walk. Clear my head."

Even then, his face still flushed with rage, he paused to press a kiss to his wife's forehead before disappearing once more, the door shut firmly behind him.

For a moment, no one moved. Lily realized that she'd kept her piece of slightly melted fudge clutched in her hand the whole time, staring at the drama unfolding before her with the frozen fascination of her first moving picture show.

"I—I apologize that you had to hear that." Elizebeth collapsed on the settee and clutched her arms at her elbows, shivering like William had let in a draft.

"You'd have come right to tell us afterward anyway," Margot said, trying to conjure up her usual bluster. "But really, Elizebeth, do you think Fabyan set William up?"

"No," she said, as if by instinct, before biting her lip. "Well . . . perhaps."

Lily looked out the window, where she could see William storming toward the bridge that led to Mr. Fabyan's private island. "William's theory makes sense to me. Not that Mr. Fabyan is a terrible man, he's just . . ."

"Controlling? Bad-tempered? *Egoistisch?*" Margot offered, and though Lily wasn't sure of all the connotations of the last in English, she assumed it wasn't flattering.

"An opportunist," Elizebeth said, and the word seemed so fitting that Lily and Margot nodded at the same time. "He's afraid of losing influence."

As Lily took her first bite of the fudge, she had to admit it had a bitter edge she wasn't expecting, as if they'd scorched it after all. Or perhaps that was simply the mood of the room at the moment.

"So long as we keep our heads down for the rest of the war, it'll be all right, won't it?" Margot asked hopefully, her lips stained with chocolate. Of all of them, she was the one who most loved the luxury that Riverbank's grounds and amenities provided.

"I would hope so," Elizebeth said slowly, considering each word before speaking it. "But I'm not so sure. This war has made George Fabyan's greatest asset useful: his collection, not of butterflies or stamps, but of people."

Lily felt both the truth and the dread in her friend's words, and she shuddered.

"We are in his cabinet of curiosities now, all of us," Elizebeth said, looking at both women in turn, "and I worry that the glass door is locked."

17

Dinah

"Life seemed so simple in those early days at Riverbank, living in luxury with all of you genius codebreakers."

Dinah hadn't been able to forget that particular line for days now, one in which Auntie Margot had implied that her mother, whose life was so humdrum that she ironed her undergarments and mended socks *before* they got holes in them, had been involved in cryptography in the first war, just like the Friedmans.

It wasn't that she'd *meant* to eavesdrop, exactly. She'd simply gone to find the cardigan she'd left downstairs during the boarders' late-night practice of the steps in the newest variation on the swing dance, the St. Louis Shag.

Margot and Mother were talking in hushed voices, and it had only taken a moment to realize it was the wrong time to intrude. As she'd backed away, avoiding the creaking stairs, she'd heard yet another mention of a mysterious place called Riverbank.

It didn't seem to be something she could simply ask Mother

about, not if she'd kept it secret all these years. A flash of inspiration had driven Dinah to Mother's old journal, vowing to take another crack at the gibberish that had stumped her so many years before.

A stroke of luck. Her tired eyes falling down the page close to midnight made her realize that the neat, printed capitals made no sense when read left to right, but if one traced the column down, words began to emerge.

Sure enough, the first journal entry described the start of the Great War, and how Elizebeth had offered her mother a job in codebreaking, which she accepted. There, the cipher stopped, and a new entry started, this one stubbornly unreadable.

At age twelve, Dinah had thought Mother had given her the encrypted journal as some sort of intelligence test because she knew her daughter was enamored of Civil War spies like Elizabeth Van Lew, Harriet Tubman, and Belle Boyd, imagining herself part of their daring exploits. Now the format of the journal made more sense.

Does Dad know?

Surely he would have to. That felt like an even bigger betrayal. Dad never kept anything from her. *But this isn't his story to tell. And anyway, Mother gave you the journal. She wanted you to find out eventually.*

Only, however, once Dinah was smart enough to figure out the code. Once she had proven herself worthy of her mother's high standards. Which, currently, after several days of returning to the journal in the evenings, she had doubts about. The second cipher hadn't followed the pattern of the first, and so far, she was no closer to breaking it.

No, no, no. Dinah crumpled another paper, tossing it toward an overflowing wastebasket, then stared down at the second entry again, willing the words to fall into place. The only legible words, other than the date, were *Shift cipher, key is a set of initials.*

The trouble was . . . she had no idea what a shift cipher actually was.

I've got to read the rest of the story. Maybe if I try writing down groups of letters backward . . .

A knock at the door interrupted her thoughts—or rather a bang, followed by a rattling of the doorknob. Dinah startled like she was an OSS overseas agent with the Gestapo on her trail. But the intruder was only Winora, marching in with a rustle of black taffeta and the overpowering smell of gardenias. "Got any nylons I could borrow? Mine are as full of holes as London after the Blitz, and I'm awful at drawing a hem up my legs with eye pencil."

Dinah slid off her chair to investigate her closet. "Aren't you an artist?"

Winora folded her arms, accenting a daring amount of décolletage peeking from the V of her neckline. "Yeah, yeah, keep the smart remarks to yourself, kid."

Luckily for Winora, while the state of Dinah's own stockings was dubious, unable to be replaced since the material was now being used for parachutes, Mother had given her a pair of her own, department-store pristine. With a twinge of regret, Dinah handed them over. A girl had to make friends somehow, and while she was making progress in her daily lunches with Winora, they'd still barely gone beyond small talk.

"Thanks, I owe ya one." Winora peeled off her heels, so unlike her usual practical brogues that Dinah wondered if she'd borrowed those too.

Dinah smiled teasingly. "Big night out?"

"You bet. One of the Radio Department fellows downstairs asked me out to dinner."

Dinah frowned in confusion, until she realized "downstairs" must refer to the lower floor of the OSS headquarters. "Are . . . we allowed to date coworkers?" Barry Longstreet clearly thought so, but he didn't seem like a trustworthy source.

Winora shrugged, wriggling into the stockings. "It wasn't in the loyalty oath, and there's no chance I'm turning down chop suey at the Lotus. They've got an orchestra and floor show every night." She snapped her fingers. "Say, I could see if he's got any bachelor friends. Next time, we could make it a double date."

"Thanks, but I'm not interested." Life was busy enough at the moment with her OSS work. No need to add a suitor to the mix.

"You work too hard, that's your trouble." The stockings donned, Winora leaned in to see the papers strewn across Dinah's small writing desk. "Like that. Looks like a real snore."

"This is . . . a personal project." Dinah tried to block her view without seeming suspicious. "A book of puzzles, you could say. My mother wrote them."

"Let me see," Winora said, removing any chance of a *no* when she snatched the journal. Her eyes scanned the lines. "Huh. Doesn't mean a thing to me."

"Same here," Dinah said glumly.

"There's someone in MO who gets all the cipher jobs, if you need a second opinion." She handed the journal back. "Say *hypothetically* I was forging documents meant to be found by the Gestapo in France."

Her tone made it clear that her department had been assigned just such a project over the past year, though Dinah knew better than to ask for details.

"I'd make a false ID for a fictional man," she went on, "then some hidden messages with false intelligence. Forgery gathers the right sort of paper and ink, gets the details right, and all that, but someone else hands us the cipher."

That sounded like just the expert to ask, if she could do it subtly. "Who is it?"

Winora's expression was all mischief. "You're not gonna like it."

Dinah guessed the answer before her fellow boarder could give it. "Not Barry Longstreet."

"One and the same." Winora patted Dinah on the shoulder. "On second thought, maybe keep trying to work it out on your own."

A horn sounded out in the street, and Winora craned her neck toward Dinah's window. A shiny black-and-white roadster that reminded Dinah of a two-tone Oxford had pulled up to the curb, with a broad-shouldered fellow wearing a homburg sitting in the front. "There's my date. Gotta go."

"Keep those stockings out of trouble," Dinah teased, and Winora crossed her heart with mock solemnity.

Alone again, Dinah began writing down any word that contained her mother's initials, trying to find a pattern. None emerged.

You could just ask Mother.

Still, somehow, after all these years, that felt like admitting defeat. Maybe it was sheer stubbornness, but this was one puzzle Dinah was determined to solve on her own.

The next morning, Mrs. Masterson was waiting at Dinah's desk, tapping her pointed leather pumps with impatience. "You're in luck, Miss Kendall. Frasier Agnew was impressed enough with your analysis of Axis rubbish that he's letting me try you on our side of things."

That would explain the new stack of documents threatening to spill off her desk. Dinah felt a sudden rush of excitement. Here, at last, she'd be doing work that mattered. "What will I be drafting?"

"News bulletin–style rumors, the best you can dream up." Mrs. Masterson indicated the files. "There's a pile of truth, at least, as much as you can trust foreign correspondents to know it. Mix in some of that with your lies. And be as quick as you can. We've got hours of *Soldatensender* scripts to supply by the end of the week."

Thankfully, Dinah recognized the name of the covert radio

station the Allies broadcasted into Germany, one of Morale Operations' most successful projects. The British SOE intelligence agency, unable to keep up with demand, had allowed the OSS to supply programing for one of their propaganda stations. From agent reports, it seemed that while German authorities knew it was coming from the Allies and forbade their men from listening, the mixture of news and catchy tunes topped the Wehrmacht charts all the same.

The click of heels indicated Mrs. Masterson's retreat. "Bring me whatever you've got by five o'clock," she called over her shoulder. "And remember: Be provocative, be vicious, and above all, be brief."

Dinah frowned. "Because shorter rumors are more memorable?"

The socialite shrugged. "No, because I'll have to read every word you submit. And I haven't got time to waste."

That parting warning haunted Dinah, echoing in the margins as she spent the next two hours glancing over the materials in her file, a hodgepodge of war information, like a scrapbook with pages out of order. Many of these pages were stamped *Confidential* or even *Secret*. Some were press releases and news articles, others detailed reports from Research and Analysis. There were interviews with POWs recently captured in North Africa, reports on death records from the Italy campaign, transcriptions of important German radio broadcasts, even one fascinating manifesto from a resistance group in Greece.

Even when she stayed at the Rumor Mill over lunch to keep reading, Dinah couldn't mine a single original rumor idea from any of the reports.

Of course you can't. What made you think you'd be good at this, anyway? When you turn in an empty paper, you'll be the laughingstock of the OSS. Then Mother will be disappointed, and you'll have to tell everyone at home and . . .

Snap!

Dinah had pressed so hard on her pencil that the lead broke, leaving a crater of a dot on her blank page and drawing a glance from the balding academic occupying the desk next to hers. *You have to stop this.*

What had Mother always said when Dinah had been stuck on a difficult algebra assignment? *"Just ask two questions: What do you know? And what does it mean?"* That was one thing about Mother. She never lost patience with a math problem . . . and usually not with Dinah either.

As usual, the two questions gave her focus. Instead of skimming multiple documents, Dinah chose one to read more thoroughly, finding at the end a map of suspected German fortifications along the coast of France. Her finger traced the lines aimlessly as she read the text beneath. Erwin Rommel, it seemed, was one of the German generals who had been reassigned to shore up defenses in France after a series of failures in North Africa and Italy.

That might be something. Dinah had read the headlines and watched the documentary *Desert Victory*. She knew Rommel's reputation as a fair fighter who didn't believe in squandering the lives of his men. *"Sharp man, and honorable too, the sort of general men want to follow,"* Dad had said about him once.

If Rommel was posted in France, awaiting the Allied invasion everyone knew would happen sometime soon . . .

"What do you know?" Answer: Rommel is popular with the German people and respected by the Allies . . . but his recent defeats have put him out of favor with Adolph Hitler.

Dinah smiled, trading her pencil for a fresh one.

The wonderful thing about rumors was that, unlike in investigative journalism, Dinah didn't have to answer "What does it mean?" only "What *might* it mean?" There was no equation to solve for X. Her work only had to be plausible, not factual.

Why not a rumor about General Rommel being under some sort of curse after his defeat at El Alamein?

Too fanciful. No one but the most superstitious would believe that.

Still, what was the harm in writing it down? She could make a final copy for Mrs. Masterson later. Once Dinah had words on the blank page, her assignment didn't seem so terrible. She just had to make her fictions better, more specific, more vivid. Her pencil scratched across the page, jotting down other potential headlines, the details to be filled in later.

Erwin Rommel badly injured in Africa, unfit for combat duty; Hitler hides this by sending him to supervise fortifications.

Sources from within reveal disagreements in the German High Command could splinter their strategy for defending France.

The defenses of the Atlantic Wall in France are unfinished and unmanned, leaving the Nazi line vulnerable to air attack.

She was doing it. She was really doing it.

By five o'clock, after filling three pages with ideas riddled with deletions and additions in the margins, Dinah presented Mrs. Masterson with a single sheet of typed rumors, focusing on only three of the recent war developments included in her file.

"Hmm," Mrs. Masterson said, plucking the paper from her. "I see you followed my advice on brevity."

Dinah forced herself not to wilt under the older woman's scrutiny. She'd always embraced the idea that fewer words were better, inspired by Lincoln's Gettysburg Address, delivered in two minutes. But had she done enough?

Mrs. Masterson narrowed her eyes at the page, making Dinah suspect she needed glasses but her vanity wouldn't allow her to be seen using them. After a few stretched-out moments, she set it on her desk. "Some of these are quite wicked, Miss Kendall. I never would have guessed you had it in you."

"Are any of them good enough be used in a broadcast?"

"Perhaps. Though I'm afraid most of our work ends up discarded when it's sent higher up." She twiddled the rings on her thin fingers, making sure all their gems faced forward. "One of the national experts doesn't find it believable, the situation changes, a deputy director is feeling contrary. Best not to get your hopes up."

All the same, Dinah felt her step a little lighter as she headed down to the bus station. At least she could rest in the knowledge that she'd done her best, learned something new, and, if she wasn't mistaken, *improved*.

As her colleagues collected their hats and umbrellas, Dinah glanced around before tucking her stack of reports into her handbag. There were plenty of news items in there she hadn't had time to draw from. Maybe if she snuck in a little late-night reading, she'd be able to catch up and really impress Olivia Masterson tomorrow.

Winora met her on the steps. They'd started taking the same bus home, though Winora straggled into the office closer to nine in the mornings.

"So, skipping out on me for lunch, huh?" was her only greeting.

Dinah had meant to tell Winora she would be busy over the lunch hour, but it had slipped her mind. "Sorry about that. I want to hear all about your date last night, though."

That seemed to pacify her, and Dinah gave the appropriate nods and exclamations of "Is that so?" to Winora's account of the Chinese restaurant and the fellow who took her there, Martin.

"He's a decent guy, you know? Smart—all the Radio men are—but easy to talk to, even though I can tell he's one of those rich-family types. We get a lot of those around the OSS."

"I'm glad to hear it." Dinah stepped out of the long shadow of the North Building, letting the sun warm her skin . . . and the hair on her arms prickled with that same uneasy feeling she'd had watching the shadow hovering around the courtyard.

With the slightest of pivots, Dinah looked over her shoulder. Three men followed a bit too closely behind them, but they were engaged in a lively conversation. *It's nothing. It must be nothing.*

A quick glance around the bus stop didn't reveal anything unusual—a high school–aged boy balancing a stack of packages, two women sharing halves of a sandwich, a portly businessman attempting to shuffle forward while reading a newspaper. A half dozen younger men, perhaps from the OSS headquarters, loitered around, but none seemed to be watching her. Most were turned away toward the street, waiting like all the other well-heeled, clean-cut fellows on their way home from a DC job that exempted them from enlistment.

What was I expecting? A lurking figure in a trench coat, like in the spy serials?

"You okay, Dinah?" Winora asked, frowning.

Apparently she hadn't been as subtle as she'd hoped. Dinah couldn't bring herself to tell Winora the truth and risk another round of mockery. "Fine, just . . . thinking. About work."

That prompted a derisive snort. "When aren't ya?"

They crowded on the bus when it arrived, and Dinah was suddenly grateful to be crammed in next to Winora, whose "scram" expression could scare off a Panzer tank division. She tried to keep her mind on the conversation until the bus lurched to a stop on Myrtlewood's street.

As she stood, two men near the rear of the bus rose after her, so Dinah told the driver to keep the change for her fare and hurried onto the street.

It was only half a block's walk to Myrtlewood Hall, and Dinah picked up the pace, not wasting time to glance behind her. Once they were inside, she pressed the door shut with extra force, keeping away from the decorative glazed windows on either side.

"Jeez Louise, woman, shoe leather's rationed," Winora complained, huffing slightly. "You trying to wear ours out?"

"I thought I felt a raindrop, that's all," Dinah said lamely. She let out a long breath, trying to slow her heart rate. Not from fear of something she wasn't even sure was real. Just the brisk walk, that's all.

"Uh-huh," Winora said, delivering her a look as she peered out the parlor windows to a partly cloudy sky. "Got any evening plans?"

"No," she answered, making a face and tapping her handbag. "I had to take home some work. I'm afraid of falling too far behind. The others in Rumors are so much more experienced than I am."

"You kidding?" Winora tsked. "All work and no play makes Dinah a dull girl."

Already, Dinah could feel her heart slow to a normal rate. This was good. More small talk, less paranoia. "I'll be all right." If she could come up with even a couple of juicy rumors from the reports in her bag, it would be worth giving up an evening. "How about you? Going out again with this fellow of yours?"

Winora ducked her head. Was that a . . . blush? "Nah. But I'm going dancing with him tomorrow night. Martin knows a place that stays open past blackout hours."

"Sounds fun," Dinah said, though she knew Mother and Dad would die if she tried any such thing herself. "Are you ever going to bring him around?"

"Maybe." A slight furrow puckered Winora's brow, smoothed out so quickly Dinah almost wondered if she'd imagined it. "But I don't think the two of you would get on. Martin's not your type." She jammed her hands in the pockets of her skirt like they were overalls and slouched up the stairs. "Well, good luck with your work."

Typical Winora, giving the bare minimum for an answer. Dinah shook her head, then retreated to the privacy of her own room. A hearty supper, a hot bath, some reading, and a good night's sleep. That's what she needed, and Washington, DC, would seem a safer place.

Still, as she passed her window, she couldn't help tugging the curtains closed. Just in case.

18

Lillian

The jaunty strains of Jimmy Dorsey's orchestra poured out of Myrtlewood's parlor archway, accompanied by a burst of girlish laughter. Lillian peeked inside, clutching a paper bag of essentials picked up from the drugstore—ones she'd noticed Dinah had not brought with her—along with a book on Civil War cryptography from the Friedmans' library.

"I wish we could invite Dinah over," Elizebeth had said, her swollen feet propped up on a footstool after dinner, *"but now just isn't the time. Perhaps next week. Do tell her hello from us."*

Lillian understood all that her friend hadn't said. No longer did she wake to creaking floors as William stumbled downstairs to pace and smoke and try to forget his troubles. He even occasionally joined the women for dinner. But he still came home from work each day pale and exhausted, certainly in no position to play host.

That did mean, however, that there was no proper setting for

143

uninterrupted conversation with her daughter except the board-inghouse, though a quick glance showed that Dinah wasn't among the girls clustered around the RCA Victor.

"Dinah's up in her room," Margot explained, after her usual effusive greeting, coming out of the dining room with a silver tureen full of Ovaltine, apparently refreshments for the board-ers. "Seemed a bit tired at dinner, but I'm sure she'll be delighted to see you."

Whether or not that was true, Lillian found herself climbing the stairs with purpose before rapping on Dinah's door.

No response.

Lillian frowned. It was nearly eight o'clock. Surely Dinah hadn't slipped out into the city at this hour? Just to be sure, she knocked again.

This time, a muted groan greeted her. The door was un-locked, and Lillian pushed it open to see Dinah splayed across her bed, barefoot, with her eyes closed.

Alarmed, Lillian took stock, but didn't see any immediate signs of illness or injury. *Drama it is, then.*

"Busy day?" she asked mildly, setting the paper bag down on the nightstand without comment. Dinah would find it later and know where it had come from. No need to make a fuss about it.

"Talk about it," Dinah moaned, stuffing her pillow under her head to give herself some amount of incline. She was wearing one of Roger's old bathrobes, a green-and-red striped affair that reminded Lillian of a faded candy cane. Or perhaps that was because her daughter always applied peppermint oil after bathing, inspired by, of all things, learning citizens of Gettys-burg used it to ward off the stench of the dead and wounded in the weeks after the battle. "Gosh, they sure work you to the bone. Even had to take home some reports tonight. Whoever said OSS stands for Oh So Social?"

"I'm glad to hear we're not wasting our tax dollars paying you to do nothing."

Dinah made a face, and Lillian considered that this was perhaps not the most sympathetic reply, but really, young women of this generation all seemed to want to work a few hours until their feet got tired. "It wasn't only that. I've had a rather stressful day."

"In what way?"

Dinah chewed on her bottom lip, then shrugged. "Probably nothing. It's only . . . I've felt a few times like someone was watching me."

Lillian had braced herself for some tale of melodrama, but she'd expected the usual workplace tensions, not a pulp crime thriller. "Nonsense. Margot lives in a respectable part of town. Did you actually *see* someone?"

"Not directly. It was more of a . . . sense. That something was wrong." Dinah sat up, gesturing in a circular motion Lillian had no idea how to interpret. "You know that prickling feeling you get when you see movement out of the corner of your eye, but when you turn, there's no one there?"

"I do not." Lillian kept her voice firm, reasonable. "If there is no one there, I conclude there was never any danger."

Inside, she felt the first twinge of panic. Lillian had heard words like this before—from Mama, during one of her spells. Always convinced some unknown enemy was after them. "Neurotic behavior," one doctor had called it; "manic spells," another had diagnosed, but though the terms varied, Lillian had known, even as a girl, what they had meant.

Her mother's tormentors were entirely inventions of her mother's troubled mind.

A careful glance at her daughter didn't reveal any of the behaviors that had marked Mama in those last days, the ones she'd watched for in herself and Dinah for decades now, wanting to have ample warning of trouble to come. No signs of neglect or indication she'd had trouble sleeping. No jerky movements or trembling hands.

Instead, Dinah shifted uncomfortably under her mother's scrutiny. "Never mind, then." She picked up a *Photoplay* magazine splayed open on the bed. "It's probably nothing."

But before she could put up a Hollywood news barrier between them, Lillian placed her hand on Dinah's arm, tentatively, as if she was afraid her daughter might crack. "Dinah, if you find actual evidence of someone following you, you ought to get a description and report them to Margot, if not the police. But . . ."

"You think it's only my imagination." Her daughter's tone was distinctly accusatory.

Did she? More like she hoped that was all this was. "I think orienting oneself to a new job is taxing on the nerves. And that you've always been of a . . . creative persuasion."

Like Roger, Dinah had been a daydreamer, spending hours with books of fairy tales and tin Civil War figurines as a child, acting out imaginary stories of drama and heroism.

"I would recommend, for your reputation's sake, that you keep your misgivings to yourself until you have definite evidence," she went on. "You're a professional woman now, and in a workplace run by men, women are open to accusations of hysteria."

There. That was diplomatically put, wasn't it? Lillian had lived by that advice for years now. The Friedmans and Roger were the only ones who knew even the vague outlines of Mama's illness. None of them knew exactly how she'd died, only that it was in a hospital from certain complications.

What you're saying to Dinah must be true. It's only the pressure of work getting to her, a momentary lapse. It won't happen again.

Whatever darkness Mama carried inside her, Lillian had to believe it was gone for good, that it wouldn't find her or, worse, her daughter. Or else all of her attempts to protect Dinah, to give her a better life where the wounds of the past couldn't come near, would be in vain.

"Mother?"

Lillian glanced up, blinking. Dinah was clearly waiting for her to say something. Once again, she'd missed the question, absorbed in her thoughts. "What was that?"

"I said, did something like that happen to you?"

It took a moment for Lillian to remember what she was asking: whether she'd been accused of hysteria by an employer. "No. Thank God."

For a moment, Dinah's gaze, sharper somehow than Roger's though their eyes were the same warm brown, rested on her so long that Lillian wished she hadn't added that last bit. "What's that supposed to mean?"

She deserves to know, doesn't she? It was one thing, avoiding speaking about her mother's mental illness when Dinah was young, but she was twenty now, about to be living on her own. Still, where to begin? It was a topic full of stigma and fear, a burden that Lillian had always tried to carry on her daughter's behalf and had hoped she'd never need to broach.

Maybe a half-truth would do for the moment, until she could decide how to explain. "It's only . . . toward the end of her life, your grandmother—my mother—struggled with a similar feeling to the one you're describing. It was baseless, certainly, but her fears . . . had a negative effect on her own health, and that of those around her."

"Is that why you never talk about her?"

Lillian took a deep breath, trying to keep back the memories she'd worked so hard to bury. "One of the reasons."

Dinah opened her mouth, then closed it. "I don't think this is as serious as that. Just something that made me nervous, that's all."

The difference between Dinah's measured reaction and Mama's paranoia was comforting. "All that to say, please tell me if the feeling intensifies, and if you think this job is too much for you . . ."

147

"I'm fine, Mother," Dinah interrupted. She stood, fluffing out her hair. "I'm sure you're right—it was just an especially stressful day. I won't say anything about it at work."

Lillian probably ought to press, but she was so grateful that Dinah didn't ask other questions about her grandmother and those dark days that she didn't have the heart. "That's probably for the best."

Dinah took a seat at the vanity crammed into the corner and pulled a packet of pins from the drawer. "Anyway, a shower went a long way to helping me feel better. I hadn't washed my hair in days. It feels fabulous." She unwound a towel from her head and let her brown hair, several shades darker due to dampness, fall to her shoulders.

"Pin curls again?"

"What else?" Dinah swiped a brush through her hair with a vigor that made Lillian wince. "Now, before you start in on me, it's not vanity, it's thrift. I could be going to a salon every other day."

Lillian couldn't resist observing, "I still think that Victory Roll style looks like you're making tunnels for mice to crawl through."

"*Mother.*" Dinah tucked up a strand of hair, pinning it slightly cockeyed to her scalp. "Don't tell me you never conceded practicality to beauty."

Lillian had been about to deny it, until she remembered. "Actually . . . I did." When Dinah gave only an unconvinced, "Mm-hmm," she felt compelled to add, "It did not end well."

Though Dinah didn't pause in her work, she seemed to perk up. "Well, go on! Now that you've started, you've got to tell."

What was the harm? It might do Dinah some good to hear a cautionary tale, and this story was among the more harmless Lillian could dig up from her past. "Well, all right. But at least let me reroll those. You've spaced them unevenly."

Back when Dinah's only fashion need had been two perfect

braids, Lillian been a champion mother. Pin curls were slightly more fiddly, but not unattainable. Dinah scraped the vanity stool next to the bed without a peep of complaint.

"It was near the end of the last war, over twenty years ago. All Margot's fault, really."

Dinah smiled. "Somehow that doesn't surprise me."

Lillian tugged out the three curls Dinah had already begun and brushed them out, separating the hair into even, manageable sections. "You have to understand, all the cinema stars of the day had dramatic, thin eyebrows. So Margot bought a cheap razor from the five-and-dime and convinced me to join her in shaving ours off."

As expected, Dinah jerked around in surprise. "No."

Lillian turned her head gently back into position. "Yes. The idea was that we'd be able to draw on perfect brows with pencil." Even saying it now, Lillian cringed at how foolish she'd been. Deep into her correspondence with Roger, she'd let Margot's talk of how "stunning" she'd look carry her away.

"What happened?"

"It looked atrocious," Lillian admitted. "And, worse, I'd agreed to go first. When I saw myself in the mirror, I screamed and pulled away, causing Margot to nick my face with the razor. It bled badly."

"I'm guessing there was no way to fix it?"

"None whatsoever." Lillian paused, not for effect, but to twist up another strand of Dinah's hair. "I skulked over to the salon the very next day and requested a cut with heavy bangs. It wasn't the style, but that and some low-slung hats hid the worst of it until my eyebrows grew back months later."

Dinah laughed, nearly dislodging one of Lillian's careful pinnings. "I think that's the best story you've ever told me. Though it hasn't got much to compete with."

Ignoring this comment, Lillian gathered the other sections of hair and pinned them down, one by one. Only the next day would tell for certain, but it looked satisfactory. "There. Finished." She replaced the remaining pins on their card. "Besides being busy, how has your job been going?"

"Smashingly," Dinah said brightly, inspecting her hair in the mirror, apparently satisfied with Lillian's work. She plucked up some clothes discarded at the foot of her bed instead of placed in a laundry bag and threw off her robe to tug them back on, heedless of modesty. "They've set me to work creating rumors for an Allied radio station. I've never had to concentrate so hard in all my life, but it's paying off."

That was just the sort of answer Lillian had hoped to hear. "It seems as if you've found something you're well-suited to."

When Dinah looked up from buttoning her blouse, she was frowning, and Lillian winced inside. What had she done wrong this time? "What I mean to say is . . . I'm proud of you. And I look forward to hearing about all you accomplish."

Dinah seemed to take extra care with smoothing her wide-legged plaid trousers. Then she mumbled, "Thanks, Mother."

Probably embarrassed at the attention. After all, Lillian wasn't usually one to heap praise. She raised her eyebrows significantly. "Enjoy the evening. You've earned it. And for goodness' sake, don't let anyone talk you into rash decisions in the name of fashion."

That seemed to dispel whatever wounded feelings Dinah might have been hiding, because she grinned. "Don't worry, I can stand up for myself."

In the quiet, Lillian stood, clearing her throat. "Well, I had better be going, then."

She half hoped Dinah would protest, ask her to stay, maybe even request another story, but Dinah just pressed her into a quick hug. "Good night, Mother. Thanks for stopping by." With a practiced hand, she tied her pinned hair under a headscarf. "Did you see if there's anything going on downstairs?"

So much for being exhausted, Lillian wanted to say. But that was just Dinah. If there was any chance for her to be around people, she would take it.

Lillian tried to remember. "The radio's on in the parlor. And there's a game of pinochle going on in the dining room, I think."

"Swell. I'm awful at cards."

The answer was delivered so cheerfully that, for a moment, Lillian assumed she'd misheard. "And that's . . . a good thing?"

Dinah tucked her blouse into the trim waist of her trousers. "Sure. No one wants the new girl to come off like some too-smart drip."

"I see." It was wisdom Lillian had never followed as a young woman. Perhaps that's why it had taken her until Elizebeth and Margot to make true friends. "Have a good evening, then. And Dinah?"

Never feel like you have to be less yourself to make others feel better about themselves.

But as her daughter turned back, Lillian amended her intended advice to, "You shouldn't stay up too late. Morning always comes sooner than expected."

As Dinah left, Lillian breathed in the lingering smell of her daughter's peppermint oil. Well, she'd done her best. Then why, as always, did she feel it was not quite good enough?

19

Lily

"The Army Signal Corps officers we trained proved capable, and guests at Riverbank always meant parties. . . ."

— Excerpt from Lillian Kendall's journal

SATURDAY, FEBRUARY 9, 1918

Lily paused in the archway that led into the hotel's ballroom, considering her options. If she fled through the lobby back to the streetcar, would anyone notice?

"Isn't it magnificent?" Margot gestured to the ballroom's golden chandeliers, her long black gloves gleaming. "I'll say this for Colonel Fabyan—he knows how to host a ball."

"It's all . . . very grand," Lily managed over the sound of the string quartet. She pressed a hand against the waist of her borrowed dress, a plum-colored evening gown with a gravy stain on one of its sheer bishop sleeves. Though she'd eaten little at dinner, her stomach felt out of sorts.

152

Several officers and their wives were already swirling about the floor in a dance Lily couldn't name. Along the wall, a row of beauties from Geneva and Aurora, invited to "even out the numbers," tittered behind their fans, waiting for unattached Signal Corps men to invite them to join in.

Lily watched as, near the center of the ballroom, William Friedman made an elaborate bow to his wife, as if he'd have to charm her to win the first dance. Ever since William had finally gotten Fabyan's blessing to join the army, and was departing in only a few weeks, he was always stealing longing glances at Elizebeth.

Beyond them, several of the uniformed young officers had noticed their entrance, marching over in a group as if eager to be the first to whisk any eligible young lady onto the dance floor. Lily recognized their faces from her times assisting in the classroom. Intelligent, hardworking gentlemen, all. And yet the thought of tromping through steps she'd never learned, all while holding a coherent conversation . . .

". . . and let's hope the punch has a kick to it," Margot was saying. When Lily didn't react, she turned, clearly annoyed that her friend was lagging several steps behind. "What's the matter with you, Lily? You look deadly pale."

"I've never learned to dance," she admitted, looking down at the card she'd been given upon entering. Some of the dances printed there—schottische, redowa, medley—were as incomprehensible to her as any cipher.

"Is that all?" Margot scoffed as if this objection were a mere trifle. "Mostly, you just step in a square and follow the man's lead. Come on, we'll find you a shy fellow with two left feet."

But Lily held up a hand to stay her reassurances. "I—I can't do this, Margot. I . . . need some air."

With that, she fled, her heart beating out a Morse code of panic within her, and headed for the grand staircase leading to the second-floor mezzanine.

After glancing over her shoulder to confirm Margot hadn't tried to follow her, she found an alcove with an upholstered armchair and collapsed into it. Should anyone pass by, Lily could escape to the ladies' room—or, as their students were wont to call it, "the latrines." Failing that, perhaps she could feign sickness, or pretend she'd received a distressing telegram, or . . .

Stop, she commanded herself, recognizing what the doctor at the reformatory had called "anxious, neurotic tendencies." Lily preferred to think of them as "runaway train thoughts," so named because once she began to fret over something, her worries picked up speed at an alarming rate.

There was no rational need for panic. She could simply remain here until a chance came to slip away unnoticed. Or, if she regained her courage, return to the ballroom as a wallflower, graciously refusing any dances offered to her.

She had just begun planning such a refusal when she caught a fragment of conversation coming from a room around the corner.

". . . not the usual place for security briefings, but we must fit in some amusement before shipping out to France, eh, lieutenant?"

Lily frowned. Someone ought to tell these Signal Corps officers how their voices carried. The hotel was full of civilians not authorized to hear classified military information. She edged out of her alcove, hoping to shut the door without drawing attention to herself.

The voices seemed to come from the first room in the hallway, its carved doorposts more ornate than the uniform oak of the guest rooms beyond. The clatter of a successful cue strike indicated it must be a billiard room.

Another voice, a bit uncertain, said, "This is about the device I found?"

Device? Lily hesitated beside the doorframe.

Growing up, she had learned it was wise to listen first and then enter a room—noting who was there, whether anyone seemed upset, what Mama's mood might be. "Children should be seen but not heard" was not just an adage; it was a necessity.

This, of course, was not the same situation. Common sense and good manners alike told Lily she ought to close the door and hurry away.

But she was near enough now to see that the door was propped open with a large brass spittoon. It would be impossible to close discreetly, so instead, she risked a glance inside. Fully half of the small, red-carpeted room was dominated by a billiard table, looking somewhat worse for the wear. Three men in army uniforms appeared to be mid-game, poles held like rifles in their arms. She retreated to safety before anyone could look her way but couldn't keep from listening.

"I imagine, being young, you'll want to get back to dancing shortly," a third voice said. This one she recognized as belonging to Major Clendenin, the highest-ranking officer who attended their little school. His voice carried like a revival preacher's into the hall, just as it had in the classroom. "But Captain Canterbury insisted you hear what we've learned regarding your report."

Lily waited for the silence between strikes that indicated both men would be concentrating on the game before them and dared another, longer look into the room. As she'd suspected, Major Clendenin was holding court at the head of the table, while a heavily whiskered man with captain's stripes made a shot that pocketed two balls. A younger officer shifted nervously in the corner, leaning against his cue like it was a walking stick.

Oh. Lily knew him as well, though not by name. Margot had given him the nickname "Wartime Wally" due to his uncanny resemblance to debonair matinee idol Wallace Reid. His uniform indicated his rank as a relatively lowly first lieutenant.

When the captain looked up with a satisfied smile, Lily

ducked back into the empty hallway. "The plot you suspected certainly troubled us . . . at first."

"May I ask what changed your mind?" Wartime Wally's voice, a rich baritone that reminded Lily of the cello from the ballroom below, held the hesitation of someone not used to casually conversing with those of higher rank.

"Indeed, indeed. There's nothing to fear, because we learned who installed the device." An undignified chortle popped out of the major. "You'll never guess."

The captain removed any chance of this by interjecting, "George Fabyan himself."

What?

"You're sure?" Though Lily could no longer see the men, she could almost hear the frown in Wartime Wally's voice.

"Absolutely certain, Lieutenant Kendall. When I notified Mr. Fabyan of the Dictograph you found, he admitted to placing it there, then blustered about wanting to transcribe some of the Friedmans' lessons for a book on cryptography."

"But one of our instructors told us the codebreakers have nearly completed a book like that."

That had been Lily, one afternoon when she'd assisted with the class when both William and Elizebeth had been occupied with an urgent, complex decryption. The fact that Wartime Wally—rather, Lieutenant Kendall—remembered something she'd said warmed her.

"It doesn't add up. Could Fabyan be some sort of spy?" the lieutenant pressed.

More laughter trickled out of the billiard room. "George? Certainly not," the raspy-voiced captain said. "He may be a loose cannon, but he's our cannon, and he's pointed straight at the Huns."

"Maybe. But I don't trust him." And with that observation, Lily's estimation of young Lieutenant Kendall went up considerably. Not many newcomers, awed by Fabyan's estate and distracted by his boasting banter, perceived how hollow it all was.

"Think, man," the major said, impatience edging his voice. "If Fabyan wants to pass along information about our cipher training, he owns the blasted place. He's attended a few sessions himself. Where's the need for covert listening devices?"

"It's just . . ." Kendall sounded flustered, but then he voiced the same question on Lily's mind. "I can't think of any other reason he'd spy on his instructors. Does he distrust them?"

"I believe that's just it. Though not in the way you might mean." Another strike of cue against ball rattled into the hallway. "As we spoke, Fabyan fished for information about whether the army was trying to 'poach' his codebreakers. As if they were a line of breeding cattle, owned by his family for generations. He's all but ordered us not to tell them about the device."

"You think he's making sure the Friedmans aren't planning to take a job elsewhere?" Lily had come to the conclusion even as Lieutenant Kendall voiced it, disbelief in his voice.

"That's about the sum of it."

The whistle Kendall let out was low and musical. "Well now. That's pretty awful."

He doesn't know the half of it. Now Lily felt ashamed for secretly wondering if Elizebeth and William might be paranoid in their suspicions.

"Believe me, Kendall, none of these codebreakers will be allowed to leave Riverbank until at least the end of the war. Maybe not even then."

Lily could feel the skin on her arms prickling from her shoulders to the pearl-buttoned cuffs of her sleeves. Mr. Fabyan couldn't really keep them here . . . could he?

"I see." There was a long pause before Lieutenant Kendall continued, "When are we going to speak with Mr. and Mrs. Friedman about this?"

Again, Lily felt she had to watch the expressions that crossed the men's faces. She edged closer, angling her head so she could see into the room and hopefully not be seen.

The answer was not long in coming. "Never," the captain answered, shaking his head. "It's not our place to stir up trouble."

The major's shot went wild, and he cursed before turning back to the lieutenant, who was wringing his army cap like a handkerchief. "He's right, I'm afraid. If we offend George, he'll boot us out of here. And we have nowhere else to go. Our teachers may be a cadre of bookish wisenheimers and liberated women, but they're all we have." He nodded at Lieutenant Kendall. "Your go, lieutenant."

As he considered this, the game forgotten before him, Lieutenant Kendall's eyes flicked up, toward the gilt mirror hung on the wall opposite the door, and Lily froze, expecting him to cry out. Instead, he looked down at his cue, shaking his head. "It . . . it just doesn't sit right with me."

The major grunted. "Such is wartime."

"He's a religious fellow—aren't you, Kendall?" the captain asked, a note of derision in his voice. "Can't stomach the idea of lying, or even withholding the truth."

The lieutenant shifted uncomfortably as both officers scrutinized him like he was standing in line for inspection. "I am, sure, but . . . actually, I was wondering something else."

"What's that?"

A sudden undercurrent of unease made the hair on the back of Lily's neck rise the moment before Lieutenant Kendall turned toward the door and said in that same simple, straightforward voice, "Whether or not to tell you I think someone has been listening to us."

Lily had always been small and fast, though she'd never had those qualities tested like this, wearing a too-long borrowed gown and rushing down unfamiliar halls.

The officers would surely spot her, given her barest of head starts, and there was nowhere in the hallway to hide. Still, she kept running toward the grand staircase, even when she heard a set of heavy footsteps behind her. "Miss! Wait! Please."

Lily did not so much as turn, skimming her hand against the banister as she ran down the stairs, a precaution against spraining her ankle.

Get away, get away. There was no way to hide that she'd been listening, but perhaps she could retreat to Riverbank, then find Elizebeth and tell her everything. She would know what to do next.

"I want to talk to you, that's all." The lieutenant's voice, though not a shout, was clearly closer. He would overtake her soon.

At the bottom of the staircase, Lily hesitated. Others were now in view—one porter was already frowning at her in disapproval. Might it be worse to create a scene in the hotel lobby than face the lieutenant? Surely he couldn't mean her any harm, not in public.

Her breath came in quick bursts, her heart pounding from exertion and nerves. With effort to control her expression, she turned. Lieutenant Kendall took the steps two at a time, arms outstretched, reminding her—absurdly—of illustrations of Prince Charming chasing after Cinderella.

There was nothing for it but to face the consequences of her actions. And Lily was quite sure of one thing: She would not be bullied.

She straightened poker stiff as Lieutenant Kendall halted beside her, but he didn't reach to grab her arm or scowl in an attempt at intimidation. Instead, he bowed. "Hello. Miss Nilsson, isn't it?"

All she could do was nod, not trusting her voice as yet. *He remembered my name.* William had introduced her in front of the class, though only once.

"Lieutenant Roger Kendall. I know this isn't usual, but might I have this dance?" His voice was entirely devoid of menace, but he stood a foot taller than her, the broad shoulders filling out his uniform testifying to a strength greater than her own.

Though Lily still had not replied, the lieutenant never looked away, and she forced herself to assess him directly, to meet those dark eyes with her own.

Oh. She almost said it out loud.

She'd expected reproach, or at least irritation, toward the eavesdropper who had complicated his evening. Instead she saw only sincerity and an unmistakable kindness. A curl of brown hair drooped down toward the lieutenant's ruddy face, one that might belong to an ordinary small-town farmer's son who'd joined up from pride in his country.

"All right," she heard herself saying, a slight quaver in her voice. She took his arm, allowing herself to be led through the lobby toward the ballroom, where a riff of strings indicated the ball had proceeded as planned.

Instead of waiting for a new dance to begin, the lieutenant ushered her onto the ballroom floor immediately, placing his hand on the small of her back and gliding to the music.

"I like a good waltz," the lieutenant said, as if they were any other couple navigating the social etiquette of dance conversation. "Easier for a clod like me to muddle through."

"Yes," Lily said stupidly. She tried to imitate those around her but found she couldn't watch them and anticipate where to place her feet next.

For a moment, perhaps noting the panic in her face or the iron grip of her hand, the lieutenant remained silent. "It's a pattern," he said at last in his quiet baritone, counting off the

160

measured steps in even beats of three. "You codebreakers are brilliant at patterns."

A pattern? Yes, it is, isn't it? This gave her mind something to focus on, and soon, her feet moved in time to the music. Lily felt her body relax. Not that she was comfortable, but there were so many other uncomfortable aspects to this situation—the slick of sweat beneath her dress cooling to a chill, the humiliation of being caught eavesdropping, the confusion about what she'd overheard—that she simply didn't have energy to fret about the dancing anymore. As Margot had advised her, she let the lieutenant lead, her muscles feeling the slight indications from where their bodies touched and responding in kind.

If only conversations could have such a predictable rhythm. This one, she was quite sure, would not.

Still keeping a pleasant smile on his face for the benefit of those around them, the lieutenant took in a breath and began. "Listen, about what happened back there. I don't know what you heard—"

"Everything," she said simply. No need to feign ignorance now. "Tell me about the device you found. What did it look like? Are there others?"

He chuckled good-naturedly, dimples appearing in his cheeks. "One question at a time. It was a round disk enclosed in black rubber." He lifted his hand from hers briefly and formed a circle with his finger and thumb. "Attached to the Friedmans' desk. A wire connected to it ran through the desk and into the floorboards, ending in an empty room next door."

She'd never heard of such an object. "You didn't know what it was?"

"Not at first. But when I showed it to Major Clendenin, he called it a Dictograph. He had seen it used by a manager at the Metropolitan Opera House to listen in on rehearsals of an upcoming play while working in his office." Unlike the major, the lieutenant had a naturally low voice, and Lily felt sure the couples nearby couldn't pick out what they were discussing.

"You mean . . . it's a sort of radio transmitter?"

He nodded. "Exactly. Connected to an earpiece that receives crystal-clear audio of everything said in the other room."

Lily blinked, processing this information. The circle Lieutenant Kendall had formed was only about three inches across. Surely something so tiny couldn't contain a device complex enough to gather and transmit sounds. "That's . . . incredible."

"Sure is." His face took on a sudden animation. "I'm a radio fellow myself—just a tinkerer, although the army's given me more training—which is how I noticed it. Whether there are others, I can't say, but I wouldn't be surprised. I bet Mr. Fabyan didn't even have the hotel's permission to install a device like that in the rooms he's renting."

Lily knew such a formality would not stop her employer. As for other devices, her room was likely safe . . . but what about the Friedmans'? Or the code room in Engledew, or the common areas of the Lodge? Her ears burned at the very idea of such an invasion of privacy.

"I'm sure this is all a bit of a shock."

She shook her head. "Nothing Mr. Fabyan stoops to will truly surprise me."

He acknowledged that with a nod. "So now you know all that we do. The question is, what will you do now?"

Lily hadn't had much time to consider, but she was sure of one thing. "I *will* be telling Elizebeth—Mrs. Friedman," she amended, in case the lieutenant didn't know her Christian name. "She and her husband are the ones most wronged if what you surmise is true."

This earned her a frown, the first one she'd seen from the lieutenant. "But if Mr. Fabyan were to hear you gave them warning, why, he'd fire you on the spot."

The scene flashed before Lily's mind, as all of her worst fears did, so often predicted and rehearsed that they could be seen in every detail—the flush of shame as Mr. Fabyan shouted at her; the hurried packing of her things; the chill of winter air as she stood in line for a train ticket, driven out of yet another home with no idea of where to go next.

And a distant memory of Mama saying, *"Folks like us, we'll never belong anywhere. Better not to try."*

"Miss Nilsson?"

Lily blinked, drawn back to the polished floors and the press of perfumed and uniformed bodies moving about them. She had stopped in the middle of the dance. As she resumed, her voice dropped to a whisper. "Are you threatening me?"

The heat in her voice seemed to catch Lieutenant Kendall off guard, for this time he was the one who stumbled. "N-no. That is . . . I didn't mean to imply . . . although I guess that's what the major thought I'd run off to do. Keep you quiet and all." The shoulders of his drab olive jacket rose with a deep breath, his face suddenly scarlet.

He's nervous too.

The thought was oddly comforting, and kept her, barely, from fleeing again.

"Listen, Miss Nilsson. I agree with you, whatever my superiors think. The Friedmans have to be told." He lifted his chin, a look of determination on his face. "But I think I should be the one to do it and face the consequences."

This had not been on Lily's mental list of anticipated statements, and she was left without a ready reply, treading on Lieutenant Kendall's feet. This time, he didn't flinch. Used to it, she supposed. "Are you sure? The major outranks you, and . . ."

"I'm not so much a coward that I can't stand up for what's right, Miss Nilsson. It wouldn't be fair to put you at risk for being in the wrong place at the wrong time. I'm the one who found the device and asked questions. I should tell them."

Lily moved through several bars of the waltz, as mechanical

as a music box, while she processed this. "The Friedmans are people of discretion. If you tell them the truth, they'll be wise about how they use it." At any rate, they wouldn't storm down to the Villa, betraying the source of their information in a rant to Mr. Fabyan.

Then again, Elizebeth was already on edge, and remembering how William responded to Fabyan scheming to keep him out of the army, Lily considered he might be prone to overreaction.

"It's awfully complicated, isn't it?" The lieutenant paused, frowning. "But I guess I'm old-fashioned. My father taught me that when you're not sure what's right, do the most honest thing you can and let God sort out the rest. So that's what I aim to do."

It seemed overly simplistic . . . and yet, Lily believed this young man meant every word. "I-I'm glad to hear it, lieutenant."

With a flourish, the quartet ended their song, and Lily dipped a curtsy to Lieutenant Kendall's bow. "I'm sorry that you got tangled up in this, Miss Nilsson, truly. I'd hoped to see you tonight . . . but not like this."

He had? She stammered out a reply, allowing herself to be led to the side of the room as couples changed places.

But before Lily could make her escape to the punch bowl, where Margot was at the center of a circle of lively conversationalists, the lieutenant caught her wrist. The intensity of his gaze made even the casual touch seem to burn. "And Miss Nilsson? It might be none of my business, but I feel like I ought to say . . ."

He glanced over his shoulder to where Mr. Fabyan stood framed by two dark walnut pillars, beaming and roaring with laughter, a full glass in hand. "Something's funny about this place. If you have the chance to get away from here after the war . . . please, take it."

20

Dinah

THURSDAY, MAY 4, 1944

Dinah steeled her nerves and rapped a knock on the doorframe of Barry Longstreet's office. "Come in," his bored tenor intoned.

She did, finding him sitting with his feet propped on an open drawer, which he quickly slammed down on seeing her. His eyes widened, an irritating smirk dominating the lower half of his face. "Well, well, what have we here?" He sprang up from his desk. "Welcome to my domain, Miss Kendall."

Despite the fact that she had deliberately left it open, he closed the door behind her, ushering Dinah inside with a hand to the small of her back.

"I won't take much of your time," she said, forcing a small laugh. "Mr. Agnew will expect me back promptly. I only want to ask a small favor."

"A favor, eh?" His eyes crinkled with delight at this choice of phrasing.

This was a terrible idea. You shouldn't have come. But after another week of making no progress on her mother's journal, she felt out of options.

A sudden worry flitted through Dinah's mind: What if Mr. Longstreet was the shadow she'd felt following her the month before? She'd only had the sensation again once in the past week and had decided to ignore it. After all, she didn't want to end up like her grandmother, however vague Mother had been about what happened to her. Still, the idea that Mr. Longstreet might have followed her to where she lived was distinctly uncomfortable.

Too late now. Mr. Longstreet stood with one hand in his jacket pocket like a suit catalog advertisement, waiting for her to go on.

"I heard you're the Publications Department's expert on ciphers."

He seemed to straighten up at this bit of flattery, almost bursting out of his perfectly tailored suit. "You've got that right."

"That's super!" She made an effort to look impressed, clutching her handbag as a barrier between them. "I'm interested in learning more about the subject, professionally."

That smirk again. "Well, I could tell you all about it. Set up a few private lessons, even."

"Thanks, but I was hoping you'd lend me a book on the subject. Something introductory." She took the opportunity to step away from him, toward the bookshelf against the wall. Reference books, mostly, but she could see from the titles on the spines that there were several by various military authorities on ciphers and decryption. One set of matching books with plain white covers looked slimmer than the others—a good sign—and she reached for them.

Mr. Longstreet's hand closed around hers, twisting it so she was forced to face him again. "Let's make a deal, shall we, Dinah?"

"Miss Kendall, please," she corrected, dislodging herself

from his grip. The snub of revoking the use of her first name—a real Victorian maiden move—usually gave fellows the right idea. Or, rather, told them they had the wrong idea.

All the same, Dinah regretted her decision not to wait until the office was empty and pick the lock to his door—a surprisingly simple trick she'd learned from Dad. Stealing the books would have spared her this trouble.

Mr. Longstreet lounged against the bookshelf, blocking her view. "Let's say I give you the whole stack of Riverbank Publications and anything else you like."

"I'm sorry, did you say Riverbank?" she sputtered. It must be the same Riverbank mentioned in her mother's journal. They'd been the experts in the last war, after all.

He didn't appear to notice her surprise. Then again, his gaze was roaming over almost every part of her body other than her face. "They're older, based on techniques from the last war, but great for beginners."

Could it really be that easy? "Sounds perfect. I'll return them to you shortly. I'm a fast learner."

"Oh, I bet you are." He tsked, angling toward her again. "But slow down, now. This is a trade, remember? What I ask in return isn't much. Just one kiss."

"Excuse me?" Fear exploded like a grenade in her stomach, and she judged the distance to the door. Should she slap him? Hit him with her handbag? Run? It was a crowded office in the middle of the workday.

Mr. Longstreet's leer of a grin only widened. "Come on, there's no need to play coy. Anyone who's friends with that McMahen girl can't be so innocent."

Now anger mixed with panic, making her stand her ground and say something decidedly impolite. "I don't care who you are or who your father is, if you ever speak to me or any of my friends that way again, I'll report you to Mr. Agnew. I'm sure he would disapprove of such unprofessional conduct."

The expression on Mr. Longstreet's face twisted into something dangerous, his fist knotted up at his side. "You wouldn't dare. As if anyone would believe—"

A knock at the door cut short his diatribe, and Dinah's knees nearly buckled with relief as Mr. Longstreet stumbled toward his desk. He'd only made it a few steps away from her when Mr. Agnew opened the door. "A word, Mr. Longstreet."

Taking advantage of the distraction, Dinah edged toward the door. "I'll see myself out."

"No need. My errand is a brief one." Mr. Agnew's voice was crisp and businesslike as ever. He didn't even seem to realize he'd accidentally rescued her. "I simply came to inform Mr. Longstreet that our agents in the field have rejected his latest project." He placed a sheaf of papers on Mr. Longstreet's desk like he was taking the trash to the curb.

Mr. Longstreet snatched them up, studying them with a scowl for a moment before tossing them to his desk. "Was the campaign called off?"

"No. The section officer simply felt it wasn't convincing enough for field use. Perhaps you should have used the full time allotted to you instead of throwing something together in an afternoon."

Dinah chewed on her bottom lip, considering. Neither man was looking at her. And the Riverbank Publications were only a few steps away. If she could just reach out casually . . .

"It was perfectly good work," Mr. Longstreet blustered. "It's not as if it has to be a *real* cipher. None of the leaked information it will be used to encrypt is accurate."

A cipher. Interesting.

Dinah plucked the slender Riverbank volumes from the shelves, enjoying the smooth feel of the covers. Mr. Longstreet might notice the books missing, but what could he do to her, really? If he complained, she could simply explain the "trade" he offered in response to her polite request. Mrs. Masterson, she felt sure, would be firmly on her side, and besides, she would return them soon. She tucked the booklets into her handbag, where they barely made a bulge.

Mr. Agnew massaged his temples with a world-weary air. "You seem to have missed the purpose of black propaganda, Mr. Longstreet. Which, given that it is the basis of our entire department, is a bit troubling. It doesn't matter if the information is not top secret; the enemy must believe it is. Which means dropping them a cipher that might have appeared as a prize inside a cereal box will simply not do."

Dinah might have felt sympathy for any other recipient of such a withering dressing down, but she had to admit it was satisfying to see Mr. Longstreet turn fire-engine red and stammer out a response. Mr. Agnew cut it off with a raised hand, like a symphony conductor. "Please deliver another draft to me by next Monday at the latest. And do your research properly this time."

"I can't!" Now Mr. Longstreet's voice was practically a whine. "There are other high-priority projects on my desk, you know."

As he listed several critical assignments occupying his time, Dinah began to think. Clearly this project was getting the attention of OSS leadership even higher than Mr. Agnew. What better way to prove herself than to take a crack at it?

Before she could overthink her reaction, Dinah blurted out, "I could do it."

Both men turn to her, faces a mirror of incredulity, which told Dinah they had forgotten she was there. Typical. Around the OSS, women tended to fade into the background.

Well, not this time.

"Do you have any experience with cryptography, Miss Kendall?" Mr. Agnew asked. To his credit, he seemed open to being surprised with an affirmative answer, though Mr. Longstreet snorted derisively.

"As a matter of fact," she said coolly, "it's a personal interest of mine. Growing up in Gettysburg, one can't help but be exposed to the history of military cryptography, and I've dabbled as an amateur myself." She had read dozens of biographies of Civil War spies, after all.

"Be that as it may, this is a relatively complex project, Miss Kendall," Mr. Agnew said. "The department needs a workable cipher for a series of falsified communications between the OSS and a northern Italian resistance group. The cipher we implement for this operation must be complex enough to be realistic, and yet simple enough to be broken by field officers."

For a moment, Dinah wavered. Despite her bravado, she really didn't have the qualifications for a project of this scale. And yet, she'd just completed a broadcast clip for *Soldatensender* about sabotage efforts of resistance groups in Italy . . . and, though she hated to admit it, Mr. Longstreet's mocking smirk had some effect on her.

"I think I can make an improvement on whatever Mr. Longstreet turned in."

This prompted a growl of outrage from her coworker. "You? That's nonsense."

Despite ignoring Mr. Longstreet's outburst, Mr. Agnew looked unconvinced. "We were hoping to find an expert, perhaps someone in a different department or in one of our overseas offices . . ."

The word *expert* gave Dinah a flash of inspiration. "I have some old family friends with an extensive library of works about codes and ciphers. I'm sure they wouldn't mind me stopping by this week for additional research."

As she'd hoped, this caused Mr. Agnew to raise an eyebrow. "And who might they be?"

"William and Elizebeth Friedman."

She held her breath, waiting. Would the Friedmans, working behind the scenes for two wars, be notable enough that dropping their names would have any effect? She had gotten the impression from Mother that William, at least, was well known in cryptography circles, though his wife, equally talented, seemed trapped in his shadow.

Yet the first words Mr. Agnew spoke were, "You know Elizebeth Friedman?"

"She and my mother have been close friends for over twenty years."

"Fascinating," Mr. Agnew said slowly. "Do you realize that she is the one who interviewed our cryptographic staff and created the official cipher used in all secret OSS communications?"

"Really? I had no idea." Inwardly, Dinah cheered. Who could've known her strike in the dark would make such a direct hit?

"Hmm." Mr. Agnew shifted his weight, giving Dinah another assessing glance. "This might change things."

"You can't possibly consider giving her my assignment," Mr. Longstreet protested.

"A moment ago, if I recall, you were trying desperately to get out of it." Without waiting for further protest, Mr. Agnew gathered the discarded papers from Mr. Longstreet's desk. "It's settled, then. I have nothing against reassigning work to someone more willing and able to complete it, Miss Kendall, particularly if you can leverage your connections for assistance on this project."

"Would speaking to the Friedmans be breaking any OSS rules regarding confidentiality?" Dinah felt she had to ask, even if it might ruin her chances at the assignment.

"In this case, no. As Mr. Longstreet so astutely pointed out, you won't be working with any actual military secrets, merely creating the system used to encrypt fake ones. Besides, I daresay both Friedmans have signed enough secrecy oaths to fill the Atlantic Ocean, given the military branches they work for."

171

"The army and navy don't share their codebreakers," Mr. Longstreet protested. "This will never work."

Once again, Mr. Agnew ignored him outright, opening the office door and gesturing for Dinah to pass through. "Thank you for your initiative, Miss Kendall. I'll let Mrs. Masterson know to lighten your workload for the next week as you add this project."

"Thank you for the chance." It was petty, but she couldn't help stealing one backward glance, just to see the fuming Mr. Longstreet staring after their exit. "I won't disappoint you."

The reason Mr. Agnew had given her the assignment was clearly because he hoped the Friedmans would contribute to it. And she'd taken it knowing there was a good chance they would be too busy with their own work to spare time for her, given Mother's reports.

What have I just done? Once Dinah reached her tiny desk, she took in a deep breath and stared at the blank paper loaded into her typewriter. Perhaps by referencing the Riverbank Publications, she'd be able to come up with something serviceable.

Dinah was so absorbed in her thoughts that she didn't notice Mrs. Masterson's approach until a blast of musky perfume indicated her arrival.

"Miss Kendall, a word. Several words, actually." Mrs. Masterson held a sheet of paper between two fingernails, almost clawlike. "As I passed your desk earlier, I found this. Could you tell me how it came to be in your possession?"

It wasn't so much Mrs. Masterson's question as its tone—almost blank, but with a subtle warning—that made Dinah straighten to attention and peer more carefully at the offending document. The text of the memorandum was too far away to be seen, but the *Secret* stamp at the top was clear enough.

Dinah frowned. To her knowledge, the detritus of paperwork scattered about her desk were all dry reports of U-boat disasters gathered by Research and Analysis from the international newswire over the past year. None of them were even classified.

"No. In fact, I don't think I've ever seen it before. What is it?"

Instead of holding it out for her to see, Mrs. Masterson merely raised an eyebrow. "It's a communique from our Radio Department. And, given its contents, it should not have left there, if you take my meaning."

So that was the trouble. "I understand, but I didn't request it, and I certainly haven't read it," Dinah repeated, making sure to meet Mrs. Masterson's eyes. "I have no idea what it was doing on my desk."

"No? I thought perhaps you'd taken it upon yourself to do some . . . extracurricular work, let's say. Trying to impress the boss." Her glance around seemed to imply that such actions occurred even among the prestigious professionals around her. "Though, of course, we don't encourage snooping into the private files of other departments without authorization."

Dinah knew Mrs. Masterson was giving her a way out, but she didn't need it, because it wasn't the truth. "Not at all. If I'd seen it before, I would have reported it."

Had the memorandum been on her desk before her trip to Mr. Agnew's office? Dinah couldn't remember seeing it—or anything out of place, for that matter—but then again, her desk was in such a state of disarray that it was difficult to tell. She glanced around at her fellow workers, as if one of them might admit to misplacing a *Secret* file, but as always, they were clattering away at their typewriters, paying her little mind.

"Maybe . . . a secretary ran it over, since they knew I worked on scripts for the *Soldatensender* program?"

"Not that I'm aware of." Her slanted glance told Dinah that she made it her business to be aware of all goings-on in the tiny windowless room that was her kingdom. "Besides, this file doesn't concern our collaborative projects but rather a . . . more sensitive Special Operations endeavor."

"Then I can't tell you how it came to be here."

A long moment of silence passed between them, in which Dinah didn't dare to so much as blink, before Mrs. Masterson shrugged. "Very well. Perhaps there has been some mistake." She tucked the offending document against her turquoise-trimmed suit, shielding it from view. "I'll just nip this back to the correct department. Do be more careful in the future."

She doesn't believe me. The realization burned through Dinah's mind and radiated from there to her cheeks in what must look like a guilty flush. "But I—"

Mrs. Masterson held up a hand. "Now, now. I don't want to hear any more about it."

The woman's tone was so authoritative that Dinah let her protest die off. Injustice or not, Mrs. Masterson didn't seem overly bothered by the mistake. Maybe it was better to let it go than to keep making a fuss.

Her supervisor's heels gave only two clacks before she turned back. "A word of advice, Miss Kendall, because I appreciate bright young things who show initiative. Have you ever wondered how I, a middle-aged, twice-divorced, born-to-poverty woman came to be in a supervisory position in the male-dominated country club of the OSS?"

As a matter of fact, Dinah hadn't, nor had she known all of those details. Apparently Mrs. Masterson assumed she was as current on actual office rumors as those their department manufactured.

"I would think . . ." Dinah stammered but was spared coming up with a reply by Mrs. Masterson's upraised hand, like a soprano whose final aria had been interrupted.

"It's because, for years, I have been ruthlessly professional—turned in each article early, cited every source, demanded the raises I deserved, treated even an inane society brief like it might become front-page news. And sometimes, it did."

The gleam in her eyes spoke of remembered conflicts and

triumphs behind bylines of days gone by. Mrs. Masterson took a step closer and rested a hand on Dinah's shoulder for the briefest of moments. "All that to say . . . don't give anyone a single reason to get rid of you, darling. Because believe me, sooner or later, someone will take it."

21

Lillian

". . . so give Dinah a kiss for me, and tell her not to flirt too much with soldiers on leave (newly minted military men are trouble—I should know!). I miss my best girls. Yours, Roger."

SATURDAY, MAY 6, 1944

Lillian glanced up to see Dinah shaking her head but smiling. She leaned back in the Friedmans' well-worn leather chair. "Oh, Dad. As if I have time for dates these days."

"Still busy at work, then?" Lillian asked, eager for this conversational opening.

All throughout dinner, the Friedmans had carried the conversation, asking Dinah about the past several years since they'd last seen her, and sharing about their close-in-age daughter Barbara and her many adventures in diplomatic work. Now, however, they'd retired to the study, and after reading Roger's letter from the week before aloud, Lillian struggled, as ever, to find something she and Dinah might talk about.

"As a matter of fact," Dinah said, leaning forward with a gleam in her eyes, "I wanted to speak to you about that. I've been getting more important assignments—actual overseas campaigns."

To Lillian's surprise, instead of ending with this vague answer as usual, Dinah set her handbag on the desk and opened it, rummaging around until she pulled out a stack of dog-eared papers. "Like this cipher assignment that got passed on to me when one of my colleagues failed to deliver a decent product."

A cipher? Despite herself, Lillian felt her heart rate increase slightly, like the thrill when Margot had placed another communique on her desk back in Engledew Cottage.

Wait. Before she could get close enough to read any of the contents, Lillian pushed the papers away, caution overruling curiosity. "Are you sure you should be sharing this?"

"Not to worry. I double-checked, and it's fine. Doesn't involve anything classified, not until they actually use the cipher. Even then, it's the senders and recipients who are the secret, not the information, which will all be false."

"I see." The tactics of Morale Operations had always confused Lillian. The straightforward world of real ciphers describing real military maneuvers seemed far more familiar. "What is its provenance intended to be?"

"I don't know all of the details," Dinah admitted. "Just that they're slipping it into the hands of German troops around Ravenna, Italy, as if it's coming from OSS communications with Italian partisan groups."

She supposed the OSS couldn't be more specific than that, but it wasn't much to go on. "Why are you showing it to me?"

Dinah shrugged. "I thought it might be useful to talk it through with someone. Do you have any experience with ciphers or puzzles? Besides crosswords, I mean."

Lillian paused to consider how she should answer. In the silence, she could hear William and Elizebeth across the hall, playing a duet on the sitting room piano—a wistful tune, their notes overlapping and flowing together perfectly. Mendelssohn, she thought, one of William's favorite composers.

Focus. Dinah asked you a question.

At one time, Lillian had planned to share her adventures at Riverbank with Dinah, giving her a journal relating some of the more exciting bits for her twelfth birthday. All of them were written in ciphers, gradually increasing in complexity. She'd hoped they might work on it together, a way of introducing Dinah to a skill that had once given her a sense of purpose.

Then Dinah had carelessly lost the journal over the summer, and by then, Lillian had realized that her daughter's interests lay elsewhere. She'd never made another attempt, and Dinah had never asked her questions about her past. Riverbank wasn't so much a secret as an untold story . . . so why did she feel so reluctant to share about it now?

Perhaps it was just the wrong time to allow those memories to resurface. In any case, this was about Dinah and her work, not a chance for Lillian to relive her glory days.

"Oh, I know a bit," Lillian answered. "One can't become friends with the Friedmans without some exposure, and your father was in the Signal Corps during the war, you remember. He intercepted many encrypted transmissions via radio, though he couldn't speak about it in detail."

"I see." Dinah didn't look away from her for a long moment, as if waiting for more. When Lillian didn't offer any, she held up the papers again. "Still, I could use some help. If you're interested in taking a look."

"Certainly." Trying not to appear eager, Lillian pulled the study's second chair closer. "Do you have your colleague's failed attempt? That seems a good place to start."

"Right here." Dinah handed over two typewritten pages describing Barry Longstreet's proposed cipher, and Lillian could immediately see why the OSS higher-ups hadn't been pleased.

It was a poem code, a transposition cipher favored by the British, and the simplest possible version of one. It took only ten minutes and a few simple guesses for her to decrypt the example text, without even referencing the rhyme—reading on in the materials, she found it had been a salacious military limerick—ostensibly necessary for the translation.

As a diversion in a newspaper's Entertainment section, perhaps it would do. As a communication intending to come across as authentic to the Wehrmacht high command stationed in Italy, it fell short.

"I think he used a poem code to try to impress Mr. Agnew, our department chief. He's mad about poetry."

Lillian set the cipher aside. "Since that clearly didn't work, there's no sense in improving on his method." There were ways, she knew, of complicating poem ciphers, but that didn't solve the problem of making the cipher feel distinctly Italian. "You probably ought to try another type of cipher altogether. What do you know about Ravenna?"

Instead of asking why that would matter, as Lillian expected, Dinah only grinned and headed for the shelf of encyclopedias behind her. "Not much at the moment, but I can find a few things out. In the meantime, do the Friedmans have anything on Italian cryptography?"

"Almost certainly. But I would have no more idea of where to look than you."

Dinah splayed a hand against her heart in mock shock. "What? And here I thought you were the human version of a card catalog."

Lillian frowned. "I assure you, I am not."

For a moment, Dinah seemed to wilt. Then she shrugged. "It was a joke, Mother. And a compliment."

A dubious one, but Lillian supposed she should take her daughter at her word. "In that case . . . thank you, I suppose. I'll ask Elizebeth if she can give you some direction."

Her daughter seemed engrossed in the encyclopedia entry and didn't even raise her head. "Super."

By the time Lillian stood in the archway of the sitting room, the song had ended, and husband and wife sat on the bench in silence, smiling at each other. It was yet another sign that William was coming out of his "fit," as he called it. Once Lillian worked her way through a few remaining projects, the Friedmans would no longer need her. Just yesterday, she had purchased a train ticket to return to Gettysburg at the end of the month, though the number of troop transports coming through the capital made it difficult.

And what will you do then?

No need to borrow trouble. She'd answer that question when the time came.

Lillian cleared her throat, regretting her intrusion as they both turned. "That was lovely."

William nodded. "Music has always helped, when I can muster the energy for it. Despite what they told me at Walter Reed, speaking to others about my own dark thoughts has only made things worse. For me, at least, it seems better to focus on what is beautiful."

When he took his wife's hand and squeezed it, Lillian felt a sudden longing for Roger. It was silly. She'd see him in a few weeks, once she'd finished her work here.

"Can we help you with something, Lily?" Elizabeth prompted, returning Lillian's mind to her errand.

"I hope so. Dinah has a . . . project at work that requires some knowledge of cryptography."

"Is that so?" Elizabeth seemed surprised but didn't ask further questions. Lillian supposed she was used to accepting incomplete explanations.

"She wondered if she might borrow anything related to Italian cipher usage. Preferably something accessible to a beginner." Dinah hadn't added that part, but Lillian knew from her own work editing the Riverbank Publications that some cryptologists' prose was as dense and unapproachable as a wall of concrete topped with barbed wire.

William was already beginning to nod, rising from the piano bench. "I think I know just what she's looking for."

Lillian followed him across the hall, grateful that it was difficult to keep up when only a few weeks ago William had dragged his feet lethargically everywhere he went.

Standing on a folding stool tucked into the corner of the study, William retrieved a volume from the library's top shelf and placed it on the desk before Dinah and Lillian. It was a bland-looking pamphlet with nothing marking the spine, just a title page emblazoned with *The Contribution of the Cryptographic Bureaus in the World War* by Yves Gyldén.

"That would be the Great War, as we're calling it now," William explained, for Dinah's benefit. "At the time, we had the audacity to hope it would be deserving of the definite article."

Dinah picked it up, paging through it. "This says 'For Official Use Only.' How do you have a copy?"

William ducked his head, modest to a fault. "I edited the translation and provided footnotes and commentary. It was originally written in Swedish."

Of course he had, likely sometime in the twenties or thirties in his "spare time."

"There's a section on Italy's codebreaking history as well as the strengths and weaknesses of the ciphers they used in the war," William went on. "You'll find most everything we know in there."

Dinah thanked him profusely, and he disappeared as quietly as he'd come, without pressing her for details on her project. "It will likely be dull reading," Lillian warned. "William's idea of a page-turner is a doctoral thesis on textual differences in translations of the Rosetta Stone."

"I am capable of reading more than movie and music magazines, Mother."

She'd made the comment flippantly, but Lillian had seen the flash of hurt in her daughter's eyes. There she'd gone again, doing more harm than good. "Yes, I know. I only meant . . . well, I suppose it was a silly thing to say." Better to turn the subject to safer ground. "Did you find anything of use in the encyclopedia?"

"Some. Ravenna is connected to the Adriatic Sea via canal. Used to be the capital of the Western Roman Empire. Famous for its mosaics and other religious art."

"That's what you know. What does it mean?"

This time, the pause before Dinah answered was longer as she glanced down at the notes she'd scribbled, then back at the OSS assignment. "How about a cipher based on a grid like a Byzantine mosaic? We could even include a postcard of a basilica wall that serves as the key."

Though Lillian tried to keep her expression neutral, Dinah was watching her carefully, and her excitement faded. "It's too complicated, isn't it?"

There was nothing to do but be honest. "I think so. Remember, the military needs to pass information efficiently. I imagine that would be doubly true for less-organized rebel groups."

"Everything is more fun in the movies," Dinah lamented.

Secretly, Lillian agreed. Most actual cryptography involved endless numbers and letters, probability and analysis, without the Hollywood spark from noir films and spy thrillers.

She decided to try another route. "Mr. Longstreet's poem code only gives you direction about what not to do. Are there any more helpful resources you could obtain?"

"Sometimes asking questions can be as powerful as giving advice," Roger had told her that once, but that was easy for him to say. He was a listener. She was a problem solver. No matter how often she tried to remember that sometimes Dinah just needed to be heard, it felt incomplete not to issue a warning or recommendation.

This, though, was different. Easier to simply guide Dinah along on a work project, especially one so closely related to work Lillian had once done.

"I suppose another department might have past examples of actual communication between resistance groups that have been declassified," Dinah said slowly. "From the invasion of North Africa, maybe. I could request them, try to imitate their style."

"An excellent thought. That sounds like just the thing."

At this pronouncement, Dinah straightened, scribbling the idea down in her notebook with a pleased smile on her face.

Did Lillian really have so much power with her words? Most of the time, she'd felt that Dinah only really cared about what Roger thought. Goodness knows he was always the first to hear her every news and confidence. But perhaps she'd been wrong.

"Seems like I've got some work before me." Dinah gathered up her papers and slipped them back into her handbag, along with the Great War booklet.

"Indeed." Lillian stood, since it was clear Dinah was bringing her visit to a close. "Most evenings, I'm here working on my crossword assignments. If you need any additional feedback, I would be happy to take a look."

"Thanks, Mother." Lillian couldn't determine from the simple response whether Dinah actually meant to take her up on the offer. "Well, I'd better get back. Curfew to keep and all. Auntie Margot can't make exceptions for me."

It was still only eight o'clock, but Lillian, feeling suddenly tired herself, didn't argue, seeing Dinah to the door before returning to the study.

It had felt good, she realized, to accomplish something related to cryptography, even if the work was secondhand. Maybe Elizabeth was right. Maybe she hadn't entirely lost her knack for analysis, even after all these years.

Dinah had neglected to put away the encyclopedia, so Lillian eased it back into its place. No sense in leaving a mess for tomorrow.

As she did, she noticed for the first time the framed photograph tucked into an alcove of the shelves. Carefully, she took it down, staring at the two long rows of one of the graduating classes from Riverbank, with the instructors seated in front.

"They kept it," she murmured aloud, finding her own image in the group, in the front with the other instructors. "After all this time." Her younger self was seated with her hands demurely folded on her dark skirt and her face in profile, while Roger, proud and handsome in his uniform, stood in the row behind her, facing the same direction. William and Elizebeth sat next to each other, and Mr. Fabyan had placed himself at the center of the group, staring directly at the camera.

No one glancing at the photograph would realize the rows of students and teachers spelled out a secret message—alternating side and front views of their faces arranged carefully to form, in a bilateral cipher: "Knowledge is power."

How young she and Roger looked. How young they all looked. Although, even then, there was trouble enough to go around. Here, in the Friedmans' study, surrounded by the ghosts of her past, Lillian couldn't help but remember.

22

Lily

"During the war, our days were made of rapid-fire letters, patterns, ciphers. Only occasionally did I stop to wonder what might come next."

—Excerpt from Lillian Kendall's journal

SATURDAY, MARCH 16, 1918

Pop!

Lily blinked, surprised at the brightness of the flashbulb's light. Still, she didn't move, keeping her head fixed to the left, awaiting instruction.

"Excellent," George Fabyan shouted so all could hear. "Well done, everyone."

She took that to mean their extensive wait was over and massaged the back of her neck. As one of the first to be posed, she'd had to wait the longest for the elaborate graduation picture to assemble behind her. The Signal Corps officers were departing Riverbank the next morning, bound for the front, so there would be no opportunities to retake the class photograph.

As they filed out of their arranged ranks, Mr. Fabyan pumped the officers' hands in cordial congratulations, accepting their thanks with gruff protests about "wanting to help my country in her hour of need."

"As if he had anything to do with it." If the voice hadn't been an octave below her own, Lily might have thought she'd spoken her own thoughts aloud.

Instead, she turned to see Lieutenant Roger Kendall, shaking his head in disgust. "It's you and the Friedmans and the others doing all the work."

"He is funding a worthy cause," she pointed out, a reminder to herself as well as the lieutenant. That, at least, was more than some millionaires could say.

"Sure," he acknowledged. "It's only that I don't trust rich folks. The way I was raised, I guess."

After their dramatic meeting at the ball, Lieutenant Kendall had found his way to her side several times throughout the evening with obvious enough attention that Margot teased her afterward about "luring in Wartime Wally."

Lily had denied everything. And yet, the next week, she'd asked Elizebeth if she could assist more often with the class at the Aurora Hotel.

If Elizebeth suspected any ulterior motives, she didn't say a word. And Lily, in turn, didn't accuse her of collusion with Margot when William assigned her to oversee a code table where Lieutenant Kendall sat.

Both husband and wife seemed to favor the young lieutenant after he had fulfilled his promise and shared, in confidence, about the listening device he'd found in the classrooms.

Afterward, Lily had joined the Friedmans in a thorough scouring of their quarters and other living areas, but their search had not turned up a second Dictograph. *"I don't see what else we can do,"* Elizabeth had said, looking defeated. *"Even if we could prove any illegal activity, which I doubt, Mr. Fabyan could certainly justify it. He always does."*

That seemed a hollow excuse to Lily, and though she hated to press her friend when she looked so exhausted, she'd felt she ought to point out the obvious. *"You could leave. We all could."*

"I . . . I have considered it. But since William is departing for France . . . it just seems simpler to remain here." She straightened her shoulders. *"Besides, we have a duty to our country, at least until the war is over."*

It was true that the Signal Corps men were now fully able to perform codebreaking in the field. Sitting in on the codebreaking classes and seeing the rapid progress the officers made under the Friedmans' teaching had convinced Lily of that much.

Before and after class, there was time for more relaxed conversation. Most of the officers hung about smoking cigars and talking to one another in the boastful way military men did, seeming to forget the petite, timid code assistant even existed.

Not Lieutenant Kendall. Instead of joining his comrades, he lingered by Lily's side, looking at her like she was the only one in the room worth talking to. She learned that his family lived in Gettysburg, Pennsylvania, where his father was a locksmith. He learned she had no family to speak of and didn't make her feel the worse for it. They traded childhood memories—Lily's carefully edited to include only happy moments—and shared about their hobbies, beliefs, and interests.

She appreciated the way Lieutenant Kendall included the officers' wives who sat in on classes as equals, asking for their opinions when he was stumped, which was often. Though he wasn't a star pupil, he took furious notes on the Friedmans' lectures. And every now and then, in the rustle of graph paper to clear off the tables at the end of the day, their hands would brush, and Lily would do her best not to let the color in her cheeks give her away.

All told, the past four weeks had been among the happiest in Lily's life. It was a relief to have something to occupy her mind other than the pressures of work and worries about the war's mounting death toll.

But now he was leaving. She knew the lieutenant was thinking about it too, from the morose expression on his face, even as officers around them congratulated one another, full of optimism that the Signal Corps, armed with new knowledge, would help win the war.

"I suppose this is good-bye," Lily said, feeling like it must be said directly. "I'm told your train leaves early tomorrow."

Lieutenant Kendall nodded, then thrust his hand into his uniform jacket. "I . . . got you something. To remember me by." He held out a small journal, bound in burgundy cloth. "For all those thoughts of yours."

She took the journal, holding it close, and realized this was the first time since Mama died that anyone had given her a gift.

Knowing he must be eager to know what she thought of it, she cleared her throat and found her voice, looking up at him with a blossoming smile. "It's lovely. I—"

A strident voice interrupted her attempt at gratitude. "Getting a little friendly with your teacher, eh, lieutenant?"

Mr. Fabyan, his immaculate black coat buttoned to his chin, inserted himself beside Lieutenant Kendall, who stammered out a reply that was cut off by the millionaire's "Not that I blame you. She's a pretty little thing."

"Miss Nilsson is an excellent teacher," Lieutenant Kendall countered stoutly, if somewhat untruthfully. Lily could explain the workings of a specific cipher to a group, but lectures about principles and procedures were decidedly the Friedmans' domain.

"Is that so?" The lieutenant's praise seemed to attract Mr. Fabyan's attention rather than deflect it. She flushed under his sudden scrutiny.

Leave us alone. Please.

But he made no motion to step aside, instead snapping his thick fingers like he'd had a revelation. "Nilsson . . . You were one of my posture girls, weren't you?"

The heat in Lily's face turned to ice.

"Well?" he insisted, squinting against the bright sunlight. "Weren't you from that delinquent girls reformatory?"

It had been almost a year since anyone had mentioned the training school in her presence. She'd spoken about her time at the school briefly with Margot and Elizabeth, but when no one had given her sidelong glances in the code room, she'd become convinced that her past had finally been forgotten.

Now, for Mr. Fabyan to say it out loud—and in front of Lieutenant Kendall . . .

"I was." She did not correct Mr. Fabyan with the full title: the Illinois State Training School for Delinquent and Dependent Girls.

"Yes, I thought so." He turned to Lieutenant Kendall, speaking in his confidential, man-to-man voice. "I had the school send several of their charges to me for six months of spinal improvement exercises and tests. They seemed quite normal, most of them. You know society, always rounding up females and labeling them incorrigible or hysterical or promiscuous or whatnot if they get into trouble. Social reform, that's what we need. More brain science too."

Lily fought to keep her knees from buckling beneath her. Mr. Fabyan was looking at her with a gleam in his intense blue eyes, as if she were a prime specimen for whatever dissections and experimentations might go into such study.

Lieutenant Kendall tried once again to break into the conversation. "I don't think—"

"After all," Mr. Fabyan went on, "look what can come out of a place like that." He knuckled Lily's cheek in what she supposed was an affectionate gesture, though she shied away. "Gold among the dross, eh?"

"I am not sure, sir," the lieutenant said frostily, stepping forcefully between the two of them, "that you'd recognize real worth if you saw it."

For a moment, Mr. Fabyan's face froze in a near-snarl. Then he stepped back, braying out a laugh. "Ha! A jokester. The army needs more of your type." He clapped Lieutenant Kendall on the back. "Go on, I've got the servants pouring out from my cellars. Help yourselves, both of you! It's a day for celebration."

With that, Mr. Fabyan stumbled off as if he'd already indulged more than was proper, leaving Lily staring at the ground. What would the lieutenant think of her now?

"It's not very Christian to hate a fellow," Lieutenant Kendall said speculatively, glaring after her employer's departing form, "but if Jesus said to love your enemies, I guess he expected we'd at least have them."

"I'm sorry you had to hear that," she said in a voice just over a whisper. Yet it wasn't only what Mr. Fabyan had said, but what was left unsaid that troubled her. All locals knew the reformatory was full of young prostitutes and runaways with identical bobbed hair, the most rebellious of whom were controlled with rawhide whips.

"*You're not like the others, Lily,*" Mrs. Halloway, one of the matrons, had said. "*Heaven knows you don't deserve to be punished for the sins of your mother. We'll get you out of here.*" And she had, by changing Lily's records to show her birthdate a year earlier. Lily's participation in the posture training experiments at Riverbank had made her aware of the opening in the kitchens, and she'd been hired shortly after leaving the school.

At the time, it had seemed like a miracle. Now that path had led her here, standing before Roger and all he didn't know, burning with shame not her own.

If only she could disappear, run back to the Lodge, and lock herself in her room. Or better yet, flee from Riverbank altogether. If Elizebeth and Margot weren't here . . . if the war effort didn't need her . . .

"Miss Nilsson?" the lieutenant asked, his hand on her arm her first indication that she'd begun to sway slightly. "Are you all right?"

"My mother . . . did not have a good reputation," Lily blurted out, feeling she must say something. "She was unwell and in debt. After she died, since I was unaware of any other relatives, I became a ward of the state. They sent me to the school. I . . ."

To her surprise, when she finally gathered the courage to look Lieutenant Kendall in the eyes, his face radiated that same steady kindness she'd seen at the ball. "Don't you feel like you need to say any more about it. It ought to be up to you to tell whoever you like about your past—or not."

"Then I'd appreciate it if you pretended you hadn't heard any of that." He must be dying to ask questions, mustn't he, after the hints Mr. Fabyan had dropped?

"I can do one better. I'm an expert at forgetting things altogether." He gave a shy half smile. "As I'm sure you know after seeing me bumble through my lessons."

This unexpected bit of self-deprecation broke the tension, and Lily actually laughed. Some of the Signal Corps men had shown immediate aptitude for decryption. They would be assigned primary responsibilities for intercepted messages at the front, the sort of position William was soon to take up. Others, like Lieutenant Kendall, would go back to regular radio communication duties, their knowledge of ciphers mostly unused except in emergencies.

"But, Miss Nilsson?"

She gripped the journal he'd given her a bit tighter. "You may call me Lily. I'd like that."

Now he unleashed the full force of his dimpled smile, and she was nearly dazzled by it. "Lily." Then the serious expression returned. "Before I do that forgetting, I just wanted to say . . . you shouldn't let anyone tell you that you are where you came from. It's not one bit true. In fact, you're the most remarkable woman I've ever met."

An unfamiliar feeling prickled behind Lily's eyes, but she would not cry, not here in front of all these people. "Thank you." It was the second gift he'd given her today, and more meaningful than the first.

If only she had something to give him in return. She'd considered it, but then decided it would be presumptuous. After all, they'd only known each other for a month, and while he seemed to regard her highly, there was no reason to think they'd ever speak again after he left for France.

Instead of seeming pleased that his words had been well-received, Lieutenant Kendall took off his cap, running a hand through his hair, a miserable expression on his face.

"What's wrong?" she prompted.

"I just don't like the thought of leaving you here. With that man."

It was thoughtful, but Lily didn't feel there was much to worry about. Today was an unusual day, full of champagne and triumph, on which Mr. Fabyan deigned to come down from his Villa to mingle with mere assistants like her. By tomorrow, he'd have forgotten all about her, she was sure. "I'll be fine."

His eyes searched hers. "Promise?"

She nodded. "I've fended for myself for a long time."

"Sure," he said, never looking away from her. "I can see that in you. But that doesn't mean you should have to."

It was that look, full of earnest admiration, that made Lily blurt out, "Will you write to me, Lieutenant? If you have time, that is."

Another cinema-star smile broke out on his face. "I'd be honored. Although you'd really best call me Roger."

"Of course," she said, allowing herself a small smile in return, when her heart was really bursting with happiness. "I'll pray for your safe return." And she was surprised to find she meant it. For a long time, she hadn't spoken to God, feeling that he wouldn't be able to spare the time for her sort. But Roger Kendall seemed exactly the sort of person God would take special care with.

"That means a lot to me. Thank you. Lily."

And before Roger joined the other officers to return to the hotel, he pressed a kiss to her cheek. Not even her lips, and yet the memory of the caress lingered long after the train had taken Roger and the Signal Corps men far away, onto a ship and off to war. A war from which many would never return.

But Roger will. Was it faith, received secondhand from Roger's more firm religious convictions, or merely a blind hope that made Lily so certain? She wasn't sure. All she knew was that that evening, as she arranged her narrow bedside table into a makeshift writing desk, she cared about the fighting in France more than ever.

As the summer of 1918 faded into fall, the daily mail deliveries from military branches steadily decreased. Some of the code room staff moved to other employment around Riverbank, but Lily had taken on the task of proofreading the pamphlets William and Elizebeth had coauthored on the process of codebreaking. "For the next generation," Elizebeth always said, though Margot insisted the next generation would be so sick of war they wouldn't dream of starting another.

The work suited Lily. It was far less stressful than last summer's chaos, allowing her to get full nights of rest without bursts of anxious panic. Besides, she found editing was another sort of puzzle, scanning each line for minute errors and suggesting clarifications. Somehow, the Friedmans had put into understandable words the frenetic activity and blind determination of their year of wartime cryptanalysis.

"Try to read it as someone without any cipher experience," Elizebeth had instructed. A sly smile appeared on her face. "Imagine yourself as your lieutenant on his first day of class, perhaps."

"He's not mine," she corrected, even as she realized that Roger himself might not make that distinction. The frequent letters she received at the Lodge, full of humorous anecdotes and questions about her life, each more personal than the last, testified to that.

Elizebeth only shrugged, letting the comment pass. She was more subtle than Margot, who pursued the subject of Lily's pen romance with tireless enthusiasm.

Though Lily had to set aside her emotions, putting herself in Roger's place as she edited the pamphlets did help her remember key areas that had confused him and recognize the jargon that demanded a definition. Lily only wished Roger was at her side to comment on the pamphlets himself.

By November, she had nearly finished her comments on *Methods for the Reconstruction of Primary Alphabets* and had gone to bed late, tired but satisfied in her work . . . only to be woken by the sounds of gunshots.

It is only a dream. Or a memory. She and Mama had spent several years in an unsavory part of Chicago.

But the distant reports sounded again as she sat up, fumbling for the lamp.

The police? An attack on Riverbank? The ghosts of the corpses in the Chamber of Horrors rising up for revenge?

Lily blinked, rubbing the crustiness of sleep out of her eyes. Foolish thoughts, all. The Allies had worn down the German forces. The Kaiser himself had abdicated, and everyone knew an armistice was imminent; all the papers said so.

Can that mean . . . ?

The thought propelled Lily out of bed, into her winter coat, which, when buttoned, seemed an appropriate replacement for a dressing gown. She could hear voices in the Lodge's hallway already, and when she opened her door, they became clearer, a cacophony of shouts by other residents, some holding guttering candles against the early-morning gloom.

"What's going on?"

"It's three o'clock in the morning. What's all the racket?"

"Is it . . . ?"

A young woman's voice, probably belonging to one of the servants, shouted from the stairwell, "It's over! The armistice has been signed over in France. The fighting's stopped."

There was a moment of silence in which it felt like the entire world paused. For the narrowest of moments, Lily could only stare, like all the others, as if they needed time to translate this simplest of ciphers.

Then Margot, clutching a floral robe, let out a wild whoop and began jumping up and down. "Three cheers!" she crowed, and a trio of cheers went up, whether it was for the American doughboys or the Allies in general or their own codebreaking headquarters, no one knew and no one cared.

Even Lily added her voice to the clamor, though she paused when Elizebeth ran up the stairs, breathing heavily. Anyone looking at her would think the news was bad, given the tears that had sprung to her eyes. "Is it true?" she asked, glancing about wildly. "The war is over?"

"It must be," Lily said, though she understood the question. After so long, it seemed impossible that a few signatures an ocean away could end all the headlines and the shooting and the fear. There was a sense of a fairy tale about it, watching her coworkers celebrating in their nightclothes as the Fox Valley Guards offered another gun salute in the distance.

"You know what this means, don't you, Lily?" Elizebeth managed, wiping tears away with a handkerchief as she pulled

Lily close. "William made it through, and now he'll come home to me."

"I'm so glad," Lily said, returning the hug a bit awkwardly.

Elizebeth blinked, her sharp dark eyes going back into focus. "I . . . I've got to write to him. We must make plans."

Margot looped her arm around Elizebeth's, limp at her side, and tugged her down the hall. "Absolutely not, Mrs. Friedman. You can get a note to your lover in tomorrow's post, but I'll not see you nipping behind a writing desk now, not when there's a party on."

And indeed, all of Riverbank, it seemed, was celebrating the armistice. Once the sun was up and a hearty breakfast enjoyed, Lily joined the other codebreakers in tossing handfuls of shredded worksheets out the window to be blown away in the November wind, a confetti of grids that no longer needed to be filled with cipher letter frequencies.

Below the window, a group of groundskeepers with noses reddened from the cold formed a jubilant barbershop quartet, warbling a mangled version of "Pack Up Your Troubles in Your Old Kit-Bag and Smile, Smile, Smile," the title of which were the only lyrics they seemed to be in agreement on. There was talk of parades going on in Geneva and the surrounding towns. It was an unexpected holiday, full of possibility and hope, and Lily breathed in deeply, savoring the feeling of being part of history.

Roger will come home soon. Though she couldn't match Elizebeth's excitement, Lily found herself smiling . . . but uncertainty still gathered in the corners of her mind on this happiest of days. The end of the war meant change, decisions, perhaps even good-byes. Despite the fact that Mr. Fabyan had made it clear he wanted his codebreakers to continue on at Riverbank after the war, surely they wouldn't remain here forever. Lily, at least, had no intention of doing so.

Which led her to wonder: What were Roger Kendall's intentions toward her—and hers toward him?

23

Dinah

When no one answered her knock, Dinah tested the handle of Winora's door—locked. No surprise there, even though most of the Myrtlewood residents didn't take the time to secure their doors.

Still, Dinah had been sure Winora would be in, given that she hadn't taken the bus home with Dinah that evening. Winora was known to cut out early from work at times, lugging her sketchbook with her to "find interesting faces" for a project.

So much for inviting her to the Smithsonian. There was a free lecture at the Arts and Industries Building for the anniversary of the last skirmish of the Civil War, a full month after the surrender at Appomattox. It had sounded like the sort of rogue military action that might appeal to Winora, and besides, Dinah didn't know anyone else well enough to invite.

Someone had to know where Winora was. But as Dinah hurried down the stairs, she could hear a tortured rendition of "Oh,

What a Beautiful Mornin'" being banged out on the piano, which decreased the chances of a Winora sighting substantially.

Sure enough, when Dinah breezed into the parlor, Betty perched at the piano, eyes closed to the sheet music propped up before her. Nearby, Anne-Marie from the second floor was draped over one of the chairs, feet on the coffee table. Her pout and watchful glances at the hallway told Dinah she was waiting for the use of the telephone.

"Hello, girls," Dinah called. "Has anyone seen Winora?"

Betty, mercifully, stopped a few measures before the end of the musical number. "No, but what else is new? She's barely been about since she started dating that fellow . . . what's-his-name, with the pomaded hair?"

Anne-Marie's eyes raised from inspecting her cuticles. "Don't ask *me*. She never introduced us. But I've seen him pick her up, and I say he's far too much of a dish to be dating someone like Winora."

This was typical sour grapes from Anne-Marie, whose own beau had broken things off with her before joining the navy, claiming the need for "freedom."

Betty sniffed. "Maybe no other girl will step out with him since he's not keen to don a uniform. If you ask me, there are too many young, single men in the capital taking government jobs that we women could perform just as well, if not better."

Dinah decided to let that one go without an answer, edging back toward the door. "So neither of you saw her go up to her room?" There was a chance she was there and had ignored Dinah's knock.

Betty frowned. "I don't think so. Then again, I don't pay her much mind."

"Honestly, Diana, I'm surprised you see as much of her as you do," Anne-Marie threw in, giving Dinah a significant look.

"It's Dinah, actually," she correctly gently, using the time to try to get a read on the other women. Anne-Marie would smear her lipstick on her nose if she smirked any harder, and Betty was about to topple off the piano bench, leaning forward conspiratorially.

Dinah chose her words carefully. "I know she seems standoff-ish, but Winora's quite an interesting character. Since we work together, it's only natural that we've become rather friendly." This was, she knew, not quite the same as saying they were friends.

Anne-Marie laughed loudly enough that Dinah worried whoever was using the telephone in the hall alcove might be disturbed. "See, Betty? I *told* you she didn't know."

"I thought everyone here did." Betty made a show of straightening the music on the piano. "Gosh, have you been living under a rock?"

Dinah hated to give them the reaction they were clearly looking for, but sometimes it was best to humor people. "What don't I know?"

She regretted asking as soon as she saw a familiar light in Anne-Marie's eyes. It was that of a woman on the hunt—not for prey, but for gossip. Whatever followed, she wouldn't be able to unhear. "The reason she's such an 'interesting character' is because she spent two years in a juvenile correctional center." Here Anne-Marie gave a drawn-out pause, her wide blue eyes fixed on Dinah for a reaction.

Thanks to her training in schooling her expression during OSS interrogations, Dinah managed not to give her the satisfaction, despite her surprise.

Clearly disappointed, Anne-Marie galloped on anyway, her words coming faster now. "A few months ago, Shirley—you know her, rooms with her cousin on the ground floor—heard Miss Schnieder on the telephone. She has to file monthly reports with the wardens on Winora's behavior, to reassure the authorities she hasn't done anything wild while she's on parole."

"We don't know what she did, or what sort of government

agency was desperate enough to hire a criminal," Betty added, with the air of someone eager to get their two cents in, "but I imagine she has some special skill they needed."

"I don't think—" Dinah began searching for words to defend her coworker, but Anne-Marie interrupted her before she could think of what to say next.

"Anyway, Winora as much as admitted it. When Shirley asked her if it was true, she only set her face like she does—" Anne-Marie paused to give a grotesque interpretation of Winora's squared shoulders and furrowed brow—"and said, 'What about it?' Then she called Shirley a name I wouldn't dare repeat."

"Perhaps she felt it was too personal a question."

If either woman picked up on the pointed implication, it didn't slow her down in the slightest. "I bet her boyfriend's actually someone from her past," Betty theorized, blinking wide eyes behind her round glasses. "Checking in on her to make sure she hasn't snitched on her gang, or trying to pull her back into a life of crime."

Dinah blinked at her. This, apparently, wasn't intended as a joke. "Don't you think that's a bit far-fetched? Winora as a mobster's moll?"

Betty shrugged. "Why else would she be so secretive all the time?"

To this, Dinah couldn't offer an explanation. Hadn't she herself thought Winora seemed overly cagey?

"You never can tell with girls like her," Anne-Marie said, her voice heavy with foreboding. "That's why the rest of us keep our distance. And now that you know, I guess you will too."

"I . . . I don't know." Dinah knew she ought to say something in Winora's defense. But it was an awful lot of new information to take in. "Anyway, it *is* good to know—"

"Ladies," a voice from the doorway intoned with such severity that Dinah instinctively straightened to her mother's standard before turning to see Auntie Margot glaring at them.

"I think I explained that this parlor was yours to use in the evenings for good, clean fun." She directed a cool look at each of them in turn. "Maybe you include gossip in that. But I do not."

Dinah wished she could slink away. How much had Auntie Margot heard? She offered a fervent nod, trying to indicate she had been dragged into this conversation against her will. Betty had already wilted, but Anne-Marie was not so easily cowed. "She really ought to know, don't you think, Miss Schnieder? I mean, living so close to someone with a criminal record . . . it's just not safe."

"And there too, we don't see eye to eye," Auntie Margot said. She folded her arms over her salmon-colored tea dress. "Miss McMahen has never been a danger to anyone. I've got plenty of reasons to believe her past is in her past. And I have a sneaking suspicion you weren't worried about Dinah's well-being. If you were, you'd have talked to me first, hmm?"

"I'm sure it never occurred to me," Anne-Marie said innocently. Edna, Shirley's cousin, tiptoed past the parlor's doorway, and Anne-Marie sprang up. "Looks like it's my turn at the phone. Ta-ta."

Betty used this as an excuse to make her own exit, the score of *Oklahoma!* left abandoned at the piano.

That left only Dinah to face Auntie Margot's still-brewing wrath. She stood studying the faded carpet. "I didn't mean to hear any of that."

The fire and brimstone hadn't entirely departed from Auntie Margot's eyes as she inspected her old friend's daughter. "Oh no?"

Dinah shook her head vigorously. "Although, I admit, I was a bit surprised . . ." She trailed off, shrugging.

"That the McMahen family business was less than reputable, or that I let Winora stay, knowing about her record?"

"Both," Dinah admitted. "I don't know what she did, exactly, but—"

"And you don't need to know." Auntie Margot stood and

rested a hand on Dinah's shoulder. "Trust me, Dinah. I've seen what good a second chance can do for a person. There was a time when the flapper version of those two talked about me behind my back, you know. And your mother's too."

"Really?" Auntie Margot, she could see—Dinah had gotten the impression that she'd spent the twenties footloose and fancy-free—but Mother? What could she possibly have done to provoke gossip?

"Really." To Dinah's disappointment, she didn't elaborate. "There won't be any trouble with Winora. She just needs a friend or two. In a way, Winora reminds me of your mother at her age."

Dinah couldn't help it. She laughed, and the attempt to stifle it added the embarrassment of a snort. "You can't mean that. The two of them are as different as night and day."

"You didn't know her then."

That was a fair point. "I suppose not. And it's not like Mother and I are best chums now."

"I've noticed. It's a shame, really." Auntie Margot shook her head. "But that's neither here nor there. I only wanted to say I hope a bunch of silly tittle-tattle won't change the way you treat Winora."

"Not a bit," Dinah assured her, offering her brightest smile. That was what Auntie Margot wanted to hear, wasn't it? Though she wasn't sure how sincerely she meant it. After all, Auntie Margot might be convinced that Winora had gone straight . . . but what if she was wrong?

Dinah eyed the new leaflet design, soon to be dropped over in the Pacific as the navy island-hopped to victory. In it, moths with the Japanese flag emblazoned on their wings were drawn ever closer to a flame, the text around the border warning of the dangers of a refusal to surrender.

This leaflet been created by field MO employees with the help of their cultural experts, who would surely know more about Japanese mindset than a cluster of journalists in Washington, DC. Still, that hadn't stopped several of her fellow Rumor Mill workers from voicing minute criticisms and changes that would hardly be worth the time to correct and reprint.

Just as she'd worked up the courage to say as much, Miss Jensen, Mr. Agnew's secretary, tapped her on the shoulder. "Mr. Agnew would like to speak to you as soon as possible, please, Miss Kendall."

She felt distinctly like a freshman being called to the principal's office, sure she'd unknowingly done something wrong. *But that's silly.* It might be quite the opposite; in fact, Mrs. Masterson was still scant in her praise, but one of their experts in German had let her know that several of her latest false news clips had been used in print and broadcast rumor campaigns. *Maybe I'm in for a promotion, or at least a commendation.*

At least this time, Mr. Agnew hadn't yet filled his office with cigarette smoke. When she cleared her throat, he glanced up. "Ah yes, Miss Kendall. The Italy team would like to know when they can expect that decoy cipher."

For the first time, real panic flared in Dinah's stomach. "I thought . . . you said I had until Monday."

He looked at her mildly through his lenses. "That's the deadline, yes. I simply wanted to see if you had anything I could present to mollify them."

"It's progressing well . . . but I'm not quite finished."

That wasn't entirely true. She'd typed up the final draft of her proposal the day before, but the Friedmans had offered to test it for her and give her feedback over the weekend. Only a fool would turn down their expert opinion. "I'll have it completed by noon on Monday, I promise."

She held her breath until Mr. Agnew gave a curt nod. "Make sure you do." Instead of dismissing her, he leaned back in his chair. "How are things in the Rumor Mill these days, Miss Kendall? Is your conscience holding up?"

"Just fine, thanks." This, at least, was something she could be confident in. "That speech you gave about liars and scoundrels was very . . . memorable. Perhaps it's not appropriate for a first day, but certainly thought-provoking."

"I think it's only fair to give new employees fair warning, especially those without a background in propaganda or psychology." Where he'd once seemed distantly polite, now Mr. Agnew focused on her like a searchlight that had caught an escaping prisoner in its beam. "And what, might I ask, have your thoughts on the subject been?"

"Well, I . . ." Dinah bit her lip. The line of reasoning had come to her weeks ago, while playing cards with her fellow boarders, though she hadn't yet tried to voice it. Anne-Marie and her set weren't the philosophical sort.

Would it sound foolish? After all, Mr. Agnew was far more educated, not to mention three decades older.

Oh, what was the harm?

"It's like poker." In the pause that followed, Dinah narrowed her eyes at Mr. Agnew. "You *have* played poker, haven't you?"

"Yes, though I can think of a hundred less tedious ways to lose money."

"How about Monopoly?"

He shuddered. "That way is much more tedious."

Dinah suppressed the instinct to roll her eyes. "I meant, have you played Monopoly before as well?"

Mr. Agnew laced his hands and placed them behind his head, leaning back in his chair. "My youngest son was eleven years old at the height of the game's popularity, and my wife persuaded me to purchase him a set for Christmas. So yes, I have indeed had the misfortune."

Dinah ignored this dismal review of one of her own favorite adolescent pastimes and pressed on. "I've decided that our

Morale Operations work is more like poker than Monopoly. In poker, everyone around the table is withholding information and even lying outright. It's part of the rules, and everyone expects it, so it isn't wrong. Whereas no one would say the same if you dipped into the bank while your opponent wasn't looking to fund your purchase of Boardwalk."

Was it her imagination, or did Mr. Agnew smile slightly? "Speaking from experience, Miss Kendall?"

She placed a finger to her lips. "I'll never tell."

"It's a fair comparison, war as a game where deception is built into the rules by mutual agreement. At any rate, it's better than the pompous stuffed shirts who say things like 'the end justifies the means' without any thought to how horrifying that ethical proposition is, taken to its logical conclusion."

Dinah frowned, puzzling through that. "I . . . think that was a compliment. If so, thank you."

"War is a dreadfully complex question. Always has been. Or, as Edward Thomas put it, 'This is no case of petty right or wrong / That politicians or philosophers / Can judge.' He was killed in action in the First World War, so I suppose he would know." Mr. Agnew's gaze lingered on the clock on the wall, as if he were the conductor of a railway and thousands depended on his ability to get onto the street at precisely 5:00 p.m. "Good day, then, Miss Kendall. I look forward to seeing your cipher work on Monday."

"I'll get it to you earlier than noon, if possible," she promised. "Say hello to your wife for me."

He grumbled out an agreement of sorts, and she smiled as the office door shut.

Maybe she and Mr. Agnew could find a way to get along after all. He, like Winora, was an addition to her theory that people were always more likeable once you understood them, no matter how standoffish they might seem at first.

When she returned to the Rumor Mill to gather her things,

the office was mostly empty. As she took out her powder compact from the top drawer of her desk, Dinah's hand brushed against the covers of the booklets she'd borrowed from Mr. Longstreet.

With all her work on the Italian cipher, she had put her mother's journal on hold. In fact, she'd nearly forgotten about her pilfered pamphlets, though she'd meant to return them as soon as possible.

Might as well get started now. She'd brought in a cushion to make the standard-issue OSS chairs more bearable, and here, at least, she'd be away from the questions of the other boarders. Perhaps she could even slip the books back into Mr. Longstreet's office tonight, with no one the wiser.

An Introduction to Methods for the Solution of Ciphers, the title read, and inside the front page, © *George Fabyan*.

Well, well, well. She really was going to learn alongside her mother, a few decades later.

A quick scan of the first few pages disclosed another revelation. *The shift cipher is one of the oldest and simplest cipher systems to understand, though it has several variants. . . .*

Dinah snorted. That was a relief. At least her mother had given her a cipher considered simple.

She sorted through the examples included in the booklet. The method did seem straightforward: Write out the letters in the key word or phrase, then copy the rest of the alphabet in order, skipping any letters found in the key. Then, assign each letter a number from one to twenty-six, essentially "shifting" the alphabet over several spaces to create more unpredictability.

But when Dinah attempted the cipher using Mother's initials, L. A. N. for Lillian Agnes Nilsson, as the key—L-1 (A), A-2 (B), N-3 (C), B-4 (D), C-5 (E), and so on—the result was still a garbled mess, even when she tried *K* for Kendall instead.

Had she misunderstood the process? But no, a check of her work revealed the same translation, and the booklet didn't describe a second step. *Fine, then.* Since the journal had been a gift to her, Dinah tried her own initials. Still no luck.

In frustration, she glanced at the date at the top of the entry. February 1918.

That triggered a memory. Hadn't Dad said once that he'd met her mother near Valentine's Day that year?

Roger Oliver Kendall it was. Once she'd gridded Dad's initials into the cipher, shifting the rest of the alphabet around it, the entry began to form coherent words.

Slowly, leaning over the journal, Dinah uncovered the real story behind her parents' first meeting. It was, indeed, at a dance—but with fewer romantic moments than Dad had implied. Their pen romance over the course of the war, however, was unexpectedly sweet. The entry stopped with celebration over the end of the war.

When Dinah was forced to squint at the last line, she realized that the Rumor Department was getting dim. Thinking the sun had gone behind a cloud, she glanced out the window and noticed the orange-gold glow of sunset starting to streak the sky. Almost two hours had passed as she lost herself in the cipher.

There seemed to be only three other entries. She was nearly halfway there.

Dinah stood, stretching. Better get home and see if Auntie Margot had saved some dinner for her. She peeped her head out of the door into the deserted hallway. The filing cabinets were shut and locked tight, the fiery half-light of a spring evening giving just enough illumination through the windows to create long shadows.

No lights, not even the glow of a solitary gooseneck lamp, indicated another MO employee had been forced to stoop over a stubborn project. Dinah hummed a Civil War marching tune quietly to herself to break the silence. There was something eerie about the empty building—she felt she could see the sinister eyes of the Office of War Information posters watching her from every shuttered window or closed doorway. *"Enemy ears are listening."*

From somewhere in the building, a sound made her stop. Something like . . . the metallic click of a drawer shutting?

You're imagining things.

No, there it was again, the creak of metal coming from the Records Room around the corner and down the hall, where confidential documents were tucked away for reference.

It's just someone working late, that's all, Dinah told herself, though she found her heart racing faster without her permission. "Hello?" she called uncertainly, feeling foolish. Now she heard the distinct squeak of shoe rubber against the floor.

"Is someone there?" When there was no answer, she forced herself toward the noise, but when she turned the corner, the stairwell door shut smoothly. Whoever had been here was gone now, and Dinah had no intention of running after them. Instead, she peered into the Records Room. The door had been left ajar—was it usually?—but everything seemed to be in place, no open drawers or stray papers in sight.

Dinah breathed deeply through her nose, picturing the air filling her lungs and coursing through her body to her head, her toes. It smelled faintly of ink and floor polish and the remnants of male agents' cologne. *All this talk of ciphers and secrecy is making you paranoid,* she scolded herself. And yet the sense of something decidedly wrong lingered in the empty office, like the echo of a harsh sound.

I'll tell Mr. Agnew what I saw first thing on Monday, she decided. Whatever Mother said, she wasn't going to ignore her intuition this time. The stakes were higher. Not just her own safety, but that of important OSS records. Even if Mr. Agnew dismissed her concerns, she would feel better knowing she'd made a report.

But though the resolution comforted her somewhat, Dinah couldn't help watching the twilight streets of Washington, DC, with more wariness than before as she hurried toward the bus stop.

Maybe it wasn't just the overseas OSS agents who faced danger and intrigue. Washington, DC, it seemed, hid secrets of its own.

24

Lily

"Riverbank remains a bittersweet place for me. I learned new skills and forged lifelong friendships on that estate. But I always knew I would not—could not—stay there forever."

—Excerpt from Lillian Kendall's journal

SATURDAY, MARCH 8, 1919

Lily placed her steps carefully, wary of the pockets of slush and mud that plagued the estate during the long spring thawing, her lips moving over her planned words like a silent prayer. *"I've been grateful for my time here at Riverbank, but now, with the war over . . ."*

The staff of the code room had signed contracts allowing them to depart for other employment "after negotiations." Lily had dismissed this vague wording as necessary for wartime security, but she soon realized there was an air of indentured servitude about Riverbank. Mr. Fabyan stated what he wanted, and others complied. If not, he meted out judgment from what others secretly called his "hell chair"—a hanging wicker seat under an elm tree, where he vented the worst of his temper.

If I don't do it now, I never will.

Lily's hand dipped into her coat pocket to touch the two items she'd slipped inside: the journal Roger had given her, still blank; and a letter written on thin Red Cross stationery. By now, she'd read it so often she nearly had it memorized.

Dear Lily,

It's over! When we first heard the news, I thought it was only a latrine rumor, but after it really hit home, you've never seen such celebrating. We toasted with watery beer stolen from a captured German trench and launched into a rowdy rendition of "Over There," the last bit especially. "We won't come back till it's over, over there."

But once we wore ourselves out and returned to our billets, all that was left was an odd sort of worry: It won't start up again, will it? When you think of all the fellows who didn't make it, and how long things have been going on, it's almost hard to believe.

It'll take some time to muster us out, but I can't help thinking how good it will be to see the family again. My, the racket Ma will make! It's a wonder God had time to listen to anyone else, the number of prayers she poured out over me these past years. Strange to think life in Gettysburg went on like it always has.

Once, I thought I'd go into radio full-time, but after all this, I'd be happy never to see another telegraph wire or portable radio set again. It's back to Pop's locksmith shop for me. There's something nice about the idea of keeping things safe after a war, isn't there?

How about you, Lily? It's all right if you haven't made plans yet, or if you'd rather not share them with me, but I won't miss my chance to say you'd be brilliant at anything you set your mind to. And that's not flattery because your letters got me through some rough days. I really mean it.

I'd love to see you when I'm back in the country, if you're willing. Maybe it's bold of me to say, but it's the truth: I miss you more every day.

In the meantime, give me any of your news when you have a chance.

Yours,
Roger

The fact that someone believed in her warmed Lily against the chill of early spring. But there was also a small part of her that worried—the letter, received in mid-December, had been her last from Roger, even though she'd replied the very next day.

You shouldn't have told him.

No, she argued back. *It had to be done.* Faced with guilt over Roger's growing regard, Lily had mustered her courage to do "the most honest thing possible" and admit to him what she hadn't to Margot or Elizebeth. Not all the truth, for fear of waking the terrible memories it might bring, but enough.

"I am not decided yet as to what I'll do after the war," she'd written. *"Your kind words notwithstanding, practical opportunities for women are limited, especially because I will likely never marry or be able to bear children. Others in my family have suffered in a similar way, and I have been told such difficulties are hereditary."*

At the time, she'd been grateful for the distance pen and paper gave her for such an indelicate revelation, posting the letter before she could have second thoughts.

Now, as weeks turned to months, those thoughts had had ample time to appear, then fester. Had she driven Roger away with her news?

Certainly, there were other explanations. Soldiers were slowly being sent back home, packed into troopships for interminable voyages across the ocean. Some had to be quarantined, the better to slow the spread of Spanish flu among returning soldiers. William Friedman had been asked to remain in France to write a technical history of the field developments in ciphers during the war.

Still, Lily hadn't realized how accustomed she'd become to a monthly update from the cheerful, plainspoken lieutenant until they stopped arriving.

Keep focused on the task before you. Lily straightened her shoulders as she stepped up to the Villa's imposing front door. She'd rather have met Mr. Fabyan in his office in the Engineering Building, but he'd been out for several days, entertaining guests. Once she assured Miss Belle Cumming, Mr. Fabyan's sharp-eyed and loyal personal secretary, that she had an appointment, she was ushered inside to the country manor's den.

Lily had worn her most forgettable gray dress, a shapeless tub frock a decade out of style, but neat enough that it couldn't be considered shabby. She'd been given it during her days at the reformatory, from one of the charity boxes of castoffs.

Mr. Fabyan's den was just to the left of the Villa's entryway, lined with diamond-paned windows that provided a sweeping view of the estate. Taxidermized heads leered down at all who entered. The millionaire sat behind a writing desk beneath a motionless peacock, oblivious to Lily's entrance.

Lily took a deep breath and stepped farther into the room. "Good afternoon, Mr. Fabyan."

"Hmm?" He looked up, blue eyes piercing, clearly annoyed at being interrupted. "Do come in, Miss . . . Nilsson." Whether he'd looked at a note in his calendar to find her name or simply searched his memory to retrieve it, Lily couldn't tell. "One moment. I must finish this."

Because he hadn't invited her to sit, Lily did not, choosing a position near the desk, but not too near, opposite where Mr. Fabyan sat scribbling. Beside a stack of scientific books and a vase engraved with gleaming lotus flowers, a pile of letters threatened to spill onto the floor. Lily had to stop herself from straightening them out of habit, then realized she recognized the recipient of the first envelope in the pile: Elizabeth Friedman.

Spelled wrong, indeed, but then, most people who didn't know her well mistakenly used the more traditional spelling of Elizebeth's first name. Lily blinked, making sure she'd seen correctly, but it was still there.

How odd. She'd assumed their mail went directly to the Lodge, as that was the address used to post them, but had imagined one of the servants at Riverbank must sort them, or perhaps Miss Cumming. She never imagined that Mr. Fabyan himself would bother with such a menial task.

Even as she processed this, Lily noted the mother-of-pearl engraved letter opener placed on top of the stack, blade gleaming like a warning. A brass teakettle perched on a burner stand on a bench nearby, steam drifting lazily into the air.

He's reading our mail.

The conclusion came to her with the force of the first bit of plaintext snapping into place for a cipher. It needed testing. But Lily was certain she was right. It simply fit many of the confusing details of the past several months. Elizebeth had wondered why Joseph Mauborgne of the Signal Corps hadn't responded to her letters, or why she and William hadn't received the job offers others in the military had hinted would come at the end of the war. But if Mr. Fabyan was reading, and likely destroying, any competing offers of employment . . .

Following quickly behind that theory came another, one that compelled Lily to step forward, risking attracting Mr. Fabyan's attention, until she was directly beside the desk.

She pushed Elizebeth's letter aside, then the next . . . and sure enough, the one underneath it had her name on it, written in Roger's distinct scrawl.

But why? What reason could Mr. Fabyan have for keeping Roger's letters from her? Or was he simply sorting through the communications, planning to deliver the innocuous ones later?

Take it. Everything in her cringed at the idea, though no one—not God or any court in the land—would consider it stealing, not with her name plainly marked on the envelope. *If you don't, you may never know . . .*

"I see you're admiring my Imari porcelain."

Lily jerked her hand back, trying to disguise the gesture with a quick bow, as if she was still in service. Mr. Fabyan's thick hand engulfed a small wooden blotter, rocking it across his signature on whatever document he'd completed, but his eyes were fixed on her.

"It—it's quite impressive," she stammered, turning her attention to the vase beside the stack of letters.

"Qing dynasty," he said, his chest puffed out like a rooster's. "Merely a trifle, a gift from my time as a diplomatic liaison to General Tamemoto after the Russo-Japanese war. I've no interest in the cheap Asian mania that's overtaken others of my set."

Lily decided not to mention that bringing an entire family from Japan to design and tend his garden might, in some circles, be considered an interest.

"All that money spent on old plates and pots." Mr. Fabyan waved his hand like the whole thing was a circus sideshow. "Some millionaires collect the strangest things, just to spend their money. I've been to T. Harrison Garrett's mansion in Baltimore. He's got a toilet made from solid gold. Can you believe that?"

This meeting was not going at all how Lily had planned. She'd hoped to enter, say her memorized piece, and flee as quickly as possible. "That is very unusual. But—"

"And what's the purpose?" Mr. Fabyan struck the desk with

such force that Lily jerked back in alarm. "A wealthy man who dies with nothing but possessions is a fool, and I am nobody's fool."

"I should say not. But—"

"Oh, there's nothing wrong with wanting one's life to matter, but I've found a better way, a more lasting monument." Mr. Fabyan leaned back in his chair, as if he were a Pharaoh casting a vision for his grand tomb. "I intend to make a name for myself by pursuing knowledge, funding new discoveries, advancing humanity! What better legacy could there be, eh, Miss Nilsson?"

Lily struggled to find an appropriate response, settling on, "That is a noble goal." There was no point in arousing the tycoon's anger, or even his attention, not now, not if she wanted to disappear.

Mr. Fabyan nodded in satisfaction. "Yes, indeed." He frowned at her, as if realizing that it was an employee standing before him, not one of the rich guests he liked to regale with his grand speeches. "Now, I'm sure you had some other reason for seeing me?"

"Thank you, sir. I was hoping . . ." Lily licked her dry lips. Goodness, why was this so hard? For years now, she'd stood toe-to-toe with encrypted messages by the dozen and demanded they reveal their secrets. Now, words seemed to falter on her tongue. "Regarding my contract of employment . . ."

"Yes, well?"

Resetting her posture ramrod-straight for courage, Lily looked the man in his slightly bloodshot eyes. "Now that the war is over, I am planning to end my time here at Riverbank. I wondered how much leave I would need to give."

Where Lily would go after this, she wasn't sure. She'd implied to Elizebeth that she'd work to save money to attend a women's college in the fall, but that prospect felt out of reach, given her limited education. When Margot had pried, Lily had hinted that perhaps her relationship with Roger had grown to an understanding of sorts.

At the moment, her only plan was a simple direction: away from Riverbank.

Mr. Fabyan stood blinking at her, as if she'd spoken in cipher and he needed time to decrypt it. Then he waved a stocky arm, reminding Lily of the windmill on the edge of his property. "None of that, Miss Nilsson. War or no war, I need all my cryptanalysts back on the Bacon project with Mrs. Gallup."

Lily could have groaned aloud were the situation not so serious. Francis Bacon again, Mr. Fabyan's favorite literary project. Even though William and Elizebeth had tried to persuade him that the well-intentioned scholar was seeing ciphers in Shakespeare's works where there were none, he stubbornly refused to listen.

"I'm sure that important work will continue," Lily said smoothly. She had foreseen this objection and had a planned response. "However, I have no background in literature." She neglected to mention that she'd read a dozen of Shakespeare's plays in the past year, borrowed from the Lodge's library, to have something to discuss with William and Elizebeth. "In fact, I never even attended secondary school."

"That so, that so?" This, at least, seemed to have gotten Mr. Fabyan's attention. He tilted his head, then stood, and his movement around the desk reminded Lily of the bears in their cages lurching forward just before feeding time. "Some might say we have the responsibility to educate you, then."

Lily tensed, unsure what to say next. Miss Cumming had departed upon Lily's arrival, a stack of packages clutched under her arm. There was no comforting clatter of servants through the door to the dining room, and the sound of the gramophone upstairs indicated Nelle was hosting a tea in the music room.

"I appreciate the sentiment, sir," she choked out, "but I don't

217

think I'd be of any use. Elizebeth and William were the great minds of the code room. The rest of us were merely assistants."

This made Mr. Fabyan pause for a moment, his brow furrowed, and Lily caught her breath. "Don't be modest, Miss Nilsson. I remember your test scores from that reformatory school. In a place teeming with the dregs of society, you stood out. Besides, I know you and Elizebeth are friends, and she's not one to associate with simpering idiots."

"True," Lily acknowledged, "but there's a difference between competence and genius. I'm sure Mrs. Gallup would assure you she wants only the best working on her project."

Mr. Fabyan worried his prodigious whiskers, scratching like they were infested with fleas. "To be frank, I don't give a—" He frowned and made a token edit due to the presence of a lady— "hoot about what Mrs. Gallup has to say. You see, Miss Nilsson, if some folks from the code room start leaving Riverbank, then everyone will want to. I can't let that happen. I've got a legacy to leave, new knowledge to uncover. Do you understand?"

Yes. He was telling her, in so many words, that she was insignificant . . . except that if he allowed her to leave, Elizebeth and William would want to leave as well.

Lily gave a curt nod, stepping back toward the door. "I apologize for wasting your time. Good day, sir."

With one last longing glance at the stack of letters, where Roger's envelope waited unopened, Lily fled.

25

Lillian

Lillian tried not to steal constant glances at the doorway, waiting for Elizebeth and William to rejoin them, instead taking another forkful of Dutch apple pie. The crumble topping, still warm, melted in her mouth.

Across from her, Dinah's slice remained mainly uneaten, its front point simply mangled about.

". . . and honestly, I think it was a little gauche for Roosevelt to complain that there aren't enough safe places for presidential vacations when gas rations are keeping everyone at home." Margot, their other dinner party guest, had kept up a lively banter for the past twenty minutes, though Lillian noticed that Dinah often struggled to make a coherent reply, shifting uncomfortably in the dining room chair.

No wonder, with two of the greatest minds in the nation sitting just one room over evaluating her OSS assignment. Dinah had asked a few questions of Lillian over a telephone call earlier in the week, but mostly, the cipher was Dinah's original work. Asking the Friedmans to test her cipher was like having Leonardo da Vinci evaluate your first pencil sketch.

"More pie?" Lillian offered, when silence descended once again.

"I *really* couldn't," Margot protested in the exaggerated tone Lillian remembered from their younger years, when the flapper's figure vied for influence with her friend's sweet tooth.

"Half a slice?"

A pause, then, "Oh, why not? Just a teensy sliver." She'd begun gushing about Lillian's "magician" ability with rationed sugar when Elizebeth tiptoed into the dining room, followed by William. He held the pages of Dinah's counterfeit cipher in his hand.

"Finished already?" Dinah asked, the disappointment obvious in her voice.

"It's a compliment to your work that it took them this long," Lillian said. "I doubt your Axis field officers will have anything approaching their skills."

"And I have the distinct advantage of being something of an expert in World War I ciphers," William added. He set the paper down on the table. "It's very strong, I think. I imagine a number of partisans saw action during World War I, so using a modified version of the *cifrario tascabile* most signal officers carried around was wise."

Dinah's cheeks pinked with the start of a blush at the compliment. "I chose the pocket cipher mainly because there was a diagram with the numbers all laid out for me," she admitted. "It helped to have a starting point. I'd have been lost without it."

"But it lends authenticity. That's what matters most for black propaganda."

Elizebeth nodded her agreement. "Very clever too, using Garibaldi as the keyword."

"Thanks. Yves Gyldén gave me the idea. He said that Italian

officers are always using keywords like *Caesar* or *Dante*. Since many of the partisan groups name themselves after Garibaldi, he seemed like the best choice."

Lillian nodded. "I hope you documented all that in your report." It seemed just the thing to impress a group of Washington bureaucrats.

"Of course."

William pushed the papers back to Dinah, and Lillian was glad to see that tonight he had a bit of color back in his cheeks, though he was still far too thin. "Well, I, for one, think you have a successful false cipher here, Dinah. Be careful, or we'll try to recruit you to the Signal Intelligence Agency."

Dinah beamed, the slight indentations of dimples that never quite matched Roger's appearing on her cheeks. She, like Lillian, likely knew that William didn't have the insincerity for empty flattery. "Thanks, but I'm retiring from code-making, and breaking, for good. It's far too challenging for a dunce like me."

At this, Lillian raised an eyebrow. "Don't underestimate yourself, dear. Look how much you've learned in only a few days." Brilliance, Lillian had learned, wasn't nearly so important as old-fashioned grit, and Dinah had inherited much of that from Roger. When she chose to focus and wanted to impress—as she clearly did with this assignment—she could comport herself quite well.

Dinah shrugged. "I just hope Mr. Agnew and the Italian field contingent think it's good enough."

"They will," Lillian assured her.

Dinah looked almost startled, then smiled hesitantly.

"Salute," William called, raising his tiny glass of sherry. "To our youngest associate. May she have a long and glorious career."

Lillian and Dinah joined in the toast, laughing, despite the fact that they only had mugs of weak coffee to heft. After the

Friedmans enjoyed their pie and Margot caught them up on the latest gossip, they parted ways. Lillian watched Dinah and Margot disappear into their taxi. It seemed her daughter had turned out to be a code girl after all, if only temporarily.

She made her excuses to the Friedmans as soon as the front door was shut, and neither objected nor invited her into the library for a game of chess, likely as tired as she was.

At least you have the letter to read.

Her steps fell a bit more lightly on the creaking stairs. Her husband's latest letter awaited her on her bedside table. Earlier in the month, Roger had sent flowers, delivered on their anniversary, but they had only come with a few lines in the florist's card. Just like during the last war, Roger's letters gave her the sense that he was in the room with her for an evening chat.

Ensconced in the upholstered chair that matched the guest room curtains, she tore the envelope and began to read.

My Dear Lily,

How I miss you! This is the longest we've been apart since the last war, and I'm likely to become a pacifist just to keep it from happening again. (Don't worry, Mom is getting on fine, but between you and me, she oversalts her soups and never remembers where my umbrella has gotten.)

I'm glad William's feeling better and that the Friedman house is free of every speck of dust and grime. You and Elizabeth and Margot stay out of trouble, now. The three of you in the same place again—I tremble to think what you might get up to. If you learned to drive, you could visit them more often—just a gentle nudge. You are, after all, the steadier of the two of us, and I'd bet once you're used to it, you'd be quite the speed devil.

How's my little Yankee doing? She's called twice and sent me a postcard—Lincoln Memorial, no surprise—but you know Dinah, all pep and positivity.

I've tucked some personal mail you've gotten into this envelope, along with a clipping from the local paper about Bobby Wiggins getting a Purple Heart, and a letter to the editor protesting the pending arrival of German POWs to Gettsyburg at the end of the month. (I have no complaints; a POW camp has meant lots of new lock installations.)

With heartfelt pleas for your swift return,

> *Your Husband,*
> *Roger (in case you're getting*
> *letters from any other Rogers)*

It wasn't a long missive, but just like with his letters two decades before, Roger could find a way to bring sentimental tears to her eyes, then make her laugh, all in the space of a few paragraphs.

Absently, her mind still on what she might reply, Lillian looked through the mail Roger had sent along. Since Margot and Elizebeth knew not to write her at home and she'd given her newspaper assignments her forwarding address, there wasn't much. Just an advertisement "to the lady of the house" about a new vermin control company in Chambersburg, the Women's Missionary Society's quarterly newsletter . . .

She paused, holding up the third envelope, stamped with the distinct seal of the Harrisburg State Hospital. It shouldn't have been surprising, given that the hospital sent letters to donors each May and November, and the Kendall family had made a substantial annual gift for the past decade. Still, Lillian had a way of forgetting—of trying to forget, perhaps.

Roger knew that Mama had been ill both physically and mentally for much of Lillian's childhood, though he didn't understand just what it cost Lillian each time she forced herself to read about the latest developments at what used to be called a lunatic asylum.

Not that Harrisburg State Hospital fit the stereotypes the phrase brought up. Lillian had researched their practices carefully and found them to be both effective and humane, with sanitary living conditions, extensive grounds and gardens for work and recreation, and dozens of specialized programs. Locals called it "the City on the Hill." The biblical reference to Christ's words about his followers' deeds shining brightly in a dark world had originally attracted Lillian's attention, for surely if ever there was a darkness that needed the light, it surrounded those who could no longer trust their own minds. She only wished Mama had known of it when there seemed to be nowhere safe she could go.

Taking a deep breath, Lillian tore open the letter and read an update on the hospital's status. The hospital's main plea was not for money, but staff, similar to the year before. Wartime enlistment had left half of their positions on the men's side of campus unfilled, and now they were even short on housekeeping staff since many local women had taken work at Harrisburg's defense factories.

Still, it ended on a positive note. *"As more veterans return from the horrors of active combat, the country is seeing more cases of battle trauma and other neurotic disorders, and with it, a rise in compassion for those recovering from such conditions. Society, it seems, may have needed a war to see our patients as sufferers to be cared for rather than burdens to be discarded."*

"Good," Lillian whispered, folding the letter back up.

It wasn't a full solution, and it was too late for Mama, who had been so fearful of the rat-infested, abuse-ridden asylums of her day. But others would be helped by the simple gift of a hospital that recognized and valued their humanity.

Even as Lillian tugged on her nightgown and brushed her hair in long, even strokes, thoughts of Mama filled her mind, as they often did when she read the updates from the state hospital. Not the happy memories, but ones from that last week that she'd never shared, even with Roger. The musty drapes, pulled tight so no sunlight trickled into their Chicago tenement. The smell of the overflowing bucket that served as a latrine since Mama wouldn't let either of them go outside. Most of all, the crying, during all of Mama's waking hours, that had eventually prompted a frightened fourteen-year-old girl to go for the doctors once again, this time for the last time. And then . . .

She squeezed her eyes shut. *Stop. You have to stop remembering. You can't change anything now, and it won't bring her back.*

No matter how often she repeated the reassurances to herself, it never held the panic back for long.

You ought to tell Roger. Wouldn't it make the burden easier to bear?

Lillian eased under the covers, clutching her throbbing temple. She knew when she should have told Roger the full truth about Mama's life and death. If not in her letters during the war, then certainly that day in the gardens, when their future was still uncertain.

Now, with both the past and the future on her mind, it felt like it would be too late. All she could do now was try to get some rest, hoping that this time, the nightmares would pass her by.

26

Lily

"I hoped I would see your father again, certainly. But as time went on, I didn't expect to."

—Excerpt from Lillian Kendall's journal

Sunday, April 27, 1919

Roger's letters were burning. Heaps of them, along with all their code worksheets, inside the gaping maw of the Villa's fireplace. Lily lurched forward to grab them with her bare hands, but she was held back by a nurse. "Take your medicine now," her soft, soothing voice intoned. "It will help you relax."

When she turned, mouth open to receive the bitter syrup, the nurse was gone, replaced by Mama, clutching Lily's china doll, the one she'd dug from the mud and cleaned so carefully. "Where did you get this? Is this how you're spending the money I earn?"

Lily tried to answer, but the words caught in her throat, and she could only watch as Mama stalked toward the fireplace, thrusting the doll inside.

It's only a dream. The thought came to her with comforting certainty, the quiet reassurance drowning out the din of Mama's angry words and the crackle of flames. *Turn toward the light. Wake up.*

Wake. Up.

Lily blinked, stretching out in a patch of sunlight. Afternoon. Yes, it was Sunday, and she'd fallen into an unexpected nap.

A loud rapping on her door told her what had jarred her out of the nightmare. She sat up too suddenly, the blood rushing to her head.

"Lily! Let me in!"

Thank goodness. It was Margot's voice. Lily hurried to the door, throwing it open to see her friend dressed in an airy frock, face all agitation.

"What is it?" she demanded. "What's wrong?"

"Boy, you really are jumpy." She grabbed Lily's arm, swinging it back and forth, and it was only then that Lily registered that her friend was excited, not upset. "It's *him*. He's here. And he wants to see you!"

Still groggy from her interrupted nap, all Lily could manage was a weak, "Who?"

Margot gave her a flat look. "The milkman." She pulled Lily back into the room toward the mirror on the wall, frowning at what she saw there. "Wartime Wally, you goof. Your lieutenant came back to pay a call on you."

Now Lily was wide awake. "Roger is here? At Riverbank?"

Margot nodded, fussing over Lily's mussed hair without asking permission. "I saw him getting off the streetcar at the Riverbank station and stopped to say a friendly hello. He asked after you right away, so I said I'd fetch you."

Roger asked for me. But that could mean anything. He might be upset that she hadn't answered his letters or confused about why the woman he'd begun to care for had suddenly disappeared. Perhaps he'd even come as a mere friend, having received and accepted her last letter with its declaration that she would likely never marry. "He . . . oh, goodness. I didn't know he was coming."

Undaunted, Margot grinned. "A surprise visit? How romantic." She gave Lily one more assessing glance. "Tuck a rose into your hair on the way. The simple, natural look suits you."

Filled with nervous energy, Lily shoved her friend, laughing, into the hallway. And yet Margot lingered, her voice becoming serious for once. "I won't tell you to say no if he asks you a certain question, Lil. Your lieutenant seems like a good fellow. But make it hard on him, at least. He'd better appreciate what he's getting . . . and what he's taking you away from."

You mean this prison? Unlike Elizebeth, Margot didn't seem to be concerned about the lives they were leading here, after the war, but Lily had to wonder: How long would free-spirited Margot be content at Riverbank, eating fresh fruit, lounging by the pool, and transcribing Shakespeare folios without becoming restless?

No time for that now. "I won't do anything rash," Lily said instead, not entirely sure it was the truth. Ever since she'd learned that Mr. Fabyan was reading and censoring their mail, her daring had grown . . . along with a wild, foolish idea, one that had seemed destined never to be fulfilled.

Lily knew exactly how she could escape this place. But did she have the courage to follow through, now that Roger was really here?

"All right," Margot said, still grinning irrepressibly. "Go. Don't keep the lieutenant waiting."

The parting comment, delivered with a wink, snapped Lily back to the urgency of the moment. She glanced despairingly down at her dowdy gingham dress, stained with ink, that she only ever wore around her own apartment. There was no time to change into something more suitable. After all, Mr. Fabyan often strolled the grounds on Sunday afternoons. The man wasn't a genius in his own right, but he had a memory like a steel bear trap. If he saw Roger, he might drive him away under some pretense.

It's all right. Roger wasn't one to be impressed by glamour and finery in any case. *"A simple country boy,"* he called himself in his letters. And perhaps her story would sound more pitiable if she looked like the charity cousin kept in the attic.

Still, she took a moment to brush and re-pin her hair, examined her eyebrows in the mirror—they had almost fully grown back since Margot's shenanigans—and made for the door.

Outside the Lodge, Riverbank was full of activity once again. The sudden bloom of warm weather had brought out dozens from Geneva and the surrounding area for a Sunday afternoon holiday, spreading out picnic blankets or wielding butterfly nets. Children dressed in sailor suits and spring frocks clamored around the bear and monkey cages, throwing peanuts and shouting encouragement as the animals performed their tricks.

Lily hurried past, with eyes for only one person.

All the while, frantic thoughts flew through her mind, fear and hope mingled together in a blur. What did Roger want to say to her? What must he think of her?

Streetcar Station 37 let out right at the entrance of the Japanese gardens, but amid the rush of pastel-clad revelers, Lily couldn't see her burly, dark-haired lieutenant anywhere. Perhaps he'd already wandered into the gardens.

"Lily?"

She turned at the sound of the familiar voice, and there he was, stepping away from a new arrival of visitors, dressed in a blue-and-white striped jacket and a straw boater hat. She'd looked past him, Lily realized, because she'd never seen him in anything other than a military uniform. He took a tentative step toward her.

229

Of course he would be uncertain. For all he knew, she had simply ignored his last letters.

Lily continued toward him—closer and closer, trusting his arms to open as she approached.

They did, feeling wide and warm as she embraced him, catching only a glimpse of his face, clean-shaven, sporting a new shrapnel scar on the chin.

"You're here," she said dumbly, breathing in the scent of him as she rested her head on his chest. Simple shaving soap, not the fancy cologne William liked to wear, but comforting all the same.

Why hadn't she thought of some pithy greeting? Failing that, there was so much to explain. But none of it seemed important anymore. "I-I'm so glad you're here."

"Really?" He coughed, covering his surprise, and she took a step back, feeling suddenly awkward. "That is, it seemed a good day for a visit. Since I was in the area. I decided to visit a buddy of mine in Chicago, help him move into his new place. He lost an arm at Meuse-Argonne. Awful stuff."

Roger might have stammered his way through more of an explanation, but he was cut off when a trio of boys in grass-stained knickers hurtled past them, headed for the pond. "Miss Schnieder told me Mr. Fabyan provides boats for visitors to take rowing on the river," Roger said at last when she couldn't manage a contribution through her dry mouth. "Maybe we could take one out?"

Margot was clearly trying to help by suggesting the idea, but that wouldn't do at all. Lily could imagine herself shaking so hard the flimsy rowboat would capsize. "Perhaps a stroll in the rose arbor first?"

He brightened at that, offering his arm. "Just the thing!"

Many of the flowers were still buds, tightly wrapped or barely emerging from their winter's rest, but the vines and trees had unfurled their leaves, and the thick stone wall near the road would provide some cover from watching eyes.

You're starting to sound like Mama. In those last days, her paranoia had steadily grown. She often fell into moods where she warned her daughter about unseen enemies, muttering conspiracies.

No. This is real. I saw the letters on Mr. Fabyan's desk.

They'd reached the vine-covered archway above the stone walkway, which provided a natural gazebo. Several other couples walked the path, headed for the bridge to Mr. Fabyan's private island, swaying to the tinny jazz music playing from the loudspeakers installed across the estate. Without saying anything, Lily steered Roger away from the tunnel, toward a small stone bench beside a row of trimmed shrubbery. Here, at least, they could speak in relative, yet proper, privacy.

Lily smiled up at Roger, who was rambling on about the trip from Chicago, trying desperately to conceal the panic rising inside her. *If you want to get away from here, you have to be graceful, composed, and elegant. Otherwise, you'll drive him away.*

"It must have been quite out of your way to travel down here," she interjected.

"Well, I—I've been worried about you. After the end of the war, when you didn't respond to a couple of my letters . . ." He took off his straw hat and stared down at it, the stiff brim crinkling under his grip. "Well, maybe you just didn't have the time."

She shook her head. "Roger, I stopped receiving your letters. And I think I know why."

His face changed from puzzled to incredulous as she told him of the mail she'd found on Mr. Fabyan's desk. "You're sure?"

"Very." When she'd told Elizebeth, she hadn't been surprised either, only angry. "I don't know what we can do about it. I had thought when William returned, perhaps . . ."

But William had returned, and while he and Elizebeth had spent a few weeks in New York City, they were back at Riverbank once more, without other job prospects. Far from the self-assured military officer Lily had hoped for to lead a confrontation with Mr. Fabyan, William had seemed oddly withdrawn and exhausted since his return, as if France had bled him of all of his courage. The Friedmans were still unsure of what to do in the future, and Lily was tired of waiting.

"I'd like to say I can't believe it, but I can," Roger muttered, glancing toward the Villa on the hill. He took her hand, holding it gently, but not allowing her to look away. "Do you feel you're in any danger, Lily? Honestly?"

He must have felt her stiffen, petrified where she sat, like one of Mr. Fabyan's newfangled concrete statues dotting the estate. No matter how hard she tried to push it away, the memory came back again, from the first time Mama had run from a hospital.

"Listen to me, girl. We learned something back there, didn't we?"

Lily hadn't been able to keep from trembling. *"What, Mama?"*

"If anyone asks you if someone's watching you, or if you're in danger . . . always say no. Even if you are. Or else they'll call you crazy. They'll threaten to take your daughter away. They'll . . ." She swiped tears away from her eyes. *"Promise me you'll remember."*

"I promise, Mama."

Lily opened her eyes—when had she closed them?—to see that Roger was still watching her, concern apparent in his open, honest face.

Lily swallowed the hurried "I'm sure it's nothing" that instinct had trained to rise to the surface. He wouldn't believe her anyway, not now. Even so, she couldn't force her voice past a whisper. "Sometimes."

Instead of looking skeptical or asking prying questions, Roger simply gave a nod as sharp as a salute. "We've got to get you away from here."

His face was red, his posture tense, and despite his dapper

summer suit, she could imagine him, for the first time, carrying a rifle, even aiming and firing it to kill. Had she made the wrong choice?

She put a hand on his arm. "Really, Roger, that's kind, but . . . we aren't slaves, and Riverbank isn't a prison."

"And yet you feel like you can't leave."

It was just like Roger to drive right to the heart of it. Lily swallowed hard. Why was it that she—that all of them—felt so bound to Riverbank?

"Elizebeth and William keep talking that way," she said slowly. "Mr. Fabyan is so well-connected in Washington that if they ever want a job in codebreaking again, they have to keep him happy. And Margot wants one more summer of luxury."

But it was more than that, even for her friends. They'd had this conversation a dozen times together, no one stating it outright, but now Lily admitted what they all seemed to sense. "It's . . . difficult for women to find a position like ours. Perhaps we've been made to feel like there won't ever be anything else. That we aren't good enough to make our way in the 'real world' outside of Riverbank."

"Well, that's a lie, I can tell you," Roger said, huffing. "In France I worked with a number of fellows who fancied themselves experts in ciphers, and none of them could hold a candle to you or Elizebeth or any of the others." Then he paused. "What about you, Lily? Do you want to work in codebreaking?"

Margot and Elizebeth hadn't asked her that recently, each assuming they knew the answer, but the one Lily gave Roger now was the truth. "No. I—I don't."

"Then now is the time to leave. Before that Fabyan gets you to sign another contract or bullies you into changing your mind . . . or worse."

Roger was responding just as she'd guessed he would, and yet, Lily couldn't help feeling a trace of guilt as she replied, "Where would I go? He . . . he never paid us much, past our room and board." The real draw of Riverbank hadn't been the salary, but the amenities, the conveniences of life on the estate, along with the prestige of working with other great minds. "I saved all I could, but I couldn't go far, and I'd need to find work right away."

"What a tyrant. I see how he's done it. Very neat, everything lined up. Like the wheels in a combination lock." Roger shook his head in disgust.

Say it. Say it now.

It was unthinkable, unladylike, even unromantic. Margot and Elizebeth would likely both be horrified, though for different reasons.

And yet, the words came, the ones Lily had imagined but never truly believed she would speak. "You could take me away from here. If you wanted to."

Roger stroked his chin, staring out at the roses, his voice as steady as ever. "I don't know if it would be proper. Maybe if I had my sister come over from Gettysburg—she's always wanted to travel—"

He really was going to make her say it outright, wasn't he? That wasn't promising.

"What if you married me first?"

Now the reality of what she was saying seemed to dawn on him, and he looked at her, mouth agape. "You . . . ? But . . . your letter . . . ?"

"Perhaps I've changed my mind. Though I realize I have little to offer, I thought we might . . ." Lily trailed off, desperately hoping Roger would rescue her by saying something, anything. His mouth remained slightly ajar, as if waiting for words to fill it, so she rushed on, trying to tame her furious blush with calm, rational words. "I know the woman isn't meant to ask, and there is much we need to speak about."

She stopped, suddenly, awareness dawning on her.

Roger was *laughing*, his shoulders shaking in silent amusement.

Of the many reactions she'd pictured, this was not one of them. She'd thought, at worst, he might turn her down with gentlemanly politeness, point out that they had spent very little time together in person, say that she was too young or not religious enough or simply that he wanted the assurance of being a father someday, something she couldn't provide. But she had not braced herself for outright mockery.

How had she so badly misjudged his intentions?

"I'm sorry," she managed, past the lump in her throat, standing. "I shouldn't have . . . I'll leave you now."

"No," he blurted, lurching forward, and when he reached out to pull her back, he caught her around the waist, turning her so gently that she caught her breath. "Lily. Please. It's only that . . . you didn't get my letters. You don't know."

"Know what?"

"That I already asked for the honor of your hand in marriage." He ducked his head, a sheepish smile on his face. "Begged is more like it, in several rambling, sentimental pages trying to change your mind. I wondered—that is, I worried—that you hadn't answered because you didn't know how to refuse me."

"Oh. Oh my." This was good news, wasn't it? But somehow, hearing that Roger had already proposed startled Lily. It muddied things to have a variable outside of her careful planning for escape.

It did, however, answer the question as to why Mr. Fabyan would confiscate Roger's mail. If his intention was to keep his cryptographers bound to Riverbank, an ardent proposal would be a clear candidate for censorship. The fact that he must have read Roger's declaration made her ears burn with embarrassment.

"Then, when I realized you never saw it, just now . . . I was relieved," Roger went on, still so close to her that she could breathe in the scent of him. "I thought maybe I had moved too fast, that this would give me a chance to give you the time you needed. But now . . ." He knelt on the damp ground of the rose garden, and Lily glanced around, worried that someone might see. But there were no prying eyes, and even the sound of springtime revelers was comfortingly distant.

"Lily, this isn't how I meant to ask you. I . . . it's all wrong. But let me say my piece." He paused, as if allowing her time to protest, but when she did not, he went on. "I've said it before, but you're the most remarkable woman I've ever met. I will do everything in my power to keep you safe and make you happy, if you'll have me. So . . . will you marry me, Lily?"

He knelt there, looking the very picture of a silhouette on a Valentine's card, handsome and young and full of hope, as if she were worth loving, even after all he knew.

And yet, Lily could barely keep her voice from trembling as she spoke the words, "I will."

He sprang to his feet, beaming. "Then you've made me the happiest man in the world." He caught her hands and pulled her to toward him, swirling her about like they were on the dance floor of the Aurora Hotel once again, and she couldn't help joining in his infectious laughter. And when he leaned in for a kiss, she kissed him back, letting the rest of the world and its worries fade, just for a moment.

Lily was the first to pull away, pushing the escaped tendrils of hair out of her eyes and glancing around. The narrow space between them seemed to fill with fears and warnings, each demanding their due. She spoke only one of them aloud. "But, Roger, what about your family?"

Roger only shrugged, still grinning impishly. "They won't be especially surprised. My mother, at least, suspected I didn't really travel out here just to visit my buddy."

He'd come all this way . . . to see her? Even after he feared she had scorned him without saying good-bye? Yet that was just the sort of thing Roger would do.

And how are you repaying him? the nagging voice in her head warned, whether her anxiety or her conscience, she couldn't tell. *By using him. Accepting his proposal to get away from here to somewhere safe . . . and to escape Margot and Elizebeth's expectations for your future career.*

No. That can't be true. I care for Roger. I do.

Lily pushed back her doubts. Now was the time to make plans and preparations. By the time the evening streetcar was set to leave the estate, they had set a date for her to steal away from Riverbank for the wedding . . . and notify Mr. Fabyan once they were long gone. All of it seemed unreal, like a nickel melodrama in a cheap theater, but Lily felt that perhaps it was the only way. As long as she could say good-bye to Margot and Elizebeth, nothing else mattered.

Margot and Elizebeth. What would they say? What would they think of her? She tried to anticipate the questions they might ask and knew there was one for which she didn't yet have an answer.

Roger had clearly fallen head over heels for her, and Lily needed him . . . but did she love him?

27

Dinah

Raised voices punctured the silence of the empty North Building. Dinah tiptoed down the hallway, placing her heels carefully so as not to disturb whoever was inside Mr. Agnew's office this early in the morning. She'd hoped to deliver her completed cipher for the Italy campaign in privacy, before anyone else in the department arrived.

For a moment, she waited a few steps from the door, wondering if she should knock or retreat to the Rumor Mill. Her indecision was enough that she caught some of the words, delivered in a slow, drawling voice that she didn't recognize. ". . . don't have to tell you it would be disastrous if the Deputy Director gets wind of it."

"I'm not concerned about your reputation, Olsen," Mr. Agnew said in the clipped, dispassionate tone she'd become used to. "What I want to know is, if these files were accessed or tampered with, would there be consequences for the war?"

238

"Possibly. They were about . . . the Jedburghs."

What an odd name. All of the chatter around the OSS was full of code words, including MO missions such as *Crossbow* and *Hemlock*. Yet, the hushed way the other man had spoken the words made Dinah feel that "the Jedburghs" were more crucial than a single propaganda campaign.

"Nothing was *missing*, you understand." There was a rustling of paper. "Here are the files that were out of alphabetical order."

There was a pause. "I can see the cause for concern. Anything else?"

"The cabinet lock showed a scratch. Could be a careless clerk and normal wear and tear. But if not . . . well, it was enough to bring me here, to ask if you've noticed anything—or anyone—suspicious."

Dinah felt her heart dip down to the soles of her pumps. He had to be talking about the Records Room . . . and the incident that was causing Mr. Olsen so much alarm sounded very much like what she'd witnessed on Friday night.

"I trust you've spoken to the clerical pool?"

"Their supervisor swears the files were put away properly a week ago, and that all filing cabinets are locked, as is procedure for any top-secret intelligence."

The word *top-secret* decided it for her. Dinah burst into the office, not caring about how she might sound. "I saw something."

Mr. Olsen, a man of Mr. Agnew's age with thinning hair and stooped shoulders, sprang to his feet, more like an agent anticipating an assassin than a gentleman standing in the presence of a lady. Not from Morale Operations, as she'd never seen him before.

Dinah had the satisfaction of seeing an expression of shock on Mr. Agnew's face before he recovered and gestured to Dinah. "Olsen, this is Miss Kendall, one of our newer hires down in Rumors."

Without so much as a how-do-you-do, Mr. Olsen interrupted, "What do you mean you saw something? What? When?"

Cringing under his sharp, accusatory tone, Dinah tried to relate what she'd seen in as journalistic a fashion as possible. The only detail she modified slightly was saying she had been "working late." True enough, just not on official OSS business.

When she had finished, Mr. Olsen's eyes opened only a fraction from their narrowed stance. "Why didn't you say anything before now?"

She could feel a blush rising, but she stood her ground. "It was the end of the workweek. I had no way to contact Mr. Agnew at home, and I worried that . . . maybe it was nothing."

Mr. Agnew sighed dramatically, like this was one more trial in his difficult life, but the look he gave her was steady. He, at least, believed her. "You're quite sure you didn't hear or see anything that might identify who was in the room?"

Dinah shook her head, then paused. There had been something, at least, though it wasn't specific. "It was a man. At least, the person was wearing men's shoes and had a long stride. I would have noticed a woman's heels."

Mr. Olsen continued to glare at her, and Dinah averted her eyes, which left her staring squarely at the files on Mr. Agnew's desk.

The topmost paper was pasted with a forward and profile photograph of an OSS agent, presumably duplicates of images used in his false ID cards, since he wore civilian clothes.

Dinah caught her breath, then blinked, looking again.

Yes. She recognized that man.

It was one of the agents she'd attempted to entrap back in Gettysburg, the older one with more common sense than his buddies who she'd recommended for a leadership role. Lee? No, Stanley. At least, that had been his code name.

Quickly, Dinah looked away from the file, not wanting to look like she was breaching security. Somehow, this made the potential break-in more personal. She'd only spoken to Stanley for a short time, but he'd seemed a decent fellow, smart and friendly. If this leak put him in danger, wherever he was stationed . . .

"Thank you, Miss Kendall," Mr. Agnew said, sweeping up the files and standing. "I'm sure Mr. Olsen appreciates any actionable information. We'll leave it to him to sort out and get back to work, shall we?" He gave the man—a department head? A deputy director?—a significant look that said he'd better get to it.

Should I recommend they change all their locks? Surely the OSS would have already thought of that and wouldn't need security advice from a small-town locksmith's daughter.

Mr. Olsen delivered a cutting glare her way, accepting the files from Mr. Agnew and holding them close to his chest like she might try to steal them right then and there. "Miss—Kendall, was it?" She nodded. "You are not to speak of this to anyone. If we find you have done so, you will be dismissed from employment. Effective immediately."

"Yes, you've made your point, Olsen, thank you," Mr. Agnew said dryly.

He huffed. "You can never be too sure. Women like to talk, sometimes indiscreetly."

"And what would you call discussing a security breach in loud tones with the office door open?" Dinah couldn't resist adding.

Mr. Olsen turned red as a stormy sunrise, sputtering out an answer, but Mr. Agnew only—smiled? Yes, he was nearly chuckling, bowing his head with the excuse of lighting a cigarette, but Dinah had seen it.

"I won't breathe a word of this to anyone, sir," she said solemnly, just to set the man at ease. This was, after all, an important matter. "You have my word."

"Then let us hope," he said in a clipped way as he clomped toward the door, "that we can trust it."

Dinah noticed that he took special pains to close the door upon leaving. When she looked back over at Mr. Agnew, he was blithely puffing on his cigarette. "I assume you have a delivery for me, then?"

For a moment, she blinked, not sure what he meant. *Oh, the cipher.* In all the commotion, she'd forgotten what had originally brought her here. She passed it to him, trying to look confident. After all, the Friedmans had approved her work, and they were experts in their field.

To her relief, Mr. Agnew set the bundle of papers on his desk without bothering to read even the first few lines. "Olsen's not as bad as he seems, though not the most pleasant under pressure. He'll sort this out. He'll have to. This sort of scandal could shut down the entire OSS." He sighed heavily. "For all that it matters. The second the tide appears to be turning in the war, I'm sure Roosevelt will let us die a quiet death of depleted funds."

Even though she knew she ought to be getting back to work at the Rumor Mill, this was too much of an opportunity to pass up. Dinah saw her chance and asked the question that had been nagging her since her first day of work. "If you think Morale Operations is underfunded and about to be shut down, then what are you doing here, Mr. Agnew?"

He blinked once, twice, three times, his eyes magnified behind his lenses. "I could almost believe you want to know."

"I do." Why else would she have asked?

Something in his watchful gaze changed. It reminded Dinah of the expression Dad got when he talked, even briefly, about his service during the war, the distant, wary look of a memory that cost the teller something to share.

"It was 1938," he said at last. "I watched two schoolchildren play a board game at a park in Berlin, moving pawns about a board and cheering. The game was called *Juden Raus*." He paused, glancing at Dinah. "That would be 'Jews Out' in English. As I watched, I picked up the general idea: The players moved the pawns toward collection points outside the city in order to win the game. For deportation, the sign said, though perhaps the children playing imagined a grimmer fate."

"Oh my." Something about the simple anecdote made Dinah's heart hurt. It felt . . . more real, somehow, than the distant headlines about *Kristallnacht* and ghettos from the years before the war.

"One of the boys was chanting a children's rhyme as he moved his last piece outside of the wall." Mr. Agnew's voice took on a sing-song quality. "'*Trau keinem Fuchs auf grüner Heid und keinem Jud bei seinem Eid.*'"

He seemed to be looking to her for a reaction. "I don't know what that means."

This sigh seemed heavier than all the rest. "Honestly, Miss Kendall, there's a war on. Oughtn't you to learn German?"

"You say that like it's something I could pick up in a weekend, like knitting or Hearts."

The brief, confused expression on her boss's face told her that he had, in fact, considered mastering a new language to be in the same category. "In any case, the rhyme meant something like, 'Don't ever trust a fox in his field, or a Jew to keep his oath.' The child—he couldn't have been older than eight—was so happy, tossing that pawn off the board into the mud beneath. He reminded me of my sons in their younger years."

"So you create propaganda as a way to counter the propaganda Hitler's government used?"

To her surprise, Mr. Agnew shook his head. "That's the worst bit of it. That game wasn't Nazi propaganda. Not a swastika in sight. It was created by a private German company turning a profit on the hate that had built up in even the youngest of citizens. I didn't see propaganda that day. I saw its effects, years later. And it chilled me."

"How terrible," Dinah murmured, shuddering slightly.

"Indeed." Mr. Agnew gave her another of his serious, calculating looks. "Evil is ordinary, Miss Kendall. Don't let anyone convince you otherwise. We might see it most loudly in radio speeches and heil salutes. But evil can also be found in denouncements and averted eyes, in broken windows and cold shoulders and nursery rhymes. Given the right circumstances, it can spring to life in our neighbors, our friends, even ourselves."

"Surely not," Dinah blurted. And yet didn't she teach the children in Sunday School the same thing: "All have sinned and come short of the glory of God," and so on? But a common human tendency toward selfishness, white lies, and bad attitudes didn't seem the same as support of a genocidal dictator.

Mr. Agnew shook his head. "I spent enough time listening to Hitler's words—and they are persuasive, articulate, powerful words, don't let the caricatures tell you otherwise—to find parts that drew on my own prejudices. That frightened me."

It sounded absurd, the idea that a reasonable, patriotic American raised on principles of democracy and equality would find anything in Nazi ideology that resonated.

And yet . . . Dad always said the key to understanding people was walking about in their shoes. What did Dinah know about the average German struggling to make ends meet in the shadow of the humiliating, devastating Great War?

No. Even if I'd been born in Germany, I would think differently. I would be part of the resistance.

Hadn't she pored over accounts of Southerners like Elizabeth Van Lew who hated slavery and secretly worked against the beliefs of their neighbors? *That would have been me*, she had always thought.

And yet . . . Miss Van Lew had died an impoverished outcast in her lifelong home of Richmond, Virginia. Her courage had cost her dearly. Rejection and loneliness—the very things Dinah feared most.

A sudden memory flashed through her mind, the way she'd

listened to the other girls rather than continuing to stand up for Winora when given the chance, afraid of what they might think.

"I think I understand," she said at last, unable to meet her boss's eyes.

He nodded crisply. "All that is far, far too many words to say that while sometimes I take a dim view of this"—he gestured to include Morale Operations, the OSS, and possibly all of Washington, DC, in his grumblings—"I keep on because I have to hope that if evil is ordinary, good might be too."

Dinah took a deep breath of the courtyard's fresh air. "Isn't spring wonderful?"

Winora munched on a bite of the apple Dinah had insisted she eat, as usual looking disgusted by Dinah's relentless optimism. "I guess."

"I hear there are plans for a trip to see the Nationals play this weekend—Shirley told me." The baseball stadium was all the way across town, to the northeast, but if this sunny weather held, it would be worth the trip. "Are you coming?"

Winora had, Dinah was quite sure, perked up at the mention of baseball, but the moment Dinah added Shirley's name, she slumped back over her lunch bag. "Nah, I don't think so."

"Is only Martin allowed to take you places these days?" Dinah teased.

That, at least, prompted a snort. "Please, I don't let any man tell me what to do. I just don't want to go."

Well, Dinah wasn't going to give up that easily. "I know they're famously awful. 'First in war, first in peace, and last in the American League,' and all that. But it's more about the company."

"It's the company I'm trying to avoid." Her gaze was a direct challenge. "There's a reason I wasn't invited."

The sour way she put it made Dinah's sunny vision of cheering, home runs, and Cracker Jack vanish immediately. "Well, I'd like to have you there."

"Huh." Winora tossed the apple core, scattering an expeditionary force of geese that had come steadily nearer. "Listen, Dinah, just because I've been to juvenile prison doesn't mean I'm a charity case."

"Of—of course not." Dinah had been resolutely trying to pretend that she hadn't heard about Winora's past, never bringing it up, even when she was dying from curiosity. Now, confronted directly, she didn't know what to say, or where to look. She settled for a fleck of Moon Pie stuck to Winora's chin. "Anyway, I'm sure it's not all that bad, whatever you did. I mean, no one thinks you . . ."

Her voice trailed off as Winora looked down uncomfortably before raising her head to give Dinah one of her famous *Yeah, what about it?* stares.

Wait. That couldn't mean . . . she wasn't a murderer, was she?

"You—you don't have to tell me." Suddenly, Dinah wasn't sure she wanted to know.

Winora shrugged. "Honestly, I'm surprised you haven't guessed by now. Ever wonder why a nobody like me was hired for the Forgery Department?"

Dinah had to admit she hadn't. After all, they'd hired her —a locksmith's daughter with no college experience from a tiny town in Pennsylvania. "The OSS is an eclectic lot."

"Darn right. Which is why they didn't have any qualms about arranging to get me let off early for good behavior . . . so long as I used my counterfeiting knowledge to help my country."

Counterfeiting. So that was the "family business" Winora had alluded to. How had Dinah not made the connection before? "That's how you learned to make such detailed sketches."

Even now, Winora didn't look the slightest bit ashamed. "I'm

not half as good as Pa, believe it or not, but identification papers and stamps, even foreign ones, aren't nearly so hard as
greenbacks, so it evens out."

"Why didn't they offer your father the job?" Not that Winora
wasn't talented, but the OSS did lean toward being a gentlemen's club, outside of secretarial and clerical positions.

Another shrug. "He's in for another ten years, on account
of shooting a policeman in the leg when he got arrested. And
my cousin was nineteen when some stool pigeon turned us in,
so he was charged as an adult too. Just got out of prison a few
months ago."

Dinah did her level best not to look horrified, mostly because
she could feel Winora watching her for any reaction.

Be calm. Pretend like half of your friends are felons. Still,
all that came out was a weak "I see."

Now that she'd started, Winora seemed to need to keep on
going. "Me, being an accessory and a seventeen-year-old girl at
the time, I got off easy. My family's never been on what you'd
call the right side of the law, but they're "Stars and Stripes
Forever" types. Pa and Uncle Ritchie both fought in the last
war, so the OSS figured I was safe to hire. Though sometimes
I think they still look at my pocketbook a little suspicious."

Dinah couldn't blame them, but she didn't say so. Still, something about knowing the full story made her breathe a little easier.
So Winora's family had engraved and printed fake money during
the Depression. Hadn't they all wished they could in those days?

"Well, the OSS made the right choice. Anyone can tell you're
doing a wonderful job," Dinah said staunchly, hoping this was
the right response.

Winora straightened slightly, cramming in another large bite
of MoonPie. "Thanks."

Now that everything was out in the open, she might as well
ask. "Why didn't you tell me before?"

For a long moment, Winora was quiet, like a pitcher assessing his opponent's mettle before chucking a fastball over the plate. When she finally did speak, her words were more measured than usual. "Like I said, I thought you'd cotton on eventually, or you'd heard and were pretending you hadn't to save face." She shrugged. "Once I realized you genuinely didn't have a clue . . . I dunno, maybe it was nice. People are always looking down their noses at me. It gets old."

Since Winora hadn't stormed away yet, it felt like another worthy risk to ask, "I take it Martin doesn't know either?" Not that they were going steady or anything like that, but Winora had been out on dates with him at least twice a week since April, though Dinah had yet to meet her fellow.

"No," she said immediately, the scowl returning in full force. "And I don't mean for him to find out. Why do you think I rush him out of Myrtlewood as soon as he shows up?"

"Are you sure that's . . . wise?"

"I don't care if it's wise, it's what I'm doing." The old stubborn tone had returned so forcefully that Dinah wondered if she'd seen a softening at all. "There's nothing real serious between us yet. I can't risk scaring him off. He's the first nice guy I've ever dated."

What was Dinah supposed to say to that? "Well, I won't be the one to tell him."

"Good." She crumpled up her lunch bag and stood, her usual way of announcing that social hour was over. "Anyway, I'm glad you know now. It's a lot of work, keeping cats in bags. Always trying to tear their way out, the mean cusses."

"The truth has a way of doing that," Dinah said, but the implication seemed to sail right over Winora's head into the clear blue sky.

During their walk back to headquarters, Dinah worried over this latest development. Mr. Agnew's words resounded in her mind: *"Evil is ordinary . . . it can spring to life in our neighbors, our friends . . ."*

And with that, Dinah couldn't help thinking of the intruder to the Records Room. Someone had broken into a lock, a distinctly criminal skill. *And one you have too, don't forget.*

Still, even though Dinah had insisted it was a man in the building, Winora was tall enough to take long steps, and she never wore heels to work, preferring instead the flat brown Oxfords she had on now.

Maybe she has a firm alibi. That would certainly make Dinah feel better. "Speaking of Martin, you got home awfully late last Friday. What were you . . . ?"

"Sorry, gotta go." Winora pulled ahead, taking the steps up to the North Building two at a time. "We've got a deadline to make on a new batch of ID cards, and I'm already late."

"Oh. Sure." Dinah waved her coworker on, letting a frown surface only when Winora's back was turned. It was likely the truth. Forgery was working double-time these days, like most of them, preparing for the invasion of France. And yet, all of Dinah's observations on body language told her it was possible Winora was simply dodging the question. Where *had* she been the night the Records Room was broken into? And what about the *Secret* report that had mysteriously shown up among Dinah's papers? After all, Winora knew which desk was hers.

But why would she want to get me in trouble with Mrs. Masterson? It didn't make sense.

It might all be nothing. But if a person could find the right connections to a spy ring or German-American extremist organizations, any top-secret OSS intelligence could get men killed.

Stop it. There was no evidence Winora had been up to anything illegal. Innocent until proven guilty, or Dinah would be no better than the gossips back at Myrtlewood. *But maybe I should get some answers before I trust Winora.*

28

Lily

"I know young people enjoy romantic stories of beautiful weddings. I'm afraid my own will disappoint."

—Excerpt from Lillian Kendall's journal

SATURDAY, MAY 3, 1919

"Do I look all right?" Lily asked, reaching to ensure no hairs had come loose from the upswept style that tugged at her scalp.

Margot swatted her fingers away. "You're beautiful. Don't touch." She inspected Lily's overflowing bouquet of blush pink roses, plucking a small bloom to tuck behind Lily's ear. "Boy, this must've cost a fortune."

"Roger's family sent it." She'd been able to spend a brief lunch alone with him at a Van Buren Street automat upon their arrival in Chicago, where he assured her that his family had been "delighted" by the telegram announcing his impending marriage.

Lily would soon find out how accurate that report was. They'd purchased two coach class tickets on a train to Gettysburg set to depart Union Station that evening. Still, whether or not the flowers were accompanied by sincere affection, she would never refuse them. Clutching the bridal bouquet was, at the moment, all that was keeping her hands from trembling uncontrollably.

Lily tried to peer into the front window, her heeled boots making the weathered porch creak, but the lace curtains were pulled fast. "I'm glad you're with me, Margot."

Margot had certainly made a production out of sneaking off on the Riverbank streetcar with her as a combination maid of honor and witness. The way she'd skulked across the estate this morning, they might have been escaping to the Chicago underworld. Elizabeth, worried that her absence for even one full day might arouse Mr. Fabyan's suspicions, had only lent Lily the cream dress she'd worn for her own wedding, its elbow-length sleeves made of tatted lace. *"So I'll be with you in spirit,"* she'd said warmly. *"May your marriage be as happy as my own."*

Even now, Lily tried to cling to that hope. But the waiting allowed her nerves to take over again, the runaway train of fears tilting inexorably down a steep slope.

You shouldn't do this.

Lily squeezed her eyes shut, and yet the thoughts kept playing like a needle placed down on the same phonograph record over and over again. *Roger doesn't know enough about you. He likely feels he must marry you out of duty. And you're robbing him of the chance to be a father.*

At least, upon feeling pangs of conscience, Lily had mustered up the courage to speak to Roger directly on that point. After they'd arrived in Chicago, Margot had left "the two lovebirds" to have lunch together.

Her fiancé had flitted about the automat, pushing nickels into slots in wall compartments and pulling out bowls of soup and slabs of pie for both of them, animated with nervous excitement.

It had felt like an awfully public place, but Lily knew it might be her only chance. Besides, the clamor of the lunching crowds created its own kind of privacy. At least that's what she hoped.

While Roger tucked in to his bean soup, she merely stared down at her spoon. "I have to say . . . that is, I feel it's only fair . . ."

The slurping stopped. Roger placed a hand on her arm, and when she'd forced herself to look up, he was smiling at her with a weight of affection she knew she didn't deserve. "It's all right. You can tell me anything, Lily."

"I was telling the truth," she began, blushing so heavily that her face felt like she'd set it aflame, "when I wrote to tell you I may not be able to . . . bear children. It wasn't a lie to drive you away."

"I would never have assumed otherwise," Roger protested, as if in defense of her honor.

Instead of reassuring her, that made her feel worse. "I didn't tell you everything." At this moment, she wished desperately that she had, when she'd still had the luxury of hiding behind pen and paper with an ocean between her and the man who now looked at her with concern in his wide brown eyes. "When I said my mother was unwell, I meant her mind as well as her body."

"I had wondered," he said quietly, "from some of the things you've said."

He had? The lack of disgust or even pity gave Lily the courage to continue. "The doctors worried that Mama's . . . weakness might be passed down to me."

"It hasn't."

She'd known he would say that, but he didn't understand, hadn't heard them talk. Mama herself hadn't started her bursts of neurotic behavior until Lily was around eight years old. "No one can know that for sure. Even if they could, there's the next generation to think about."

In the crowded automat, what followed was less a long silence and more like watching Roger in a silent film while the sounds of their fellow patrons slurping soup and clinking nickels into slots provided the clamor of the theater around them. Finally, he ventured, "It's something we'd have to consider. . . ."

"No. There is nothing to consider, Roger. There is no choice." She had to keep going now, speaking the hardest bit of truth. "The second time Mama was hospitalized, the doctors persuaded her to agree to a . . . procedure. For herself . . . and for me."

For a moment, Roger blinked, clearly not understanding. Then a flush spread across his cheeks, embarrassment that she shared, that had kept her from saying the word *sterilization* out loud.

"How old were you?" His voice was hoarse now.

"Fourteen."

Even now, the memory caused Lily's heart to clench within her, though she could only remember a doctor with a severe, downturned mouth hovering over her before all faded to a throbbing blackness. She'd woken to the sound of her mother sobbing beside her, the anesthetization drug dulling her thoughts.

Roger's eyes narrowed further, and he shook his head. "Only a child. And with your mother unwell. How could anyone with even a lick of conscience do something so awful?"

That's when Lily realized it hadn't been embarrassment she saw in Roger, but anger.

"It didn't hurt." Mama had complained of pain during her recovery after they'd been released, but Lily attributed that to her usual histrionics, and she quietly set about doing the usual household tasks and staying out of Mama's way for a week afterward.

Though she had no visible scar to remind her, Lily had always mourned the children she would never have. But Roger needed to be able to choose, even if it meant rejecting her.

She toyed with the napkin beside her tray. "It's not too late. To change your mind about marrying me, I mean. Margot could see me off, and I'm sure I'd find a position of some sort."

"I could never—"

"Please, Roger, let me finish." If he interrupted her now, Lily knew she'd never gather the courage to speak of this again. "You—you are so kind to offer to help me, but a marriage built on regrets surely cannot last long. And you would be a wonderful father."

Roger paused for a long moment, and Lily could only imagine the dreams that rose to his mind of being greeted after work with a chorus of young voices, tossing a giggling daughter into the air, taking a son to his first baseball game.

"Lily," he said at last, squeezing her hand. "No one is guaranteed healthy children. They're a blessing from God when they do come, and if we never enjoy that gift, I'll love you all the more. I meant everything I said in that garden, and I don't mean to change my mind."

And in that moment, she had known: Roger was a good man, the sort she'd felt would be out of reach for her. Nothing she could say would drive him away.

But he doesn't understand, the darker whispers in her mind insisted, both then and now that she was minutes away from speaking her vows. *Later, once the initial emotions fade, he'll have second thoughts . . . and it will be too late.*

Lily opened her eyes and leaned against the porch railing, where Margot seemed to tilt and pitch before her. "I . . . don't feel . . ."

"You are *not* going to faint on me," Margot said so matter-of-factly that it tethered Lily back to consciousness. "Now, breathe. Deeper. That's it." Her friend had yanked off her silk hat, flapping it as a makeshift fan before Lily's face. "Did you eat breakfast, lunch, anything?"

"Only a few bites." She and Margot had risen before dawn, the better not to encounter any of the other residents of the Lodge, and Roger had been so distracted at the automat that he hadn't noticed his intended's meager appetite.

"That sure doesn't help." Margot studied her a moment like a doctor performing an exam, then scowled. "He didn't bully you into saying yes, did he, Lil?"

"No, not at all." Lily could reassure her of that much. "Roger is the kindest man I've ever known. But . . ." Once again, lacking a crossword clue or frequency analysis to supply the right words, Lily grasped at the best she could find. "It's all happening so fast."

Margot nodded sympathetically. "And you're not much for change, are you?" Lily nodded at this understatement. "Listen, Lil, I'm no expert. But I know you. You're braver than you let on and the most faithful friend anyone could want. Roger's a lucky man."

Whether or not Lily herself believed that, Margot did. That reassurance gave her enough courage to adopt the graceful, upright posture the scientists at Riverbank had drilled into her, and, when the reverend's wife eased the door open, step inside the parsonage parlor.

Even admitting to the practicality, Roger couldn't agree to stopping by the courthouse for their marriage ceremony. *I'm a bit old-fashioned,* he'd confessed. *"Oh, I know God's everywhere, but a promise feels like it matters more given in front of a minister."* He'd gotten his war buddy, Frank, to call in a favor with a Methodist preacher. As they weren't members of his congregation, they couldn't be married in the church, but he'd agreed to officiate in his own parsonage.

Lily was secretly grateful, if only because all those empty pews would have given her the willies. As it was, the pink-cheeked reverend's wife had done her best to make the parsonage cheery, scattering white doilies over the furniture and placing a vase of bluebells on the mantel. She now beamed at Lily from her station on the piano bench, where she'd struck up a rendition of Mendelssohn's "Wedding March."

Turning into the parlor, Lily saw their other witness, Frank, standing at attention before the fireplace, next to the pastor. His sleeve was knotted at the right shoulder, showing what the war had cost him.

And there, next to him, was Roger, dressed in his army uniform and looking more handsome than ever.

She nearly tripped over the hem of the borrowed dress, taking in a sharp breath. Grateful the walk to get to him was a short one, she gave Margot her flowers and gripped Roger's hands before instructed to do so, desperate for something strong to hold on to.

He squeezed them reassuringly as the piano notes faded. Were those . . . tears in his eyes?

You don't deserve him.

You shouldn't do this.

I have to. That's what she'd told herself over these agonizingly long weeks since meeting Roger in the garden, that it was a simple practicality of escape. But the truth was simpler—either more selfish or more beautiful. She could admit it now, staring up at Roger's comforting brown eyes. She *wanted* to marry him, this man who was so deeply safe, who wrote and spoke from his heart and listened with care, and, for some reason, adored her. This was her chance at the life that Mama and the doctors and the reformatory matrons had told her over and over again she'd never have.

As the reverend opened his Book of Worship and the piano notes faded, Roger leaned closer. "I wish I could have given you more," he whispered, and she could close her eyes and picture what he meant: a clapboard country church crowded with Roger's friends and family, an altar bright with candlelight, strains of joyful music filling the air.

She squeezed his hands, searching for some words of reassurance when she herself felt her emotions in such turmoil. "You are all I need."

"We gather here today to celebrate the holy union of a man and a woman before God," the reverend began, and Lily tried to put her worries aside and focus on the vows she was soon to recite. She would strive to be the best wife for Roger that she possibly could, the wife he deserved.

Because to Lily, promises, once made, were not easily broken.

29

Dinah

MONDAY, MAY 22, 1944

Dinah hit the carriage return on her typewriter with more force than necessary, grinning at the last lines of her script: *There's no shame in it, soldier. Why, for all you know, your own girl is one of our members too. So just follow me. . . .*

After she'd turned in the Italian cipher to Mr. Agnew, Mrs. Masterson had assigned her to write a dramatic radio sketch depicting the activities of "The League of Lonely War Women," the clever invention of a female MO officer in North Africa. The rumor was simple: Wehrmacht soldiers on leave would find leaflets letting them know that if they wore a red heart cutout on their lapels, a representative of the league would find them the "companionship" of a willing German woman, a wife or girlfriend of a fellow soldier.

Of course, the organization didn't exist. *"But if they think it does . . . how many will wonder if their sweetheart is embracing another while they're gone, in the name of patriotism?"*

Mrs. Masterson had shrugged, a devilish little smile on her face. She dropped her voice. *"These academics and politicos are brilliant, but I have a hunch you've seen more Hollywood dramas, hmm? Do it justice."*

So the night before, while the other boarders painted their nails and listened to sketch comedy on the radio, Dinah had jotted down notes in the margins, trying to hit just the right notes of pathos in the dialogue between a lonely soldier and cheating German wife. Now, as Mrs. Masterson read over the draft, her ever-ready red pen hovering motionless, she knew she had succeeded.

Finally, Mrs. Masterson looked up. "Our translators might have a few suggestions for cultural context, but to my eye . . . it's a hit. Well done, darling."

Though she knew it was unprofessional, Dinah couldn't help grinning at the praise. "It would fit perfectly aired right after Marlene Dietrich's 'Time on My Hands.'" The German-American star had recorded an album of songs in her native language for *Soldatensender*, including a mournful, romantic ballad.

"That's up to Radio to decide," Mrs. Masterson said archly, but then she gave the slightest of smiles. "But I'll make the suggestion." She waved Dinah off. "Go on, to the duplicator with you."

Some of the more senior staff members insisted on assigning such work to a member of the secretarial pool, but once Dinah had the machine explained to her, she preferred to save time and do it herself. She nearly skipped down the hall, imagining the voice actors reading her script.

Which, unfortunately, caused her to stumble around the corner into Barry Longstreet.

He tipped his hat with an exaggerated bow. "Hi there, sweetheart." There was something sour in his expression, though it seemed to be impersonating a smile.

She nodded coolly and kept on walking. "Good morning."

This time, she knew she wasn't imagining a smirk on his face as he turned toward his own office. "We'll see about that. Oh, and I heard that Mr. Agnew wants to speak to you."

How odd. Mr. Longstreet hadn't spoken to her since she'd taken his Italian cipher project, though she had caught him glowering in her direction from time to time. Had Mr. Agnew really requested her, or was Mr. Longstreet just making a poor joke?

She decided to err on the side of caution, changing her route. After all, the department head had approved her false cipher, though with his usual reserved demeanor. He might have another code-related assignment for her, and this time, she was ready to say yes with confidence. The night before, she'd solved another of her mother's journal entries using a frequency analysis. True, the entry was only seven sentences long, a brief account of feeling unable to leave Riverbank because of Mr. Fabyan's machinations, but it was the first cipher like the ones Mother had broken in her code room so long ago. Maybe soon she could take the role of MO cipher consultant away from Mr. Longstreet.

When she bustled into the office, a bright smile on her face, Mr. Agnew looked directly at her, a cigarette already clenched in his mouth, forming the wrinkles of his face into rather a haggard look. "I have a few questions for you, Miss Kendall."

Something in his expression stilled her. His mouth was set in a hard line, his eyes narrowed. Instinctively, Dinah stiffened. Bad news, perhaps? From home, about the war?

"All right," she said uncertainly.

Mr. Agnew took a long drag on his stubby cigarette before snuffing it out. The wait, paired with his unreadable expression, seemed painfully long. "Did you take a book on ciphers from these offices for your personal use?"

She thought a moment before replying. Now Mr. Longstreet's smirking demeanor made more sense. He had, apparently, noticed the Riverbank pamphlets had briefly gone missing and had the temerity to turn her in. Still, why now, when she'd taken them over two weeks ago?

"I did borrow some booklets from Mr. Longstreet. Without his permission," she added, for the sake of full disclosure. "But only because he wouldn't let me use them when I asked." Dinah wondered if she should mention the man's attempt to extort a kiss from her, but she already felt humiliated enough. "He must not have mentioned that I returned them all last week in tip-top condition. I'm assuming you've already spoken to him."

"I have. Doing a bit of extracurricular reading, Miss Kendall?"

She flushed despite herself. "I was hoping to further educate myself on ciphers." This was true, if incomplete, because it felt ridiculous to admit she was working on solving ciphers her mother had given to her at twelve years of age.

That should clear things up. After all, Mr. Agnew was smart enough to have a healthy suspicion of Mr. Longstreet's motives in accusing her.

She expected Mr. Agnew to quote some poetry and wave her back to her work, but instead he continued, "And have you removed anything else from this building for any reason?"

What an odd question. "No. Never. I—" Midway through her denial, Dinah realized it wasn't true. "Actually, I took a stack of field agent transcripts back to my apartment to complete over the weekend once." Realizing how that might sound, Dinah found her words coming faster. "I knew I'd fall hopelessly behind otherwise. I didn't show them to anyone, I swear."

Indeed, as she'd feared, Mr. Agnew's face darkened. This, she could tell, was the real offense, though how he'd suspected it, she didn't know. "It would have been far better to ask for additional time than to remove confidential documents from OSS headquarters." He stood, even his slight stature seeming to loom behind his desk. "Are you aware, Miss Kendall, that doing so was a violation of federal statutes protecting military information? Documents that you signed upon the start of your employment here?"

"Not until now." But it seemed obvious in hindsight. How could she have been so stupid? She could see her chances of future cipher assignments slipping away. She'd been as bad as the Confederate Army when they requisitioned a printing press in Chambersburg just before clashing with the Union troops at Gettysburg, using it to print thousands of paroles for the prisoners they'd assumed would surrender to them.

Focus. Now wasn't the time to journey to the past, not when her present was so urgent.

"And what about the *Secret* memorandum from another department that your supervisor found on your desk several weeks ago?"

"She told you about that?" Dinah blurted, before realizing it sounded like an admission of guilt. Still, from the way Mrs. Masterson had spoken, she'd seen the older woman as an ally.

"Only when I inquired about the aforementioned breach of protocol."

"Like I told Mrs. Masterson, I don't know how the memorandum got there." Now, under Mr. Agnew's withering gaze, the truth seemed even more unbelievable than it had when she'd spoken it in the Rumor Mill. "Honestly, Mr. Agnew. Mrs. Masterson claimed she found it on my desk, but I never requested it. Or took it," she added, just to cover any suspicions he might have. "It must have been some kind of clerical error."

"I see." This time, when Mr. Agnew paced a few steps closer, she had to stop herself from cringing away. "Is there anything else you need to disclose, Miss Kendall?"

His scrutiny felt different when aimed directly at her. "No," she said, this time sure she was telling the truth. "The *Secret* report must have been a mistake. And I'll never remove any documents from the office again, I promise."

He paused for a long moment. "I'm afraid you won't have a chance. I remain grateful for the work you've done here, and I'm sure Mrs. Masterson would agree. However . . ."

No. This couldn't be happening.

And yet Mr. Agnew's words marched on, toneless but firm. "Because of your violation of the secrecy protocols of this office, your employment with the OSS has ended, effective immediately." He looked at her, and Dinah felt for a moment that he was almost sad to deliver such a verdict. Then the expression disappeared, replaced by his stern frown once again. "Do you understand?"

"Yes, sir." What else was she supposed to say? Though some of Mr. Agnew's suspicions seemed unfair, this was mostly her own fault. After all, hadn't she signed dozens of secrecy agreements on her very first day? The embarrassment of it burned her face as she turned away.

Funny. Dinah had been braced for just this conversation nearly the whole of her first week, worried she hadn't done enough, that she'd finally make enough mistakes for Mrs. Masterson to turn her out of the Rumor Mill. But as the weeks had gone by, her typing speed had improved, her work had received accolades, and each new batch of rumors had become easier.

She had thought . . .

Well, that she had finally become useful.

"I will notify Mrs. Masterson immediately, so do not feel the need to do so yourself. Please gather your personal belongings and leave everything else for your replacement."

"Of course." How would she do so under the watchful eyes of her colleagues? Maybe they'd all be too busy to notice. Maybe they wouldn't care even if they did. "Good-bye, Mr. Agnew."

"Good-bye, Miss Kendall." He opened the door for her, adding quietly, "Do take care."

After hurriedly emptying out her desk and leaving her final

assignment with the secretarial pool, face downturned, she took the stairs rather than risk being trapped in an elevator with a curious coworker. *I have to get away from here.*

Halfway to the bus stop, she realized that Winora would inquire after her at lunchtime. What would Mrs. Masterson tell her?

It's too late now. All Dinah could think of was going back to Myrtlewood Hall and the privacy of her room to have a full three-hanky cry. Hadn't she thought this job was too good to be true? That she could only fake her way through it for so long before being found out? Maybe this was God's way of moving her back to something more suited to her abilities, where she couldn't do any harm.

The entire bus ride was a miserable exercise in holding back tears in front of complete strangers. Dinah had no sense of someone watching her now. She probably never really had—it was only her inflated ego that made her feel she was important enough to be followed.

When she arrived back at the boardinghouse, Auntie Margot was, judging by the clattering in the kitchen, washing the dishes to prepare for dinner, allowing Dinah to slip upstairs unnoticed.

Dinner.

Dinah groaned. Mother was coming to dinner tonight. For once, Dinah had been eager to answer the inevitable questions about work with a detailed résumé of her latest accomplishments and Mr. Agnew's reaction to her Italian cipher.

Now, everything had changed.

How am I going to tell Mother?

The tightening of fear in her chest answered the question for her: *I won't. At least not until I've found another job.* It might take a few little white lies, but sometimes, anything was better than facing the truth.

30

Lillian

Lillian gathered the breakfast dishes into a precarious stack, breathing in the lingering smell of coffee, cinnamon, and bacon. William, she was satisfied to note, had eaten all but a few crumbs of his second helping. Now he buttoned up his suit coat, which she flattered herself to think didn't hang quite as loosely on his slim frame as it had when she arrived.

"Good morning, ladies. I'm off." He kissed Elizebeth's forehead. "Busy day today."

His wife made a small adjustment to his tie. "Isn't it always?"

He chuckled in acknowledgment and ducked through the door while Elizebeth expertly pinned on her hat as a precaution against the breezy spring day. "How did you get the bacon, by the way, Lily? We haven't had a cut that fine in years, practically."

"I've made friends with your butcher. He set it aside for me." She'd learned that trick from Roger.

Elizebeth shook her head. "You are a wonder, Lily."

"Says the celebrated codebreaking genius of the nation."

Instead of giving her an answering smile, Elizebeth glanced over at her, pausing a moment before saying quietly, "Comparison is a dangerous game, I've found."

"Dangerous?" Lillian plucked up the discarded napkins to avoid meeting her friend's eyes. "I was only teasing, dear. I'm quite content with my life as it is."

"Are you sure?"

Those three simple words made audible a question that had nagged at Lillian most of her married life, and though she had a glib affirmation ready, it simply wouldn't come. "Most of the time."

Elizebeth continued to watch her steadily, and Lillian sighed. "It's only . . . Dinah is away on her own now, and my mother-in-law does more than her fair share of the cooking and cleaning. And Roger . . . it's been a busy few years. I feel as though we barely know each other." She set down the plates on the table, surprised to find her hands were trembling slightly. "I suppose coming here has made me think more of what might have been."

"Yes. I see."

Lillian tried to think of how she might change the subject, ask if Elizebeth needed to get to the bus stop, even retreat to the kitchen, but there didn't seem to be a graceful way to do so.

Instead, Elizebeth's Shalimar perfume scented the air as she stepped closer, laying a hand on Lillian's arm. "I can't tell you what might have been if you'd chosen a path more similar to mine, Lily. But since we have been writing monthly letters to each other for twenty years, I can say this much: You have done good work. From tending to Dinah when she was a colicky babe to the way you applied yourself to bookkeeping to save Roger's family business. Even the way you capitalized on the crossword craze in the twenties and organized your church's soup kitchen after the Crash."

With every word, memories of the past two decades played across Lillian's mind like a flickering movie reel. She had felt a sense of purpose, of accomplishment during those years, hadn't she? It was only when she opened Elizebeth's and Margot's letters that she started to doubt whether she was living up to her full potential. "But they're such small things."

Elizebeth's brows twitched downward briefly as she considered. "Are they? Maybe. But our lives and all of history are made up of small things done by small people." Her gaze lingered a long moment on the family photograph on the wall, Barbara and John looking so grown-up compared to the way Lillian remembered them. "I've wondered too, from time to time, if I made the right choices. I think all women do."

"I'm sure you did."

"I hope so." Elizebeth took up her handbag from where it rested by the breakfast table, eyes thoughtful. "Perhaps what's most important is what we do with the time we have left."

Those words, and the ruminations they sparked, made Lillian linger over the breakfast dishes, aimlessly repolishing the everyday spoons like they were Thanksgiving-dinner silver. Most days, she had felt that marrying, raising a child, and giving all she could to a sleepy rural community mattered. Sometimes, though—especially in the long, dark months after Dinah's birth or the lonely evenings when no one else was at home—she had wondered.

Maybe her efforts truly were enough after all.

Shaking herself, she wiped her dishwater-wrinkled hands on her apron. There was no sense in idling.

But when Lillian went through her mental inventory of tasks, she realized the pantry was stocked as well as ration coupons would allow. All the mail had been sorted and answered. Every square inch of the Friedman's house had been swept, scoured, or scrubbed as required.

With only a few days left until her departure, Lillian found

herself in the unexpected position of having absolutely nothing to do.

*Perhaps I really should go sightseeing like Elizebeth is always
suggesting.* In her first years of marriage, before Dinah was
born, Lillian had visited Elizebeth and Margot in Washington
more frequently. This was her chance to see what had become
of some of their old haunts.

An idea occurred to her. What had Margot said? *"Lily, my
dear, you tell others you care about them in cipher when they
need it in plaintext."*

It couldn't hurt to see if Dinah might be available to join her
over her hour lunch break. She had been unusually quiet during
dinner at Myrtlewood on Monday night, hesitant, perhaps, to
share stories of her work around the other boarders. A more
private meeting might be just the thing.

Lillian glanced at the clock. It was still only a few minutes
until seven—the Friedmans rose at dairy-farmer hours. The
boarders would be just finishing breakfast. Before she could
change her mind, Lillian hurried to the Friedmans' study and
placed the call.

One of the other boarders answered the phone and left her
dangling for so long that Lillian worried she'd forgotten all
about her mission to fetch Dinah. She was about to return the receiver and try again when Dinah's perky voice came on. "Hello?"

"Good morning, Dinah. It's Mother."

"Is something wrong?" Her daughter's voice was tense with
concern.

"No, certainly not." Oh dear. Had her greeting sounded so
grim? "I had only thought—if you're free—that I might take
a streetcar past OSS headquarters and introduce you to a favorite restaurant of Elizebeth's and mine for lunch today. It's a
tearoom once called the White Peacock—there's a new name,
and it's under new management, but it's decorated with articles
from the old White House stables and is very charming."

She was saying too much, babbling as ever when she didn't know how else to fill the awkward gaps that would inevitably follow. And indeed, when Lillian paused, the other end of the call fell painfully silent.

"It sounds lovely, Mother," Dinah said at last, "but I really can't. I—I haven't been taking lunch breaks lately, I'm afraid."

"Oh. I see." She cleared her throat. "Even busier than usual, then? I hope the success of the cipher project has something to do with it."

"Something like that."

"I know you can't give me any details. That's all right. Perhaps another time." Although when she'd have the opportunity again before leaving town, she couldn't say. Would Dinah want her to visit again? Lillian supposed it depended on how long the war lasted . . . and whether Roger came with her.

As she hung up, Lillian scolded herself for her disappointment. She, of all people, ought to understand that women had to work harder and longer than anyone around them to show they were worthy of the roles they'd already earned. She should be proud of Dinah.

It was nothing personal. Probably.

Therefore, there was no cause to take it personally. Lillian could visit the tearoom by herself. Perhaps the peace and quiet would be just what she needed.

She'd only just begun deciding which of her three standard hats would look the least shabby when the phone rang again, disturbing the quiet.

Lillian hurried to answer it. Perhaps Dinah had changed her mind. Perhaps she'd decided it was worth making time for her mother after all.

"Hello?" she asked, trying not to sound too hopeful.

"Lillian, thank goodness."

She frowned. "Is this . . . William?"

"Yes. There's a . . . bit of a situation." His voice was higher

269

pitched than normal and tense, his words coming quickly. Another nervous breakdown?

She lowered her voice, as if there were anyone on her end who might overhear. "Are you all right, William?"

"Yes, yes, I'm fine. It's only . . . the army would like to consult with you on a sensitive matter of national security."

She blinked, staring at the receiver. "I'm sorry, I must have misheard. The army needs *my* help?"

"Believe me, Lillian, you're uniquely qualified to advise us on this particular matter."

If William's tone hadn't been so serious, Lillian might have laughed. Uniquely qualified? Did the army want a demonstration of how to make cardamom buns, or a personalized crossword puzzle? Perhaps they were interested in the history of Gettysburg or needed an emergency cleaning woman.

Try as she might, Lillian couldn't think of a single sensible reason William would recommend her help. "I'm afraid I don't—"

To her surprise, he rattled off an address, not for the Signal Intelligence Agency that he worked for, but for the Military Intelligence Services. "Can you get here within the hour?"

The fact that William, who was usually painfully polite, had interrupted her, gave her pause. "I-I'll do my best."

"Good. Because I can't stress enough the urgency of this conversation."

As Lillian replaced the receiver, she couldn't help but wonder what she was getting herself into.

The army's Military Intelligence Services headquarters was more impressive than the improvised code room of Engledew Cottage, but only in size. It consisted mainly of bland, windowless offices and desks crammed together in a boxy maze, populated by men in uniform rushing to and fro like they were all hand-delivering telegrams from the front.

Yes, William's civilian duds were distinctly out of place here, and Lillian felt ostentatious wearing a maroon suit and pumps as he escorted her down a hall with no nameplates next to the doorways. "I've told them of your work with us during the Great War, and that you are a personal friend," he spoke over his shoulder, not slowing down since the moment she'd met him under the hawkish gaze of the front secretary. "That ought to signify something, at least."

"Yes, but William, aren't you going to tell me what this is all about?" He'd refused to do so over the phone, but Lillian felt a desperate need to be prepared for whatever was to come.

He shook his head. "I'm afraid I can't. This isn't, strictly speaking, Signal Corps business, but Colonel McCormack asked for help. I'm not sure what details you'll be permitted to know."

Lillian nodded, given that acceptance was the only option currently available to her. William would have given her more details if he'd felt he could. She would simply have to wait.

Not, as it turned out, for long. Her introduction to Colonel McCormack, a solidly built man wearing round, horn-rimmed glasses, consisted of William's exchanging of names, a murmured "how do you do," and a crushing handshake. Then the colonel sat back heavily in his seat, indicating a chair across from him where she might do the same, as William bowed out, shutting the door behind him.

"Mrs. Kendall, I must impress upon you the utmost confidentiality of what I'm about to relate to you. Are you prepared never to speak of this meeting with another living soul?"

If she'd suspected William of exaggerating the importance of this meeting, she didn't anymore. The colonel had the look of someone who hadn't slept for days and wasn't planning to until a crisis was over. "Yes, of course."

To her ears, her voice was less than convincing—more sober than confident—but perhaps that's what Colonel McCormack was looking for, because he gave a sharp nod. "We'll have you sign the security oaths before leaving, but I trust Bill. Any friend of his is a friend of mine."

That, at least, allowed Lillian to relax somewhat. *Listen to what he's saying, then think about how you'll respond.*

As the colonel continued, the mellow tone of his voice reminded her of a radio announcer: deep and rhythmic, relating "just the facts."

"Last week, our British colleagues at MI5 brought us some alarming information. They, like many of our troops, find crossword puzzles to be a diversion from the monotony of air raids. It was in this way that they discovered several common code words used as clues in *The Daily Telegraph* puzzles. A coincidence, they decided."

Lillian straightened. So her theory about crossword puzzles hadn't been far off after all.

"But then, a few weeks ago, more code words appeared, ones more specific and alarming—particularly as all of the words related to a . . . mission of a very sensitive nature. They fear that the puzzle compiler might have leaked information to the Nazis."

The colonel paused, watching her, as if to see that she understood, and Lillian was sure she did. He must be referring to the invasion of France. Everyone knew it was coming, although the details of when and where were cloaked in the highest secrecy.

At least, they were unless this crossword puzzle showed otherwise. Though Lillian wasn't a military strategist, it didn't take one to realize how disastrous a leak of such enormity would be, the number of generals who must be, even now, panicked at the thought of moving forward or changing plans that required months of careful coordination.

"I see," she managed. "And have they questioned the compiler?"

He nodded. "MI5 has found no obvious link, and Mr. Leonard Dawe emphatically denies any knowledge of military plans or intent to cause harm. This, as I'm sure you can understand, is less than reassuring to General Eisenhower."

"I can see why." At least if MI5 had uncovered a clear conspiracy, they would have had actionable information.

"Because of your experience with both the transmission of secret messages and creating crosswords, we had hoped you might offer your opinion on the matter."

Goodness. Lillian took in a breath. Never had she thought her humble bit of side income would have such national importance. "Am I permitted to ask for examples of the keywords used? That would help me determine the relative coincidence of choosing them by chance."

"Gold, sword, Juno, Utah, Omaha, mulberry. And . . ." He paused briefly, then continued, his voice blandly level, though the pause lent a certain significance to the word he added next. "Overlord."

Oh dear. Worse than she'd hoped. With the sheer number of code words that must be associated with a complex military maneuver, one or two overlapping words might be chance, but this many, and over a short period of time? It seemed impossible. Not to mention that two of them were American place names, which would be rarer, she supposed, to find in a British newspaper.

Lillian asked the next logical question. "And, to be clear, these were all code names? The names of actual ships, harbors, and so forth weren't present anywhere in the puzzle?"

"Correct."

That, at least, was the best-case scenario. If the crossword was intended to leak sensitive information, it seemed unlikely that code words alone would be helpful. Then again, she'd learned in the first war reoccurring words often unlocked whole encryption systems.

"May I see one of the puzzles?"

Colonel McCormack handed her a folded sheet of newsprint, dated May 22. The answers had been blocked in, with a wide circle around the clue *Red Indian on the Missouri* and the answer, *Omaha*. A scan of the rest of the clues showed the usual variety Lillian would expect—references to the arts, famous figures, and a scientific term, with a bit of wordplay thrown in.

She didn't stop there, however, shutting out the actual words and focusing only on the letters and lines. No message formed in the capitals in any given vertical line. She tapped a rhythm on the edge of the desk with her fingers, remembering.

"What are you doing, Mrs. Kendall?" Colonel McCormack asked after a moment.

"Making sure the blacked-out boxes used to separate the grid don't spell anything in Morse code," Lillian admitted, aware it might seem silly, but every angle had to be explored.

He grunted—impressed? Irritated that she hadn't yet answered his question? Lillian couldn't be sure. "It would be a highly inefficient way to convey a message," she said at last, when she was certain she couldn't find any other encrypted words. "Newspaper editors sometimes suggest changes to a puzzle at the last minute, which could jeopardize the intelligence. Not to mention the fact that it's so public—I can't imagine the Nazis are unaware that many Allied servicemen are crossword aficionados. And the structure of a puzzle allows for little context on the words used."

"Our thoughts exactly." He stroked his chin, and Lillian noted its prominent cleft. "I was an attorney before becoming a military man, Mrs. Kendall, so I'm quite aware that unsettling coincidences can and do occur. And yet . . . this many?"

That was the question of the hour, wasn't it?

To answer it, Lillian returned to two other questions: *What do you know? And what does it mean?* "Tell me more about

Mr. Dawe, in particular. Anything about how he constructs his puzzles."

"I'll give you everything MI5 related to us." The colonel glanced down at a memorandum in front of him, scanning the lines. "He's a regular contributor to the *Telegraph* puzzle section, in his fifties. Has been the headmaster at a boy's school for a number of years, relocated from London to Surrey to avoid the Blitz. He's known to be very orderly, almost a disciplinarian, but also well respected by his students." He read off the paper, "According to a member of the school's board, 'Dawe is a man of extremely high principle, and one could not imagine anyone less likely to be involved in anything incorrect.'"

Lillian nodded. Mr. Dawe sounded like the sort of man who she might have chatted convivially with at one of the Friedmans' holiday parties.

Then again, most traitors likely seem ordinary at first.

So no motive. Time to move on to opportunity and means. "Are there any Allied troops stationed in or near Surrey?"

Colonel McCormack tilted his head, and Lillian had the sense she was at least not embarrassing herself with her questions. "Yes. There are US troops stationed throughout Surrey. Dawe could conceivably have gotten the information himself, though MI5 finds it more likely that he had a contact closer to the army and was simply used to broadcast messages passed to him, as he rarely left the school grounds."

"Do we have any other reasons to suspect him of treason?"

"None whatsoever. Dawe has no foreign connections, no grudge against America or Britain, no evidence of any other suspicious behavior during the war. By all appearances, he is an upstanding citizen who seemed genuinely baffled when he was detained and questioned."

"And he's an academic and administrator," Lillian added. "He's no actor—not even a politician or businessman used to putting on a front of charm for others. That MI5 has no reason to doubt him after a thorough interrogation is suggestive of his innocence."

"That's the trouble in a nutshell. Our experts' impression of Mr. Dawe is that he's innocent, but the scant evidence says otherwise—and the stakes are higher than you can imagine. We have to know what the Germans might know, and we have very little time. . . ."

To decide whether or not to call off or reschedule the invasion.

Lillian didn't let herself dwell long on the seriousness of the chess game she'd stumbled into. Instead, she tried to form a picture of Leonard Dawe in her mind: a balding, middle-aged man sitting down at his desk with a cup of tea in some corner of his busy day to jot down clues on lined paper. School finances were tight, the boys complained about strict rationing, and this puzzle was due by the end of the week. . . .

She opened her eyes, unsure how long they'd been closed. "The boys. The boys at the school."

"Yes?"

"Tell MI5 to ask Mr. Dawe how he came up with his solutions."

Colonel McCormack frowned. "I'm not sure I see the connection."

"It's an arduous process to create a crossword," Lillian explained. "Especially when one makes a regular job of it, creating many puzzles over the course of the year. The danger is that you will repeat yourself: referencing the books you've read, the places you've visited, the adjectives you most often use, and so on."

Though she was sure he had a hundred things to do, Colonel McCormack didn't show any signs of impatience at this sudden detour into the process of creating crosswords. "And how do you combat this issue?"

"What I do, and what I suspect Mr. Dawe did, is bring in others." She thought of Margot and her endless supply of Hollywood celebrity names, or the way Roger could be counted on for biblical references. "I'll ask friends to clear their minds and say the first few words that come to mind. Those become my solutions, and I write clues to match. This way, some of the work is done for me, with a bonus of including words that wouldn't have leapt readily to my mind."

"You think Mr. Dawe asked his students to supply words for the puzzles?"

Lillian nodded, unable to suppress a smile of eagerness.

"But wouldn't that move our problem back a step? Could one of them be a spy?"

"I suppose it's possible, though not the most likely solution by far, and not just because of the boys' age. Have you noticed how boys react around men in uniform, Colonel?"

That prompted the first slight smile Lillian had seen from the legally minded military man. "Certainly, Mrs. Kendall. Most of them gawk like their toy soldiers have leapt to life and are walking around them. They can't stay away. I was just the same at their age."

She pictured the crowd of Gettysburg schoolchildren and high schoolers who swarmed around the rare sight of uniformed soldiers on leave from Camp Sharpe, treating them like movie stars, bragging about being deputy plane spotters and volunteering with scrap drives, chattering nonstop.

And, sometimes, listening.

"Often adults pay them very little attention. You said there are hundreds of soldiers stationed in the area. Isn't it possible that these boys might have heard code words used by the soldiers and officers in Surrey? And if so, that those unusual words might come to mind when their headmaster called them in to rattle off solutions for his puzzle?"

Yes. This was it, Lillian could feel it. The only way to resolve all the information they'd been given about the *Telegraph* panic—not a coincidence, but not deliberate espionage either.

"It sounds plausible," Colonel McCormack agreed, with enthusiasm that didn't seem feigned. "Dare I say likely. Like the solution to a Sherlock Holmes story."

Lillian felt certain the famous detective couldn't feel any more thrilled than she did at the moment. Hadn't Roger insisted there was a reason she'd come to Washington, DC? *Well, Roger, maybe you were right.*

Colonel McCormack scribbled furiously on the notepad at his side, perhaps something to give to his secretary to type up. "We'll relay the information to MI5 and have them question Dawe as soon as possible. If it checks out . . . perhaps we can all sleep easier at night."

"I can only hope so." *Please, let it be the right answer.*

This time, Lillian braced herself for the force of the handshake as Colonel McCormack stood to show her out. "Thank you, Mrs. Kendall. You may have given us just the insight we needed."

"I'm honored to be of use."

But instead of leading her back through the maze of offices, the colonel paused, focusing his gaze directly on her once again. "There are precious few who know the most critical details about this mission. A major general was recently demoted and sent away from the front for merely speculating about the date while tippling at a cocktail party."

Lillian forced a wry smile. "Luckily for the future of the free world, I don't drink cocktails."

He did not seem amused, towering above her slight frame, his voice rising with the dramatic tones of courtroom arguments. "We are at a precipice, Mrs. Kendall. The outcome of the war may rest on the success of this invasion as well as the lives of thousands of our men. Therefore, we require your full confidentiality on this matter."

This time, she nodded soberly. "I understand. I'll be as silent as the grave."

After all, she was used to keeping secrets.

Dinah

The envelope trembled in Dinah's hand, as if it were the yellow Western Union all women with a man in the military feared.

> *We regret to inform you, regarding your recent civil services test for clerical and verbal aptitudes, that your score was not sufficient to be eligible for hiring through our agency. For information on retaking the test, please . . .*

Dinah crumpled the letter and her hopes with it.
She had failed. Again.
You shouldn't be surprised. Despite a week of practicing the skills involved, the moment the proctor had set the exam in front of her, everything she'd learned seemed to flee away. She'd wasted so many precious minutes sorting words by alphabetic order that she'd had to circle answers to the last dozen questions at random. Not that it mattered. Those had been computation

problems, where a lucky guess would be her only chance of a correct answer anyway.

Even worse, as soon as Dinah made one error in the first line of the typing portion, her jangled nerves had been unable to recover. She'd misspelled the word *regards*, for goodness' sake. Still, she'd held out hope that others had performed similarly, faced with a time limit and the pressure of an employment agency looking over their shoulder. That, apparently, was too much to ask.

"Bad news, I see." She startled to realize that Auntie Margot, who had delivered the letter, was still standing in the doorway, dressed in dirt-stained dungarees, her pale blond hair bound in a neat, defense-worker kerchief. "Want to talk about it?"

"Only some disappointments in the job hunt." Though she'd dodged Mother's questions the only time they'd seen each other since she'd been let go, she couldn't avoid giving some explanation to her landlady for why she was lurking around the house during working hours. "Don't worry, I can still pay rent."

At least, she could pay next month's rent. Her shopping trips for new business clothing, made in anticipation of a long career in espionage, had made a dent in her savings.

"I wasn't worried." Auntie Margot turned like she was going to leave, but hesitated, tapping a finger to her cheek like something had just occurred to her. "Only, say . . . does your mother know yet?"

All of it, including her overly casual tone, smacked of bad acting. "Partially." Mother had to have realized *something* was wrong by the uncomfortable way Dinah had been acting, dodging her questions and avoiding her invitation for a lunch meeting.

"I don't know how you think she'd react," Auntie Margot went on, "but I've got a feeling you're wrong."

That proved Auntie Margot didn't understand her mother,

at least not her parenting philosophy. "I'll keep that in mind. Thanks."

A cup of coffee, reheated from breakfast. That's what Dinah needed. Maybe paired with another crack at her mother's journal. Anything to forget the letter with *not sufficient* written in perfectly typed letters. Soon, the other boarders would be back from work to distract her, complaining about their endless workload or asking her opinion on a new shade of lipstick.

Not Winora, though. She'd been oddly cold around Dinah lately, barely mumbling a hello when they passed in the halls. At first, she'd attributed it to a bad day, but the third time it happened, Dinah wondered if Winora was distancing herself from the OSS leper for fear her dismissal might be catching. Still, Dinah found the lunch hour to be an especially lonely time.

"Good evening, Miss Schnieder!" a man declared cheerfully from the entryway. Dinah paused at the top of the stairs. Had she heard that voice before?

Quietly, avoiding a creaky step, Dinah tiptoed down to the first of the staircase's landings. From there, she could see the profile of a young man wiping his feet on the welcome mat. With his head tilted down, she could only see blond hair and a strong nose and chin.

"Once again, you're early," Auntie Margot said, reverting to the strict-spinster tone Dinah had noticed her adopt when gentlemen callers were involved.

"Sure, sure, I'll wait outside. I know the drill. I'm sure Winora will be here any minute."

Ah. So this was Martin, Winora's mysterious boyfriend from Radio. That explained the recognition she'd felt. Dinah had probably passed him on the OSS steps or in the halls without even realizing it.

A sudden impulse made her want to saunter down and introduce herself, just to see the kind of fellow who'd be a match for her coworker.

Don't even think about it. It would be just her luck that Winora would walk in and accuse her of flirting with her man. Instead, Dinah crept back to her room, realizing too late and with a groan that she hadn't stopped by the kitchen for coffee.

Another time. She made herself comfortable at her desk, turning to the back of the journal. There was only one entry left in the little book, and Dinah had a hunch, based on the date, what it might contain. After all, she'd just spent three days working out a decidedly unromantic account of her mother's wedding day, nothing like how Dad told the story. He'd always described a returning solider, won over by Mother's poetic letters during his time abroad, sweeping his true love off her feet in a whirlwind romance.

Mother, on the other hand, described the ceremony like a business transaction, except for one enigmatic line.

Your father was the first one to love all of me, even the parts he did not fully understand.

Even in her most personal of revelations, it seemed, Mother still hid things from her daughter.

With notes from the Riverbank ciphers laid out in front of her, Dinah wrote out columns of letters, willing the entry before her to give up its secrets.

Lily

"The new decade brought change. A new life and a new home in Gettysburg for me, where George Fabyan could never influence me again. Recovery from war, votes for women, and jazz mania for the nation. Sometimes, our lives change dramatically, as in my escape from Riverbank. Other times, they change with a realization, quiet and slow."

— Excerpt from Lillian Kendall's journal

TUESDAY, JANUARY 9, 1923

Home. I have to get home.

Lily stumbled off the curb on her way to the train station, pushing down a sudden churning of nausea. No need to draw attention to herself in public.

Her sickness was natural. She knew that now. Not a disease nor the start of a nervous breakdown. That was something to be grateful for. After all, the news she'd received this morning was good . . . wasn't it?

Lily had waited over a month after she'd begun to suspect before making an appointment in Harrisburg, discreetly, taking the train and giving Roger another reason for the errand. There was no cause to disappoint him if she was wrong.

But the doctor had confirmed what she already knew in her heart to be true: Lily was pregnant.

She'd blinked against the harsh, new electric lights of the examining room. "But I was . . ." Even now, she was unable to force herself to say the word *sterilized*, not only because of propriety, but because of the memories it recalled. "I was told I wouldn't be able to bear children."

"It seems you were misinformed," the doctor said, his voice cold and clinical, as if he were pronouncing a death sentence instead of good news. "I can see no medical reason you should not be able to bring this baby to term."

No medical reason.

The words rattled about in Lily's mind like marbles in a jar all the ride home and kept rattling as she paced the hall of the brick colonial she and Roger had made their home.

What had really happened when Mama had been admitted to the hospital all those years ago?

Whether the doctors had felt it indelicate to explain to a fourteen-year-old or they simply couldn't spare the time, she had never known exactly what the sterilization surgery entailed. The nurse had explained Lily's monthly courses would continue to come as usual and that recovery time would be relatively short, speaking slowly as if she might not be capable of understanding even that. Had something gone wrong with the procedure, a simple medical error?

No. That couldn't be. There would be some sign, surely, for the doctor to see, physical damage or scarring. Lily had always thought it strange that, after her head stopped throbbing from the anesthesia, she hadn't felt any other pain.

Lily closed her eyes, forcing herself to travel back to the Illinois hospital that had admitted her mother during one of her raving periods. She remembered the operating doctor only in vague terms, an older man in a white coat, but she could picture the deep frown on his face as she had wept, fearful that if she went to sleep for the surgery, she would never wake up. She'd assumed he had been angry at her hysterics.

Now Lily imagined the scene differently. What if the doctor had taken pity on the mere girl brought before him against her will? Perhaps he rejected the popular ideology that society should decide who was fit to reproduce and hadn't gone through with the operation, his own act of private rebellion.

There was no way to be sure, nearly a decade later, yet the scene *felt* true. And as evidence, there was the simple, shocking reality that Lily was pregnant.

If that is what happened, the doctor should have told me. I needed to know. Roger *needed to know.*

"What do I need to know?" Roger's voice asked, calling her back to her present world, full of floral curtains, fresh eggs from local farmers, and books read together on Sunday nights by the fire.

She'd clearly spoken out loud. Mutterings sometimes escaped her when she had a desperate need to process her thoughts. It was still difficult, even after nearly four years of marriage, getting used to the fact that few spaces were completely private.

When she turned, doing her best to mask her concern, Roger had removed his coat, newspaper in hand. "Don't tell me. You've got some new business scheme."

That, at least, allowed Lily to put a hand on her hip and fire back, "If I did, you ought to thank me for it in advance."

The retort brought out the dimples to Roger's cheeks. "Granted. It's a marvel what you've done to the old shop, Lily. Even Dad agrees, and he once told me an adding machine was 'an unnecessary frippery.'"

That explained a great deal. "Thank you, dear."

Lily had worked for a year on a bookkeeping correspondence course, completing exercises with ledgers, invoices, and fake money sent to her via the post. The certificate she'd earned was less valuable than the knowledge to clean up the financial muddle of the Kendall and Son Locksmith Shop. While Roger and his father both had excellent reputations for their work, neither could keep an accurate accounts book.

Now that the subject had been effectively changed, Lily knew she could direct the conversation to business matters if she chose. But such diversions of Roger's attention would only last for so long. It had been over two months since her last cycle. And besides, she thought, glancing at her husband, who was reaching to turn on their brand-new Silvertone radio, she wanted to tell him, if only because his reaction would remind her that this was a joyful day.

If she believed what the minister at Roger's church said on Sunday, then Providence had decreed that, against all odds, she would be a mother. That meant that good must come of this.

Yes. She *would* believe that.

She took Roger's hand, tugging it from the radio's dial. "I have something very important to tell you."

Lily leaned against the kitchen wall to catch her breath, glaring at the stubbornly un-scrubbed bit of floor in the corner. *Just leave it be.*

Over the past six months, she had expanded to a size that, with each glance in the mirror, seemed enormous and left her unsure that she'd be able to stand if she knelt to the ground. Roger would have a fit if he knew she was still cleaning only a few weeks before their baby's birth.

"Why on earth," she muttered, taking off her apron and rubbing her sore muscles, "do some women seem to enjoy being pregnant?" Elizebeth, who had given birth to a little girl just a few months before, made it look easy, somehow remaining stylish despite the tent-like dresses for expectant mothers.

For Lily, carrying a child had been nothing but misery. The nausea her mother-in-law had insisted would disappear by the fourth month had only worsened and was joined by throbbing backaches and difficulty sleeping as the pregnancy progressed. No one, not even Elizebeth and Margot, now living in nearby Washington, DC, could look at her baggy eyes and swollen feet and say she "glowed."

This was far from the gentle, feminine experience she'd been told to expect. Perhaps Mama had similar difficulties while carrying Lily and that was the reason she had always seemed to resent Lily as a child. Or maybe it was simply that Lily was an obstacle to the freedom she craved, another mouth to feed, a burden her troubled mind wasn't willing or able to carry properly.

But I won't be that way. No matter what hardships the baby had caused her, this "miracle," as Roger called it, had given her a chance to prove herself worthy of the title of mother.

With the kitchen gleaming and her in-laws insisting they dine at their house, to "spare you the work," Lily retreated to the nursery, where her narrow writing desk still occupied one wall to show what the room had once been intended for. Underneath the locksmith's ledger was the family Bible, and she opened it to the first page, where Roger had tucked the paper where they'd listed ideas for the baby's name. Several of each gender were struck out, but they hadn't yet agreed on one from those that remained.

"Would you . . . want to add Clara?" Roger had asked tentatively in one of their early conversations. *"To honor your mother?"*

Lily had closed her eyes. Roger was the reason Mama's name was included in the family Bible, even without the respectability of a husband's name beside it. Clara Nilsson, 1869–1914. A simple notation, but oh, how many memories and regrets and fears were contained in the thin line between those numbers.

Without any money for a proper burial after her death, the hospital had taken Clara Nilsson's body to be interred in an unmarked grave on a state plot for occupants of a local poorhouse. Lily hadn't yet been back to visit, though Roger had asked, and she thought she might never. Now, Lily couldn't help but fear that if she passed on the name, it might carry Mama's mental struggles with it, like an infectious disease transmitted by contact with the very letters in her mother's name.

"No," she had said, smiling tightly. "*I don't think it would suit our child.*"

Enough of this. Her mother-in-law's advice that thinking only of pleasant topics during pregnancy would lead to a contented, happy baby was likely an old wives' tale, but it couldn't hurt to take precautions. Lily shut the Bible, pushing it aside, and took up her ciphers instead.

She'd brought out the journal Roger had given her before going off to war. Every week, she added more of the story of her time at Riverbank, each entry hidden behind a cipher, starting with the simplest and progressing in difficulty.

As she experimented with a Playfair cipher on the back of a used envelope, Lily felt a sharp drumbeat kick to her ribs. "Patience, now, little one," she said in mock warning, rubbing her growing belly. "We've got to get along, you and I."

Sometimes, Lily tried to picture what their child might be like, whether he or she would have Roger's smile and genial disposition or Lily's blue eyes and sharp mind. Perhaps both.

But her fondest daydreams were reserved for what they might do together. Someday, this baby, born into a world after "the war to end all wars," would be old enough to learn about ciphers and puzzles, and they'd go through the journal together, learning skills and sharing memories.

And Lily would be a good mother. Whatever came next, she would take her responsibility seriously.

But what if you fail? That whisper of doubt was getting louder now as the due date approached, keeping Lily up at night more often than the pain of cramping legs or an overly active child.

Lily shut the journal and held it tightly to her chest. *I will not fail. Not at this. I will not be like my mother.*

33

Lillian

TUESDAY, MAY 30, 1944

Lillian shook her head at the ridiculous taxidermized monkey inside Myrtlewood's front entrance. George, Margot had called him. After George Fabyan, Lillian presumed, though his death in the thirties meant he wasn't around to take offense at the jab.

A fitting tribute, in a way, she mused as she wiped off her boots. In the end, all his threats hadn't been able to stop his codebreakers from drifting away from Riverbank, one by one. Even William had plucked up his courage and resigned after another year, easily securing a position with the army, while Elizebeth worked for the coast guard. Like the monkey on the wall, Mr. Fabyan was terrifying but ultimately harmless. Perhaps that's why Margot had chosen the name.

Lillian listened for signs of her friend, who unsurprisingly hadn't answered her knock, even though she'd known when Lillian planned to arrive. No clatter of construction or renovation betrayed Margot's whereabouts, though in the parlor, someone was plunking a simple melody on the piano. "Beautiful Dreamer," an old Stephen Foster song, one she'd sung as a lullaby to Dinah.

But it couldn't be her daughter playing. It was only a quarter till three. Dinah would still be behind her desk at Morale Operations.

Still, Lillian couldn't help peering into the parlor. Sure enough, Dinah sat at the piano, clearly putting in great effort to recall the position of the notes.

As the song continued, memories returned. Mama had possessed a lovely singing voice, though she rarely used it in those later years, a tremulous soprano that made every song sound like the closing aria of an opera—always a tragedy.

"Beautiful Dreamer, wake unto me / Starlight and dewdrops are waiting for thee."

Lillian could almost feel the blanket pulled up to her chin as Mama, smelling of roses and face powder, leaned over and kissed her forehead. It was one of her most peaceful memories of childhood.

"Sounds of the rude world heard in the day / Lull'd by the moonlight have all passed away."

Dinah remembers too. Whatever resentments or differences might have come up between them, her daughter recalled the tune of the song that Lillian sang each night, tucking her to sleep.

When had she stopped?

Probably after Dinah and Roger had come back from their tour of Civil War battlefields. They'd been gone for so long that she'd gotten out of the habit. Or maybe it was that Dinah had returned tanned and taller and looking so unlike a little girl that their nightly ritual hadn't felt right anymore.

At the piano, Dinah stopped and cocked her head, then swiveled on the bench to face the arched doorway.

Lillian stilled, as if she'd been caught in some crime. *Nonsense.* This was a public space. "I—it's been years since I heard that song."

Dinah clattered the fallboard over the keys so abruptly that Lillian was surprised she didn't smash her fingers. "I practiced this one the most. Apparently some of my lessons stuck with me."

Without the music, the silence felt unbearable. "You're home early from work," Lillian observed, to help the conversation along. "I came to say good-bye to Margot, and then you, though I expected you later. My train leaves tomorrow."

"Oh." Dinah shifted, her eyes on the floor. "I'd forgotten."

Something was clearly wrong, and Lillian had the distinct feeling she was missing the obvious answer, like the last incomplete word in a crossword with half of its letters already filled in.

Just then, Margot's heels clicked down the hall. She breezed into the parlor with a voluminous length of floral fabric draped over her arms. "Lily, darling, you've just got to see these new drapes I got for a song!" When she noticed Dinah perched stiffly on the piano bench, she stopped short. "Oh! I see the two of you found each other. I'll . . . just leave you to it."

"You don't have to—" Dinah blurted, hand stretched toward Margot like she was a life raft in the stormy waters of the Pacific.

"Please, feel free to stay, Margot," Lillian said at the same time, finishing her daughter's thought.

"No, I don't think I will," Margot said breezily, but as she passed through the doorway, she cast an uncharacteristically concerned look Lillian's way. "So glad the two of you have a chance to . . . chat."

The distraction, at least, had given Lillian time to assess the situation. Other than her pallid complexion upon spotting Lillian, Dinah seemed perfectly healthy. From Dinah's reports of Mr. Agnew, it seemed unlikely he would allow her home this early. Either she was playing hooky from work, or . . .

Lillian thought back to the odd way Dinah had dodged her questions at dinner the week before. "You're not working for the OSS anymore, are you?"

Dinah stood, crossing her arms over her chest as if there were a sudden chill in the room. "Well, you were bound to find out sooner or later. Yes, I was fired last week."

The bitterness in her daughter's voice made Lillian flinch, even though she knew it wasn't directed entirely at her. "But why? Things were going so well."

"That's what I thought too. But I made a mistake that cost me my job." Dinah lifted her chin in challenge. "Go on. I can take it."

"Take what?" Lillian asked blankly, hating how vacuous she sounded.

"The lecture. I'll even nod and look remorseful at all the right times."

What had come over her daughter, to talk back like this? "I don't . . . all I want to know is . . . why didn't you tell me?"

At first Dinah didn't answer, scowling like it was a trick question. But when Lillian allowed the silence to linger, she sighed. "For one thing, I was hoping to tell you after I'd found a new job. That way you and Dad wouldn't throw a fit and insist I come back to Gettysburg."

Throw a fit? As if she and Roger were children prone to tantrums.

And yet . . . perhaps Lillian was being too harsh on Dinah. This must have been quite a disappointment. Lillian took a steadying breath and tried to soften her tone. "I'm glad you're not giving up on government work altogether. It's normal to encounter setbacks early on in one's career. I wouldn't take this to heart."

That prompted a noise somewhere between a laugh and a snort. "Of course *you* wouldn't. You don't understand what it's like to finally find something you were good at, only to have it taken away."

Lillian probably ought to have said something sympathetic, but the dismissive way Dinah said it, as if her mother had never in her life done something of value, made Lillian blurt out in a sharp tone, "Yes. Yes, I do."

Dinah shook her head. "That's not the same. You had a choice when you left co—" Dinah trailed off suddenly, glancing back toward the piano.

Codebreaking. She'd been about to say codebreaking, Lillian was sure. "How did you find out?" Though the answer seemed obvious: Margot must have told her.

Dinah walked back to the piano, taking down a slender book from the rack, where sheet music ought to be. A book Lillian had thought she'd never see again. It might have been a tome from the doomed Library of Alexandria the way she couldn't take her eyes off it. "My old journal. How . . . ?"

Dinah came closer, holding the journal out. There was no doubt it was the same volume. "I solved all of them on my own."

There was a note of pride in her daughter's voice, but Lillian was still struggling to accept the first, more simple reality of the journal's existence.

She closed her eyes and remembered. Waiting at the Gettysburg station to see the two faces she loved so much come toward her, sun-kissed and grinning. Listening to their boisterous, overlapping greetings. Realizing how much she'd missed them . . . but scolding Roger for the evidence of a chocolate indulgence smeared around Dinah's mouth.

On the way back home, both had chattered away about the grand times they'd had touring Civil War battlefields and fishing and staying up far too late. Even then, she'd felt a twinge of jealousy that she hadn't been there with them.

"I don't suppose you had any time to work on the journal, then?" Lillian had tried to say it casually.

Little Dinah had only seemed confused. *"What journal?"*

"The one I gave you for your birthday."

"Oh, that." Spoken like it was no more than a movie stub,

saved only by the most sentimental for scrapbooks. *"I must've left it out by the creek near Fredericksburg. We never could find it."*

Lillian had pictured the careful ciphers, her secret story she'd poured out during sleepless nights, bleeding down the page in blurred ink.

"Sorry, Mother. I hope it was nothing too important."

"No," Lillian had said, unable to manage even a strained smile. *"I suppose it wasn't."*

Even now, the disappointment pricked her heart afresh, like someone picking off a crusted scab and finding that blood could still well up.

"How did you . . . ?" she began, then started over. "I thought you lost this years ago."

"No," was all Dinah offered in response.

Perhaps it had simply been misplaced, somehow. It had been so long since Lillian had written the journal entries—at age twenty-three, she'd been another person entirely, nearly—that she struggled to remember what, exactly, she'd disclosed. "And . . . you read the entire thing?"

"I just finished the last entry." Dinah handed Lillian the journal, papers poking out from it in Dinah's illegible scribbling. "Don't look so shocked."

Lillian closed her mouth, which had indeed gone somewhat slack, but from the absurdity of the situation, not disbelief in her daughter's ability. "I'd intended for us to work through the ciphers together."

"You never said so. I figured that since I couldn't read them, I'd failed some sort of summer vacation homework." She shrugged, but Lillian could see the hurt in her daughter's eyes. "That's why I . . . well, I never lost the journal. That was a lie. I just wished I had."

Why not just admit you couldn't solve the puzzles? Lillian wanted to ask.

Then again, Dinah had only been twelve years old at the time. Only a girl.

Only a girl who felt her mother disapproved of her.

Much like Lillian had been once.

Before Lillian could process this realization, Dinah went on, "The point is, I know the whole story now, all the things you never told me about Riverbank. Speaking of keeping secrets."

"That's not remotely similar, and you know it." After all, Dinah had been so busy with her own life that she'd never bothered to ask about her mother's.

But that wasn't true, not really. Lillian had simply wanted to bury her past, to start afresh with Roger and her miracle child. Learning the journal was lost was as much a relief as it had been a tragedy, because it gave her an excuse not to go back to those times in her own memory.

Still, silence was different from direct deception . . . wasn't it?

With effort, Lillian looked away from her journal and directed her attention back to Dinah's face, fixed in that sulky glower so familiar these days. "But we're wandering from the topic at hand. Purposely, I think." Dinah didn't deny it. "Did you expect me to be angry that you lost your job?"

"Maybe."

This, at least, was a place where Lillian might be able to help the situation by staying calm. Goodness knew it was her only parenting skill. "Well, I am not, though I wish you'd felt free to tell me. If anything, I'm disappointed in the OSS. You have skills that would be valuable to any organization. It sounds as though you don't even know why you were let go—"

Dinah, who had been making a thorough study of the carpet as Lillian spoke, jerked her head up. "Like I said, I broke a secrecy protocol. Not intentionally, of course, but a rule's a rule. They'll probably find someone much more qualified to replace me."

This didn't disturb Lillian in the slightest. "That's what you were told. But the OSS is a bureaucracy, and I was part of one for long enough to see its tangled network of politics, nepotism, and budget cuts. There could be a dozen reasons to get rid of a talented young woman."

"Mother, you weren't there," Dinah said flatly. "Mr. Agnew cited policies, documents that I'd signed and hadn't obeyed."

Lillian paused. Perhaps there was some truth to that. But at the moment, with tensions in Europe so high and newspapers predicting a domino chain of events that might end the war, the OSS needed all the help they could muster. "I'm sure we'll be able to clear up the misunderstanding. Perhaps if your father or I give them a call . . ."

This time, when Dinah's gaze snapped back to hers, the old fire was back in her eyes. "No, Mother." She stepped closer, her words coming fast and loud. "You have to face facts. There was no mistake. Maybe the truth is that your daughter is a failure. That she can't follow the rules or keep a job longer than a few weeks."

Lillian took a step back, clutching the journal to her chest, like someone trying to block a blow. "I didn't—"

But the words her daughter spoke next cut deeper. "I know you've always wanted me to be more like you, so you could be the perfect mother with the perfect daughter. You very nearly said so in the last journal entry. Well, I'm not. I can't be."

"That's not fair." Despite her best efforts, Lillian felt a flare of anger at the way Dinah had turned this against her once again. Whatever she'd read, she'd surely taken it out of context. "You're the one who hid the truth from me, when I would have only wanted to help."

"I don't *want* your help." Dinah's voice had risen loudly enough that Lillian was afraid Margot might overhear. "The longer you've stayed, the more I've felt you looking over my shoulder in disapproval. I need to do this for myself."

There was no time to think. Only barely enough for Lillian to say, in her most composed voice, "What are you saying, dear?"

Dinah leveled a hard stare in her direction. "Go home, Mother. Please. I don't need you anymore."

34

Dinah

WEDNESDAY, MAY 31, 1944

"Could you pass the syrup?" Dinah had to address this question to Winora's shoulder, since she had angled her chair in the opposite direction. Still, there was no way Dinah was going to gag down plain oatmeal.

No response. "The syrup, please," Dinah said, louder this time, enough to attract the attention of some of the other boarders.

With a grunt, Winora picked up the jar and deposited it slowly in front of Dinah's plate, like her joints had become as sticky as the handle.

"Thank you." *I suppose.*

Across the table, Shirley gave her a sympathetic "Can you believe her?" glance.

Dinah decided she'd give talking to Winora one last try on the safest topic imaginable. "Awful, isn't it, all the rain we've been getting?"

But before Dinah had finished her question, Winora pulled out her chair with a loud scrape and stalked out of the dining room.

"All right, then," Dinah muttered, staring after her.

Shirley leaned closer, elbow on the table. "Don't pay her any mind. She's been in a bad mood since she broke up with her boyfriend."

Anne-Marie rolled her eyes. "I'll bet anything *he* broke up with *her*." This declaration was delivered in a low tone with a wary glance at Auntie Margot at the head of the table. Apparently she'd learned some caution from their last encounter.

"Oh." Dinah prodded her oatmeal with her spoon, suddenly less hungry. Maybe Winora's stormy demeanor lately hadn't been personal at all. She couldn't help but wonder which of the two had ended things—and how. Not that Winora was likely to tell her. They weren't exactly confidantes these days.

That's all right. Dinah had quite enough to do today to keep her mind off her former coworker. She'd scoured the want ads in the newspaper and found several to apply for. Not government work, but certainly a switchboard operator or a stenographer would pay well.

But what will I do for references? She could hardly ask Mr. Agnew, not after the way they'd parted, and her only other employer had been Dad. Maybe Colonel Forth from the Catoctin Mountain training base would put in a good word for her, especially if he hadn't heard the details about her dismissal.

This latest hurdle distracted her so much that she almost ran into Auntie Margot before stopping short in the hallway, nearly causing her to drop a stack of magazines. "I'm so sorry."

"I could say the same," Auntie Margot said, grinning sheepishly. "You see, I almost forgot. A letter came for you two days ago." She plunged her free hand into the rickrack-lined pockets of her day dress, retrieving a packet of spearmint chewing gum

300

and a small screwdriver before producing an envelope. "I meant to give it to you right away, but you know how things are."

Dinah took it, expecting to see her father's handwriting. He'd written her updates every couple of weeks since her arrival, each styled as a mock newspaper with *Breaking News from Gettysburg* at the top.

Instead, the script read *Miss Dinah Kendall* in an unfamiliar cursive.

Dinah hurried to her room to open it in privacy, torn between fear and hope. Perhaps the employment agency had reconsidered, or a position had opened up that didn't require a high score on the civil services exam.

But when she saw the name and address written neatly in the upper righthand corner of the stationery, her eyebrows shot up. Both belonged to Mr. Frasier Agnew.

Dear Miss Kendall,

I'm sure you are surprised to hear from me. However, in the time since your employment with the OSS has ended, I have had certain misgivings about the circumstances surrounding my decision.

My wife, Hazel, and I would be pleased if you would join us for dinner this Wednesday at 6:00 p.m., or, if you are unavailable, another date at your earliest convenience. Perhaps that will afford us a chance to discuss this "off the record," as they said during my journalism days. Also, Hazel is eager to meet you.

I understand if such a meeting seems confusing or unappealing, but I assure you that I only want the truth. I hope I can rely upon your desire for the same. Please let me know if you are able and willing to attend.

Sincerely,
Frasier Agnew

"Lincoln's beard, if that isn't the strangest . . ." she murmured, rereading the message again to make sure she hadn't missed anything. It sounded as if there was more to her firing than had originally met the eye . . . just like Mother had suggested.

She let the letter fall onto her mattress, frowning. Now that her head had cooled somewhat, Dinah was already feeling guilty for the way she'd lost her temper with Mother. It would just figure that, on top of that, Mother would be right after all, at least in part.

Dinah checked the date again. The invitation was for this evening. Not much time to think things over. Still, she couldn't deny being wildly curious, and the mention of Mrs. Agnew's attendance made the whole thing sound on the level.

Well, there's only one way to find out.

As she stepped out of the taxi, Dinah let out a low whistle. Nothing said "old money" like a three-story brick row house in the Georgetown neighborhood. Mr. Agnew, a former newshound who rotated the same five ties, one for each day of the week, hadn't seemed the type. Then again, there was a reason people jibed about the OSS being a wartime country club.

She let the ornate gold knocker fall with several firm raps and waited, glancing toward the bay windows above perfectly trimmed shrubbery. Mrs. Agnew had sent a brief but warm telegram in response to her acceptance this morning, so she knew they would be expecting her.

She was just about to try again when Mr. Agnew opened the door, without his suitcoat, his sleeves rolled to his elbows. His features froze in place. "Miss Kendall?"

Oh dear. Had she smeared her lipstick? Maybe she shouldn't have worn any. Dinah resisted the urge to pull her compact from her handbag and check, instead giving him her sunniest smile. "Good evening. Am I too early?"

Her former boss simply stood in the doorway, blinking dumbly, even though it was a cloudy evening. "What are you doing here?"

"You invited me?" She had meant to say it confidently—perhaps it was some sort of test?—but the sheer bewilderment on Mr. Agnew's face made it emerge with a question mark.

"I assure you, I did no such thing."

For a moment, Dinah felt her own sanity pitted against Mr. Agnew's blank-faced denial. Even her lively imagination couldn't have fabricated an entire letter.

"No," a voice behind him said, "but I did."

Mr. Agnew stood aside to reveal a woman dressed for dinner, pearls and all, pushing herself forward in a cane-backed wheelchair. Her graying hair had been swept up in an immaculate style, a chiffon neck scarf knotted above her dove-colored suit like a Sears ad for "mature lady" fashions. But the deep smile lines around her eyes gave her the look of a girl twinkling with mischief. "Aren't you going to invite our guest in, Frasier?"

"It seems you already have," Mr. Agnew said, voice tight as a bowstring.

Dinah knew she ought to make her excuses and leave . . . but on the other hand, Mrs. Agnew beckoned her inside. "How do you do, Mrs. Agnew." She directed her greeting exclusively at her hostess, bending toward her slightly.

"I'm so pleased to meet you, dear," she said, clasping her hand. "And you can call me Hazel."

Behind her, Mr. Agnew shut the door with a firmness that suggested he was doing so more to prevent the neighbors from eavesdropping than accepting her presence. "Will someone please tell me what is going on?"

Mrs. Agnew wheeled herself deeper into the house with ease.

"That is a conversation for dinner, Frasier, surely. You'll need to add another place setting to the table."

The Agnews, Hazel explained, ushering her into a spacious dining room, kept a cook as well as a housekeeper, since "I'm not as able to get around these days, and Frasier really could scorch water."

They made small talk for a while, both of them deploying the usual niceties like this was a regular social call instead of . . . whatever it was turning out to be. Then Mr. Agnew transferred his wife into a sturdy Queen Anne armchair at the head of the table. What he whispered to Hazel as he leaned in closely to her, she couldn't guess, but she noted the care with which he performed the nightly ritual.

Dinner was already laid out, steaming, before them, and Dinah waited for Mr. Agnew to choose the seat on Hazel's right before taking the chair opposite him, directly beneath an elaborate chandelier.

Mr. Agnew gave a rather stiff blessing over their meal, including a pointed aside about the Christian obligation toward guests, however unexpected.

"God does have a sense of humor, you know, dear," Hazel said when he'd finished, taking a delicate sip of split pea soup. "Consider the platypus."

Mr. Agnew scoffed, looking at Dinah like she was a hobo who had knocked at his back door for scraps. "I'm supposed to find this funny?"

"Oh, eventually." Hazel directed her attention to Dinah. "Now. Dinah. I suppose the proper thing would be to let you eat your dinner in peace before explaining."

"No need to hold off on my account," Dinah said innocently, sipping her soup. *Delicious.* She clinked her spoon against the bowl again, holding it up to cool. "I'm fully capable of listening and eating at the same time."

Gradually, due to Hazel's obvious delight in her scheme,

Dinah's feeling of awkwardness had faded. It was, by now, *fun* to see dignified Mr. Agnew at a loss.

"Very well," Hazel said. "I know this is quite unusual, but so were the circumstances around your dismissal. Frasier told me about it—he never keeps anything from me unless it's a government secret—and it didn't sit well with either of us."

"I never said any such thing," Mr. Agnew insisted.

"No, but you kept mulling it over and scowling. Since you didn't seem interested in pursuing the matter further, I thought it best to—what do they say in journalism, dear?—hear it straight from the horse's mouth." She smiled at Dinah.

This, apparently, was her cue to speak. "As the resident horse, I don't know what I can tell you. I was careless and didn't think about the consequences of my actions. As far as I'm aware, that's all there is to it."

Though she tried to say it nonchalantly, Dinah could feel prickles of heat rushing to her cheeks. She shoveled in more soup, thick and creamy, to cover for it. Would it be rude to tear off a piece of bread to sop up a portion? Probably.

In the pause, Mrs. Agnew angled a significant look at her husband. "Well?"

"She could be lying."

"For heaven's sake, Frasier. You've made your career exposing corruption. Tell me frankly: Do you see any indications that this girl has any idea of the conspiracy she's been accused of?"

Conspiracy?

"No," he admitted. "But I might be wrong."

"It's good to hear you admit *that*, at least." She gestured to a platter of oysters, which Mr. Agnew passed to her. Dinah took only an ornamental serving. To her, eating shellfish felt like forcing down briny gelatin.

No one spoke for a few moments, the clink of silverware the only sounds. When Dinah couldn't bear the tension any longer, she spoke. "All right, let's have it. Apparently there's something I don't know. Why was I really fired, Mr. Agnew?"

She had caught him mid-bite, though he didn't tip the raw oyster into his mouth, instead cutting a prim bite with a knife and fork. "For one thing, because I didn't feel I ought to report you to the FBI for treason."

If Dinah had had anything in her mouth, it would have been spewed quite ungracefully across the table. "Excuse me?"

"You're starting in the middle, dear," Hazel pointed out.

With another heavy sigh, Mr. Agnew set down his oyster fork. "The day before your dismissal, Miss Kendall, I received a letter at my office from a concerned citizen who listed numerous reasons you were a danger to the OSS."

Dinah sat back in her chair, taking this in. "I . . . I was anonymously denounced? Is this Washington, DC, or Nazi-occupied France?" She didn't wait for him to answer that. "Was any of it credible?"

"It didn't appear so at first," Mr. Agnew replied. "But your confirmation of some of the letter's contents certainly gave me pause."

"You have a copy of the letter here, I suppose?"

Mr. Agnew jerked with a cough, but if he'd momentarily choked on his oyster, he recovered quickly. "I do. How did you know?"

"'Everything in triplicate' seems to be the OSS's motto." Truthfully, it was a guess, but if he had spoken about it in detail with his wife, the odds that he'd brought it home to show her seemed high. "Can I at least have a chance to see it and respond?"

This seemed to trigger an attack of conscience for her boss, which Hazel broke with a gentle, "Go on, Frasier. It can't do any harm now."

"No, I suppose it can't."

While Mr. Agnew stood to retrieve the letter, Dinah enjoyed

a heaping helping of summer squash hash, courtesy of a local Victory garden Mrs. Agnew and a friend tended together. Might as well enjoy what she could. Dinah had a feeling whatever she was about to read might make her lose her appetite.

Only a few minutes passed before Mr. Agnew returned, setting a typewritten letter beside her plate like a second napkin. Dinah picked it up and began to read.

To Whom It May Concern,

I write with the grave news that one of your employees, Miss Dinah Kendall, is untrustworthy and should be removed from employment immediately.

The very fact that I know to whom to address this letter is the first reason for concern. Miss Kendall speaks often of her employment with the OSS, bragging about the work she does to receive attention from her friends and especially young men. I have seen her bring documents from work to her personal residence on numerous occasions, some of which were stamped SECRET. What she does with that information, or who else might see it, is anyone's guess.

Beyond this, I have personally witnessed her engaging in questionable activities, such as bringing a camera to areas around the Navy Yard and taking surreptitious photographs; making jokes about stealing our nation's most treasured documents evacuated from the Library of Congress; and reading a book on cryptography, possibly with the intent of sending information in code.

For these reasons, I suggest the OSS look into Miss Kendall's record, restrict her access to sensitive information, and scrutinize all of her past contributions.

I trust that the OSS will refrain from revealing the source of this information to Miss Kendall. Should she face consequences for her actions, whether they were

*malicious or merely careless, I fear she might find me
and enact revenge.*

*We are often reminded that it is the duty of every
American to preserve our freedoms. I believe Dinah Kendall is a threat to the goals of your organization and the
safety of our nation. For this reason, I remain,*

A Concerned Citizen

Stunned, Dinah held the letter between two fingers, looking
back and forth between her hosts. "Well, the writer didn't spare
any melodrama," she finally managed.

Mr. Agnew nodded, clearly watching her reactions closely.
"Granted."

"Not that you have to believe me, but I might as well set
the record straight." Dinah scanned the letter again to make
sure she hadn't missed anything. "First, I haven't told anyone
outside of my immediate family—and the Friedmans, which
you authorized me to do—that I'm even working for the OSS,
much less bragged about the nature of my work. Second, I don't
own a camera and haven't taken any pictures here in DC. And
finally, yes, I took some booklets on ciphers from Mr. Longstreet's office, but only because his repeated harassment made
it impossible to simply ask for them."

"And the Library of Congress joke?" Hazel asked.

At first, that had puzzled Dinah too, until she'd remembered
the screwball romantic comedy she'd outlined to Winora involv-
ing the theft of the Constitution. "That one is true too. It was
amusing in context, I promise."

And, it hadn't escaped Dinah, it was a detail only Winora
would know. But . . . something bothered her about that theory.
The letter didn't *sound* like Winora, for one thing.

She's smarter than you give her credit for. She might come
across as Boston-accented tough, but there was a reason the

OSS had hired her. And anyway, wouldn't this explain why Winora had been avoiding Dinah?

But she'd think about that later. What mattered now was persuading Mr. Agnew, who was scratching at the slight stubble on his chin, looking at least a decade older than he did behind his commanding desk. "As you know, I already admitted to taking home the files, but I promise, I had only the best of intentions."

"So you said." He held up a hand, as if to silence the protests he knew Dinah might raise. "Even in journalism, we must take anonymous tips seriously, though we investigate them carefully. In this case, however, there was little objective information I could confirm."

"And didn't that raise your suspicions?"

He acknowledged her objection with a nod. "Again, at first. Then I considered the fact that Olivia Masterson called you 'naturally gifted' at spinning false stories. And when you confessed to some of the infractions . . . well, I began to wonder: What if they were all true? Given what I did know for certain, I felt I had no choice but to fire you."

It all sounded very reasonable and by-the-book, but there was one thing that still bothered Dinah. "And yet, shouldn't you have contacted the FBI if there was doubt about my loyalty? Especially with the incident in the Records Room and the tampered files?"

"You are correct. I did not file a report, not even internally."

Dinah studied him. He had spoken the words almost philosophically, as if they were discussing a distant political question rather than her actual life. Once again, she felt trapped into asking the obvious question, "Why not?"

When the pause stretched too long, Hazel cleared her throat. Mr. Agnew looked pained, as if this conversation was taking a physical toll on him. "Because," he said at last, "when it came down to it, I couldn't truly believe you were a spy. Still, I felt I had to take some action out of an abundance of caution—

and the rules you admitted to breaking were certainly enough to warrant your firing. At the time, it felt like an appropriate compromise."

It was difficult to hear, but Dinah had to admit that it made a certain sense.

At the head of the table, Hazel pushed aside her plate, still half full, with a clatter. "Frasier, the young lady deserves an honest answer."

"That *was* honest," he protested.

"Perhaps. But it wasn't complete."

"I suppose not." This time, Dinah noticed, Mr. Agnew didn't look directly at her, but rather at the china cabinet behind her. "As I told my wife, Miss Kendall, I chose to fire you in part *because* I felt so strongly that you were innocent. As someone who prides himself on rationality, I am suspicious of feelings, especially my own. There are few people I genuinely like."

"*Very* few people," Hazel added, eyes twinkling once again. "You should hear his commentary on my guest list after a dinner party."

Ignoring his wife, Mr. Agnew pressed on. "But even though we had nothing in common, I liked you. Saw potential in you, after only knowing you for a few short weeks. That bothered me. I worried . . . that if there was something terrible you might be capable of, I'd simply overlooked it like a sentimental old fool."

"There isn't," Dinah said, though the reassurance sounded hollow, even desperate given the circumstances. She'd never thought about her natural charm as a curse before. How many people secretly thought her natural warmth was insincere? Winora, probably. "I'm not a spy, Mr. Agnew. I promise."

Mr. Agnew shrugged. "Since nothing could be proven one way or another . . . I chose the easiest path. I am prone to do this at times and usually regret it." This was spoken with a tender look at his wife, full of history that Dinah could only guess at.

After a moment, Mr. Agnew cleared his throat, all business once again. "In any case, I should have at least given you the chance of a fair investigation."

"You have now. Or at least, your wife has." Dinah still felt herself reeling, like she'd just stepped off a midway ride at the York State Fair. "The question is . . . how can I untangle what happened here? Where do I start?"

"Where indeed?" Hazel echoed, turning to Mr. Agnew as well.

Mr. Agnew only shook his head. "I understand the desire to find out where this slander originated. I would likely do the same. But I would caution you: In order to be rehired with the OSS, all of this would need to be brought to light, including the actual infractions you committed. I doubt the outcome would be positive."

"I'm sure you're right." The judgment still stung, but Dinah understood it. "Still, I need to know."

"I had hoped," Hazel ventured, "that it would be quite clear to you, at least, what was happening and who was responsible."

If only it were that easy. "There's really only one person who could know all of this," Dinah said slowly, "but I don't know why she'd want to slander me."

Her boss had returned to his dinner, but paused now. "Has there been some dispute over a man?"

"Mr. Agnew!" she blurted, shocked at his forwardness.

He held his hands up in defense. "It is a powerful motivator, you can't deny that. 'Hell hath no fury like a woman scorned' and all that."

"Absolutely not." Still, the mention of a man drew Dinah's mind back to the strange figure she'd felt following her. Was there any connection there?

"Then I suppose the only way to arrive at the truth is confront the person most likely to be responsible," Mr. Agnew said, decisive as ever.

"Are you sure that's wise, dear?" Worry creased Hazel's forehead for the first time as she cast a glance at Dinah. "Mightn't Dinah be putting herself in some sort of danger by asking questions?"

"From a government girl? I very much doubt it. It sounds like a case of petty jealousy."

"It had serious consequences for me," Dinah reminded him, and was rewarded with something that resembled penitence on Mr. Agnew's face.

She stared down at her rejected oysters, trying to decide not only what to do, but what to feel. Now that she had so much new information, none of it fit together into a neat picture.

Mother would know what to do next.

But Mother wasn't here, chased away by Dinah's rash words. Even if she still had been in the city, it would be humiliating to admit her need for advice. No, for once, Dinah was truly on her own. Isn't that what she'd said she wanted?

"Would you care to stay for dessert?" Hazel offered hopefully, jarring her out of her thoughts.

It might have been rude, but Dinah stood before being in-vited to. "Thank you, but I feel I ought to be going. I'm not especially hungry."

They exchanged the usual good-byes, made surreal by the occasion of their dinner party, though Dinah believed Mrs. Agnew when she said she'd be "delighted" to have Dinah over for tea someday "under better circumstances."

Mr. Agnew walked her to the door, telling her to keep the slanderous letter when she tried to give it back. "Might I sug-gest: If you have suspicions that some sort of sabotage of your character is at work, start with the who, then turn to the why."

Which was, Dinah realized, just another way of repeating her mother's two favorite questions:

"What do you know?"

Very little, it turns out.

"And what does it mean?"

That I'll be having a chat with Winora as soon as possible.

35

Lillian

WEDNESDAY, MAY 31, 1944

Lillian shifted on the hard seat, wishing she'd removed her crossword notebook from her luggage before stowing her bag. The portly businessman beside her had fallen asleep within two minutes of their departure, legs splayed into the narrow space between seats. Dusk had turned to night, the shadowy suggestions of a landscape passing by the grime-streaked window.

That left Lillian with nothing to dwell on but her own thoughts as each clack of the rails took her farther away from a daughter who no longer needed her mother.

We'll repair things in time, Lillian reasoned, as she so often did after arguments with Dinah.

Still, this time, Dinah's attack felt distinctly *unfair*. After all, Lillian had tried so hard, for so many years, to befriend her daughter, to provide for her and give her good advice and challenge her to live up to her potential.

*She's moved on to a new life, a new season, and so must
you. That's all.*

By the time the conductor announced the Chambersburg
station, Lillian felt overstewed in self-pity. She stood, stretching
muscles sore from disuse, and joined the many travelers pressing toward freedom. The sudden rush of blood to her head,
combined with the heat of dozens of bodies, made her lurch
forward unsteadily, her knees threatening to give out.

"Lily!" a familiar voice called, its owner waving to her from
the platform, his arms outstretched for her to fall into. Roger.
Her wonderful, kind Roger, solid and rooted as a battlefield
oak.

Lillian stumbled in her hurry to rush to his side, his greeting
interrupted when she sobbed into his chest, the pent-up resentments of years finally forcing their way out.

"Well, well," Roger said, sounding as bashful as he'd been
as a bachelor veteran. "What's all this?" He pushed back Lillian's hair, which had fallen into disarray around her face. "Not
happy tears, are they?"

"N-no. I—I'm glad to see you, but . . ." She pushed away
from him and breathed in deeply, trying to force her emotions
to come under control, her posture to return upright, these
blasted tears to stop welling up. It was the late hour, it must be,
and the stress of travel. She hadn't slept well the night before
either, playing Dinah's words over and over in her mind.

"Come here." Roger held her more tightly this time, until
the marching rhythm of his heart subsumed the jaggedness of
her breathing, smoothing out her crumpled places.

When she pulled away, she found she could stand up straight
once more. "I-I don't know what came over me. I'm all right
now. Really."

He gave her a wary look but trusted her enough to go fetch
her luggage. He'd parked the Buick on the street by the station
and opened the sedan's door with flair, likely to prompt the wan

smile she offered in return. *What do I need to tell him? How will I explain it all?*

"Whenever you're ready to talk, I'm ready to listen."

Lillian clutched her handkerchief in one fist, keeping it at the ready. As they rumbled down the road back to Gettysburg, all her carefully constructed explanations fled away, and she told Roger the stark facts: how Dinah had come to resent her presence in the city, her daughter's lies, and the confrontation over the journal and their final argument.

"She . . . wanted me to leave. Told me to get out—I assumed she meant Washington, but maybe it was out of her life entirely." Even now, she couldn't bring herself to look over at Roger, afraid of seeing pity in his eyes.

"I'm sorry, Lillian. I'm sure she didn't mean it. Maybe you're being too hard on yourself."

This was exactly what she'd expected to hear from Roger, ever the peacemaker. Wearily, she leaned back against the seat. "You don't understand." It was so much more than this one argument.

The anxious, bitter, runaway-train thoughts poured out of her now, and for once, she didn't try to keep them in. "I never tried to be wealthy or powerful like George Fabyan. I didn't even have ambitions of doing important work or leaving a mark on the world like Elizebeth and Margot. All I ever wanted was to be a good wife and mother. I worked so hard and sacrificed so much, and even that one small dream . . . well, look what it's come to."

The last line came out more like a whisper, an awful relief, like giving in to a bout of nausea.

Roger was quiet for a long time, and she didn't rush to fill the silence. What would she say? She had nothing left to give.

"It's not a small dream, Lily," he said at last. "Your love for this family matters more than you know." Lillian looked up at her husband's kind eyes, feeling a lightening inside her, until Roger continued, his tone hesitant. "But also . . ."

"What?" she prompted, bracing herself for what might follow.

He lifted his hand briefly from the steering wheel to rub the back of his neck. "I don't know how to say it, exactly. It's just . . . if motherhood is your whole purpose . . . well, that's an awful lot of pressure. On you. And maybe on Dinah."

A denial sprang to her lips, but something held it back: the strong, key-in-the-lock feeling she always got when Roger was right. How long had she felt that motherhood was both a joy and a heavy burden, an overwhelming responsibility with terrible consequences for failure? Maybe from the first confusing moment she'd learned she was pregnant.

"I'm a simple man, Lily, you know that. God first, family second . . . and it's easy to mix up that order. Easy and usually full of good intentions, but dangerous."

Put that way, it sounded so straightforward, as Roger's wisdom always did. But Lillian had no idea what it meant practically—what to do next or how to stop the ache she felt inside. Because there was still more that Roger didn't know, that she couldn't expect him to understand since she'd never spoken the words out loud.

Maybe it was the darkness, the fact that she didn't have to look at her husband, or maybe she was just so tired of holding it all back, but Lillian felt a sudden courage.

"But I was supposed to do better. Than . . . than my mother."

The fact that Roger glanced over at her, surprised, told her he realized the bravery it took to force out those words, at least on some level. "It's a hard thing, taking a new path. Your mother didn't give you much of an example to work with."

Lillian bit her lip. It wasn't the words so much as the tone— that old, familiar kindness—that urged her to continue.

"It's worse than you know. Mama . . ." So soon after her resolution, Lillian found herself faltering. Where to begin? There were so many years of stories she'd never told, a library of hurts and fears and neglect.

"You know Mama wasn't well. I . . . I've never told you just what that meant." The words, once cracked open, flew out of her, like the sorrows of the world out of Pandora's box. "When I was only a girl, she became paranoid, thinking someone wanted to kill her. An anarchist boyfriend she'd once had, I think it was. We never stayed in one place for very long. She would break into a run when we were out in public. Talk to herself. Lash out at me on her bad days."

When the silence stretched too long, Roger prompted her with, "You've told me before that there were good days. Was that true?"

"Some. She'd throw herself into her latest employment, usu-ally as a store clerk, for weeks, even months at a time, hardly ever at home, then go through times when she'd lock herself—and me—inside our tenement, until I had to sneak down the fire escape to buy food."

"Oh, Lily." Roger's voice was tentative, as if he was afraid he might startle her. "What happened to your mother? I know she didn't ever get the treatment she needed."

"No." Lillian thought of William's experience in Walter Reed. "Even today, very little is known about how to heal the mind. Three times, she was taken to a hospital. The first, she left in the middle of the night without being released. The sec-ond, the hospital forced her to agree to sterilization. The last time, when she was at her worst, barely intelligible, the doctors suggested an operation on her brain. As her only next of kin, even though I was underage, they asked me to give permission. And—I did."

That choice, made out of equal parts hope and desperation, had bowed Lily down in a way deeper than Riverbank's posture scientists could ever correct. It was the secret she had never shared, the guilt that she'd tried for years to bury, but even an unmarked grave couldn't hold it.

"It was supposed to help . . . but she was so weak . . ." Lillian paused, attempting to reign in her emotions once more. "She didn't survive. I'm not sure the doctors cared, though they told me she'd passed 'peacefully.'" Lillian didn't bother to hide her skepticism at the report. Peace had never been a visitor to her home. Not before Roger.

"And that's when you were taken to the school for dependent girls."

She'd told him of the strict schedules and harsh punishments at the reformatory, so now she only had to nod. "When I turned seventeen, I began working at Riverbank. It was the first time I was truly free."

But her childhood had left scars. Not physical ones, no. It seemed even the terrible operation she'd thought had altered her life forever was only a sham. But no matter how often Lillian insisted she could forget, that by telling no one the deepest hurts of her past, not even her journal, she knew the truth: Her mother's legacy still haunted her.

After a long silence, as if to make sure she had really finished, Roger pounded a fist on the steering wheel, tilting them briefly off course. "I wish I could take it away. Or . . . do something."

Lillian blinked away a few persistent tears, unwilling to let herself dissolve into sentimentality again. "You can't change the past, Roger. As it is, when you entered my life, you changed my future. I couldn't ask for more."

The slightest of smiles creased the familiar tracks into his face. "My wife, always practical." The Buick lurched to a stop, and only then did Lillian realize that they'd arrived at home. She would have enjoyed soaking in the familiar old house with its neat porch and shutters in need of a new coat of paint if her husband hadn't redirected her attention with a gaze of determined steel. "But, Lily, I want you to hear me . . . you are not your mother. Not only are you a different person, but you've made different choices."

Lillian's breath caught. How good it was to hear those words, spoken out loud.

And yet he hadn't been there, hadn't heard the anger in Dinah's voice. "But what if . . . ?"

"No. Nothing is going to change my mind on that." Roger reached over to take her hand, squeezing it tightly. "Sure, maybe you've still got something to learn, like all the rest of us. But you've loved Dinah fiercely from the very start."

Lillian tried to find words to reply, turning away with the excuse of opening the car door. If only she could believe it. As they walked up to the house, side by side, her voice dropped to a whisper. "What if, after all that, she doesn't love me?"

"Oh, Lily." Now Roger stopped on the porch, putting his arms around her, like they were a courting couple sneaking one last doorstep kiss. "She does. I know it. But me saying that won't help, will it?"

She allowed herself to nestle her head against his chest and felt a weight lifted, not fully, but enough to answer honestly. "Not especially. Right now, I feel as if . . . I should never have gone to Washington at all."

Roger's voice was thoughtful, not the dismissive optimism she'd braced herself for. "Just because you and Dinah argued doesn't mean you shouldn't have been there for her when she needed you. And, believe me, she did—and does."

He was probably right, Lillian knew, but the words refused to travel from her head to her heart. "But it's so *hard.*"

"That's people for you." Roger chuckled warmly. "But just because a relationship is hard doesn't mean it's bad. You'll always be her mama, Lily."

Another few moments passed, dark and silent, with fireflies gently winking into view around them, before Roger added, "I wish you'd told me sooner. About your mother's death and all."

"I know," she said miserably, the guilt of twenty-five years washing over her despite Roger's gentle tone. "I should have been honest with you. You deserved better—"

"Lily." The word was quiet, but a command, and even in the

dark, she could see him angle his head toward hers. "That's not what I meant. I've always known there was some trouble or struggle you faced, that was just . . . beyond me."

"Because I never told you the whole truth."

"Maybe. Still, every time I caught you staring sadly into the distance and I couldn't help, I would stay up at night wondering . . ."

"Wondering what?" Had he suspected the truth all this time?

The arms around her waist slackened briefly. "Whether it would have been better if you hadn't married me. If you'd felt free to marry someone else, someone who would understand you better."

Never had she dreamed her confident, charming husband could feel that sort of doubt. "Oh, Roger. You couldn't really think that."

"You have to admit, the circumstances of our wedding vows weren't exactly typical."

"No. But even then, I believed I loved you." She could feel him stiffen, and hurried to add, "I say it that way because it's nothing compared to the love I feel for you now. Roger, you're everything I needed you to be. God brought us together. I'm sure of that. And . . . when I'm with you . . . I'm home."

Closing her eyes, Lillian could see Roger again as he was twenty-five years ago, dressed in his uniform on their wedding day, smelling of shaving soap, his eyes full of tears and hope.

They hadn't known what they were doing, certainly. What young couple does? But they had chosen each other that day.

And, Lillian thought, as she kissed her husband on their front porch, they were still choosing each other, even now. And for the moment, that was enough.

320

36

Dinah

Every boarder, Dinah had learned, had a "tell" in their footsteps. Anne-Marie breathed asthmatically through her nose, Betty took tiny mincing steps, and Winora McMahen clomped up the stairs like the cops were after her.

That made it easy for Dinah to lurk in her doorway the next evening, ducking out to interrupt Winora as she fumbled with her key. "Listen, Winora, I know you don't want to talk to me, but I've got something important to ask you."

She'd hoped to see the first twitching signs of nervousness or guilt, but her neighbor's face was as blank as an empty page in her sketchpad. "Yeah? Whaddya want?"

Not exactly a warm welcome, but Dinah would take any opening. "Can we speak privately?"

"Fine," Winora grunted, swinging the door open. Other than a heap of discarded clothes scattered about, Winora's room

321

was sparse and smaller than Dinah's, uncluttered by personal possessions.

But the walls! Two of them were full of papers taped haphazardly about, all of them in pairs. Dinah stood gaping at them for a moment, then stepped closer to examine them. A torn-out page from a children's book featuring a family of ducks in brown tones had become a charcoal drawing; a bright red steam engine and its cheerful operator was rendered in pen and ink. There were even small pencil sketches of watercolors that Dinah recognized from Beatrix Potter books. Other than the change in medium, Dinah wasn't sure she'd be able to tell the difference if presented with each separately.

"These are amazing," Dinah said, temporarily distracted from her interrogation.

"Huh?" Winora turned from where she'd cleared laundry off her chair, turning it away from the desk. "Those are nothing. Just practice." Dinah sat, allowing Winora to glower down at her. "Now, what's this all about?"

All morning, in the quiet after the others left for work, Dinah had planned what she might say. With the OSS recruits she'd attempted to trap back at Gettysburg, sometimes the best approach had been the direct one, in hopes of catching the subject by surprise. She'd decided to try the same here. "Why did you slander me to Mr. Agnew?"

There wasn't even a flicker of recognition on Winora's face. "What are you going on about?"

"There's no point in lying," Dinah said calmly, folding her arms. Maybe that would also make it harder for the larger woman to bodily drag her out of the room. "I've read the letter you sent. Outside of blatant lies, it contained a few exaggerated facts. Facts only you could know."

"What letter?"

Dinah let the silence linger, staring her former coworker down, but Winora's nose was scrunched up in bafflement. Either she should buy a one-way ticket to Hollywood, or she was genuinely in the dark about the defaming letter.

And yet how could anyone else have the information it contained?

Unless Winora told someone.

But then . . . who would have any reason to accuse her so maliciously? Mr. Longstreet? Maybe, but Winora disliked him just as much as Dinah did. There was no way she'd blab anything personal to him.

There was only one way to settle this. Carefully, Dinah pulled the anonymous letter Mr. Agnew had given her from her pocket, creased down the center. "See for yourself."

Winora snatched it up, still scowling. "This isn't some kind of funny business, is it?"

"Believe me," Dinah said, feeling suddenly exhausted, "I haven't found any of this the slightest bit funny."

While Winora read the letter, Dinah eased around in the chair. Perhaps it was because of her lingering suspicions, but she couldn't help taking a look at the papers scattered across Winora's desk.

Unlike the ones hanging on the wall, these were characters Dinah had never seen before, sketched in what she could now identify as Winora's strong, dark-stroked style. A hot dog seller driving off a pigeon. Two girls with buckteeth skipping rope. A cheerful Great Dane.

A second glance showed Dinah that there were a few people she recognized, though not from children's books. The first was the imperious dame who wore a calf-length mink on their bus line. Underneath it, a sketch of Mr. Agnew, eyebrows furrowed, a cigarette clamped in his exaggerated mouth.

And there, in the middle, was a young man, broad-shouldered and handsome, holding a door open. Dinah squinted, picking up the paper to examine it more carefully. His suit was immaculate, though his wide, flirtatious smile revealed a crooked front tooth.

Dinah dropped the paper, her thumb leaving behind the slightest of smears. *Oh no.*

Martin Seigel, Winora had written in capitals beneath the illustration, confirming Dinah's suspicions.

The man in the sketch was Winora's ex-boyfriend—and also the OSS recruit Dinah had informed on back in Gettysburg.

That's why his voice had sounded so familiar the day she'd heard him in the entryway. She'd heard it letting secrets slip at the Wills House soda fountain three months before. He'd gone by Ralph Something-or-Other then, but she'd known that wasn't his real name.

But why was he here, working for the OSS?

Dinah had thought when she reported a recruit for blabbing information, he'd be dismissed from the organization. Apparently, that assumption had been wrong. Probably, Colonel Forth had judged that Martin-not-Ralph only needed to be removed from a Special Operations role that required secrecy. Or, worse, judging from Winora's description of him as "one of those rich-family types," maybe his parents pulled strings to keep him at an OSS desk job and therefore exempt from military service.

Either way, his sudden reappearance in her life made Dinah's head ache with implication. *It couldn't be . . . could it?*

"Hey!" Winora's voice, all outrage, disrupted her line of thought. "Don't look at those." She shoved Dinah aside and scooped up the illustrations from her desk like they were military secrets. "Haven't you ever heard of privacy?"

"I—I'm sorry," Dinah stammered.

"Anyway, you might as well beat it, because I sure didn't write this." Winora pushed the letter back at her. "I swear."

"No," Dinah said slowly, "but I think you know who did."

"Oh yeah? Who?"

The answer had come to her as clear as the final chapter in a mystery novel. "Martin." Mr. Agnew had it the wrong way around. If you started with the why and then moved to the who, it all made sense. Or, at least, began to.

Winora's eyes narrowed. "What's that?"

This was going to be tricky. "Listen, I know you might not want to hear anything bad about your ex-boyfriend . . ."

She only snorted. "You kidding? He dropped me like a hand grenade, out of nowhere too. Something about expecting a promotion soon and wanting to focus on his career ambitions, but I knew better." She narrowed a glare in Dinah's direction. "*Someone* told him about my family's business."

"If that's true, it wasn't me. Cross my heart." Dinah made the gesture, realizing how childlike it might seem, but her mind was so occupied that she didn't care. "Winora, I've got to know. Did you tell Martin anything about me? For example, the work I took home from the office or the books on ciphers I read?"

"It might've come up," she said, shrugging.

"Yes or no, Winora."

She jammed her illustrations into a desk drawer before turning back to Dinah. "Okay, fine. Martin saw you one day and asked about you. I tried to make you sound like a dull stick-in-the-mud type to get the attention back to me. A girl doesn't need the competition."

It was a checkmark in the "aye" column for her theory, though not definitive proof. "He worked in Radio, is that right?" Winora nodded, so that at least gave Martin access to the *Secret* file that had made its way to Dinah's desk.

"And did you stop speaking to me because you heard I was accused of leaking confidential information, or even spying on the OSS?"

The arms cocked defiantly on her friend's hips gave enough of an answer. "Is it true?"

"No," Dinah said, with as much force as she could muster, careful to continue looking Winora directly in the eye. She pushed down a prickle of resentment that Winora had been so quick to believe the rumors instead of standing by her side. Then again, they hadn't even known each other for two months. What could she expect? "Almost everything in the letter is a lie. Except for the details that only you *and Martin* knew."

There was a pause as Winora seemed to take this in, slow realization dawning before her eyebrows knitted together again. "That's the stupidest thing I ever heard. Martin didn't have any reason to go after you like that. He's never even met you."

"I'm afraid he has." She took a deep breath and plunged in, giving Winora every detail that might be relevant: her report on Martin during his training, the feeling she'd had of being followed, the unauthorized document on her desk that got her in trouble with Mrs. Masterson, and her conversation with the Agnews.

When she'd finished, instead of firing off a volley of questions, Winora only stared, the springs of her bed creaking as she sat down.

"So you think Martin only went out with me to get at you?" she finally asked. "And to dig up enough dirt to write this?"

Dinah winced. Unfortunately, that was the logical implication of what she was saying. "It's possible." It would explain why he'd unceremoniously dumped her once Dinah was taken care of, but she didn't add that part, trying to spare her friend's feelings.

Winora swore, crumpling the paper in her fist. "I knew it was too good to be true." She stood up, pacing the tiny confines of the room, the glare meant for Martin landing instead on an innocent illustration of a bull sniffing a flower. Dinah was surprised it didn't shrivel to ashes. "Okay, so he *could* have sent this letter. Why—just to get even? Feels like a lot of work."

Dinah shrugged. "I might have cost him his job with the OSS's commando unit. Maybe he thought a Radio Department office job was a step down, so when he saw me show up at headquarters . . ."

"He saw the chance to do the same thing to you that you'd done to him," Winora finished.

Dinah frowned. She hadn't thought about it that way. For all her smugness about spying on spies, she'd forgotten how quickly the tables could turn. "For the record, I think Martin's a real cad for breaking your heart."

"Oh, I didn't give him that. Only a solid counterfeit." Winora faced her, mouth set in determination. "Still, now this feels personal, you know? Dumping me is one thing, but using me . . . that's another. We've got to get this guy."

"I don't know what we could possibly do." In a way, finding out Winora had been the culprit would have been easier. Dinah might have persuaded her to go to the OSS and take back the slander in the letter. "Mr. Agnew believes me, I think, but the claims in the letter were sensational, and"—she had to admit—"some were true. Even if I could work in Morale Operations again, there would always be talk. Maybe I should just cut my losses."

Winora's frown only deepened. "But then that lying snake gets away with everything. Can't we make some sort of complaint?"

"We don't have any proof, only a lot of hearsay and conjecture."

"And Martin's a smooth talker." But Winora wasn't looking at her anymore, studying the letter instead. "Now, *that* could be something . . ."

The hint of intrigue in her voice drew Dinah in, and she glanced back at the letter. Winora indicated several spots in the text.

"What exactly am I looking for?"

"Come on, girl, you've got eyes. Don't you see it?"

Dinah only shook her head.

"Whoever wrote this has a typewriter with a bent key lever. Every single *T* is crooked as a cop on the make."

"Oh," Dinah said. Now that it had been pointed out, yes, she could see that the letter leaned slightly to the left. "Why does that matter?"

"If we could find the typewriter this was written on, that would be proof, yeah?"

"Maybe," Dinah conceded. "Or at least, it would help to confirm any claim I made. But even if you searched his office, I don't think Martin would have used an OSS typewriter for this."

"Probably not, but . . ." Now the grin on Winora's face had taken on a distinctly sly angle. "Martin tried to get me to come back to his room once, in a hotel converted into apartments. Sure seemed surprised when I slapped him in the face on his doorstep. Which means I know where he lives."

Throughout this speech, Dinah hadn't been sure where it was going. Now she hoped she was wrong. "You don't mean . . . ?"

"Paying his place an unexpected visit might be the only way to get answers." Winora held up the letter, dangling it in front of her. "Question is, how badly do you want them?"

It's a good thing Winora isn't the only one with skills some would consider criminal.

Dinah couldn't help taking one last glance up and down the hotel's hallway to make sure no one would disturb her.

"I told you, I'm keeping watch," Winora hissed from behind her. "Just make this quick."

"I'm trying." A whistling cleaning woman had passed by a moment before, but they hadn't seen or heard another soul. It was nearly ten o'clock, and most of the residents of the Regal Hotel seemed to be government workers with regular office hours. Winora herself had feigned a nasty cough to call off work, sounding so realistic that Dinah had wanted to check her for a fever.

Now here they were, about to perform their first breaking-and-entering job.

Well, a first for Dinah at least. Winora would neither confirm nor deny her experience when asked.

Dinah plucked a sturdy hairpin from behind her temple, letting a stray curl fall out of her Victory Roll. She pictured Dad beside her, watching with his keen brown eyes, asking the occasional question rather than giving corrections. He'd tested all of his lessons for the OSS on her.

Safecracking took ages to learn, and more effort and patience than Dinah had been willing to give. But picking an ordinary lock? That was easier than most people imagined. All one really had to do was understand the mechanics of the type of lock, then insert something that, like a key, could apply the correct pressure to the catch pin.

"You have the most important talent you need already," Dad had assured her. *"I've seen it in the way you connect with others so easily."*

She had frowned. Navigating social situations felt like the only area where she had any kind of knack, but still . . . *"That doesn't have anything to do with breaking into a lock."*

"Oh, but it does," he'd said, eyes twinkling. *"They both use the same skill. Listening."*

So Dinah leaned closer to Martin's door and listened, prodding the hairpin in at the right angle through the keyhole, and feeling her way in deeper, picturing the metal shafts and cylinder it was passing through inside the door. Then, after shifting the pin in place and tilting it ever so gently to the side, she heard it. The unmistakable click of release.

"Well done, little Yankee" she could almost hear Dad saying.

But would her straitlaced father approve of what she was about to do? Mother certainly wouldn't, regardless of Dinah's good intentions for justice.

Better not think about that. What was done was done.

Winora was already inside, and Dinah ducked in quickly after her, if only to escape the danger of scrutiny from other residents.

The front room was just the sort of place you might expect a bachelor to live in. Despite the fact that Winora claimed Martin came from "one of those Founding Father aristocracy families," the décor seemed typical of any four-star hotel: generic oak furniture, dark patterned carpet intended to hide stains, a framed watercolor of the Potomac in a garish frame. While there was no kitchen, a narrow cabinet and table with two chairs formed a breakfast nook by the window, a hasty accommodation that attempted to transform the suite into an actual apartment.

"It'll be in his bedroom, I bet," Winora said, dismissing their surroundings with barely a glance. The first door she tried led to a small bathroom, which she gave barely a glance before swinging open the door on the left. As Dinah followed Winora inside, the lingering smell of expensive, spicy cologne filled her nose, the scent familiar, if not comforting. Dinah was not following a wild, unsubstantial guess.

Martin was Ralph from Gettysburg. She was sure of it now.

Martin's gracefully curved mahogany writing desk seemed too fine to fit with the other hotel furnishings. It took up most of one wall, the chair pressed nearly against the bedframe. Best of all, right in the center was a typewriter.

Winora, her black leather driving gloves looking oddly out of place—*"We've got to keep our prints off,"* she'd said—wasted no time cranking the platen knobs and banging out a brief message on the paper already inserted in the machine.

Dinah's breath caught at a sound like a creaking board, but when seconds ticked by without a disturbance, she tried to relax again. Their unorthodox entry into the apartment had put her on edge.

"It's him, all right," Winora confirmed, tearing out the page and fluttering it around for Dinah to see what she'd written in the center of the paper.

GOTCHA, with a clearly crooked *T*.

She continued, "Plus, the paper's the same weight and . . ." She rattled the blinds on the window to let more light into the room, holding the paper aloft as if searching for invisible ink. "Mm-hmm, yep, that's the right watermark."

As she held up the paper, a bit of text near the top caught Dinah's eye. Winora hadn't taken the time to insert a new sheet of paper for her test, and it seemed that Martin had been in the middle of composing a message, just a few lines at the top of the page.

Except . . .

"Let me see that," Dinah said, snatching it from Winora before she could protest.

Yes. Martin hadn't written actual words, only groupings of letters in pairs of five, forming a meaningless jumble . . . but one Dinah had seen before.

Martin was using a cipher.

"But why would he do that," she whispered, "unless . . . ?"

A terrible intuition came over her, something that would help resolve at least some of the out-of-place details. "Winora, we've got to search this room. Carefully."

Her friend's eyes widened. "You crazy? We've got what we need. Better get out of here before we leave a trail. In and out. It's neater that way."

"I know, but . . ." Dinah indicated the lines of cipher. "Doesn't this look odd to you? Like he was composing a secret message for someone." She thought again of the Records Room, of the tampered files that hadn't yet been explained. Had she smelled the same heady cologne that day too?

Winora shook her head. "Nah. Not Martin. He's too clean-cut for anything like that."

Dinah resisted the impulse to point out that there was a

great deal she hadn't realized about her former beau. "Maybe. But as long as we're here, we're going to be thorough." Dinah reached for a desk drawer, only to have Winora nudge her aside.

"Not on your life. Let me do it." In response to Dinah's questioning look, she added, "I've got practice leaving places undisturbed, okay? He'll never know I was here."

Sure enough, Winora was unexpectedly gentle with her search of the desk, moving as few items as necessary and re-placing them as she went, even turning an ink bottle so the label was facing the exact angle as it had been before. Then, suddenly, she tensed, her hand stilled in midair.

"Dinah. Look at this."

A corner of colored paper was poking out from under the blotting mat, and Winora tugged it out slowly. She held up a map of France, one edge ragged, as if it had been torn from an atlas. A pen circle rounded out an uncomfortably narrow area along the coast, with a few others crossed out with a bold slash. "Looks like Martin was very interested in seaside France."

The very region everyone knew would be invaded by the Allies in the next several months.

Dinah felt dizzy. She'd come with the faint hope that she might get her old job back, or at least that Winora would stop pestering her about bringing Martin to justice. Now, everything Dinah thought she knew shifted slightly, and the picture became darker, more menacing.

"He wasn't doing this to get revenge on me. Or, not only for that reason," Dinah said, stepping away. "The leaked informa-tion, the disappearing files . . ."

"You were right." Winora's voice was grim. "Martin's a spy. But how would he know anything about the location of a pos-sible invasion?"

"I don't know," Dinah admitted, backing toward the door. "But we've got to get away from here. Now."

This time it was Winora who shook her head. "There's got

to be more somewhere. Spies always leave paper trails, and I bet I can find his. The OSS made a film, see, for training the commandos. Martin would have watched it just like the rest of them."

"How do you know about that?"

"I made the ID cards for it." She replaced the map with care, rearranging the fountain pens on top of the blotter with precision. "It was my first assignment, just a movie prop, as a sort of test. But I watched the whole thing, and there was a section teaching agents where to hide something *in a hotel room*." She opened the window and began feeling along the frame outside. "Give me ten minutes, doll, and I'll have enough proof that the FBI will be fighting the police for a chance to arrest him."

"All right," Dinah said, backing toward the door. "I'll see what I can make of the cipher."

Winora's voice followed her into the sitting room. "*Don't* touch anything."

Her knees already bent to perch on the sofa, Dinah sprang up guiltily.

"In fact, don't breathe on anything. Treason or no, this is illegal, and if I get arrested again . . ."

That made sense. The stakes would be higher for Winora than for Dinah if a suspicious neighbor happened to report them.

Standing and pacing the suite's living room, Dinah tried to make sense of the cipher. It seemed clear Martin had been interrupted in the middle of writing his message, leaving her with only a fragment. With no starting point and only a few repeated letters, Dinah felt at a loss.

If only Mother was here. She'd have this solved in five minutes.

Dinah tried to remember what she'd learned from the Riverbank Publications, but it was all so new, and the letters began to swim in front of her the harder she tried to focus on them.

After a few minutes of no progress whatsoever, Winora slunk into the room so soundlessly that Dinah didn't realize she was there until she removed a painting from the back wall near the window. "Oh, now *this* looks like something." She began prying at a sheaf of papers wedged into the frame.

"Are you sure you should disturb anything?" Dinah asked. "Maybe we . . ."

She paused. This time, she was sure she heard footsteps, firm and heavy, out in the hallway. *Probably just a neighbor passing by.*

But that hope was stilled by the mechanical clatter of a key turning in a lock. Winora swore and ducked behind the ornamental screen beside the dinette table.

In the center of the room, Dinah only had time to crumple the half-written cipher into her pocket before Martin Seigel strode through the door . . . and stared at her.

37

Lillian

Lillian rubbed her tired eyes against the brightness of early morning. Her stomach lurched, less from the potholes in the road and more from the certainty that she was making a terrible mistake.

It's too soon.

I should have sent Roger alone.

I shouldn't be going at all.

Yet she had made her choice the day before, and now, tucked into their old Buick, it felt too late to turn back. Unbeknown to Dinah, she and Roger were bound for Washington, DC.

As they puttered out of the Gettysburg city limits, Roger rolled down the windows of the sedan and whistled a cheerfully off-key rendition of "It's a Long Way to Tipperary." "There's no better way to see the countryside than behind a steering wheel, don't you think, Lily?"

Lillian hummed noncommittally. Though, now that he mentioned it . . . "That reminds me of a question I meant to ask."

"Fire away, captain."

Lillian took in a deep breath, bracing herself for the teasing that was sure to come. "Could you . . . teach me how to drive?"

Roger might as well have been a boy given a fistful of candy bars. "Could I? Anytime! How long have I been trying to get you to give driving a go?"

"Since the day we married, nearly." And she'd always adamantly refused.

Still beaming, Roger shook his head. "You'll be a whiz at it, just you wait and see. What made you come around to the ol' horseless carriage after all these years?"

"Now that Dinah is out of the house, I was thinking of taking up a volunteer opportunity." She paused, feeling that putting it into words would be a point of no return. "In Harrisburg."

"Would we have the gas rations for it?"

It was a logical question, given that this trip to DC had only been possible because, in warmer weather, Roger walked to work, allowing him to save up gasoline. "I've thought of that."

"Of course you have," he said fondly.

"Given the distance, I'd have to appeal to the ration board to issue us a B ration sticker. But I think I could make a strong argument. Failing that, Ada Pendleton makes anti-aircraft guns at a manufacturer in Harrisburg." Lillian ought to know; the garrulous matron worked it into conversation whenever possible after church. "I could carpool with her."

"Then I say it's a capital idea," Roger enthused, as usual, jumping all in without knowing the details. "Don't think I haven't noticed you moping about lately, waiting for something to do. This sounds like just the thing. What's the work involve? Another soup kitchen?"

Time for the full truth. "No, just cleaning. It's . . . at the Harrisburg State Hospital for the mentally ill."

"Ah, I see." His eyes darted to her, worry evident there. "Will that be hard for you?"

"Yes," she admitted. "But I feel I have to try."

She'd reread the letter from Harrisburg State Hospital several times upon returning home. Until the end of the war, they needed immediate, practical help to make up for the labor shortage. And Lillian had the time, the abilities, and the desire.

There was nothing more she could do for Mama. But there were others who could be helped.

"Good enough for me," Roger said, tapping out a jaunty beat on the steering wheel. "Next thing you know, you'll be running their billing department, then getting a degree and examining patients."

"Perhaps." The joke wasn't so implausible. Still, to avoid the crippling feeling that often overwhelmed her when making long-term plans, Lillian had decided further choices were for a different day. The tasks would be menial, certainly. But it was work she was good at, and she was beginning to believe that it mattered, even if no one noticed or praised her for it.

In a way, that decision had led to the one to return to Washington, DC, to speak with Dinah. Like the first break in a complex cipher, Lillian had at least one certainty to cling to, something she could do with her life in this new season. That made it easier to commit to the next choice. Her daughter might not want to hear it, but Lillian needed to speak some words that had long gone unsaid.

She'd thought of calling Myrtlewood, but Roger had dismissed this idea. *These sorts of things are better in person. I meant to visit sometime this summer anyway. Might as well be now.*

For once, Lillian had let Roger's carefree "why not?" attitude overrule her need to plan and second-guess. After all, there was something to the Scripture about not letting the sun go down on one's anger. Time apart, she felt, would only foster resentment between Dinah and her.

Still, despite Roger's determinedly cheerful banter—"Take a look, Lily, hardly anyone drives at the nationwide speed limit. War or no war, thirty-five miles an hour is far too slow."—the closer they came to Margot's neighborhood, the more tightly Lillian clutched the wrapped package of fudge she'd brought as a peace offering.

"What if Dinah doesn't want us there?" Lillian asked abruptly, cutting off instruction about shifting gears so smoothly an open milk bottle wouldn't spill a drop. Realizing she hadn't phrased the question honestly, she began again. "What if she doesn't want *me* there?"

Roger only shook his head. "If I know Dinah, she's already regretting some of the things she said. Though she'd never admit it, not unless you made the first move. Too stubborn."

"Maybe the only personality trait she inherited from me," Lillian said wryly.

"I don't know about that." He winked at her. "You're a wonderful woman, Lily. And a wonderful mother, just like I always knew you'd be."

As they drove, Lillian tried to rehearse what she might say to Dinah to explain her presence so soon after being sent away. *"I know you're a grown woman, and I haven't come to lecture you."*

Too defensive? Probably.

"When we parted, both of us spoke hasty words, and I wanted to clarify what I meant, rather than leave it open to supposition."

Too businesslike. It sounded like the opening to an official memorandum.

Oh, what was she going to do? She had come up with a serviceable few lines at one point, probably right before she'd drifted into a restless sleep the night before. Now, it was all forgotten.

Lillian was about to ask Roger what he would say in her

place, then rejected the idea. She was not her husband. It was time to stop hiding behind him and find her own voice. Whatever she said to Dinah, it would have to be honest, and it would have to come from the heart.

You'll know what to say when the time comes.

The thought was so unexpected that for a moment, Lillian thought Roger had spoken. But no, he was focused on navigating the traffic that had slowed them to a crawl ever since they'd entered the highways around the capital.

And despite the crowds and horns that usually made her clutch the leather seat with white knuckles, and despite the knowledge that she was inching closer to a difficult conversation, Lillian found herself overwhelmed by a deep, unshakeable peace.

Was this what Roger meant when he spoke of Providence at work with such certainty? Here, at last, the runaway train had ground to a halt, the brakes pulled by the hand of a mighty engineer, and all was quiet.

Lillian would tell Dinah she loved her. That was what mattered most.

This time, Lillian noted with satisfaction, when she and Roger arrived at the Friedmans' house, William's roses were in full bloom, and the windows gleamed in the morning sun. As promised when she'd telephoned the night before, Elizabeth had left the key under the mat, and Lillian and Roger let themselves in.

"I'm so afraid we'll be imposing," she admitted, removing her hat. "After all, it's only been a few days since I left, and William's health is so delicate. . . ."

Roger cut her off with a low whistle, dropping their bag on the entryway floor. "Wowee, Lily, this place is spotless. You really outdid yourself." He gave her a kind, but significant look. "Seems to me, if anything, the Friedmans might feel in your debt after all of this."

"Thank you." She took a deep breath, trying to let his words sink in. In the end, though, it wasn't about debts and favors, lining up ledgers with one another to make sure they were equal like one of her bookkeeping correspondence exercises. Lillian was not a bother for simply needing help. She was Elizebeth's *friend*.

"Perhaps I should call Dinah to see if it would be a good time to come over."

Her husband squeezed her hand, not fooled by her matter-of-fact tone. "I'll be right here if you need me."

Lillian marched into the den, straight for the telephone, without pausing, because any delay or distraction might keep her from phoning Dinah at all.

As expected, Margot answered the call, slightly out of breath, indicating she'd been interrupted in some project. "Hello, Margot. It's Lily. I'm . . . in town again."

"Back so soon?"

"Yes, Roger drove me up. It was rather a last-minute decision." Her cheeks flushed slightly. "I had some . . . unfinished business with Dinah."

"Good for you, Lil." There was pride in Margot's voice, as if she'd personally orchestrated all of this.

Time to follow through. "Would you tell her there's a call for her?"

"I would if I could, but she's already gone out. Left about an hour ago with another one of the boarders."

"Oh. I see." Perhaps she was already applying for another job or had secured an interview. Inwardly, Lillian chastised herself. This was what came of not planning in advance. "Did she say when she'd be back, or where she's going?"

"No, sorry. But I'm sure she won't be gone long."

"Will you give us a call at the Friedmans' when she returns, or if you hear anything from her?"

"The very moment."

Lillian's shoulders slumped as she replaced the receiver. The delay meant there was nothing left for her or Roger to do but pray and wait and try not to worry.

As always, that was easier said than done.

38

Dinah

Friday, June 2, 1944

"You." Martin's voice was a cocktail of surprise and disgust, but at least his moment of stunned silence had given Dinah time to compose herself.

"Hello, Martin," she said, grateful her voice came out level. "I have to say, that name suits you. I never did think you looked like a Ralph."

Keep calm, keep talking, keep him from finding Winora's hiding place. It wasn't much of a plan, but it was the only one she had at the moment.

She stared Martin down, trying to anticipate his next move. He was wearing a perfectly tailored camel-colored suit, and he stood stiffly frozen between her and the doorway. Would he call the police? Reach for a hidden weapon?

Since he seemed to be doing neither, she decided against trying to dodge around him. With his greater height and weight, he'd almost certainly be able to stop her.

"How did you get inside my apartment?" he demanded.

"No need to be rude." Slowly, so he wouldn't become alarmed, Dinah crossed to the side of him, gesturing to the door, and as she'd hoped, Martin turned with her, putting his back to the screen where Winora was hiding, her silhouette faintly visible behind the gold-and-black painted motifs. "I meant to shove a message under your door, but when I realized it was unlocked . . ."

He scowled. "I never leave my door unlocked."

Dinah was about to quote Mother—"*It only takes one instance of carelessness to ruin a habit*"—when he snapped his fingers. "You broke in, didn't you? Just like your old man taught all of us."

That was no use, then. Somehow, perhaps in whatever stalking he'd done to find her, Martin had figured out that Dad was the OSS lockpicking instructor. "Fine, you caught me. So maybe I let myself in. But I found what I wanted."

Making a quick decision, she removed the paper from her pocket, folded so only Winora's GOTCHA was visible, a message that felt incredibly arrogant now. "Did you know each individual typewriter has unique quirks? Yours is a crooked letter that showed up in the anonymous letter to Mr. Agnew."

To her surprise, instead of growling in anger, Martin relaxed, his shoulders releasing their military-tense posture. And was that a flicker of relief in his eyes?

Realization washed over her. He thought that was all she knew, the only bit of the puzzle she'd figured out.

Better keep it that way.

"I'll take that, thank you," he said, plucking the paper from her fingers and tearing it into quarters, letting them drop to the carpet. "Saw me at the OSS, did you? I thought you might, eventually."

Dinah shook her head. "No. I looked out the window when you picked up Winora a few weeks ago." That much was true, though he'd been inside his fancy car and too far away for her to see. "It took me a while to realize where I recognized you from, but once I did . . ." She shrugged. "I knew *someone* filed a report that led to me being fired. You, at least, had a motive."

He swore. "Sure, and then Winora sent you here. I never should have told that dumb broad where I lived. Careless of me."

"Watch your language," she scolded, more for something to say than any other reason, because Winora had stepped out from behind the screen and was moving along the wall in plain sight, only a few yards behind Martin.

Don't react. Don't stare. Whatever Winora was up to, Martin turning around and seeing her seemed like the worst possible outcome.

"I—I expected you to be at work this morning," she continued, forcing her eyes back to Martin. To Dinah's surprise, her words prompted a smug, twisted smile. When had she, or Winora, ever thought this man was handsome?

"Haven't you heard? I'm not working at OSS headquarters anymore."

Somehow, she got the idea that this was not good news. "You've lost your job, then? It's about time."

Instead of creeping forward with a blunt object to cosh over Martin's head, Winora seemed to be fiddling with the latch on the large double-hung window near the breakfast nook. A thin assortment of papers was pinned beneath her other arm, presumably whatever she'd found taped behind the painting.

"In fact, I've been promoted," Martin went on, "to the position I should always have held: a radio operative on a Special Operations team. Now I'm just awaiting orders—and deployment overseas."

A jerk of motion caught Dinah's attention. Winora still held the papers, but was shooting Dinah a look that shouted, *Do something!* as clearly as if she'd hollered it out loud.

But what, exactly, was she supposed to do? Get Martin out of the room? At the moment, she couldn't think of any way to make that happen. Make additional noise to cover Winora's movements? That, at least, she could try.

"I'm sure you're very proud of yourself," Dinah said, clapping slowly. She then launched into a hearty rendition of "For He's a Jolly Good Fellow" as Martin stared incredulously at her. Even Dinah couldn't hear a sound as Winora yanked open one of the windows.

She's going to drop the evidence outside. Not a bad idea, especially if the papers could be recovered, though the idea of sensitive documents fluttering down to a back alley mud puddle or blowing into the street made Dinah cringe. But then what? They would both still be trapped here.

"What are you—?" Martin blurted, staring, but Dinah only sang louder. The slightest of breezes swirled in as Winora stepped up on the dinette and . . . began to climb out the window?

". . . and so say all of us." The song faltered as Dinah choked in surprise, forgetting the next section of lyrics.

Thankfully, Martin chose that moment to intervene, raising his voice. "Are you out of your mind?"

She folded her arms, giving him a petulant look. "Just angry, thanks."

"Well, can it," he growled. "If one of the neighbors knocks, I'll have to tell them I was just calling the police on you for breaking in."

Slowly, still visible on the other side, and not teetering like she was balanced on a ledge, Winora pushed the window shut. By the time Martin flinched at the slight noise, the only visible movement outside the window was an overweight pigeon flying past. He turned back quickly, clearly wary of taking his eyes off Dinah.

Since Winora hadn't fallen to her death from the third floor, the only logical conclusion was that the former hotel room must open out onto a fire escape. Which meant Winora might get away—but she had left Dinah alone with a Nazi spy.

She'll get help and come back, Dinah told herself. *The police, maybe.*

Except even if Winora had found something incriminating, she probably wouldn't go to the police, not with the chance that she'd be sent back to prison for breaking and entering. At best, she'd call in an anonymous tip, but there was no guarantee the authorities would act on it.

Dinah had to get out of this one on her own. Somehow, she had to convince Martin that she didn't suspect him as a spy so he'd let her walk away from his apartment unharmed.

It's just another propaganda job. You can do this.

"I bet you were disappointed when the *Secret* document you planted on my desk didn't get me kicked out right away," Dinah continued, making sure to cover any possible noise of Winora's escape.

He only shrugged. "It should have, but I wasn't counting on it. Everyone knows Madame Masterson plays favorites. But Agnew listened to me, didn't he? And it was one more strike against you."

"Says the person who got demoted by the OSS before finishing training," Dinah goaded. "Back in Gettysburg, you spilled all the OSS's secrets the moment you let your guard down. You'll never make it in Special Operations." Although she was now certain that Martin had no intention of keeping any of America's secrets to himself, revealing them not by a simple slip but with intention to those who could use them for harm.

Now, at least, a flush of red in Martin's cheeks indicated she'd prodded at a sore spot. "Says you. On paper, I'm over-qualified for the job—fluent in German and French, two years' experience in a New York radio station, a college degree from

Colombia University." He nearly spit out the words, and Dinah couldn't help taking a step back. "It turns out, the only reason I was demoted was because a nosy little turncoat from Gettysburg whined about me to the upper brass during my training. One who was recently fired for suspicious behavior. When I reapplied for consideration for a Special Operations unit, they couldn't find any reason not to accept me."

Hadn't Winora said he was a smooth-talking charmer? If the psychologists who tested new recruits hadn't seen past Martin's façade, then Dinah's evaluation had been the only voice of dissent. "Was that your plan all along when you got me fired? To be promoted back to your old unit?"

He shrugged. "It crossed my mind. Really, though, it was enough just to see you put in your place, and Agnew too. My buddy Barry Longstreet says the old man's been moping ever since."

Now that he'd had a chance to brag, it was time to shift the conversation. "What are you going to do now? Threaten me to keep quiet, I suppose. Now that I know the truth about your dirty career move."

As she expected, Martin snorted in disbelief. "How the tables have turned. When you ratted on me, was that a dirty move too? You have no idea what you cost me."

A prime spying opportunity, most likely. "You wanted to impress your important family, is that it? Or maybe attract women after the war with stories of your heroics."

This time, his eyes held the unmistakable glint of irony, like he was barely restraining himself from telling her all. "Something like that."

"I could still make a report to the OSS accusing you of slander without the evidence from the typewriter," Dinah said, trying to sound like she was mustering up a last bit of bravado. "Even if it's your word against mine, the truth is on my side."

"And then I'd have you arrested for breaking into a private

residence. Which, you might not know, is a felony." He tapped a finger against his chin. "How were you planning to spend the next ten years, Dinah? In prison? Because that's where you'll end up if you even try to report me."

Whether or not he was pulling this number out of thin air, Dinah had to admit: Outside of any concrete evidence of Martin's activity as a spy, she was the only one who had done anything illegal.

That's good. Let him think he took away your last hope. What sort of reaction would be most satisfying to an egotist like Martin?

She clenched her hands in fists, letting her voice waver. "I could go to the papers . . ."

"It won't do any good, Dinah." His patronizing tone nearly made her gag. "Without access to my typewriter, you have no proof—and even that was only the weakest sort of proof to begin with. Try saying anything, and you'll only look like a desperate ex-government girl peddling a wild story."

His eyes rested, for the briefest of moments, on the painting Winora had ransacked only moments before, but his face relaxed. Apparently she'd replaced it at exactly the right angle.

Pretending she hadn't noticed, Dinah went on, babbling again. "Mr. Agnew might believe me. He could convince—"

"Shut up," he ordered, the phrase coming out with explosive force, and she did so, pressing her lips tightly together. "Listen carefully. If I get the slightest hint that you've gone to the government or the police, I'll find a way to repay you and everyone you love. I've found you once. I watched you, followed you everywhere, found out all about you. I can do it again. Besides, I have . . . *connections.* Believe me, Dinah, you won't see the knife until it's deep in your back."

He meant this metaphorically, Dinah was sure, but the dispassionate way he said it gave her chills.

Time to admit defeat. Dinah made her tone bitter and cutting so it wouldn't seem she was surrendering too easily. "Fine. But you're wrong if you think I'll stick around and beg for another chance. I'm leaving DC for good, back to Gettysburg, where people appreciate me. You've won, Martin. I hope you're happy."

"I am, actually." His crooked tooth showed once more in a smile. "Because the sad truth is, even after all your good intentions and little lockpicking games, you're simply not a threat to me. Harmless. Useless."

He nodded toward the door, and she turned toward it, skin prickling at the idea of turning her back on this awful man. "I think you've outstayed your welcome. Run along now."

Dinah forced her shoulders to slump and her head to bow. Better to let him think she was resigned, that he had won.

But . . . hadn't he? She and Winora might have gotten away unharmed, but as far as she knew, Winora hadn't found anything definite they could use against Martin. Was he right after all? Had her hard work been useless?

No time for that now. As soon as Martin's door had slammed behind her, Dinah increased her pace, running down the hallway like there was a fire on the third floor. Any moment now, Martin might check the cache behind the painting and find it missing, or notice his bedroom had been disturbed. It was possible he wouldn't notice for a few hours, but Dinah wasn't about to take that chance.

When she reached the revolving door at the entrance of the former hotel, Dinah pushed her way through . . . only to collide with a figure standing on the sidewalk outside. "Hey! Watch it." Never had Dinah been so glad to hear the Boston accent aimed her way as Winora gave her a critical once-over. "Glad you made it out."

"No thanks to you." Dinah didn't slow down in the slightest. Let Winora struggle to keep up. She was going to put as much distance as possible between herself and the Regal Hotel.

"Figured you could handle yourself. If you hadn't come out in a few minutes, I'd have rung up housekeeping, made up some story to get them to check out Martin's room." Huffing slightly, she drew level with Dinah. "Nice job with the singing. You were flat, though."

"Well, excuse me for not taking voice lessons in anticipation of distracting a Nazi spy."

The joke was wasted on Winora, who glanced over her shoulder, as if they might have a tail. "So Martin doesn't know what we've got?"

"Not yet. What *do* we got—that is, have?"

Winora waved the papers in Dinah's face, though all she could see were other cipher groupings like the one they'd discovered in Martin's typewriter. "A whole lotta gibberish. Letters, mostly, it looks like, between Martin and another sender who uses cheaper paper. Found some of them stashed behind the painting, the rest inside the flap of a book's dust jacket back on the desk. Amateur stuff. Someone's gotta be able to make sense out of it."

"Yes," Dinah said, smiling for the first time since she'd heard the rattle of the apartment door lock, "and I think I know exactly who."

39

Lillian

FRIDAY, JUNE 2, 1944

Lillian had stared at *The Washington Post* crossword clue—
like a wing—for five minutes without a single workable idea
when the knock came at the door, a secret-police pounding
that made her wince.

Steady, Lily. She hadn't been this jumpy since she'd been
convinced George Fabyan was trying to trap her at his estate.

Roger barely looked up from his newspaper. "Probably an
encyclopedia salesman."

"I'll check." Lillian sprang up, grateful for something to do.
A glance at the clock told her it had been less than an hour since
their arrival, but it had felt like ages, waiting on the phone to
ring with news from Margot.

When she opened the door, there stood Dinah herself, flanked
by one of her fellow boarders, the one with the unruly black
hair—Winifred? Wendy? Lillian couldn't quite remember her
name. She clutched several sheets of paper to her chest.

351

Margot must have told Dinah we were here. But why had she brought a friend?

"Told you they might be home," the other woman crowed, pushing past Lillian to enter. "Always pays to check."

But Dinah was only staring at her mother like she was one of the ghosts rumored to have haunted Riverbank. "Mother? What are you doing here?"

For a moment, Lillian only blinked, confused. *Oh. She expected to find Elizebeth.* This was the Friedmans' house, after all. Lillian's carefully rehearsed explanations fled in light of this new development. "We . . . that is, your father and I thought . . . perhaps a visit?"

A moment's confusion passed over Dinah's face, but it was gone in an instant. "It doesn't matter. Am I ever glad to see you."

"You are?" Something in Dinah's demeanor raised Lillian's suspicions—and the way she hurried inside, locking the door and throwing the deadbolt, even testing it. This from the girl who often accidentally left her bedroom window open during a summer rainstorm.

Was Dinah convinced someone was following her again? The similarities to Mama's affliction had troubled Lillian, but when Dinah hadn't mentioned it again, she'd dismissed it as a one-time instance of her daughter's overactive imagination.

"You mean your codebreaker friend isn't here?" the other woman demanded, scowling suddenly.

Ignoring her, Lillian turned back to her daughter. "What's wrong, Dinah? Why were you looking for Elizebeth?"

"Dinah thought she might help us," her friend said breezily, "because it looks like we've caught a Nazi spy with his pants down."

"Not literally," Dinah hastened to add, just as Lillian felt her eyebrows shooting upward. "It's only . . . Winora and I found some documents. Ciphers. And they seem to be very suspicious."

Something about all of this wasn't adding up. "And how did you obtain these documents?"

Sure enough, Dinah glanced away briefly. "It's a long story. We haven't got much time if we're going to get this fellow arrested."

"Which he deserves," her companion—Winora—added with enthusiasm. "And then some."

Roger had entered the room by now, taking in the flurry of words and activity with his usual measured calm. "Then why not give us the quick version?"

The two young women exchanged glances, clearly realizing that neither Lillian nor Roger would accept no for an answer. It was Winora who spun the tale, almost in one breath, a wild story of an Axis sympathizer infiltrating the OSS by flashing around his family name and credentials, only to be demoted by Dinah's report. How he'd gathered information to aid the Germans by surreptitiously copying documents, eavesdropping, even cozying up to Winora—and gathered information on Dinah at the same time.

The first time Lillian couldn't keep herself from interrupting was when they described their idea to test the typewriter in Martin's apartment.

"You went *alone*? Without telling anyone where you would be?"

"We didn't know he was a spy at the time. And I left a note in my room with the hotel information," Dinah said feebly, "just in case."

Which Margot had clearly not seen, or she would have told Lillian of it. By the time she had, it would likely have been too late.

"It was a solid plan," Winora insisted, in a voice like a carnival hawker trying to convince her latest mark. "'You never can have a foolproof plan,' my pops always says, 'cause the world is full of fools, and sometimes you're among 'em and don't know it yet.'"

"Wise words," Lillian said dryly. "And I suppose you simply broke down this fellow's door?"

"No," Roger interrupted. "She picked the lock. Didn't you?" Dinah only ducked her head, as much a confession as Lillian supposed she would get, and her father chuckled appreciatively. "That's my girl."

"*Roger.*" Didn't he realize that such shenanigans were *illegal*?

"I mean . . ." He coughed, rearranging his features into a stern expression. "That was a very dangerous thing to do."

Good heavens. Lillian felt the distinct need to sit down, overwhelmed by the suddenness of it all. She sank into one of the parlor chairs, taking in a deep breath.

"Anyway, the short of it is, we found more than we bargained for." Winora set the stack of papers she'd been clutching on the footstool before her with a *thwack*. "Take a look at these."

There was a map of France, an envelope, and pages of typewritten ciphers. Drawn as if by one of the magnets Roger used to collect metal shavings at work, Lillian reached for them, scanning the letters, looking for the early hints of patterns.

"If you can prove we've got the goods, then we can call the cops, the army, maybe even—" Winora shuddered like she was naming a famous criminal gang—"the *feds*. Someone who can nab Martin before he gets away."

"It won't be long before Martin notices the papers are gone, if he hasn't already," Dinah added.

That explained her sense of urgency, but not the paranoia. "But he won't know it's you who took them, correct?"

Again, another secretive look passed between them. "Oh, he'll know," Winora said.

Lillian opened her mouth to ask another question, then shut it again. They'd have time to sort out this predicament later, likely with the authorities involved. "I'll see what I can make of these."

"May I help?" Her daughter's voice was hesitant, yet hopeful.

Lillian looked up from the papers, her mind already beginning to work through possible divisions between words. "I would appreciate it. We'll find the answers together, or not at all."

From the grin on her daughter's face, Lillian felt that, for once, she'd said just the right thing.

"We'll need everyone to pitch in, actually." She looked over at Roger, who froze in the doorway.

"I thought I might 'pitch in' by making some tea." In response to Lillian's imploring look, he backed away farther. "Come on, Lily. I was never more than a second-rate codebreaking dabbler, even twenty-five years ago."

"Don't sell yourself short, dear. It may come back to you. Besides, I get the feeling that this Martin's efforts were on the more basic end of the cryptography spectrum."

"You bet," Winora chimed in. "He's more the kind to have mailed in for an Ovaltine decoder disk than be a real pro."

They could only hope so. Until they could get ahold of the Friedmans, they were a quartet of rank amateurs and has-beens with a daunting—and time-dependent—task before them.

Attempting to imitate Roger's usual optimism, Lillian straightened her shoulders. "Let's see what we can do, shall we?" Without waiting for a rousing agreement, she led them into the den, the desk now immaculately cleared off, giving them plenty of room to spread out. "Where should we start?"

"A longer message," Dinah suggested, and Lillian smiled. So she *had* learned something from the process of translating the journal.

"What about this one?" Winora said, passing them a full typewritten page, folded in thirds. "This was the one I found in the book dust jacket. It's got the crooked letter from Martin's typewriter, so he was probably about to send it to someone. Envelope's not sealed or addressed, though."

Lillian frowned. "Of course not. We should be so lucky."

With no address or location information, it would be difficult to find the "big fish" as they called it in Elizebeth's line of work, the real source of any spy network getting information into the hands of Axis operators. Martin clearly had a contact he was communicating with.

Don't get ahead of yourself. At the moment, Lillian had only Dinah and Winora's assurances that this Martin character was involved in anything illegal. It was time to let the ciphers speak for themselves.

Lillian drew out pencils and thick, white erasers, all in their correct places after she'd reorganized the room, and set the cipher next to a blank sheet of paper. "Roger, will you start the frequency analysis? Winora, arrange the remaining letters by date, if possible. We'll need all the context we can gather if we're going to make quick work of this. Dinah, you and I will try to isolate the reoccurring vowels."

The Friedmans' den was a code room once again—but this time, she was the one in charge.

Despite his protests, it seemed Roger hadn't forgotten the basics of his training all those years ago. "Like riding a bicycle," he muttered, his finger pointing to each letter in turn. Even Winora made herself useful, bringing in additional chairs from the dining room and taping papers together to make larger worksheets to use in lieu of a blackboard.

But it was Dinah who impressed Lillian the most. As soon as Roger had finished listing each letter's occurrence, she pointed to the longest columns. "The messages must be in English, not German, right?"

Lillian nodded. "Most likely." That was a mercy. No need for an emergency phone call to Myrtlewood to get Margot's expertise.

Wait. Myrtlewood. "This ex-boyfriend of Winora's . . . does he know where you live?"

For a moment, Dinah blinked, in the dazed way of someone who has been recalled to reality from the separate world of numbers and letters. Then understanding lit her face. "I already thought of that. We telephoned Auntie Margot from a pay phone and told her to lock the doors, in case Martin shows up looking for us."

"Very good." Lillian only hoped Margot would comply instead of taking matters into her own hands. The young man should count himself lucky if she didn't assault him with her gardening spade.

She directed her attention back to the cipher. Winora's occasional exclamations and Roger's mutterings faded away, and there were only the groups of letters to be split apart and the sound of pencils scribbling possibilities. She wrote down guesses more often than Dinah, but her daughter's occasional, hesitant contributions were often accurate.

Though Lillian couldn't be sure how much time had passed, it felt like only a few minutes before they'd assembled a dozen possible letter substitutions and begun to divide the five-letter blocks into the length of actual words.

"Wait." Dinah pointed at one of their tentative divisions. "This word here turns up *flament*. Which is nonsense."

She frowned, shifting her focus back to their worksheets. "Are you sure it's not *fragment* or something similar?"

"Not according to what we've worked out."

Indeed, a check confirmed her daughter was right. "Maybe we need to start again, or at least look at where the word is divided."

"No." The single word, coming from Winora, was blurted out with such stricken panic that even Lillian looked up. "Flament is a name. A French name. Is . . . could the word before it be *Gilbert*?"

Lillian glanced at the worksheets. They hadn't yet solved for G or B, but all the other letters fit. Her lips moved soundlessly, checking those letters against the other gaps in the message. All of them formed intelligible words, seemingly physical descriptions of several men listed by name. "How did you know?"

"Because I was on the team making their fake ID cards," Winora admitted. She swayed slightly, leaning against the desk, staring at their worksheets in horror. "I—I told Martin about some important identity cards I'd forged when he asked what I actually did at work. Just the code name for the project—Jedburgh—and the fact that I'd had to learn some French for it. I'd had a little too much to drink, and I was showing off. Since he was OSS too, I thought . . ." Her hand flew to her mouth. "I think I'm going to be sick."

"Not on the documents," Lillian said firmly, but the implications of Winora's words were beginning to sink in. French, she'd said. That meant these OSS agents were undercover in Europe's most critical battlefield . . . just before a possible invasion.

Colonel McCormack's words, and even more, his somber tone, came back to her. *"We are at a precipice, Mrs. Kendall. The outcome of the war may rest on the success of this invasion."*

"So that's what he copied from the Records Room," Dinah said, another statement that was nearly meaningless to Lillian. "They were filed by code name, and once he had that . . ."

"I've done it now," Winora moaned. "What if he's already leaked their names to the Nazis?"

"There's no need for hysterics." Lillian tried to keep her tone objective. "As you pointed out, this doesn't appear to be a copy of a letter already sent. Whoever Martin's contact was, he likely didn't get this information or the map of France you saw."

"You think so?" Winora asked, her voice still colored with desperation.

Lillian nodded, hoping it wasn't merely wishful thinking. "We can't prove it yet, not without getting Martin into custody. If the Allied invasion of France has been compromised, or if the Germans can positively identify the OSS agents in France, the government must know about this immediately."

She thought of the crossword panic overseas in Britian. How many close calls, how many near leaks and espionage attempts would the Allied invasion be able to survive to pull off an operation of such magnitude?

For a moment, silence reigned in the den as they all realized just how critical their evidence had become. Roger was the first to break it. "Could the Friedmans help?"

"If you can manage to get ahold of them. I don't know if they take calls at work." Perhaps they ought to have started there, but Lillian had been hesitant to bring her old friends in without anything concrete. This cipher was certainly shaping up to be just that—not to mention deeply alarming.

Roger nodded sharply, ducking out of the doorway. "I'll do what I can."

"Telephone is by the stairs," Lillian called after him, in case he'd forgotten.

With one message decrypted, the others, though shorter, seemed easier, all of them simple substitution ciphers, not the complex, randomized structure that could only be created with a machine. Most seemed to be Martin's correspondence with an unnamed American resident of German extraction, who Martin only referred to by the initial *T*. His replies indicated skepticism that Martin could produce any information of value to "our mutual interests," along with a refusal to introduce him to other "more direct" contacts. Once, Martin referred to "the Bund," likely the German-American Bund, an isolationist extremist group that had thrived before Pearl Harbor.

"This is good," Lillian pointed out, hoping it would ease some of Dinah's tension. "It seems that whatever he has already given to T wasn't of special use. Your Martin seems to have been more an annoyance than a linchpin."

"Because he hadn't sent his contact the invasion information," Dinah concluded.

"We can only hope so."

Winora had long since disappeared into the kitchen to "rummage something up from the pantry," leaving the two of them alone. Her daughter slumped forward in her chair, turning to the next document in the stack, but Lillian stopped her. "There's enough here to convince the FBI of the seriousness of your evidence, perhaps even to make an arrest."

"What if it's too late? What if he realizes he was compromised and runs away?"

"Then there's nothing more we can do." It was the honest, practical answer, but the defeated look on Dinah's face made Lillian wish she had something more hopeful to offer. They sat in silence, the broken and unbroken ciphers scattered before them on the desk.

Say it.

Her stubborn side voiced an argument. *Now certainly isn't the time.*

Then again, when was she likely to have a better opportunity?

Lillian cleared her throat, standing to face Dinah, who had risen to gather up their worksheets. "Also, related to the ciphers and the journal . . ." It was a poor start, but Lillian had to continue, or she might never find the courage again. "I'm sorry I made you feel you hadn't lived up to my expectations."

Dinah was already shaking her head. "It's all right, Mother. We were both upset, and . . ."

"No, no, let me say this."

Dinah's mouth closed, and she turned to look, really look, at her mother for the first time. The scrutiny almost made Lillian glance down at her hands, folded with nothing better to do but clutch each other for support, but she maintained eye contact. "The truth is, when I became a mother, I had an idea of how everything ought to be. The French lessons, the arithmetic drills, the endless piano scales . . . I put you through all of that because my mother didn't seem to care what I did or what I made of myself. But I cared. I wanted you to thrive, to find something that you were passionate about. In the process, I believe I made you feel you had to earn my approval. And I'm sorry for that."

Dinah nodded slowly, and a wry smile lit her face. "I haven't exactly made things easy for you. That last conversation especially. I . . . it was a little harsh."

True. But this wasn't about Dinah. "That's behind us now. I'm proud of you. I hope you know that. And, more importantly, I love you."

She tilted her head, as if surprised. "Of course. I've always known that."

Lillian cleared her throat. "Good. That's . . . that's all I want." Hesitantly, she opened her arms, and Dinah stepped into them. The embrace was brief, but the familiar smell of peppermint oil made Lillian's eyes moisten with the watery beginnings of tears.

"They're here," Roger called from the hallway, his voice breaking into the moment, causing Lillian and Dinah to step apart.

"Who?" Lillian asked, hoping for Elizebeth's familiar face. If anyone could calm her rising anxieties, it would be her old friend.

"The FBI. I told William to pull whatever strings he could. He trusts you, Lily."

Enough to risk his career sending a federal agent to his house to investigate suspicious papers obtained by a twenty-year-old lockpick. "Thank God for that."

"What do I do?" Dinah asked, peering out the window. Two men stepped out of a dark sedan, slamming the door and hurrying up to the house like they expected to find the accused spy tied up inside.

"You'll have to talk to them," Lillian said matter-of-factly, looking at Winora too, who had come into the den. "Alone. Tell them everything you told us—and anything you left out."

"I—I'd rather have you with me. If you don't mind." In that moment, Dinah looked like the barely budded young woman she'd been on her first day of high school.

The rap on the door certainly had an intimidating effect, and Lillian heard Roger greet the agents, ushering them inside.

Lillian shook her head. "You and Winora are the witnesses. If they ask our process for decrypting the ciphers, I'll come in, but not until then." She squeezed her daughter's hand. "You can do this, Dinah."

Perhaps Roger's idea of making tea wasn't so bad. They could all use something soothing just about now.

As Lillian slipped into the kitchen, she heard a gruff male voice say, "So you're one of the girls who called in about a spy?"

"I'm one of the *women* who gathered evidence of an infiltrator to the OSS, yes," Dinah said, all trace of nerves gone from her voice. "Perhaps you'd like to hear about it."

"That's my girl," Lillian whispered, and for the first time during this ordeal, a smile curved onto her face.

40

Dinah

"You mean you can't tell us *anything*?" Dinah demanded as William and Elizebeth sat down at the dinner table. Even though she'd always been intimidated by her mother's brilliant friends, she didn't try to temper the disbelief in her tone.

Mr. Friedman's moustache twitched slightly, as if he were suppressing a laugh. Surely he wouldn't look so amused if Martin had gotten away . . . would he?

"It's the FBI, dear," Mrs. Friedman said gently. "They're notoriously tight-lipped."

"But *you* know," she couldn't resist pointing out.

Mrs. Friedman exchanged glances with her husband as they passed around a dish of mashed potatoes. "A limited amount of information, yes. Because of our work with the Bureau as consultants."

"Dinah, this is a matter of national security," Mother added in a pacifying tone. This time, Dinah restrained herself from huffing a weary sigh, because she knew it was just Mother's way . . . and that she was probably right.

"National security my eye," Winora responded tartly, and the look of horror on Mother's face told Dinah she was probably regretting extending this dinner invitation to her friend, even after everything that had happened. "They wouldn't have a thing on Martin if it wasn't for us."

"Perhaps it'll be in the papers soon," Dad said, clearly trying to console them. "Those newsies can't resist a good fifth-column spy ring."

Elizebeth gave only the barest of nods. "I wouldn't doubt it. Tomorrow, perhaps."

"Then what's the harm in giving us an early preview?" Winora pressed, leaning against her elbow while she chewed a full mouth of food. "Some reporter somewhere already knows."

"If," Mr. Friedman said, taking a measured bite of roast beef, "I felt it were appropriate, I could say only that the suspect was apprehended at his parents' summer home on the Chesapeake Bay, attempting to collect his personal belongings—and his mother's sapphire jewelry set, which he may have been intending to sell to finance a possible disappearance."

"William," Mrs. Friedman said in a warning tone.

He wiped away her scrutiny with a dab of his napkin. "Hypothetically, you understand."

"So," Dinah said, giving Mr. Friedman a look of appreciation, "he did realize we were on to him."

"Or at least that he was missing some very sensitive documents. If the FBI hadn't acted on your tip immediately, he might have gotten away."

Dinah decided it was the right time to try pressing her luck. "Hypothetically, would they have found out anything about who Martin was corresponding with?"

Mr. Freidman paused for slightly longer this time. "Given that he was apprehended while in the act of destroying a

German-American Bund storm trooper uniform, they have some individuals in mind. Many of the Bund's former leaders have been imprisoned for the duration of the war, so it narrows the field somewhat."

The "harmless nationalistic" organization she'd learned about back in Gettysburg would be connected to all of this.

"They may hope that Martin himself might be persuaded to give up information." Mr. Friedman shrugged. "He seemed to be a lone operator attempting to prove himself . . . but he might lead the authorities to other persons of interest. Regardless, I think you'll see some exaggerated accounts of the FBI's daring exploits over the next few days."

"I don't suppose they'll mention us?" Dinah asked, trying not to let her eagerness show. There was something dramatic about being named in a real, actual newspaper article. Imagine what her friends from home would think.

"With J. Edgar Hoover in charge, I sincerely doubt it." Mrs. Freidman made a sour face. "At most, it would be, 'With the help of information from alert citizens.' That sort of thing."

To Dinah's surprise, Winora nodded in satisfaction. "Good. I've got to keep my nose clean."

"But you were on the right side of the law this time," Dinah pointed out, adding, with a glance at Mother, "that is, mostly."

"Yeah, I know," Winora said glumly. "If word gets back to Pops that I helped the FBI . . . The OSS is one thing, but the feds are something else."

"You should both be quite proud of your quick thinking," Mother said. "Though perhaps not for all of your methods."

Dinah tried her best to look ashamed. After hearing that Winora was Martin's girlfriend, the FBI agents hadn't pressed them for information on how they'd entered Martin's apartment, either making their own assumptions or simply accepting that the ends justified the means. Still, she had to admit that their risk-taking had very nearly had serious consequences.

"It won't happen again," Dinah said solemnly, and meant it.

"Aw, it wasn't so bad." Winora had almost a fond expression on her face. "In fact, it made me want to ask for a transfer to Special Services. To get in on some of the real action, you know."

Dinah was surprised to find she didn't agree. Reading about espionage was quite different from being so close to danger. Some dreams, it seemed, changed with time.

Yet even as the dinner conversation changed to lighter topics, Dinah couldn't help asking the same question her mother had asked in her journals during the waning days of the Great War: What would her next dream be?

⸻

It was, Dinah had to admit while wrenching her arm to reach the back of her hair, much more difficult to pin up her curls without Mother's help.

A couple of days after the excitement with Martin's arrest, the papers had indeed announced the FBI's sensational discovery of a suspected spy in the capital, though there would be more information released around the trial. For a brief moment, it had been front-page news . . . until today, that is.

Dinah checked to make sure she had her copy of the *Post* on her vanity, ready for tonight's address. She'd decided not to change into her nightwear just yet. Even though it was nearly ten o'clock and she wouldn't be leaving the parlor, her father's old robe felt too informal.

With life more or less back to normal, Dinah had paid the rent for June, committing to stay at Myrtlewood for at least the rest of the month while continuing to search for a position. Yesterday, she'd had her first real prospect, by way of a telephone call from Hazel Agnew, of all people.

"An old friend of mine is a docent at the Smithsonian," she'd

said. *"Apparently they have an urgent need for an assistant to one of their archivists to process a large estate donation of Civil War artifacts. I told her I knew of a bright young woman I could highly recommend, but I wanted to ask you first."*

*"*Thank you for thinking of me.*"* The polite response came automatically as Dinah considered the option. It wasn't anything she'd thought of before, and wouldn't be war work, strictly speaking. And yet, to be surrounded by all that history . . .

"It sounds like rather a lot of filing and inventorying," Hazel went on. *"At first, I thought the work might be too ordinary for your talents, but when I voiced that thought aloud, Frasier said you might appreciate the value of the ordinary more than most. I'm not entirely sure what he meant by that, but he said you would know."*

Dinah hadn't made a commitment yet . . . but she had an interview scheduled the next day, and she intended to look her best. Victory Rolls it would be, help or no help.

A knock at her door jarred Dinah out of her thoughts, and Shirley threw open the door, her cheeks flushed. "Hurry, Dinah, or you'll miss the whole thing."

Was it already that late? "I'm coming." She snatched up her newspaper and rushed down the stairs, leaving half of her hair hanging loose. The other boarders were arranged in the parlor, where every available space was filled, dressed in a mix of daytime wear and pajamas to accommodate the late hour. Most held newspapers with headlines of Eisenhower and Normandy and "the greatest invasion force of the war" shouted out in bold type.

"The address will begin in two-and-a-half minutes," Anne-Marie informed them all with the exactitude of a railroad conductor.

"Shouldn't we turn on the radio?" Dinah said, kneeling on the rug directly in the center of the room. "I don't want to miss a word." All day, rumors about the Allied landings at Normandy, supplemented by early newspaper reports, had been all anyone could talk about. Out on the streets, on the buses, and even in Myrtlewood, there was an electric feeling, equal parts fear, from knowing such an assault would have a high cost, and excitement. Dinah couldn't help wondering what it had been like at the OSS headquarters.

"Honestly," Betty said, adjusting her curlers, "I think it's all a lot of trouble for nothing. They never tell us anything real in these sort of addresses."

There was some truth to that, but at the moment, Dinah would take any scrap of information she could. After all she and Winora had gone through . . .

Wait a minute. Dinah glanced around to confirm. "Where's Winora?" She'd been so preoccupied with her own thoughts that she hadn't noticed her friend wasn't present.

"In her room, probably," Anne-Marie said in the slow, throaty voice meant to imitate Lauren Bacall that really made her sound like she was sleep-talking.

"Did anyone invite her?" Dinah demanded, though she already knew the answer.

Silence from the other women, unbroken until Betty glanced nervously at Auntie Margot, who was leaning against the far wall. She usually left her boarders to their own devices in the evening, but this broadcast was too important to miss.

"I can't imagine she didn't know," Betty said quickly. "It's all anyone's been talking about. Maybe she just doesn't care about war news."

"She's just being her usual antisocial self," Shirley interjected.

This time, Dinah wasn't going to let the comment go, turning to face the others. "Or she knows that some people might make her feel unwelcome."

Betty laughed nervously, and Shirley scooped up a handful of popcorn, jamming it into her mouth. "I don't know what you're talking about," Anne-Marie said coolly.

"I think you do," Dinah countered. "It's a shame too. Winora is more interesting and talented than anyone our age I've ever met. And I'll bet she's *very* interested in hearing about the invasion." *For personal reasons*, just like Dinah, though she couldn't add that part, couldn't explain why the two of them felt that they, in a small way, had contributed to the campaign's success—or at least prevented a tragic failure.

"You bet I am." The voice in the doorway made all of them turn, and Winora marched in, dressed in tattered plaid pajamas, holding a box of MoonPies. "Thought today was worth celebrating." She made no attempt to pass the treats around, simply plopped the box in the middle of the coffee table and sat down next to Dinah. "Well, what are we waiting for? The show's almost started."

Auntie Margot obliged, giving Dinah an approving wink as she passed by. She adjusted the radio dial, where a broadcaster's resonant bass was introducing the president. Soon, President Roosevelt's voice came into their parlor strong and clear. "My fellow Americans: Last night, when I spoke with you about the fall of Rome, I knew at that moment that troops of the United States and our allies were crossing the Channel."

"Hey," Winora whispered into the dramatic pause, "I made this for you."

Dinah was about to tell her to hush and not interrupt this historic moment when Winora passed her a small sketch done in pencil with her characteristic dark lines and heavy shading.

"It has come to pass with success thus far," Roosevelt continued.

The subjects of the drawing were immediately recognizable. It was Dinah and her mother, hunched over a worksheet together, their faces focused. Somehow, in the flurry of shading and lines, Winora had captured the tension and excitement of the moment: two codebreakers working together to crack a cipher.

369

"It's amazing," Dinah whispered back.

Winora jutted her chin out in acknowledgment of Dinah's praise. "No one will know what we did, but that doesn't mean you can't remember it."

"And so, in this poignant hour, I ask you to join with me in prayer."

Dinah knew right where she'd put the drawing—in a frame, next to her Union summer photo with Dad. Somehow, it seemed to belong there.

There was a rustling of newspapers as the women turned to the prayer that had been printed in all the major newspapers, their voices joining with the president's as they read along. "Almighty God: Our sons, pride of our nation, this day have set upon a mighty endeavor, a struggle to preserve our Republic, our religion, and our civilization, and to set free a suffering humanity."

Even Winora's tone was more subdued than usual, as if she was picturing the men, some hardly more than boys, storming the beaches, firing and falling and shouting, trying to take back Europe for the Allies.

"They fight to end conquest. They fight to liberate. They fight to let justice arise, and tolerance and good will among all Thy people. They yearn but for the end of battle, for their return to the haven of home."

Home. Over in Gettysburg, Mother and Dad were likely reciting these very same words, gathered at their country church with parishioners Dinah had known all her life. There was something deeply comforting in that, in joining together with so many others in the same words of petition and hope.

". . . a peace that will let all of men live in freedom, reaping the just rewards of their honest toil. Thy will be done, Almighty God. Amen."

When Dinah glanced around, everyone in the room seemed solemn, but not sad. Even Auntie Margot, swiping at her eyes with her handkerchief, was smiling, and Dinah thought she knew why. The way Roosevelt spoke of peace and the fact that Allied troops were even now fighting to liberate France, it felt like the fighting might actually end in victory. Maybe his speech hadn't relayed many details, but it had rung true with hope.

Then what? Would she stay in DC, go back to Gettysburg, travel to another place entirely? Dinah wasn't sure.

And yet . . . she couldn't help thinking of the journal on her desk upstairs. Her own confident, capable mother had been young and uncertain once too, staring out at the aftermath of her own war with a choice before her. It must be all right to feel that way. After all, Mother had started a new life, a good one, and that meant Dinah could too.

As the other boarders stood, closing their newspapers and wondering aloud about Axis opposition, air attacks, and the casualty numbers that would come in the next few days, Dinah looked instead at Winora's sketch. The future was a cipher for everyone, really, a jumble of unknowns.

Maybe all she had to do was gather the courage to begin.

Author's Note

This novel was possibly my most ambitious yet, with two time-lines and many scenes based entirely on actual occurrences. I'll speak to some of the history behind the novel here, but be sure to visit the "History" page of my website (AmyGreenBooks .com) to find out more about what is fact and what is fiction.

I tried to take great care with Elizebeth and William Fried-man's characters, both genius codebreakers who served their country from WWI through the 1950s. As described in the novel, William was hospitalized for acute depression in early 1941 and battled intense feelings of anxiety and despondency throughout his life, often triggered by exhaustion from stressful periods in his cryptography work. Both Friedmans were extremely private about William's struggles, rarely seeking treatment or mentioning the periods of reoccurring depression to their friends and family. Throughout his life, William described Elizebeth as "my rock," especially during these difficult times. Their romance and married relationship is a beautiful picture of two brilliant individuals caring for and supporting each other.

I tried to be fair in my portrayal of larger-than-life George Fabyan as well, even though he serves as an antagonist to my

main characters. He was a complex man, both fervently patriotic and eager to advance knowledge . . . and also moody
and controlling. The incidents when he bugged the Friedmans'
classroom and read his codebreakers' mail are also historical.
Of him, Elizebeth said many years later, "He was always doing
things for you, and things you couldn't get out of accepting. You
knew you didn't want to, and that you'd be sorry, but never-
theless, you'd be carried through." These and other firsthand
testimonies shaped the way I portrayed Fabyan's character.

Riverbank was turned into a scientific laboratory for a number of experiments, including the use of underage girls from a
local reformatory school for a posture correction regimen. As
for the other details about Riverbank, I loved including some
of the many quirks of the beautiful country estate, which I had
a chance to visit and tour—it's open to the public.

For the WWII timeline, the German-American Bund's activities included Hitler Youth–style summer camps, subversive
propaganda, and a 1939 anti-war rally at Madison Square Garden that drew more than twenty thousand participants. The
group was dying out by 1940 and was officially disbanded by
the government after Pearl Harbor, but many of its members
maintained fierce anti-Semitic and pro-Nazi leanings. While
Martin is a fictional character, several former Bund members
were arrested and convicted for participating in three different
spy rings in the early 1940s.

No known spies made it into the OSS, but several appli-
cants were dismissed in the course of the training and interview
process for either fascist or communist leanings to avoid such
an occurrence, so it is possible someone could have slipped
through. Dinah's role attempting to trap agents into revealing
too much in Gettysburg is based on a real test the Catoctin
Mountain–trained OSS fellows faced while on leave.

As for Morale Operations, all of the campaigns mentioned
in the novel were real, from the Hitler-critical toilet paper to

the successful radio station that delivered rumors along with popular music. The MO team members I included in the novel are fictional, but several women had influential roles in developing MO campaigns, including Barbara Lauwers, who developed my favorite propaganda scheme, the League of Lonely War Women. (I moved up its timeline a few months so I could mention it in the novel.) In addition to the administration staff in DC, Morale Operations also had an office in New York City. For simplicity's sake, and to be able to show the wide variety of projects the department undertook, I combined the two locations into one.

The British "crossword scare" just before D-Day also really happened just as described in the novel. The Allied investigation did eventually decide no critical information had been leaked. It was only afterward that anyone made the connection to the boys at the school overhearing the military code words that appeared in the puzzle, a conclusion I allowed Lillian to reveal.

I'm grateful to the guides at the Fabyan Villa Museum and the authors of the many books on codebreaking and the OSS that I used for research (*The Woman Who Smashed Codes* by Jason Fagone and *The Propaganda Warriors* by Clayton D. Laurie were among the most accessible, if you're interested in reading more). Any mistakes that remain are my own.

Also, many thanks to my editorial team, particularly for their graciousness in rearranging my editorial schedule so I could turn in the manuscript before the due date of my baby. In addition to the leadership of Rochelle Gloege and Kate Deppe, I had the joy of working with Jen Veilleux and Hannah Ahlfield on this one as well. I'm also grateful for all the hard work put into this by the marketing team at Bethany House. You are consistently a delight to work with. I can't begin to list all of the art, design, sales, and administrative team members who are a part of getting this book into your hands, but as always, I'm deeply grateful for their efforts.

For my personal thanks, I'd like to shout out family and friends for checking in on me, saying, "Wow, interesting" when I excitedly dispensed the latest bit of research trivia, and giving me the practical gift of extra time to write as I approached deadlines. Ruthie, my critique partner and brainstorming buddy, gave excellent feedback on this story, as always. I'm so grateful to be a part of a supportive community of writers and non-writers alike.

Finally, thanks to you, readers, for taking time to get to know these characters and step into the past with me—I couldn't do it without you. Please visit my website and drop me a line on my contact form there. I love reading and responding to reader mail.

Discussion Questions

1. What did you like or dislike about the novel's inclusion of two different timelines, the main story in WWII and flashbacks to WWI? Did you have a favorite between the two?

2. How would you describe Lillian and Dinah's relationship at the beginning of the novel? In what ways did they grow closer throughout the story?

3. The Author's Note mentions that Elizebeth and William Friedman and George Fabyan are historical figures. Does knowing this change how you view the events of the novel? If so, how?

4. Both Lillian and the Friedmans deal with a stigma around mental illness during their era. What was most interesting to you about their struggles? Do you think this issue has gone away?

5. Until recently, Elizebeth's contributions were nearly entirely forgotten, with William getting much more credit for the work he accomplished. Elizebeth tells Lillian, "History has a way of forgetting all but the emperors

and generals . . . and the occasional brilliant playwright. Women in particular often change the world
quietly, without recognition." Has that been true in
your experience? Are there other little-known women in
history you would like to read a novel about?

6. Mr. Agnew says of his work at Morale Operations: "I
   believe truth is the most powerful force on this earth.
   Still, the lies we manufacture in Morale Operations
   might give us the edge we need. Because sometimes,
   the truth is that our enemies are winning the battle. If
   we let them know it, they might win the war." Do you
   agree or disagree with his (or Dinah's) justification for
   using deception during wartime?

7. Did you have suspicions about who might be behind Dinah's feeling of being followed? At what point did you
   realize the truth?

8. Margot insists Winora and Lillian have a lot in common,
   despite having very different personalities and life experi-
   ences. Can you see any evidence for that comparison?

9. Given the opportunity, would you be a better fit for
   codebreaking at Riverbank or rumor creation with the
   OSS? Or would you turn down both jobs?

10. Early in the novel, Roger's mother tells Lillian, "There
    is great honor in being an ordinary woman." How does
    this theme play out throughout the novel?

11. Do you think Roger and Lillian are suited for each
    other? Were you hoping they would get together, de-
    spite the difficult start to their relationship?

12. Near the end of the novel, Roger assesses Lillian's main
    problem as one of putting her family and role as wife
    and mother before anything else, even her faith. Do you
    agree? What are some signs she has been putting too
    much pressure on that particular dream?

13. Which historical details did you find the most interesting?

14. Do you have any predictions about what Lillian and Dinah will choose to do after the events of the novel, perhaps even after the war?

For more from Amy Lynn Green,
read on for an excerpt from

The Foxhole
Victory Tour

During World War II, Catherine Duquette and Maggie Mc-
Cleod come from different worlds but are thrown together
on a USO variety show touring North Africa. While they
each have secret reasons for accepting the job, neither antici-
pates the danger and intrigue they'll encounter performing
so close to the front lines.

Available now wherever books are sold.

1

Maggie McCleod had exactly twenty-four measures to get her heels back on. The trouble was, she had to keep wailing on her trumpet at the same time, which made the whole operation much more complicated.

As she riffed on the crescendo of "Rhapsody in Blue," she tried to work her bare left foot deeper into the high heel. The motion was hidden from the audience by the hem of her gown, but her grimace as her toes jammed partway in could be spotted by anyone with a keen eye. Swollen again. No surprise after the band members had been forced to run to catch the train to Minneapolis.

Come on, come on. A measure skipped by without her as she fumbled with the strap, trying to force it over her heel.

It was easy enough to wriggle the shoes off at the start of each concert, right after Maggie took her spot on the stage. Just a discreet motion shielded by her gown's long hemline while the audience listened to Catherine Duquette, first-chair

383

violinist, give her polished introduction to the Swinging Sweet-hearts. Replacing the heels before the final bows was trickier, but Maggie had never had this much trouble.

In front of her, conductor Martin Simmons tilted his head back theatrically with the final swell of the upbeat tune, his baton twitching wildly, as if trying to juice the last bit of energy out of "his girls." Beyond him, the audience filling the plush seats of Northrop Auditorium clapped enthusiastically.

"A good show," they'd say during intermission. *"Didn't those girls play like men?"*

At least, that's what they'd say if she didn't give them some-thing more interesting to talk about by tripping to the micro-phone. It was tradition for the soloist of the previous piece to dismiss the audience for intermission, reciting the standard lines their promoter churned out. Tonight that was Maggie, shoes on or off.

On Simmons's cue, Maggie curtsied with the others, deeper than usual, letting her hook the heel's strap with her finger and give it a frantic tug.

No one else could hear the tiny snap, but Maggie froze. *Perfect. Just super.*

She silently cursed Simmons for choosing the ridiculous uni-form, their promoter for showcasing it on publicity kits, and even women like Catherine who made walking in heels seem effortless.

Simmons, arms spread apart in his circus ringmaster stance, was staring at Maggie, punctuating her cue with his thick eye-brows. One of her fellow brass players elbowed her in case she'd forgotten.

There was nothing for it but to scoop up the broken heel, let-ting it dangle from her free hand, and limp to the microphone.

The gathered audience stared, and she gave them a smile. Might as well defuse the tension. "Never fear, everyone, I wasn't injured. Just a wardrobe issue." She held up the shoe, and the concern turned to chuckling. "Not the most practical of uniforms, but you all came for the glamour, and the Swinging Sweethearts deliver at any cost."

It wasn't how she was supposed to start the speech—the script called for her to mention the venue and thank everyone for being there—but it felt good to say it out loud, despite the slight discomfort on the faces of the first few rows past the stage lights. She'd always hated the posters with condescending slogans like "While our boys are off at war, the women have joined the band . . . and these sweeties sure can swing!"

She warmed to the speech, drawing closer to the microphone to make sure even the back row would hear. "I hope you've enjoyed our all-girls extravaganza, even if it was just our name that drew you in. Come to think of it, you don't see Tommy Dorsey or Glenn Miller changing their band names to 'The Bachelors of Rhythm' or 'The Dashing Dreamboats.' Maybe it would sell more tickets—or maybe that's just for us women."

More laughter, and this time she glanced across the stage at Simmons, who was frozen in place. Good thing he couldn't actually murder her with his baton in front of this many witnesses.

Anyway, this was his fault. He was the one who dressed them up like dolls, scolded anyone who seemed to be gaining weight, and told their promoter to feature posters with photographs that made them look more like pinup girls than serious musicians. "The crowds come to get an earful *and* an eyeful," she'd heard him say.

Well, he was getting an earful now, and it served him right.

Mr. Simmons was already gesturing frantically to the band to leave the stage, but the women's eyes were mostly on her, including a horrified Catherine Duquette, cupid-bow mouth in a perfect O.

Better finish this quickly.

"The program will continue after intermission. So listen to

us—close your eyes if you need to—and see if you don't get the best music you've ever heard from this all-girl band." She gave a small bow. "Thank you."

The applause that followed was probably the same volume as usual, but it felt different. Special. It was for her specifically. Not just her as one instrument in dozens, another gown in a sea of sweethearts.

She refused to look over her shoulder at Simmons as she filed backstage with her fellow band members. As she did, Catherine turned, clutching her violin case. "Was that . . . planned?"

Catherine looked the very image of demure womanhood, her auburn hair pinned with a pearl hair comb, with only one curl falling out by her ear. Even that was probably intentional. She'd never gone onstage with a wrinkle in her gown, much less lost a shoe and embarrassed their conductor in front of an audience.

"Of course not. Help a girl out, would you?" Without waiting for an answer, Maggie grabbed the shorter woman's shoulder, steadying herself as she pulled off her other shoe without tearing her gown's hem. That done, she flared her toes against the scuffed boards of backstage, enjoying the freedom of being gloriously barefoot. "Thanks."

"Why did you . . . ?" Catherine began, then bit her lip and tried again. "That wasn't the speech we're meant to give."

Noticed that, did you? Maggie fought rolling her eyes and just shrugged. "It came to me, that's all. Didn't you like my improvisation?"

"I don't . . . it's just . . ." She seemed to give up on explaining the faux pas and settled for "Mr. Simmons will be upset."

"That's why I don't plan to let him find me." Maggie hiked her skirt up enough that she wouldn't trip over it and gave a little wave. "See ya onstage." With that, she made a beeline for an abandoned stack of scenery, an ideal place to hide until the end of intermission.

Maggie leaned against the wall, breathing out deeply. She'd actually gone and done it, said what she'd been thinking for ten long months now.

For once, she wished her father had been in the audience. He hadn't fully approved of her joining the Sweethearts, but he'd always raised her to speak her mind. But he was still back in Chicago and hadn't even been able to break free from his mission work to attend one of the shows they'd put on near her home in the Windy City.

As confident as Maggie had tried to sound to Catherine, she couldn't help worrying. This was her third job since she'd moved out on her own a year and a half ago. She hadn't cared when she was fired from the soda fountain for slapping a handsy customer or when she walked out from the munitions factory when she found out the male employees were paid more. Those had been ways to pay the bills, nothing more. But the Sweethearts, despite their ridiculous name, had been her dream, a chance to play music professionally. If she'd ruined it by running her mouth again . . .

"It'll blow over," she muttered, willing it to be true. She could talk her way out of nearly anything, after all.

At least, that's what she hoped.

2

Catherine Duquette pretended to admire the Northrop Auditorium chandeliers as the audience streamed past her, hoping against hope that no one would talk to her.

It wasn't strictly required, but Mr. Simmons always liked his girls to mingle with the crowds during intermission to make connections for future bookings. That wouldn't be so bad, except it required her to speak coherently to strangers.

Still, there was no way around it. Better to make an appearance and be seen by Mr. Simmons, murmur a few thank-yous to compliments on the show, then hurry backstage with some excuse or another.

To pass the time, Catherine took covert glances at the gowns worn by the women of the audience, some draped in furs to keep the chill of the winter night away. The frigid season and the seriousness of wartime ensured that most of the colors and prints were subdued shades of blues and grays. But she caught a glimpse of a stunning cream dotted-swiss gown with a tiered skirt, and a gold number with a sweetheart neckline designed to show off a sapphire necklace.

The men she mostly ignored, except that, as usual, her heart raced slightly when she saw a glimpse of Brillantined black hair. A moment later, the turn of a head and the appearance of a rotund belly proved it wasn't Leo.

Of course it wasn't. He couldn't be here, lounging in a Minneapolis performance hall. He was somewhere across the ocean. At least, she prayed he was, and not in a field hospital or buried in foreign soil.

Don't think about that. Whenever her mind drifted to Leo during shows, her performance suffered.

A flash of color caught her eye, and Catherine squinted at the woman emerging from the auditorium's side door just to be sure. Yes, she knew that fur coat, a dark tuxedo-front mink with turned-back cuffs over a burgundy gown. That her mother was wearing an old coat proved she was at least attempting to cut back on new fashion for the war effort.

Catherine bit her lip. She'd worried about coming back to the Twin Cities, although she hadn't said a word about the Sweethearts' schedule to either parent.

The second Mother's eyes caught hers, they sparkled, bottle green like a traffic light and outlined with winged liner to make them seem larger. "Catherine!" she squealed, nearly trampling several audience members to clear a path to her, arms spread wide for a hug. Catherine breathed in the familiar scent of Evening in Paris, the one constant in her mother's life. "You were magnificent, as always."

"I didn't know you'd come," she said, forcing a smile.

Her mother had already changed her expression to an exaggerated pout. "Come now, be honest, *ma chérie*. Were you *ever* going to tell me about your show? Ah," she said, waving a manicured finger in the air before Catherine could speak. "I've guessed it. You were embarrassed of your *maman*."

"No, of course not. I—I thought you were living in New York until . . ." Catherine choked on the ending she couldn't bring herself to voice: until the divorce proceedings went to court.

"Ah, I see," Mother said, leaning in conspiratorially. "I am, of course, but those dratted lawyers are always making me pop back into town. Imagine how delighted I was to have this to look forward to." She took Catherine's arm to lead her out of the flow of traffic, pausing to greet an acquaintance Catherine pretended to remember and waving at a couple across the room before turning back to her daughter. "Honestly, it was divine, seeing all you ladies up there. I couldn't have been prouder."

"Thank you," Catherine murmured, all that was usually required of her in conversations like this.

"Do you remember how your father groused about starting lessons when you were so young. 'Vivienne, imagine the *expense.*'" Her imitation of Gerald Duquette, complete with gruff, smoke-grated voice, was quite good. "I told him that it would be worth it one day, and wasn't I right?"

"Yes, Mama." That was always the right answer . . . as long as Catherine's father wasn't around.

Whether it was that stray thought or a familiar lurching gait that caught her attention, Catherine found her gaze drifting toward the crowd—and the one man striding determinedly in their direction.

No. Not both of them. The sick feeling in her stomach intensified as he took measured steps across the gleaming terrazzo floor toward them, but she discarded a momentary thought of fleeing.

"Catherine," he said coolly, not even directing the slightest acknowledgment toward Mother.

"What are you doing here, Father?" It was terribly rude, but Catherine hadn't been able to help blurting it out. Father never read the entertainment notices in the newspaper. His order was strictly Business, News, and sometimes Editorials, but never something as trivial as music or theater.

"*I* certainly didn't invite him," Mother inserted, as if this were at all in question. Her face didn't wear the same stormy glower as her estranged husband, but she'd taken on a haughty, head-tilted posture that had the same effect.

"Arthur brought me a playbill with your photograph in it," Father said, disgust lacing his voice, as if she'd been plastered across town on a circus flyer clad in a lion-tamer's bikini instead of a perfectly respectable glamour shot with her violin.

Catherine felt a fleeting burst of anger at Father's favorite employee, but poor Arthur likely had no idea of the tension he'd caused. She turned up the brightness of her smile to a level that would break blackout regulations. "Yes, our promoter thinks people respond best to a local connection."

"I see." Catherine knew that tone well. It meant Father had weighed all the details and passed final judgment. "I just finished speaking to that director of yours—"

"Conductor," Mother corrected, forcing her way back into the conversation and angling her narrow shoulders to step between the two of them. "Honestly, Gerald, even an uncultured boor like you should know that. I suppose you think intermission is called the seventh inning stretch."

Father ignored her, a skill which, Catherine had recently realized, had allowed him to remain unhappily married to Mother for twenty-two years. "He told me he wasn't aware you were only touring for a year."

Catherine felt her ears burn and knew it would only be a matter of seconds before the flush crept up her neck and to her cheeks. "I—I meant to tell him. The timing just never seemed right."

That wasn't entirely true. Some part of Catherine had hoped that she'd be able to negotiate with Father, or even that, with the divorce proceedings taking up so much of his time, he might forget.

A foolish hope, she now realized as she looked at her father's immovable face. He had more gray around his temples than she remembered.

"I see. Well, I took the liberty of breaking the news to him. He wasn't happy, of course—all the more reason you ought to have given him notice from the start—but he said he certainly wouldn't want to keep a young woman in his band without her parents' approval."

The words made Catherine flinch. Persuading her father to agree to one year of touring "to get this music business out of your system" had seemed like a dream come true. But here she was, eleven months in and barely started. When she took her place onstage, none of the difficulties of the tour came to mind. She could only think about the dear friends she'd made in her fellow musicians, the improvements in her skill, the sheer freedom of touring through glittering ballrooms and big cities across the country . . .

Mother brushed Father aside with the flat of her hand, a gesture that might look playful if you overlooked the spite in her tone. "Oh, stop being such a boor, Gerald. No amount of bluster can keep my Catherine away from music, can it, *ma chérie*?"

Catherine searched for a response, but Mother didn't seem to need one, her attention fixed on her estranged husband.

Father, on the other hand, hadn't taken his eyes off Catherine, his words clipped and businesslike. "It is, however, not up to you. Catherine and I had an agreement, and I'm sure she wouldn't be so foolish as to break her word, not with her future at stake."

The words were very proper. No promise of disinheritance, no reminder that most musicians at her level wouldn't be able to survive on their salary, no threats. Those wouldn't come out until she dared to cross him.

Just now, Catherine was feeling remarkably low on daring.

She wasn't like Maggie, who could speak her mind and grit her teeth against the reaction. Her parents' slowly rising voices were already attracting stares, and she licked her dry lips in an attempt to speak. "Can we discuss this after the performance, please? I really ought to—"

"There's nothing more to discuss," Father interrupted. "One month, Catherine. That's final."

Mother sniffed. "Delightful. Then I'll be sure to tell the concertmaster of the New York Philharmonic to schedule Catherine's audition for mid-March."

"My audition?" Catherine asked, hating how helpless her question sounded. Surely her mother hadn't. . . . She wasn't ready, not for performances at that level. Her year with the Sweethearts was the first time she'd ever·played with other musicians.

"I was just going to tell you before we were *interrupted*." She glared at Father, then turned back to Catherine. "It's a magnificent opportunity. I may have been forced to give up my career after getting married, but I still have my connections."

That was a slanted version of the real story. From what Catherine had heard, her mother, a Parisian-born opera singer, had been struggling financially and had married Father as a way out. But Catherine knew Mother had told her rendition of the story so often that she believed it was true.

"I must say, he was fascinated when he heard I had such a talented daughter. 'Where have you been hiding her away?' he asked." She gave her usual trill of a laugh. "Of course, the real question was, *Who* was hiding her away?"

Father's voice was little more than a growl at this point. "That's unfair, Vivienne. I've always wanted the best for Catherine—which doesn't include the life you lived in Paris, half-starving in a tiny apartment with a ruined reputation."

Catherine cast desperately about for a way of escape and saw two of the Sweethearts' woodwind players whispering to each other and discreetly pointing in their direction. Were they close enough to hear?

If not, they soon would be. Vivienne Lavigne-Duquette and Gerald Duquette were known in society gossip rags for their tempestuous public rows. Catherine usually managed to play the peacemaker and remained invisible whenever possible.

Not this time. She struggled to breathe as more and more people turned and whispered, gesturing to her parents, who now stood directly facing each other, their voices continuing to rise.

"You mustn't pretend, Gerald. You want *your* best and always have. The rest of us might as well not even exist."

Father scoffed. "Really, Vivienne, you seem determined to make it impossible for *anyone* to forget about you, even if that means making a scene."

"I really must be getting back," Catherine finally said. Both pairs of eyes turned to her, sharp as daggers, cutting the courage out of her so she could only add, "Enjoy the rest of the program, Father, Mother."

Now. Now. She had to leave now. Before they shouted after her, before she was in the middle once again. Catherine nearly tripped over her hem in her hurry to escape, blinking back tears.

What was she going to do? If Mr. Simmons had already agreed to dismiss her from the Sweethearts—and she didn't doubt her father could bribe or coerce him to do so—then she had very few choices before her. She could return to the Duquette mansion on Summit Avenue and marry a suitable husband like her father wanted. Or she could run off to New York and live with her mother and whatever man was currently in her life, riding her coattails into a prestigious audition she wasn't prepared for.

Her parents were dividing her and her future up like she was another bank account or vacation property for their attorneys to quarrel over.

A few deep breaths backstage were all she could spare before one of her fellow violinists tugged her to join the others for the second half of the performance. Catherine took her seat in the front row, smoothed her skirt, and ran a hand across her violin's lustrous finish to soothe her shattered nerves.

The bitter tightness returned to her throat, like a bowstring pulled until it snapped. How would she focus on concertos and key signatures now?

The way you always do, she reminded herself, settling into her place and smiling vaguely as Mr. Simmons stepped up to lead them in tuning their instruments. She breathed in deeply, tucked her violin close against her, and let her bow join the discordant cacophony necessary to produce beautiful music. For a few moments, she could play something ugly, venting her emotions into those loud, uncensored notes.

Then, when the curtain rose, Catherine would forget that her mother and father were in the audience, waiting to confront each other again after the final curtain. She would forget the impending deadline, the audition, everything but the music. And she would play the best she ever had.

Amy Lynn Green has always loved history and reading, and she enjoys speaking with book clubs, writing groups, and libraries all around the country. Her debut novel, *Things We Didn't Say*, was nominated for a 2021 Minnesota Book Award and won two Carol Awards. *Things We Didn't Say* and *The Blackout Book Club* received starred reviews from both *Booklist* and *Library Journal*. Amy and her family make their home in Minneapolis, Minnesota. Visit AmyGreenBooks.com to learn more.

Sign Up for Amy's Newsletter

Keep up to date with Amy's latest news on book releases and events by signing up for her email list at the website below.

AmyGreenBooks.com

Follow Amy on Social Media

 Amy Lynn Green @AmyGreenBooks

Be the first to hear about new books from Bethany House!

Stay up to date with our authors and books by signing up for our newsletters at

BethanyHouse.com/SignUp

FOLLOW US ON SOCIAL MEDIA

   @BethanyHouseFiction